John Cuddy novels by Jeremiah Healy

Blunt Darts
The Staked Goat
So Like Sheep
Swan Dive
Yesterday's News
Right to Die
Shallow Graves
Foursome
Act of God
Rescue

Published by POCKET BOOKS

A JOHN FRANCIS CUDDY MYSTERY

JEREMIAH HEALY

RESCUE

POCKET BOOKS

New York   London   Toronto   Sydney   Tokyo   Singapore

This book is a work of fiction. Names, characters, places and incidents
are products of the author's imagination or are used fictitiously. Any
resemblance to actual events or locales or persons, living or dead, is
entirely coincidental.

POCKET BOOKS, a division of Simon & Schuster Inc.
1230 Avenue of the Americas, New York, NY 10020

Copyright © 1995 by Jeremiah Healy

ISBN: 0-671-89875-2

First Pocket Books paperback printing June 1996

10 9 8 7 6 5 4 3 2 1

POCKET and colophon are registered trademarks of
Simon & Schuster Inc.

Cover photos: road by Doug Plummer/Photonica; boy by Issaque
Fujita/Photonica

Printed in the U.S.A.

*For the men and women of
New England School of Law:
past, present, and future*

RESCUE

1

I F I'D BEEN WEARING A SUIT, NONE OF IT WOULD HAVE HAPPENED. Actually, that's not quite right. Some of it, maybe even most of it, still would have happened. I just wouldn't have been involved in it.

Usually I wear a suit, because a lot of what a private investigator does comes from lawyers, and lawyers in Boston expect you to look, and therefore dress, the way they do. That early September afternoon, though, I was driving south toward the city on Interstate 93 in blue jeans and an old chambray shirt. I was out of uniform because I'd been helping another investigator named George-Ann Izzo on a surveillance in one of those Essex County suburbs with views of meadow grass that make you think of the African veld. We were trying to serve process on a wandering civil-case defendant, and the last thing we wanted him to think as he looked out the window of his girlfriend's house was that we were lawyers or agents of lawyers.

George-Ann had relieved me at three P.M., so the sun was slanting in the right-hand window of my silver Prelude, the last year of the first model. I had the moonroof back and every window and vent open. The air was still warm but not hot, the trees still full but not turned. I'd been paying less attention to the traffic, which was light, and more attention to the overpasses, which were many, because I'd already gone by a state trooper hiding on the southbound side of one of the abutments. The cruiser's radar gun was angled for catching speeders who hadn't noticed that New Hampshire's limit of sixty-five dropped down to the Bay State's fifty-five ten miles back. Then I rounded a curve, and the topography gave me a good half mile of lead time to make up my mind.

An old car was stopped on the shoulder of the road, a flat on the left rear wheel making anybody working on it vulnerable to the "slow" lane traffic. Only nobody was working on it, just what looked like a young woman and a younger boy standing behind the bumper, staring at their bad luck.

Ordinary tow trucks don't ply the interstates, and it might be a while in these budget-crunched times before a statie not on radar duty would drive by. I looked down at my old clothes and thought how I had a margin of at least an hour before I was supposed to meet Nancy Meagher that night.

Taking a breath of the nice air, I put on my blinker and edged over to the right.

As the Prelude slowed down behind them, the young woman turned to look at me. She was more a teenager, wearing a faded green T-shirt, torn blue shorts, and sneakers, maybe five-five with baby fat bulging on the upper arms, thighs, and calves. Her dishwater blond hair was pulled back into a ragged ponytail by one of those elastic ribbons I've heard Nancy call a "scrunchy."

The boy was about ten, give or take a year, in jeans and a red T-shirt. His hair was butch-cut and the color of growing wheat, his hands jammed into the front pockets of his pants. He kept his nose pointed at the flat tire instead of my car, only his left eye swiveling toward me, like a horse does when you approach it from the side. I felt a vague memory stir, something from the past that wouldn't quite come.

I parked behind the Dodge Swinger, my front fender jutting out a little to create a zone of safety around their left rear wheel. Up close, the Dodge looked older than its nearly twenty years, the yellow paint rusting over, the chrome heavily pitted, the tonneau cover on the roof scuffed and peeling every few inches like a blackened onion. The radio antenna dated from the days before you could retract them, and somebody long ago had stuck one of those plastic daisies on it, the things that were supposed to help you spot your car in a sea of them outside a mall or theater. Problem was, the plastic had faded to the point of translucence, and it was hard to picture anyone driving the Swinger, even just for shopping.

Getting out of my car, I said, "Do you have help on the way?"

The girl watched me warily, crossing her arms as soon as I started talking. The boy kept his head toward the wheel as his eye strained to keep me in sight.

I approached them. "Can I give you a hand?"

The girl looked past me, back to the north. "We got a flat."

A neutral, lifeless voice. "I can see that. You have a spare?"

She hesitated, but didn't even look toward the trunk, much less go to open it. "Not sure."

Obviously, I was making them nervous. Squatting down, I compared the flat and the other rear tire. Both were worn through most of the tread, nearly down to the thread. "If you do have a spare, I hope it's in better shape than the ones you've got on her now."

The boy suddenly said, "It's not a her."

A rural New England accent, clipped on the syllables but not harshly, more like New Hampshire than Maine. He stepped back without looking, nudging into the girl, who'd been standing between me and the license plate. It was a New Hampshire registration all right, the motto LIVE FREE OR DIE in raised green letters against the cream background.

He pointed toward the plate. "See, it's our Batmobile."

The license number read BAT-611. "I see what you mean."

He said, "It's taking Melinda and me away from—"

"Eddie, hush!"

A little hurt, the boy turned to her instinctively. When he did, I saw the reason he'd been keeping his left profile toward me. There was a birthmark, one of those reddish blotches like

Gorbachev has by what used to be his hairline. Only Eddie's covered most of his right forehead, crossing the eyebrow and continuing under the eye onto his right cheek, like an outline of the state of Texas. As soon as he noticed me noticing it, Eddie turned back toward the tire, showing only the left profile again, the eye still swiveling.

The vague memory nagged at me some more. "Tell you what, Eddie. If you guys have a spare, will you help me put it on?"

He started to turn toward me, then stopped. "Really?"

"Really?"

"You'll really let me help you?"

"Sure. We'll just have to be careful, with the traffic and all."

He turned all the way to me. "Okay."

I smiled at him. "Good. Now, let's see what you've got by way of equipment."

Melinda fiddled with a ring on the middle finger of her left hand, a gilded, plastic thing that might have come in a box of Cracker Jacks. "We don't have no money to pay you."

"I wasn't expecting any."

"So long as you don't expect nothing else."

There was some defiance in her words, like she'd had to say them before and they hadn't worked. Eddie was looking up at her, biting his upper lip.

I said, "Just trying to help."

Melinda glanced north again, then down at Eddie and the flat. "Yeah, okay. Thanks."

I extended my hand to her. "Probably be easier to shake now than later. John Cuddy."

She took my hand awkwardly, releasing it quickly. "Melinda. This is Eddie."

The boy said, "Eddie Straw."

She said, "Eddie," with a warning in it.

I shook his hand. "Pleased to meet you, Eddie."

He held my hand longer, putting a lot of strength into the shake. "It's short."

"Short?"

"Yeah. Short for . . ." Letting go of my hand, he ran the palm of his across the birthmark. "You know, 'strawberry.' "

I nodded. "What do you say we get on this tire?"

Eddie nodded abruptly, maybe copying me. "I say we do."

I looked at Melinda. Going around to the passenger's side door, she opened it and leaned across the seat to the ignition. Her hand came back out with a leather tab having just two keys on it. Even so, she tried the wrong one first in the trunk lock. The second caused the lid to spring, and I looked inside.

There were some old newspapers and an ice scraper and a couple of quart cans, probably containing oil but hard to say because the labels had long ago rotted off them. A set of jumper cables was shy one of the alligator clips, and the whole interior had that musty smell of a boathouse nobody's visited all winter.

Wading through the newspapers, I came up with first the jack and then a lug wrench, a relief since my Prelude's tools probably wouldn't have fit too well. The spare was underneath everything, locked down with a couple of wing nuts and looking a little better, but not much better, than the rubber on the wheels. Fortunately it was mounted on a rim. When I got the tire out, I bounced it on the pavement.

Eddie said, "Why are you doing that for?"

I said, "Give me your hand."

He paused, looking at his hand, then did.

I put it on the rubber at the rim. "Now push."

He did.

I said, "What do you think?"

"I don't know."

"Do the same thing on the right tire."

"The good one?"

"Right. The good one."

Eddie moved over to the wheel and down onto his knees, crab-walking carefully on the gravel. "I think it feels kinda soft."

"Which one?"

"The one you took out of the trunk."

"I do, too."

Melinda had her arms crossed again, rump against the fender. "Can we drive on it?"

"I think so. Once this spare's out in the sunshine a while and rolling over a hot road, it should inflate enough if you go easy till the first station."

The wary look. "Station?"

"Service station."

"Oh. Oh, right."

"There a blanket?"

Suddenly more wary. "Why?"

"Because I don't have one, and it'll be easier on my knees if I can cushion them against the gravel."

"Oh. Oh, sure, hang on."

Melinda went to the backseat, lifting a dingy knapsack with her right hand and yanking something with her left. She came back out with a blanket, but pretty quickly, as though no other luggage had to be moved to free it.

Like everything else about the car, the blanket was old, a stadium plaid that once would have been handsome on a bed at a lake house or hunting camp. I folded it into a two-foot-by-two-foot square.

Kneeling on the square and using the lug wrench, I loosened the nuts. Southeast first, then northwest, northeast, and southwest. The fourth one was the most trouble, but I finally got it to turn.

Over my shoulder, Eddie said, "You ain't gonna take them off?"

"Not yet."

"How come?"

"Because it's safer to loosen them before you jack up the car, but safer still to leave them on so the tire doesn't fall off as the rear end's going up."

He didn't say anything, but when I twisted my head around to look at him, he was nodding gravely.

I set down the wrench and mopped the sweat from my eyes. "Okay, now comes the jack. If the car was on an incline, we'd have to chock the wheels."

Eddie looked at me vacantly.

I said, "If the car's facing uphill, what might happen if I raised the back end of it?"

He studied the car, frowning, then lit up. "The Batmobile might slide on you."

"That's right. So where would you put the chock?"

"What's the chock?"

"Like a rock or a piece of wood, to wedge under the good tires."

The boy studied again, shorter this time. "Behind them."

"That's right. You learn fast, Eddie."

"That's not what my—"

"Eddie!"

He turned toward Melinda this time like she'd slapped him.

Melinda looked from Eddie to me to him again. More softly, she said, "You can't be bothering Mr. Cuddy while he's trying to do his work."

Just the grave nod.

To break the tension, I said, "This is where I need your help, Eddie."

He brightened. "What do you want me to do?"

I spoke to Melinda. "I don't suppose you have the manual that came with the car?"

Just a shrug.

To Eddie I said, "Can you get down on your knees behind the car, let me know when I have the jack centered under the axle?"

"The what?"

For a kid who sounded country, he didn't seem to know much about how things worked. "The long bar that connects the left rear tire to the right rear one."

"Okay."

I got on my belly and crawled under the car, intentionally positioning the jack a little off. "How's that?"

Eddie's voice said, "You want it in the middle, right?"

"Right."

"I think it's too far over."

"Which way?"

"Toward you."

"How do you mean, Eddie?"

"I mean, you got to push the thing a little more away from you."

I centered it this time. "How's that?"

A pause. "That looks pretty good. Yeah."

I cleared away the gravel from the pavement to get a stable base. Recentering the jack, I worked the handle until the weight of the Swinger was just lifting, then slid out from under.

"Good job, Eddie. But from now on, you have to remember one thing."

"What's that?"

"Don't let any part of you get under the car. Even when it's jacked up, the car can slip and come down on you."

The grave nod. "I understand."

I raised the car to where I had three inches of airspace under the bad tire. Eddie helped me roll the good tire over to it.

I said, "This space between the flat tire and the ground is so we can put on the spare without having to jack any more."

"Because it's bigger than the flat one."

"That's right." I took off the southeast lug nut first and handed it to Eddie. "If we had a lot of tools, it wouldn't matter much, but out here, we need to keep track of which nut came off which lug."

He stared at the metal in his right hand.

I said, "How can we do that?"

Eddie looked back at the wheel and nodded four times. "Four . . . nuts, right?"

"Right."

He looked around, then down at himself. "I've got four pockets in my jeans."

"Good idea. Which order you going to use?"

Eddie thought about it, then used his left palm to slap left front, right front, left rear, right rear.

I said, "That ought to work."

He stuck the first nut carefully into his left front pocket.

We followed the same routine with each lug before rocking the flat gently until it came off. I laid it on the ground between their car and mine.

Eddie said, "Why are you doing that for?"

"You mean instead of putting the flat in the trunk?"

A nod.

I pointed under the car. "If I put something heavy in the trunk, I throw off the weight and maybe make the jack move."

He looked underneath the chassis. "And that might make the car slip, right?"

"Right."

As we moved back to the good tire, Eddie said, "You a mechanic?"

"No. Why?"

He bit his upper lip again. "It's just ... You sure know a lot about cars, is all."

"Everybody should know how to change a tire, Eddie, no matter what kind of work you do."

"What kind of work do you do?"

"I'm a private investigator."

When he didn't respond, I turned my head to look at him. He was staring at me, awestruck. I lifted the spare onto the lugs.

Eddie said, "You're kidding?"

"About what?"

"About being a private eye."

"No, I'm not. Here."

He accepted my ID folder as though it were a newborn chick.

I said, "Open it."

His lips moved while Eddie read to himself. "Just like Magnum and Rockford and all those guys."

Cars he didn't know, but even in small towns they have television. "It's not like that in the real world, son. Pretty tame most of the time."

Holding open my ID, Eddie said, "If something ever ... If I ever got lost or anything, would you come help me?"

"Sure."

His voice got more serious. "Promise?"

I felt that vague tug of memory again. "Promise."

With the grave nod, Eddie folded the ID and gave it back to me.

I fit the nuts back onto the lugs hand-tight, then stood and stretched.

Eddie said, "Aren't you going to use the thing on them?"

"The lug wrench?"

"Yeah, the ... wrench."

"Once the car's back on the ground."

He looked at the wheel, then under the chassis again. "So the jack doesn't slip, right?"

"Maybe you should be the mechanic, Eddie."

"Maybe. Maybe I will."

It was the most hopeful thing I'd heard him say.

Melinda's voice said, "Eddie, come here, will you?"

He left me. Ratcheting the jack handle to lower the car, I heard Melinda say, "Mr. Cuddy?"

"Yes?"

"Eddie and me are just going down into the trees a minute."

I was about to say "How come?" then caught myself in time. "Sure. I'll still be a little while here."

I watched them move down the slope of the shoulder into the bushes and disappear. Finishing with the handle, I started to crawl under the chassis to retrieve the jack. I heard a vehicle swerve into the slow lane as it passed me, then hit its brakes farther south. From beneath the Swinger I watched a GMC Sonoma pickup, navy blue with a camper shell in its bed, back up fast along the shoulder until its rear bumper was only ten feet or so from the front of the Dodge.

I slid out from under and started to stand as the driver's door of the truck opened and a man's head and shoulders came out. The head wore an Atlanta Braves baseball cap over shaggy, reddish hair, buck teeth, and jug-handle ears. His aviator sunglasses would have kept his eyes from me even if the afternoon glare hadn't been in mine. The shoulders were broad under a green and black lumberman's shirt, a little warm for the weather even with the sleeves rolled up, show-ing tanned, wiry forearms.

He stopped cold when he saw me, then sat back into the truck with the door open and tried a grin. "Need any help?"

There was a southern edge to the voice, and I checked his license plate. Lots of mud dried over the numbers, but an-other New Hampshire registration from the colors.

"Thanks, but I think we're all right."

He looked around. "We?"

"The people I'm helping."

"A Good Samaritan, huh?" He pitched it just this side of sarcasm. "Where they at?"

"Taking a bathroom break."

I watched him process that. It seemed to me he wanted to look back down the slope, but stopped himself.

Then he dipped his head. "Don't like to see another Granite Stater broke down, you know?"

"Uh-huh."

"Well, Live Free or Die, right?"

"Right."

The guy shifted back into the cab and closed the door, driving off to the south a lot more conservatively than he'd driven in. I looked down at the rear plate of the Dodge, then walked around to the front. From the way my Prelude was positioned, he couldn't have seen the Swinger's rear license, and at the speed the pickup was going he would have had to be pretty quick to notice the front plate was from New Hampshire.

I was back at the trunk of the Dodge, everything just about loaded into it, when Melinda and Eddie came out of the trees and up the slope. As they reached me, I closed the trunk lid.

Glancing north, Melinda said, "All done?"

"I think so."

"Well, thanks for your help."

"You really need to get that flat fixed."

"Okay."

"The other tires, they're not going to last you long, either."

She went over to the driver's side, glancing north again before opening the door. "Thanks for the advice."

"Wait a minute till I clean off my hands, and I'll follow you into the city."

"No, we got to get going."

I said, "You have a place to stay tonight?"

A defiant expression that suggested she'd had to practice it, too, when things really counted. "We're gonna be fine, Eddie and me."

I looked over to him, then held up my dirty hand so he could see why I couldn't shake. "Take care, huh, Eddie?"

The grave nod, then he bit his lip some more. "Good-bye."

Eddie got in the passenger's side and closed his door. Melinda hit the gas, spraying gravel as she moved the Dodge out into the slow lane. A plume of oil smoke coughed out the tailpipe, the acceleration not what it might have been despite my feeling that Melinda was trying to make up for lost time.

I watched their car until it was out of sight around the next curve. Then I went to my own trunk for a rag to wipe my hands, trying to bring back the memory that Eddie Straw had triggered.

2

"HOW'D YOU GET YOUR HANDS SO DIRTY?"

Taking the classroom desk-chair next to Nancy Meagher, I said, "Some people had a flat on 93. I stopped to help out."

She smiled and shook her head, which made the shoulder-length black hair wave gently over her cheeks, the freckles on either side of her nose playing peek-a-boo with me. Straight from the office, she was still dressed in a charcoal gray suit with ruffled white blouse and pearl earring studs. The wide-spaced blue eyes blinked once, then her left hand drifted over to my right, squeezing it between two smudge spots.

I said, " 'Only one soap's gonna get these hands clean, mister.' "

Nancy cocked her head. She's a lot younger than I am, and this time her eyes told me that she didn't get the quote.

"It's from an old commercial for Lava, Nance."

"And that's some kind of soap?"

"Right. They used to advertise it on—"

"Okay, folks. Let's get started, please."

Caryn, our instructor, walked with her red-tipped pointer

to a sales-meeting easel at the front of the classroom. On the far side of thirty, she was dressed in a rugby jersey and blue jeans. The fourteen other students were already in their seats, spiral notebooks open like Nancy's and mine.

"Last time we discussed the differences between a Beach Dive and a Boat Dive, Calculating Your Buoyancy, and Underwater Hazards." Caryn flipped to the next chart, which had "scuba" spelled out as "Self-Contained Underwater Breathing Apparatus." Moving her pointer, she said, "Tonight we're going to cover Deep Diving, Depth Tables, and the Repetitive Dive Tables. First though, are there any questions from last time?"

One of the other students raised his hand and asked an incomprehensible question about Boyle's Law, which has something to do with temperature, the air in your tank, and water pressure. I say "something" because taking the course was Nancy's idea, a way to prepare for the Caribbean vacation we'd promised ourselves as a break from Boston's upcoming seven months of winter. *Magna cum laude* at New England School of Law before becoming an assistant district attorney, she'd been acing every test we'd had in the course while I'd been getting just about enough questions right to stay alive. I was a little better in the pool than the classroom, though, so I thought I'd probably make it through to the open-water dives all of us would have to complete for certification.

Caryn had moved off the question to a review of the other laws (Charles's and Dalton's) we'd seen, then tied in Henry's Law on a liquid under pressure absorbing gas proportional to that pressure. Which led to a discussion of the bends and the need to calculate your bottom time (the time you leave the surface until the time you leave the bottom), Caryn stressing the importance of the repetitive dive tables if you go back under before twelve hours have gone by.

In a whisper, Nancy said, "I think you should be writing this stuff down."

I looked at her notebook. It reminded me of a monk copying a manuscript. "Nance, if we dive only once a day, we don't have to worry about the twelve-hour thing, right?"

A frown.

Caryn took us through countless examples of multiple dives using the tables. I got hopelessly lost after the third one, so I studied the other students. There was a couple in their fifties, which saved me from being the oldest person in the room. A bunch of yuppies, male and female, who seemed a clique. Two college girls, one a little heavy, the other like an Olympian. Two men who might have been a couple, buddying up for the pool exercises but otherwise keeping to themselves.

Caryn neared the end of our two hours, suggesting we always check to see if a decompression chamber was available on any island we visited. She also recommended not diving shortly before getting on an airplane, which sounded eminently sensible to me.

"Okay. Any questions on what we've covered tonight?"

The same male student asked another convoluted question about the repetitive dive tables. The two college girls rolled their eyes at each other, then looked toward me and giggled. Caryn noticed, the male student didn't seem to.

Nancy leaned over. "Next thing I know, you'll be passing notes to them."

Caryn finished her answer, then said quickly, "Okay, let's hit the pool."

The classroom was in the Boston City Hospital complex. The Center for Adult Education uses the complex because the hospital pool is deep enough to simulate about half an atmosphere of additional pressure. The city morgue's nearby, but both Nancy and I had been there often enough professionally not to mention it to each other as we split for our respective locker rooms. Everybody reassembled in the pool area wearing just swimsuits and carrying personal mask, fins, and snorkel.

Caryn was there as well, changed into a sleek, one-piece Speedo. "Okay, how many of you brought knives tonight?"

Her voice echoed off the tiles in the damp, chlorine-laden air. Five hands went up, two tentatively.

"Please strap them on, the inside of the calf opposite your major hand. So, if you're a rightie, strap the knife on the inside of your left calf. That way you can access it if you have to, but it won't catch your weight belt if you have to ditch the belt during a dive. Remember, *always* wear the knife in open water, whether diving or just snorkeling. Monofilament fishing line is tough to spot and tougher to snap if you get tangled in it on a reef or a wreck."

Hands to her hips. "Okay, don all your equipment—pack, tank, and belt—except for mask and snorkel, and hop in for the drill."

The "drill" the first night of class four weeks ago was swimming three hundred yards without equipment and without stopping. Nancy and I made it, but I was surprised at how demanding it had been and not surprised that six of our original twenty-two students couldn't do it, being counseled quietly by Caryn that they needed to improve their endurance before maybe registering for the course the next time it was offered. After that first night, the drill built on each thing we learned.

Caryn said, "Okay, everybody's in. Off the sides of the pool and drown-proof."

Drown-proofing consists of hanging in the water, fins toward the bottom, legs relaxed, face just under the surface and head just breaking above it. Exhaling through the nose and mouth, you push downward with both hands in front of you, lifting your face from the water and breathing in deeply. You hold that breath as you relax, your body sinking but the natural buoyancy of your filled lungs bringing you back up to the original position. You then repeat the sequence, something that supposedly can be done for hours unless hypothermia or a particularly big fish intervenes.

After ten minutes, Caryn said, "Okay. Get your masks and snorkels, then regulators in and dolphin-kick."

At the side of the pool, Nancy reached up for her stuff. She spit into the mask, rubbing the protein-rich saliva over the eye-side of the lens to keep the glass from fogging under water. Then Nancy slid her hand down her air hose until she found the regulator, putting it in her mouth and trying a few breaths to check, again, that the air valve was working. Around the rubber mouthpiece, she said, "Let's go, Flipper."

I really didn't like the dolphin-kick much. It requires you to keep your legs together and pretty stiff while you undulate your body from the waist to move underwater the way a dolphin can. Of course, a dolphin doesn't have the same kind of spine we do or a metal tank banging against it. Or a torn-up shoulder and knee that were just beginning to feel right a few months after I'd injured them.

When we all had surfaced again, Caryn said, "Okay, now I want the doff-and-don. Three times each as soon as you're ready."

Nancy and I breathed through our snorkels until our respiration calmed down. I pointed to her, and she nodded. Putting the regulator back in her mouth, she dived to the bottom of the pool, doffing all her gear, tank last and over the head. Then a final breath from the regulator, which is taken from the mouth and folded over its hose on top of the tank pack. Then an ascent to the surface, breathing out the air that was breathed in under pressure and thus is expanding because of somebody's law. Three breaths at the surface, her face bearing an oval outline from having worn the mask for a while. Her hand formed the "okay" sign of thumb and index circled, other three fingers pointing outward. Then a free dive to the bottom, replacing the regulator and donning all the other equipment again. Clearing her mask of water by breathing hard through her nose, Nancy came back up.

At the surface, she said, "That's one for me."

I did the same doff-and-don sequence that she had, and then we alternated for two more times each, finishing ahead of everybody except the older couple, who I began to suspect were ringers.

This was our last night in the pool, the following week just a multiple-choice exam followed by a review of the right and wrong answers to the questions. Caryn had us do some simulated rescues and other exercises, and then it was time to shower, change, and go home.

Sitting next to me in the Prelude, Nancy said, "My place or yours?"

I drove north on Massachusetts Avenue. "Either is fine with me. I just have that service-of-process surveillance tomorrow."

"Then let's make it mine. I'll be on trial with an armed robbery starting in the morning."

"Dinner?"

"I don't have anything in the freezer. Take-out okay?"

"Fine. Thai or Szechuan?"

"Your choice, John."

"Thai then. Wine?"

"I've got white, but it's not chilled."

"We'll stop for some."

Her hand ventured over to mine on the stick shift. Nancy and I had been together for a year and a half. The spark was still there, stronger than ever for me and I believed for her as well, but the relationship also had grown broader and deeper in the last few months. We now had a certain easiness between us, a domestic chatter that somehow wasn't as shallow as it might seem to others. More the comfort-zone level of exchange two people can enjoy without having to worry about making conversation, as I'd had with my wife, Beth, before the cancer made me a widower.

I turned right onto Boylston, passing the Hynes Convention area and the renovated Prudential Center. They've done the stonework facade in *Miami Vice* pastels, the poor Star Market looking like it took over an abandoned nightclub. After a left onto Fairfield and another onto Newbury, Nancy got out to place our order at The King and I. Circling around the one-way streets, I stopped in the wine store at the corner of Exeter Street, buying a chilled bottle of chardonnay before circling back and picking Nancy up outside the restaurant.

We headed to South Boston, the food smells wafting up from the take-out bag. At her place, the third floor of a three-family house, Nancy fed Renfield, her slightly gimpy cat, and then dished out the honeyed pork with mushrooms, pad Thai, and white rice as I opened the wine. We ate at Nancy's living room coffee table, quickly at first, then more slowly, lingering a little over the chardonnay as I put shredded pork in front of Renfield on the floor.

Nancy swirled some wine in her glass. "You're doing a good job of spoiling him."

"He deserves some spoiling. He's been through a lot."

Renfield had needed an operation on his rear legs to correct a congenital problem that manifested itself after I dropped him once. I'd been the only one around to take care of him after the operation, and the cat had "imprinted" on me, as the vet called it. What you had to admire about Renfield was the way he came back from essentially having his back legs broken and the kneecaps reset. He couldn't jump much, but he hadn't lost the sense of being a cat that had caused Nancy to name him after the character in *Dracula* who eats small mammals.

A smile toyed with the corners of Nancy's mouth. "You've been through a lot, too."

"The shoulder and knee are just about fine."

"I meant all the physical stuff in the pool tonight."

"You did everything I did."

The smile got saucy. "Does that mean we both should be too tired for any more ... physical stuff?"

I smiled back. "I'm not if you're not."

Setting down her glass, Nancy said, "You know, I probably shouldn't tell you this, but I overheard the college girls talking about you in the locker room."

We both stood. "Do I want to hear it?"

Nancy took my right hand in both of hers and walked me toward the bedroom. "I think so."

"All right, what did they say?"

"They both thought you were in great shape for your age."

We got to the bedroom door and went in. "For my age."

"Yes."

"You had to tell me that part."

Nancy started undoing the buttons on my chambray shirt. "Just reporting accurately."

"Well, they don't know what they're talking about."

"They don't?"

"No. For their age, I'm in great shape. For my age, I'm a god."

A laugh in her throat as she started on my belt buckle. "Greek or Roman?"

"We deities disdain any categorizing by mere mortals."

The zipper. "I think maybe Mars."

"Mars?"

The slacks. "God of War, John."

"Why?"

"Because . . ." The laugh again. "Because of the heft of your . . . mighty sword."

I stepped out of the slacks as Nancy moved over to the bed and sat down, lips trembling.

"Nance?"

"Yes."

"This is getting embarrassing."

She looked me up and down. "Zounds, what a physique."

"Nance, enough, all right?"

Around the strangled laugh. "All right."

I slipped out of my briefs.

Nancy managed all of "Gadzooks" before keeling over sideways on the bed, hysterical.

Afterward, we lay cuddled side by side under a sheet and a light blanket. In a snoozy voice, Nancy said, "They also thought your scars were sexy."

"Who did?"

"The college girls. They think you must have led a 'totally awesome' life."

"They're right on that, anyway."

"I wanted to tell them where each came from, but I didn't know."

I shifted a little. "You know some of them."

Nancy worked the covers down a foot on my chest. "Yeah, but not even most of them. This one, for example."

"Third grade, fell off my bike."

"Onto what, a bayonet?"

I didn't say anything.

Nancy moved her hand southward. "How about this one?"

"Paper cut."

"Over your ribs?"

"Severe paper cut."

A pause. "John?"

"What?"

"Does it bother you to talk about your scars?"

"No. It reminds me of how they happened, which aren't among my greatest memories, but I don't mind your asking about them."

"Why not?"

"Why not what?"

"Why don't you mind my asking about them?"

"Because they were a part of my life, and now you're a part of my life, and I want the current, important part to know about the past, less important parts."

"Good answer." Another pause. "Then how come you joke around about the scars instead of telling me what they're from?"

"Because it might . . . it kind of sounds like bragging somehow if a guy talks about things he's been through."

"Oh, well, as long as it's 'guy stuff,' then I can see why I shouldn't know."

Not heavy-handed, just soft and deft and deadly. "Okay, pick another one."

"Topic?"

"Scar."

Nancy ran her fingernails up over chest, throat, and chin to the eyebrow. "This one."

"What one?"

"This." She pushed on a calcium deposit. "I've always wondered about this little bump between your eyebrows."

"It's not exactly a scar, Nance."

"Tell me anyway."

"Okay. It's from when I was in Saigon. Another MP lieutenant—Justo Vega, he's a lawyer down in Florida now—Justo and I were in this bar, kind of a quiet one where the MPs could drink off-duty without getting into brawls with the troopers on R and R. We got to arguing about professional wrestlers: who was the toughest if it wasn't all orchestrated, who'd be the hardest to take in a street fight."

"True guy stuff."

"Verily. Anyway, we went through Antonino Rocca and Lou Thesz and so on, but Justo kept saying BoBo Brazil was—"

"BoBo ... ?"

"Brazil."

"This is a real person?"

"Yes. Justo kept saying BoBo Brazil would be the toughest because of the Coco-butt."

"The ... ?"

"C-O-C-O-B-U-T-T. Brazil would be nearing the end of a match, and his finishing shot would be a head-butt to the other guy's forehead, like bashing a coconut."

"I get the picture."

"Well, Justo and I disagreed on that, so we started practicing the Coco-butt on each other, to see if it really would work."

"You practiced it?"

"We did. No more than six or eight times, I think, before the bar owner started to wonder about the people his government had invited to come over and fight for it."

"Six or eight times."

"Yeah. Justo kept saying, 'You must be patient, John; BoBo himself, he did not learn this in one night.' I think we even got to the point where we were pretty good."

"But?"

"But I was drinking, and either Justo kind of missed or I did, because you're supposed to use the crown of your forehead for the actual impact."

"And that's how you got the bump between your eyebrows."

"Yes."

"I take back what I said before."

"About what?"

"About you being Mars. It's more like you're from Mars."

"You asked me a question, I gave you the real answer."

Nancy didn't say anything for a while. Then, "You know, each time I've asked you about the war, you've always deflected it a little at first."

"I thought I already explained that."

"You did, it's just . . . it's hard for me, for anyone my age, to keep asking somebody your age about the war if we're . . . put off when we first bring it up."

"Nance, it was hard for me to ask my father's generation about World War II, because the really good ones—the good soldiers, I mean—never brought it up themselves."

"And you don't either, John. And I can understand why you wouldn't. But when you're asked about it directly, specifically, it's okay for you to talk about it. I want to know about those parts of you, too."

I closed my eyes. "Message received. I'll try."

Another pause, longer this time. "John, you haven't been down to see . . . the Wall, have you?"

The Vietnam Veterans Memorial in Washington, where all the dead—Suddenly Eddie Straw's left eye was swiveling in front of me, and it all came back, the vague memory now roaring through my head.

Tet, the lunar new year in January, 1968, when the Vietcong attacked Saigon with rockets, mortars, and small units of infantry. All of us piled into jeeps or two-and-a-half-ton trucks, hitting the streets as soon as we could. I dropped off two troopers, both PFCs, from my deuce-and-a-half at an intersection near Tu Do Street. As MPs, none of us had anything heavier than forty-five-caliber sidearms, and we were all jumpy as hell.

One of the PFCs was a French-Canadian kid from northern Maine named Duquette. His first name doesn't register, but I remember the other MPs calling him "Frenchy." Duquette was facing the alley near the intersection, his left eye swiveling like Eddie Straw's as he strained to keep me in sight while watching for trouble.

"John."

Duquette said, "Sir, we've only got three clips of ammo each. You'll be back for us, right?"

I wasn't more than a few years older than he was, but I remember saying, "Don't worry, son, I'll be back."

Duquette said, "Promise?" and tried to grin, the one eye still swiveling.

I said, "Promise."

"John?"

The next time I saw Duquette was six or seven hours later, faceup in the gutter, a cruel sash of AK–47 rounds stitched diagonally through his chest, the forty-five lying jacked open and empty near his hand. He'd run out of ammunition before I'd gotten back for—

"John!"

I turned to Nancy. "What's the matter?"

"You zoned out on me. I was saying your name and—"

"I'm sorry, kid. I just . . . Never mind. I'm okay."

Her voice was very quiet. "You don't even remember my question, do you?"

"Your question?" I took a moment. "No, I don't."

"I asked you if you'd ever been down to visit the Wall."

Jesus. "You're right, I did forget. And no, I haven't seen it."

Still the quiet voice. "Last message of the evening?"

"Okay."

A kiss on my ear. "Maybe you should."

"Why?"

"To get rid of some of the scars I can't play with."

Nancy dropped off before I did, just after I realized she was right.

3

I SAID, "YOU SURE YOU DON'T WANT IT?"

George-Ann Izzo, five-seven, a hundred-fifty pounds, and dark-haired, looked down at the Styrofoam cup of Dunkin' Donuts coffee, then back up at me. Between clenched teeth, she said, "I want it. I just better not have it."

George-Ann's teeth were clenched because her jaw was wired shut. The wiring, and rubber bands, were necessary because a jerk she'd tried to serve with a contempt citation in a matrimonial case had swung on her, breaking her jaw and going in for more before George-Ann dislocated his shoulder. Earlier on the stakeout, she'd told me about having to use a Water Pik instead of a toothbrush and how sensitive she'd become to things that stain your teeth.

I said, "Coffee stains, huh?"

Just a nod.

We were sitting in my Prelude, me at the wheel. I'd come by to relieve her, and George-Ann was going over what had happened the night before. The house we were watching was in front of us and slightly raised on a knoll. A nice garrison with three acres near the end of a winding country lane, it belonged to the new, fortyish girlfriend of a man who stayed at various places around the country without seeming to live in any one of them. According to the plaintiff's lawyer, who'd gotten a superior court judge to appoint George-Ann as special agent for service of process, the man (Harry was his first name) might be staying with the girlfriend (Irene), and the lawyer even had a candid photo showing the two of them for identification purposes. After two days on her own, however, all George-Ann had seen was the girlfriend going to and from work, walking a female rottweiler on a stout leash, and bringing back take-out food in a Mercedes registered in Irene's name. The telephone went unanswered, and knocking on the door brought nothing but barking. That's when the lawyer got my name added to the special agent order, and I joined in to provide almost round-the-clock surveillance. Either one of us would be able to hand Harry the summons and complaint in a case that would tie him up in fraud allegations until roughly the new millenium.

But first we'd have to tag him, and so far, we hadn't even seen him.

I said, "Irene's at work?"

"Yeah. Left an hour ago, after walking the dog." George-Ann opened her handbag, rummaging around and laying things out in her lap. One of them was a plastic box with a hinge on it.

"You starting on intravenous drugs, George-Ann?"

"Huh?"

"The case."

"Oh. That's not paraphernalia."

Her sentence through the teeth came out, "Thaz nah par-phen-nail." I said, "What is it, then?"

"My kit. It's got scissors to cut the anchor bands in my mouth, in case I start to choke on my meals of milk or soup. Otherwise, I'd start to throw up and the puke would have no place to go but down into my lungs. Probably should have some wire cutters in the kit, too."

"Lovely."

A shrug that meant, "Part of the job." And, in a way, it was.

George-Ann came up with her keys and shoved the rest of the stuff back in the bag. "I'm out of here. Do me a favor, get this guy today?"

"I feel lucky."

"I feel like shit."

She opened the passenger door and went back to her car. I heard it start and watched it make a three-point turn in my rearview mirror, then disappear.

There isn't much to do on a stationary surveillance. The subject can always slip out one of the doors you can't see, but when you're alone, there's also not much you can do about that. You have to keep your eyes on the house, so reading's not an option. Some people play bridge in their head, others go over pivotal baseball or football games they attended or watched on the tube. I bring a boom box and some audio cassettes, usually instrumental, because I find I can lose my boredom in them while my eyes and brain stay on the job.

George-Ann had gotten several originals of the summons, in case we ended up leaving a set of documents in the mailbox or between the storm door and inner door of the house. The lawyer told her to do that as a last resort, but my guess was that it would be last-resort time soon, even though I wasn't sure from my one year of law school whether documents just left at the house of Girlfriend A would be sufficient service on Boyfriend B. I was halfway through the second tape of the morning, a nice piano album by Liz Story, when the forces of good caught a break.

The front doors of the house opened a little more than a crack, and the rottweiler bounded out, a jeweled collar around her neck, obviously intent on something. She barely got past the path to the house before evacuating herself graphically on the lawn. Using hind legs to kick some grass, the dog did a patrol of the property, more playful than watchful, and then headed back up to the house, where the doors magically opened and closed again.

Interesting, when you considered that George-Ann told me Irene had walked the dog only an hour or so before.

I gathered together the sets of documents and turned off my boom box. Leaving the Prelude, I quartered my way toward the front of the house as though it were a machine-gun nest. Then I sat behind a forsythia bush and waited. Fifteen minutes, half an hour, forty-five.

That's when the doors cracked open once more, and the rottweiler came bounding out again. She was intent on the same task, enough so she didn't notice me until finishing her round of walking. I was down on my knees by then, patting the ground in front of me. The dog bounded up, tongue lolling outside her mouth. She battered me at the shoulders with her head, then bounded away and back, wanting to play despite her obvious diarrhea. I waited till she calmed down some, then scratched between her eyes with my left hand while my right was slipping one set of the court papers under her collar. Once I had them secured, I stopped petting, and she gave up on me and returned to the front doors. They opened again, and the rottweiler went inside. I waited for a count of three, then moved along the front of the house, my back to the horizontal siding, until I was just beside the entrance.

The inner door came open all the way, the storm one flying outward as Harry of the photograph burst through. About fifty, he was maybe an inch shorter than my six-two-plus but built a little huskier than he seemed in two dimensions, with solid forearms under the Ralph Lauren Polo shirt and twill slacks. Henry was clutching, you might even say crushing, the papers from the dog's collar in his right fist, looking wildly up and down the lane.

From ten feet behind him, I said, "You're it, Harry."

He whirled around, shaking the fist that held the documents toward my face. "You think this is fucking service? You think this'll stand up? You fuckhead, you got another think coming!"

"Harry, two things on that. One, I've got a second set of papers right here. Two, I'm between you and the door."

He took a look at the door. "That's kidnapping!"

"I'm not taking you anywhere, Harry."

Another idea crossed his face. "False imprisonment!"

"I don't see anything stopping you from leaving."

His eyes flitted left-right-left, but without enthusiasm. "You fucker, I'll get you for this."

"Harry, you can extend your hand, and I can lay these papers in it, or I can stuff them under your collar, too. Your choice."

He fussed and fumed, but after another few seconds, he extended his hand, and I served him.

Harry said, "Goddamned fucking bitch."

"It's not the dog's fault. It's—"

"I'm not talking about the dog. Fucking Irene. She has to give her fucking hound a taste of the take-out. I tell her, 'Irene, the fucking spices are gonna be too much for it,' but no, she has to give her little 'lovebug' some of the curry shit I could barely eat."

"Tragic, Harry. The Greeks should have done a play on it."

"Wasn't Greek."

"Sorry?"

"Wasn't Greek food. It was fucking Indian."

I left Harry contemplating the unfairness of life.

Driving away from the house, I was feeling pretty good. I tried a pub in one of the northern suburbs for lunch, finding a pay phone to call George-Ann and leave the news with her answering service. Then I bought a Boston *Globe* from the honor-system box by the phone and brought the paper back to the bar to read while I waited for a turkey club sandwich. The place had Bass ale on tap, so I ordered a pint. Halfway through both the pint and the first section of the *Globe*, I stopped cold.

The story hadn't made the front page, or even the third one, since no firearms or allegations of gang involvement or racial overtones jumped out at you. There was a grainy photo, though, showing a light-colored van that I knew was actually white and its dark-colored lettering that was actually blue. The van belonged to the Chief Medical Examiner's Office, and it was parked alongside the Fort Point Channel, which flows into the harbor by South Boston. The miniheadline of the story read UNIDENTIFIED WOMAN FOUND IN CHANNEL. There weren't many details: A couple of casual night fishermen casting from a bridge noticed the body floating near some rocks, the face disfigured pretty badly. The kind of story that gets three inches one day and maybe a mention the next, usually to the effect that "police officials have no further leads on the identity of the victim or the cause of death." The kind of story you barely even read anymore. Except for one thing.

In the right foreground of the grainy picture, a bit fuzzy because the photographer was focusing on the van, you could just see a faded plastic daisy sticking up from an antenna. The story didn't say anything about a little boy with a birthmark.

When my sandwich came, I ate every bite, but there didn't seem to be much taste to it.

Not stopping at my office, I drove directly to South Boston. The Homicide Unit is located in the old Broadway police substation. Our then-mayor reopened some substations a few years back, despite the budget problems, to give the citizens in underserved neighborhoods a greater sense of security. Since all the officers in the Southie one are plainclothes detectives who don't ride the streets, however, it's kind of hard to see where the greater security comes into play.

I walked down the hallway with lockers on either side of me and up to the medium blue door with the dark blue sign that says in white letters HOMICIDE UNIT. I rapped on the door before going in, although I didn't hear anybody tell me to enter, and I'm ever more convinced I'm the only one who bothers to knock.

Usually the place is crawling with men in sports jackets and the occasional suit and one woman in a blazer and skirt, typing and yelling and sometimes even laughing in front of the pale blue walls and cork bulletin board. That day there was only one man sitting in an old, black-padded armchair, talking into the receiver of an older black phone. He was a little younger than I am, with a ruddy complexion and those puffy, unformed features all newborns and some jaded cops seem to share. His name was Guinness, and I'd run into him on a case a while back. There are twenty-one detectives in Homicide, seven three-officer teams. Of all the cops I'd met in the unit, the only two I couldn't stand were Guinness and his lieutenant, a guy named Holt.

Guinness hung up and stared at me. "Your fucking rabbi's not around."

I figured he meant Robert Murphy, a black lieutenant. "How about Bonnie Cross?"

"She's out, too. Maybe you didn't hear, half the unit's over in Rox', account of the Zulus and the Ubangis went at it pretty good last night."

Roxbury was a predominantly black neighborhood. "Love to hear you say that when Murphy's here."

"Well, he isn't. What do you want?"

"Can you tell me who drew the woman in the Fort Point Channel?"

"The floater by the bridge? I did, as a matter of fact. Thank Christ she was pretty fresh. Nothing worse than a ripe floater."

"Can you give me any details?"

Guinness creaked back in the chair. He was wearing a tweed jacket with elbow patches, but didn't quite pull off that professorial air. "Yeah, but why should I?"

"The story in the paper said she was unidentified."

"They got that right."

"I maybe can identify her."

Guinness looked at me. You could almost see the smoke coming out his ears as he tried to decide whether talking with me would make his job easier or harder. He fixed on easier. "How might that be?"

I told him about the breakdown alongside Route 93, the plastic daisy, and the guy in the GMC pickup.

Guinness said, "Maybe it's not your girl. This one looks like a jumper—or maybe an accident—but nothing to show she had help."

"Look, the guy pulled away before she did. That gave him

time enough to scout an overpass and hide on the south side of it like a speed trap. He just has to wait till she goes by, then follow her into town."

"Yeah, but we didn't find any sign of this kid Eddie, birth-mark or not."

"So?"

"So why wouldn't your pickup guy drown the two of them while he was at it?"

"I don't know."

"And they're from New Hampshire, why ice even just the girl in Boston?"

"Because it's a big city. Because he figured with all the deaths down here, this one might not be noticed."

"Yeah, well, he got that right. A little more tide last night, and this floater'd been on her way to Portugal and out of my hair."

"Guinness, look. Can we treat this one like it's a homicide, just long enough for you to clear it?"

"What do you mean?"

"Take a ride with me, over to the channel."

"A ride? You got rocks in your head or what? I got pa-perwork up the wazoo here that I'm not gonna file, much less clear, by Christmas. You got any idea, any fucking con-ception, how many *real* cases I have? Guys who didn't decide to end it all by pumping five rounds from a nine mil into their fucking chests from twenty feet away. Wives who got beaten to death by their husbands over a botched dessert or maybe what cable station they were gonna watch that night. You think I got the time to ride all over hell and back with you on the chance, the remote possibility, that my floater last night wasn't a suicide or an accident?"

"Guinness, the bridge is, what, a mile from here? Maybe? I'll even drive you."

He mulled it over, though I was pretty sure the last couple of minutes was just an act. "Tell you what. You take me to the morgue first. We look at the floater, you tell me whether or not she's your girl. She is, then we'll ride over to the bridge. What do you say?"

The best I was likely to get. "Okay. My car, then?"

He inclined his head toward a set of hooks where usually ignition keys on big wooden blocks would hang. "We'll have to. All ours are over in the Congo there."

The morgue was built back in the thirties. It was almost new in November, 1942, when the bodies from the Coconut Grove fire were taken there by the hundreds, at least as many people standing in line outside the mortuary that next Sunday morning, waiting to identify friends and loved ones. Now, though, the morgue is literally falling down on the pathologists and technicians who work inside it, gaps in the hung ceiling where the rectangles of Styrofoam have crumbled onto the examining tables and slabs. They've been talking for years about moving the place out to Framingham on state-owned land that would be a cheaper site than building or renovating in Boston. Until then, the medical examiner struggles with an inadequate budget and a pared-down staff and conditions more appropriate to the end of the nineteenth century than the predawn hours of the twenty-first.

I noticed a couple of cosmetic touches since my last time there. Somebody had cleaned the two fifteen-inch sphinxes that crouch at the head of the staircase, even slathered a little paint on the swinging double doors. But the air was still the same. Unnatural temperature and humidity, too warm in summer, too cold in winter, too heavy all the time.

Guinness spoke to a technician, using phrases like "the floater" and "not family." The technician ran a finger down the top sheet on his clipboard and then motioned us to follow him. In the body room itself, the honeycomb of beige square doors was set in a wall of beige tiles, and the handle on the door would remind you of an old-time icebox. The technician pulled down on the handle, and the drawer snicked out on its casters, coming to a sudden, vibrating halt between Guinness and me.

The technician whipped the sheet back over the body and down to the waist. There's no sense of modesty in a morgue, no further indignities that can give the dead any final offense.

Just glary lighting searing vivid memories into the minds of even occasional visitors like me.

I looked down. There wasn't much left of the face, the eye sockets empty, the features and the teeth staved in here, pushed out there from the fall or the rocks or the creatures you prefer not to picture. The hair seemed a shade darker, but it had been in the water for a while. The body type was about right, the flesh more flaccid in death than in life as I remembered her. There were no surgical marks on the chest or scalp.

I said, "When's the autopsy?"

"Not scheduled," said the technician.

I looked up at him. "How come?"

Guinness said, "Not that it's any of your business, Cuddy, but in case you haven't been keeping up with the news, the M.E.'s got stiffs stacked around this place like fucking cordwood. Unless I can give him a reason for cutting on this one, she stays a virgin."

I looked at Guinness this time, then back down to the body. The left hand had an irregular bleach mark where the Cracker Jacks ring would have been.

I said, "Was she wearing a ring on that finger when you found the body?"

Guinness said, "What kind of ring?"

"Any kind."

"No. No jewelry."

"Car keys?"

"There was nothing on her."

"Wallet even?"

"What's the matter, you deaf or what? Nothing is nothing."

Very evenly, I said, "How about a scrunchy."

"A what?"

"One of those puffy ribbons a woman wears to keep her hair back."

"No. She was just in shorts and a T-shirt and panties."

"Colors?"

"Blue shorts, I think. The T-shirt might be green or blue, I never saw the clothes dry."

"Shoes?"

"Just some kind of old sneakers."

I thought about it. The guy in the GMC pickup staves in her face, wrecking the teeth for dental matching. Then he takes everything off her that seems distinctive but leaves the bare minimum of clothing. That way, if the body's found, it looks like it went in the water and bounced off the rocks on its own.

"Well?" said Guinness.

"I think it's her."

"Finally. What's her name?"

"Melinda."

"M-E-L-I-N-D-A?"

"I guess so. Never saw it written down."

"Last name?"

"Never heard it."

"What?"

"I said I never heard it."

"The fuck you jerking me around for, Cuddy? You say you can ID her, and you don't even know her fucking last name?"

"Maybe there'll be something in the car."

"What car?"

I looked at him steadily. "The one at the bridge by the channel."

Guinness seemed as though he was going to protest over that, too, but something about what he saw in my face led him to pass on it.

I said, "Can you show me?"

Guinness took a loud breath, pushing open the passenger door of the Prelude and walking to the railing on the bridge to join me. He pointed vaguely toward the right bank of the channel. "Fishermen said they spotted her over there first. Just thought it was a barrel or something till she got closer."

"They pull her out?"

"Shit, no. One of them stayed here while the other one went and phoned 911. The one that stayed made out he was some kind of hero for watching over things alone."

"Can I have their names?"

A smug grin. "When you give me hers."

I took a breath myself. "Where was she when you got here?"

"Still in the water, hanging-ten with her face against the rocks and pilings."

"The uniforms didn't beat you here?"

"Hey, like you said, our station's only a mile away."

I oriented myself to what the photo angle in the *Globe* had been, then turned around. There was the faded daisy, on the antenna of the Dodge Swinger, slumped into a parking space. I walked toward it, Guinness following behind me and making noises like you'd hear on the twentieth mile of a forced march.

When I stopped at the Dodge, his voice said, "This the car?"

"Yes."

"You sure of that?"

I gestured toward the daisy. "This is it."

"All right. Let me get the plate."

As Guinness took out a pad and moved to the rear bumper, I said, "B-A-T-6-1-1, New Hampshire."

He looked down, then back at me. "The fuck it is."

"What?"

"This is a New Hampshire tag, all right, but you're not even close."

I walked over to him. He was right. SLH-237.

I said, "I don't get it."

Guinness said, "I do. You been jerking me around on this from the word go. And I'm pissed, Cuddy, very fucking pissed."

"I'm not jerking you around." I bent down. There were fresh nicks on the screws holding the plate on, and some mud around the edges of it. "This plate's been changed."

"Yeah, right."

I moved to the front of the Dodge. "This one, too."

"In your dreams, Cuddy."

"Guinness, look. I'm telling you, this is the car, but the guy in the pickup must have switched plates."

"With what?"

"Maybe his own truck. His plates had mud covering them, and there's some on these."

"Oh, so he commits a fucking murder, *then* takes the time to switch his own plates for the ones on the murdered girl's car?"

"Maybe the plates on his were stolen already."

"Yeah, or maybe he just keeps a couple sets in inventory, in his toolbox there for whenever he needs them."

"Guinness, all I know—"

"Why does the guy leave the fucking car here at all, huh?"

"Why?"

"Yeah. Why doesn't he drive it the fuck away from where he kills the girl or at least dumps her?"

"He was alone. Or he didn't have time. Or Eddie was giving him—"

"Or the Easter Bunny was hopping along Summer Street after playing tennis with Santa Claus at the Boston Athletic Club, and the guy didn't want his boyhood idols to think less of him."

"Guinness, don't you see it? The guy in the pickup was trying to throw you off."

"Yeah, well, he did a helluva good job of it, Cuddy. A helluva good job. Because I'm thrown off like I went over a fucking cliff. Now take me back to the office."

"We're here, can't we at least go through the car?"

"On what ground? The doors are unlocked, feel free to come back and fucking browse. But all's I see in there in plain view is a couple of candy wrappers. And I get no smell of decaying flesh from the trunk and no fucking grounds to pop it, especially if the owner just happens to stroll over from Anthony's or Jimmy's picking the remains of a lobster roll out of his teeth and asks me what the fuck I'm doing vandalizing his vehicle."

I looked into the car through the driver's side window. The

blanket I'd used from the backseat was gone, along with the knapsack Melinda had lifted off it.

"Will you at least run the plates for me?" I said.

Guinness exploded. "No! What I will do is take out this fucking Glock cannon the commissioner made us all learn how to fire and blow a fucking hole through you unless we're in your Japmobile in the next ten fucking seconds."

I looked at him for five of those seconds, then shook my head and started back for the Prelude.

4

G
UINNESS HAD ME DROP HIM OFF AT A COFFEE SHOP TWO
blocks from the Homicide Unit on West Broadway. He
didn't bother saying good-bye.

I found a parking space down another block and a pay
phone that was working. Dialing directory assistance for New
Hampshire, I got four numbers for the Division of Motor
Vehicles there. The first woman who answered bounced me to
a second, who bounced me to a guy in the Information Office.

"I'm a private investigator in Boston, and I need to run the
registration for a couple of your vehicles."

"No problem. They're public records up here."

"Great."

"Just come to our counter, 10 Hazen Drive in Concord,
between 8:15 and 4:15 any weekday. If you're going to want
information on more than one registration, it's five dollars
per vehicle, and be sure to get here by four."

I didn't have to look at my watch to know I wouldn't make
it. "Any other way besides being there in person?"

"By mail, but it takes longer, on account of your request
has to arrive here, go down to the mail room, and then out
to the division and eventually the unit involved."

"How about accessing your computer from down here?"

"Sure, but only through NLETS."

"What's that?"

" 'National Law Enforcement Teletype'—or is it 'Telecommunications'? I can never keep it straight, I'm one of the dinosaurs goes back to the real teletypes, you know? Anyway, National Law Enforcement Teletype or Telecommunications System. Any police department down by you can access NLETS and NCIC at the same time."

"For any wants or warrants."

"Or whatever the new jargon is. You a dinosaur, too?"

"Kind of. Thanks for your help."

"We aim to please."

I hung up the phone and looked over to the substation, then back at the coffee shop. I figured I had at least half an hour before Guinness would be finished.

"It's open."

I came through the door marked LIEUTENANT MURPHY. The man himself was sitting behind his desk, using the one pen from the penholder in front of him, the other slot in the holder having a miniature American flag stuck in it. Murphy wore a long-sleeved shirt with a collar stay under the paisley tie, the jacket to a windowpane tweed suit laid over a chair next to the desk. He looked up, waving the black hand that seemed to swallow the gold pen.

"Sit down, Cuddy. Be just a minute."

I took one of the other chairs, iron gray metal with green pads that matched neither the black padded one Murphy used nor the olive drab file cabinets on one wall. My chair did match the shelves of green Massachusetts Statutes Annotated behind his desk. Almost.

Whatever Murphy was writing seemed to give him trouble. "Lieutenant, I can come back another time."

"No. Be done with this—aw, shit. It can wait."

Watching him put down the pen, I said, "What is it?"

Murphy frowned. "Birthday card. My godson, Arnett."

"I hate writing cards."

"Me, too. Truth is, I'm not exactly crazy about Arnett himself."

"Bad kid?"

"Not exactly a kid, either. Boy's twenty-nine years old. Dropped out of high school, bummed around, got his equivalency, bummed around, dropped out of college, bummed around some more. Had three jobs, two of them things I fixed up for him, then finally quit the last one, and guess what?"

"He's bumming around."

"Might be some hope for you yet, Cuddy."

"Tell him not to join me. Profession's tough enough as it is."

Murphy leaned back in the chair, lacing his fingers behind his head. "Which brings us to why I have the pleasure of your company."

"Kind of."

"What do you want?"

"A girl was fished out of the Fort Point Channel last night."

"Stop."

"Guinness and I—"

"I said, 'Stop!' "

I did.

Murphy came forward in his chair, the hands folded on the blotter in front of him. "Seems to me the last time you got me involved in another squad's case, it blew up in my face."

I didn't answer him.

"Seems to me it was Guinness and Holt then, too."

"I'm not trying to get you involved, Lieutenant. I just want to run a couple of plates with the New Hampshire registry."

"So go talk to New Hampshire."

"I did. They won't do it over the phone."

"Take yourself a ride."

"They'd be closed by the time I got there, and the mail's too slow."

"So, account of it's Friday afternoon, you want me to put in a request, huh?"

"That's right."

"My name'd have to go on it. Ask Guinness to do it."

"Already tried that."

"How about your friend, ADA Meagher?"

"That wouldn't be professional, and you know it."

"No, but it would be fine and dandy to have me help you out."

I got up to leave. "Okay, Lieutenant."

Murphy's eyelids slipped down, giving him a lazy look. "Cuddy?"

"Yeah?"

"Am I the only other cop you know?"

"No."

"Then try knocking on somebody else's door."

It was a good suggestion. "Thanks."

Murphy looked down at the card. "Boy never really had a chance in life."

"I'm sorry?"

"My godson. His daddy was from L.A. and named him after Jon Arnett, halfback for the Rams."

A blond-haired, clean-cut guy. "I remember him."

"Yeah, well, then you see what I mean."

"Afraid not."

"Come on, Cuddy. How's a brother supposed to make anything of himself, his daddy goes and names him after a *white* running back?"

"Calem Police, Sergeant Dwyer."

"Can I have Paul O'Boy in Detectives?"

"Wait one."

After some electronic burping, I heard, "Detectives, O'Boy speaking."

I pictured a stubby guy in clashing clothes with only a few wisps of hair at the front of a perfectly round head. "This is John Cuddy."

"Christ. Now what, the gang thing again?"

"Nothing from them. Just a simple request."

"We're all out."

"You haven't heard it yet."

"Tank's empty, Cuddy."

"You owe me, remember?"

"I remember the guy you went in to save was already dead."

"And the other two weren't."

No answer.

I said, "And nobody on your end had to fire a shot or file a report on a shooting or—"

"Okay, okay. So maybe you're entitled to a little slack. What is it?"

"Simple. I need to run two plates with New Hampshire."

"What, they don't have a procedure for you guys to follow on that?"

"They do. But they won't jump through hoops for a private out-of-stater, and I need the answers haste-posthaste."

"What?"

"I think it's Shakespeare."

"Then go ask him."

"O'Boy."

A labored sigh. "Cuddy, it's Friday afternoon, for chrissake."

"Your computer can't talk to their computer?"

"Yeah, but we usually do those things off-hours when there's no emergency."

"This is kind of an emergency, O'Boy."

A guttural noise. Then, "Tell you what. I can try to slip them in with our next batch of requests, so nobody notices my name's on yours."

"When would that be?"

"Tomorrow morning."

"Can you call me after that?"

"Cuddy, I'm taking the wife on a getaway weekend to Boothbay Harbor."

"They have phones in Maine."

"You don't follow. It's more like she's taking me, kind of a second honeymoon. She thinks the 'getaway' part sounds naughty for a cop."

"You can't manage one call to your department and another to me?"

"I'm kind of hoping not to be able to, if you get my drift."

I thought about it. "Monday, first thing?"

"I oughta be able to do that. Soon's I get in, I'll check with our computer jock, see what he's got."

I didn't see any faster service by dealing with the registry myself. "Okay, but first thing Monday, right?"

"Right, right. Piece of advice?"

"Go ahead."

"You gotta learn to chill out, Cuddy. Every case isn't a matter of life and death."

Images of PFC Duquette in the gutter and the woman in the morgue and a little boy with a strawberry birthmark crossed my mind. "No, not every one."

5

THAT SAME FRIDAY NIGHT, NANCY SAID, "YOU SEEM FIDGETY."

"I don't feel fidgety."

We were sitting on stools at the bar of a place called the Irish Embassy near Boston Garden. They'd redone the interior after buying one of the old 99s, a chain all over the metro area. Truth to tell, if you have a liquor license within three blocks of the Garden, you don't need much more than a roof and a bathroom to pack the people in, even when the Celtics and Bruins aren't playing.

Nancy looked at me over the rim of her pint of Harp. "If you're not fidgety, how come you didn't answer my question?"

I set down my Black and Tan. "Sorry."

She looked at me some more.

I said, "Okay, what was your question?"

"Do you really think they're serious about a new Garden?"

"This time?"

"This time."

Over the past twenty years, a rotating cast of developers and politicians have regaled the public with news conferences about building a new facility for basketball and hockey. The current arena is old and cruddy, with restricted sightlines. It's also where I remember seeing Bill Russell and Dave Cowens and Jo Jo White and Larry Bird on the parquet floor laid over the ice surface when Johnny Bucyk and Bobby Orr and Derek Sanderson and Gerry Cheevers weren't using it. Not to mention the Ringling Brothers Circus and the Moody Blues and even some—

"John, what's the matter with you?"

"What?"

"You're zoning out on me again."

I turned to her. We'd both changed into casual clothes after work to hear some Irish music, the rest of the people around us dressed in everything from designer suits to sweat suits. Nancy was wearing white duck pants and a cotton cowl-neck sweater in one of those in-between reds I never get right. I had on a chalk-striped shirt and corduroys that were almost too warm for the night but not quite. "I was just thinking of some old times."

She got a little wistful. "The ones before me."

"Not exactly, Nance. I'm worrying something that gives me a bad feeling."

"A case?"

"Not yet."

The wistful look turned a little hurt.

I said, "I know we agreed to share things, kid. It's just that this might be a direct conflict of interest for you."

"How direct?"

"A Boston death that the police aren't treating as a homicide."

"But you are."

"It just doesn't feel right to me."

A better smile. "So long as I still feel right to you."

"No problem there."

There was some feedback noise from the stage at the back of the bar, and a guy in his twenties with home-cut hair moved to the microphone, shrugging the strap of a guitar over his head. Adjusting the mike for his height, he said, "And how are you now?"

A smattering of applause.

"Ah, you think you're feeling fine already, wait till you hear me sing. They loved me in Amsterdam."

A guy's voice yelled out, "Amsterdam?"

"Yes, in Holland, it is. Wonderful people there. I'll tell you, if the Dutch lived in Ireland, they'd still own half of Europe, but if the Irish lived in Holland, we'd all be drowned by now."

A roar of laughter. The singer launched into a revolution song I hadn't heard before, and the crowd fell immediately quiet.

Nancy leaned into my ear and said, "What's the name of this?"

"I don't know, but it's not considered polite to talk during one."

Nodding, she leaned back.

Saturday morning, we walked to a hardware store, Nancy buying me a pair of white, cotton work gloves so I could keep my hands clean the next time I changed a tire. Then we drove north in the Prelude, taking Route 1 to 128 North and Route 133 toward Crane Beach. It's a magnificent stretch of sand and dunes donated by the Crane family, the folks who brought the world all those porcelain urinals and toilets in the older public buildings. In summer the beach is packed with sun-worshippers who don't mind that the water's too cold for swimming or that for a couple of weeks the place is infested with greenheads, big flies that would remind you of pit bulls with wings.

It was overcast, just cool enough to chase the bathing suits and replace them with optimistic beachcombers, determined joggers, and elderly race walkers. Nancy and I left the car in the parking lot and climbed the slatted-board path between two dunes to the water.

Across the bay to the north and west is the Plum Island Reserve, protected home to dozens of species of marsh and beach birds. We turned east to walk into the wind first.

Nancy took my hand, swinging it a little like we were

square dancers doing a promenade. "What's bothering you, John?"

"Nothing."

"You kept me up all night."

"I was twitching in my sleep?"

"Twitching? Try kick boxing. What's going on?"

"That case—or what might be a case."

"The one I could have a direct conflict on."

"Right."

"I think I'd rather have a conflict than bags under my eyes."

"Oh, I don't know. They might give you that air of maturity a jury wants to see in a lawyer they're expected to trust."

We didn't say anything more for a while, walking among the broken crab shells, lavender tampon applicators, and used condoms garnishing the tide lines of seaweed. A father and son were flying a kite, not even needing a running start in the breeze.

Nancy said, "I was talking to a clerk on the civil side last week."

"About what?"

"The problem with unclaimed exhibits."

"From trials, you mean?"

"Yeah. After a case is tried and nobody appeals, the attorneys almost never take the stuff back."

"So, you shred it."

"Not just documents, John. Crushed bicycles and clogged airplane carburetors and faulty ski lift chairs, you name it and it's pushing through the walls of the cubbyholes they have."

"Bullshit, Nance."

"Meaning?"

I stopped, waited for a jogger to go by us. "Meaning you're just making small talk."

Her eyes searched mine. "What's wrong with that?"

"You're doing it to annoy me."

"Why?"

"Because I'm not telling you what's bothering me."

"You told me."

"No, I didn't."

"Sure you did. You—"

"You know what I mean."

The smile that just tweaks the corners of her mouth. "And you know what I mean."

"If we have a relationship . . ."

". . . then we share things, regardless of professional inconveniences."

"I don't think they taught that in law school."

Nancy used a thumb and forefinger to tug at my chin. "If you'd finished, you could say for sure."

We started walking again, my hands in my pockets, her left arm linked in my right. I went through the whole story, Melinda and Eddie Straw and the red-haired guy and Guinness at the Fort Point Channel.

Nancy waited for me to finish. "Because I know you, I'd say you have a point. If I didn't know you, I'd probably agree with Guinness."

"Diplomatic."

"John, is that all of it?"

"What do you mean?"

"All this upset over a boy you barely know?"

"He reminds me of someone."

"Who?"

"An MP of mine, back in Saigon."

Instead of pushing on that, Nancy said, "You want me to do anything about the woman from the channel?"

"Officially, you mean?"

"Yes."

"No. Somebody's running the plates the old Dodge had on it the two times I saw it. I don't see what else I can do till Monday."

Nancy squeezed my arm against her. "I have a few ideas, but out here they'd require a blanket."

We stopped again, and I kissed her. Breaking off the kiss,

Nancy looked up and down the beach, then back at me. "Maybe we could make do without the blanket."

Sunday morning I jogged along the Charles River and did a round of the Nautilus machines while Nancy worked on the armed robbery case for a few hours. Sunday afternoon we went to the last picnic of the season at the house of one of her former law professors who lives in Milton. He's black, and when he moved up here from Philadelphia he inherited "Bertha," his aunt and uncle's old-fashioned barbecue machine. It's a monstrous double-barreled jobbie that slow-cooks about a thousand baby-back pork ribs for three hours until armed guards can no longer insure their safety. We mingled with other professors, alums, and some current students. Leaving early, both of us were in bed by ten so Nancy would be fresh for court the next morning.

I was sitting in my office that Monday, having gone through the Saturday mail that included three charge card solicitations, two vacation "steals," and one advertisement sent by the Fall River Historical Society, still pushing Lizzie Borden memorabilia from the hundredth anniversary of the axe-murders. I was about to start writing the report on an arson case when the phone rang.

"John Cuddy."

"Cuddy, you better have a good explanation for this."

"O'Boy. How was the weekend?"

"The weekend was fine. They got this nice inn—more like a motel, but they call it an inn, the wife calls it an inn, I call it an inn—with this restaurant looks like a tugboat next door. Good food, good everything."

"Then what puts you in so foul a mood?"

"Might have been professional courtesy to let me know what was involved in that check you asked me to run, you know?"

"If I knew, I would have told you. What's up?"

"What's up is a request that's got my name on it, and now I see from the NCIC that one of the plates was reported lifted from a car parked at a mall in East Jibib someplace."

"Which of the plates?"

"S-L-H-2-3-7. Came off a 1990 Buick LeSabre owned by a Manchester woman named Squires, Emily D."

"And where is the mall?"

"Just off 93, south of Manchester."

About an hour north of where I'd helped Melinda and Eddie. "How old is this Squires?"

"Hold on, hold on. She's married . . . sixty—no, that was when the registration was . . . Wait a minute—seventy-two years young."

"How about the B-A-T-6-1-1?"

"That one's just on the Motor Vehicle, not the hot list. Belongs to a Dodge Swinger registered to Finn, Oswald M. D.O.B.—for chrissake, he's eighty-six. What've you got, some car-jackers out of a nursing home?"

"Where's this Finn from?"

"Elton."

"Where's that?"

"What am I supposed to be now, your geography teacher?"

"Just a second."

I went through the Rand McNally I kept in a desk drawer. The atlas was five years old, but the towns hadn't changed names much. Elton was maybe thirty miles northwest of Manchester. Melinda and Eddie might have come from there in Finn's Dodge, the redhead boosting a plate for his truck from the mall where the Squires woman parked her car. Then Redhead kills Melinda down here, switches the plates, and leaves the Dodge with the wrong tags to be traced, if at all, weeks—

"Hey, Cuddy, you still there?"

"I'm here, O'Boy."

"What am I supposed to say if Mrs. Squires wants her plates back?"

"Tell her they're on Mr. Finn's Dodge."

"And where is that?"

"Parked next to the Fort Point Channel."

"Fort—over by you in Boston, there?"

"Right."

The guttural noise. "I don't know the woman, but somehow I got the feeling she isn't gonna like that."

"O'Boy?"

"Yeah?"

"How about an address on Oswald Finn?"

6 ═══════════════════════

I DROVE NORTH ON INTERSTATE 93, NOTICING HALF A DOZEN places on the other side of the road where the redheaded guy in the GMC truck could have waited to pick up and follow Melinda and Eddie southward into Boston. Crossing the New Hampshire line, I stayed on 93 through Manchester. After twenty minutes or so, I saw an exit for Elton and two other towns, the exit ramp having at its bottom another sign with Elton to the left and the other towns to the right.

Turning left took me onto a two-lane road, wild meadows and small ponds on either side. I opened the moonroof to enjoy the slower speed. The air was bracing, less like the last day of summer and more like the first day of fall. The lanes grew narrower, then started to climb, pines and hemlocks now bordering the road. I went another six miles before descending toward a little town that looked as though it had jumped off a tourist's postcard.

White steeple like a whooping crane towering over all the other buildings, some red brick, others clapboard in white, blue, and yellow, all with black shutters and close to the street. Stately maple and oak for shade, the shrubbery in front of most houses trimmed lovingly. There was a blinking light at the center of Main Street, where the octagonal gazebo on the green bespoke brass band concerts a century ago. Across from the green was the municipal office building, stolid in gray granite, a hunk of oak with curlicue lettering advertising library, town clerk, and police. I left the Prelude in a visitor parking slot and walked into the building.

Red arrows on the corner of the entryway pointed every which way. I took the one toward POLICE.

The door with the stenciling on it reminded me of my pebbled-glass one at the office, a fine web of chicken wire visible through the translucent glass. I knocked and heard, "Come on in."

The voice was male, that low, intimate tone of an airline pilot explaining to the passengers why he'd suddenly climbed three thousand feet without warning. The only man in the outer office was standing behind a waist-high counter, his right hand holding a telephone to his ear, his left hand beckoning me as he nodded in my direction. He was about forty, no more than five-seven but burly, his forearms under a short-sleeved, powder blue uniform shirt—the kind you see on men used to driving nails or shooting pucks. A big semiautomatic filled a strapped holster on a Sam Browne belt. His pants were dark blue with a cavalry stripe down the sides, the shoes a Corfam black with no apparent lifts in them, which I found admirable. The hair on the blocky head was chocolate-colored, crew-cut with a moat of baldness around the patch of hair at the top of his forehead. Beyond the moat, the hair rode over tiny ears, the sideburns in front of them almost hiding them.

Into the phone, he said, "Well, what do you have that'll get it out? . . . You can't smell it? I can smell it, and I've got to be riding around— . . . Well, try that, then, and give me a call back. . . . Soon's you can. . . . Right, thanks."

Hanging up, he blew out a breath. "Had a couple of teenagers drinking beers out behind the high school Saturday night. Nothing so wrong with that, rather see them on beer than dope, I guess, but one of them got upset enough as I was driving him home that he urped up in the back of my cruiser. Stinks to high heaven, and the boys at the car wash don't know what all to do about it."

"Disinfectant's the only thing I remember working, but it's going to smell, too."

He looked at me. "Be the lesser of two evils, anyway. You with a department now?"

"Never was. Back in the service we had mostly jeeps, and you could take down the canvas, air them out some."

"MP?"

"Yes."

"Overseas?"

"Among other places."

He considered that, stuck out his hand. "Kyle Pettengill."

"John Cuddy."

After we shook, Pettengill said, "What can I do you for?"

Folksy of him. "I'm a private investigator in Boston. I have what might be a case I'd like to talk with somebody about."

"Well, I'm somebody. Will I do?"

"Don't see anyone else."

"And you won't. Girl's out sick, some kind of Asian flu already this year. I'm kind of the day shift. Come on in my office."

I walked around the counter and followed Pettengill to another pebbled-glass door that had K. PETTENGILL, CHIEF lettered across the middle.

He pointed to his title on it. "I'm a little shy on Indians."

"Sometimes easier that way."

"It is. Most folks wouldn't believe that, but it is."

Pettengill's office had a lower ceiling than the outer area. The floor was carpeted but didn't look vacuumed, with dog hairs I could see and grit I could feel as I walked on it, even in dress shoes. On top of his desk were a small sun-bleached American flag and a brighter New Hampshire state flag, both with magnetic bases. Between the flags was a blotter, some paperwork and pencils, and an opened bottle of Dr. Pepper, the sixteen-ounce size. There were two guest chairs in front of the desk, both old wood, just the backs padded in brown leather.

Pettengill said, "Before you get comfortable, you might show me some ID."

I took out my holder and handed it to him. He went to the chair behind his desk and sat down, copying the information from my license onto a pad of yellow-lined foolscap. Then he pushed the holder back across the desk to me. I put it away and chose one of the chairs.

Pettengill set his pencil down so it wouldn't roll. "Okay, what do you have?"

"I helped a young woman named Melinda and a boy named Eddie with a flat on 93 down near Boston last Thursday afternoon. A redheaded guy in a blue pickup pulled over, too. He seemed interested but then moved on. I think the woman's body was found in the Fort Point Channel that night."

"You think?"

"Face and teeth were smashed in."

Pettengill nodded. "Fingers?"

"Intact."

"Go on."

"There was no sign of the boy near the channel, but the car I saw them in was parked by where the body was found, only the plates had been switched."

Pettengill considered that. "And one of the plates led you to Elton."

I was impressed. "That's right."

"Just who's your client in all of this?"

I thought of PFC Duquette and Eddie Straw. "I'm not sure."

Pettengill considered that, too. "Describe the woman and the boy."

I did.

"And the redheaded guy in the pickup."

Again.

Pettengill rubbed his chin like he was trying to remove makeup. "Would you like some Dr. Pepper?"

"A little early for me."

A nod. "Reminds me of what used to be my favorite drink."

"What was that?"

"Canadian Mist and Coke. Call them 'blabbers' around here, account of you have more than three of them, you start blabbing about near anything."

"But it's not your favorite drink anymore."

"Uh-unh."

"What is?"

"Dr. Pepper."

My turn to nod.

Pettengill's hand brought the soda bottle close to his lips, then stopped. "You see, I liked those blabbers just a mite too much."

"There a reason you're telling me this?"

"There is. The driver of your pickup sounds an awful lot like Lonnie Severn."

"You know him, then?"

"From back when the blabbers and me were constant companions. I've been sober two years, four months, and . . . huh, I've lost count of the days. Bad sign, means it's been too long since a meeting."

"AA?"

"Yeah. Works for me."

"And for this Severn, too?"

"No. No, I got him to attend a couple meetings around here, my regular one, and another over to Bristol, but the program didn't seem to be right for him."

"The man I saw didn't strike me as being under the influence."

"Oh, he wouldn't have been. At least, I hope not. No, Lonnie found his own way. Found it through Jesus."

Pettengill watched me for a reaction. I don't think I gave him one.

He took a swig of the Dr. Pepper. "I'm not sure exactly how religion's helped Lonnie, but he's doing all right for himself. Got a good used trailer out of town a ways, nice new pickup you saw. Straightened himself out."

"I think I'd like to talk to Lonnie."

"Maybe. First things first, though. Who belonged to the plates on the car you saw?"

"One was an older woman from Manchester who had them boosted off her car in a mall lot."

Pettengill watched me some more. "Who was the Elton one?"

"Oswald Finn."

"You had the name already, you have the address, too?"

"Yes."

"So you could have found Oz Finn on your own."

"Probably."

More nodding. "I'm wondering how come you stopped in to see me first?"

"Professional courtesy, Chief."

"Meaning, you're not licensed in New Hampshire."

"That's right."

"An honest answer. I like that."

"Just reciprocity. You recognized the driver of the truck and told me his name."

"I did."

"You recognize Melinda and Eddie, too?"

"Eddie, yes."

"There a reason you didn't give me his name?"

"There is. I figured we'd go see Oz Finn together. Depending on what he says, we might see Eddie's folks, and then again we might not."

"Why start with Finn?"

Pettengill reached for a blue straw Stetson. "Because I've known Oz a lot longer than the others."

"Should we take my car?"

"Unless you sorely miss the smell of beer puke."

7

MAKE A RIGHT ONTO MAIN HERE."
Before moving into the traffic flow, I waited for a weary Ford pickup from the late sixties to ease by me. "Old one."

Pettengill shrugged. "Lots of old ones around here."

I looked at the buildings on the street as we passed them. Most had stock in the windows, not too many FINAL SALE or OUT OF BUSINESS signs. "Things seem pretty prosperous, considering."

"Considering the recession, you mean?"

"Right."

"Well, we aren't as bad off as some towns, that's for true. But we don't have a ski mountain close on, or a university like Durham or even a college like Henniker. No, what we've got is some clean air and country roads and two thousand or so good souls."

"Sounds like enough."

"Not quite." He motioned with his hand. "Now this left, just past that lightning maple. Should take the poor tree down, before it falls on somebody."

"What do you mean by 'not quite.' "

"Huh?"

"What do you mean by the air and roads and good people not being quite enough?"

"Oh. You got to understand Elton as a small town in New Hampshire. Fine state, blessed with a lot of natural beauty but too few natural resources. Quarry petered out around the time they finished the town building we were just in. Mills did fine till the Great Depression in the thirties, then went south to the Carolinas. We had a nice little factory here made some kind of computer thingies till the company that opened her went bust down by you. That factory, it carried this town a good fifteen years, but it's gone and that's it. What the state gives the towns to spend on education hasn't been what it should be for a couple generations, and that's coming home to roost. Then—"

Pettengill stopped. I said, "What's wrong?"

"Nothing's wrong. I just didn't mean to be going on like that."

"It was interesting. I didn't mind."

"Man who used to drink and doesn't anymore has a lot of time on his hands. I fill it up reading, but that doesn't mean I should be blabbing about current affairs the way I used to about other things when I'd be three sheets."

What Pettengill had been talking about didn't seem to me like a man showing off his education, informal or otherwise, but I didn't press it. "Anything I should know about this Oswald Finn before we meet him?"

"Nothing that won't be apparent."

It was an old clapboard house, one full story and half of a second. The half wasn't quite vertically proportional to the first, as though the upper part was added on by someone else later. The roof was missing some shingles, and others were cracked here and curling there. Pettengill and I climbed the steps to the shallow, open porch that held a broken-down wicker chair and a gut-sprung easy chair, the fabric faded beyond color.

"Mind that board before the top. She'll give on you a little."

I stepped up and over it.

"Not like Oz to be inside on a day like this. Lord knows we'll be seeing few enough more of them."

Pettengill opened the screened door and banged hard on the inside one. I didn't hear anything, and apparently he didn't either because he banged louder.

Turning to me, "Oz is a bit—"

A voice said something from well past the inside of the door.

The chief put his mouth to the crack of the jamb, shouting. "Oz, it's Kyle Pettengill. I'd appreciate a few minutes of your time."

There was a rattling of the knob, and Pettengill pulled back his head before the door shuddered and then heaved open. I didn't hear the sound of any locks first.

The man on the other side of the door looked like a human basset hound. The skin on the forehead nearly drooped over the eyebrows, the jowls hanging so far they swung as he moved his head from Pettengill to me and back again. The eyes were hawkish, but the right side of his mouth seemed to tic along independent of the left, and the hands that gripped the top rails of the four-footed walker were gnarled and colored in swirls of red and purple. He wore a white dress shirt with frayed collar and a brown cardigan sweater with frayed cuffs over stained, baggy suit pants.

Then he smiled, yellowed false teeth, and you could see a young man trying to get out and have a good time for himself. "Kyle, sure is a pleasure to see you."

The voice was raspy, but not loud.

Also in a normal voice, Pettengill said, "Oz, this is John Cuddy."

"Mr. Cuddy, pleased to meet you. Forgive me for not shaking, but I'm afraid the arthritis has made me a little ragged on the amenities."

"Not to worry."

"Well, we'd probably be more comfortable inside than out."

The three of us moved directly at the pace of the walker

into a living room whose furnishings were bought on time before I was born. The arms of the plush sofa and matching chairs were covered by crocheted doilies, the rug worn and the coffee table scratched. But the doilies were white and starchy, the rug clean, and the table polished. The arthritis forced Finn to make getting into his chair a five-count exercise, which included doing a one-eighty with the walker and then a slow recline until his butt was past the point of no return and he settled into the cushions. Pettengill took the sofa, me the other chair.

Finn used his right foot, wearing a Leatherette bedroom slipper, to nudge the walker out of his line of sight but not his reach. "So, Mr. Cuddy, what brings you to Elton?"

I looked to Pettengill, who nodded. Returning to Finn, I said, "I thought you might want to know where your car is."

The old man blinked, the folds of skin making it nearly as much of an exercise as getting into his chair had been. "My car. It isn't out back in the garage?"

I looked to Pettengill again. He said, "Oz, when's the last time you were out to the garage?"

Finn allowed as how it had been a while.

I said, "Mr. Finn—"

"I'd feel more comfortable, you were to interrogate me using 'Oz,' if that would be all right with you."

When I paused, Finn filled the space. "You see, a man gets to be eighty-six, he kind of likes to feel the peer of the men he talks to, doesn't remind him as much of being so old."

"Fine. Oz—"

"Also might help my comfort level to have an idea just who you are, Mr. Cuddy."

I guessed the first-name basis didn't run both ways. "I'm a private investigator from Boston. Something happened down there that I'm looking into up here."

A cloud worked its way across Finn's face. "Something having to do with my car."

"I'm afraid so."

"Tell me. Straight."

I looked to Pettengill a third time. He nodded again.

Watching Finn, I said, "I stopped to help a young woman and a boy with a flat tire just north of Boston. That night, someone matching her description was found dead near the same car, but the boy wasn't."

Finn's lower lip came out a little, like a toddler pouting. "My car."

"Yes. I recognized it from the daisy on the antenna."

"Ma's sunflower."

"I'm sorry."

"My wife—we always called each other 'Ma' and 'Pa,' from Ma and Pa Kettle. You know what I mean?"

"I saw a movie with the characters. Marjorie Main was one, I think."

"Yes, well, when we started calling each other that, it was a joke. Got to be less of a joke as we got on in years. Anyway, Ma stuck that plastic thing on the antenna the day we bought the car. Got some kick out of the name, too. Dodge 'Swinger.' Not that we ever were. Other than together, I mean. Loved the car, but never cared for the flower, myself. Then, after Ma died, I just couldn't take it off. The car was the last big thing we'd bought together, you see. Would have seemed like ... betrayal, somehow."

"Can you tell me about Melinda?"

Finn looked off, through the window. "Reminded me a bit of Ma when she was her age. Came up to my door last spring—Melinda, now, not Ma, of course. Ma's been dead these past ... Anyway, Melinda came to my door, she was dirty and tired, an old rucksack weighing her down, but she had her head up, sort of ... I'm not sure what word I'd use."

"Defiant?"

"Yes, defiant. Or 'spunky,' that's one Ma would have used. Melinda had spunk. Was down on her luck but hadn't given up. Said she'd be happy to do any work I had for food." The pouting lip. "Dear God, Kyle, I hadn't heard anybody saying that since 'thirty-three."

Pettengill nodded. He seemed good at it.

I said, "Do you know Melinda's last name?"

"Never told me one."

"How about where she was from?"

"From? You mean hometown?"

"Yes."

"Never said."

"How about more recently?"

"No, we didn't talk much about her ... what would you call it, her 'background'? I got the impression ... I'm not sure how you say something like this today, but I think she'd had ... a hard time of it, and not just before she came to see me."

Pettengill said, "Abuse, maybe?"

" 'Abuse.' I guess that would be a polite word for it, Kyle. I had the feeling people, maybe even family, had taken advantages off her." Finn looked out the window again. "Sex things."

I gave him a moment. "But you never asked her about it."

The hawkish eyes came back to me. "Would you?"

Pettengill said, "Oz, did she end up working here?"

Finn eased off. "Yes. I don't have much needs doing, just the household stuff that fell away a bit since Ma passed on. But I couldn't turn that girl from my door, so I skipped this room and the bedrooms and got her working on the kitchen and bathroom. I didn't exactly follow her around, but it was pretty clear she was doing a good job on things and sure wouldn't finish before sundown, so we had some beef stew—Dinty Moore, they put out the next best to homemade—and she just wolfed hers down, like it was the first hot meal for a while. I asked her if she could come back the next day, keep going with the work. And Melinda said she could, then asked ... then asked if she could maybe sleep on the floor of the spare room back by the kitchen, save herself some time getting here in the morning. Well, it didn't take a genius to figure she had no place of her own to stay, so I told her to use the upstairs bedroom—I have to stay all on this floor with the arthritis—and gave her a towel and facecloth and showed her where the linen was. She thanked me, and there was a tear coming down her cheek. ..." Finn traced a bent index finger down his own face, pantomiming it, then snorted once and dropped the hand to his lap. "Anyway, she stayed that night, and we had toast and cereal the next day, and she started on this room. After that, we just . . . kept going."

I hadn't wanted to interrupt him, but he seemed finished. "Oz, did many people know she was living here?"

"Couldn't say. I sure didn't tell anybody. Elton's four times the size it was when I was growing up, but it's still a small town, and folks in a small town love their gossip."

"Did she ever have any boys here?"

The hawkish eyes again. "Not under my roof."

Pettengill said, "Did Melinda know Lonnie Severn?"

"Severn? I hope not."

I said, "Then you never saw him around here."

"No. There's something off about that boy, and I don't just mean from his drinking." Finn looked to the sofa. "No offense, Kyle."

Pettengill nodded. For a man with a great voice, he didn't seem to use it much.

I said, "What do you mean by 'off'?"

Finn came back to me. "I don't know the word for it nowadays, but 'peculiar' is how he struck me, first time I met him. The kind who when he was a child would get his pleasure pulling the wings off flies or frying ants on the sidewalk with a magnifier glass."

Would get. "Severn's not from around here, then?"

"No. I think he come up with the rest of them for that computer place."

"Up from where?"

"Don't know. South, someplace, account of his accent."

Consistent with what I'd thought meeting him on the Interstate.

Pettengill said, "You ever see Melinda with anybody, Oz?"

"Anybody?"

"Anybody at all."

Finn shook his head, the jowls swinging some more. "This house isn't exactly made for entertaining, Kyle. Only one I can think of is that Eddie Straw."

I tried to watch Pettengill. He didn't react more than you would from someone saying "Have a nice day."

I said to Finn, "When was this?"

"Oh, over the summer. That boy ... Was he the one with Melinda and my car?"

Carefully, I said, "The boy told me his name was Eddie."

"Well, you couldn't miss him, it was. Got this birthmark through his face. Damned shame, too, because he's a nice boy. Guess God works down past skin-deep."

"Did Eddie and Melinda become friends?"

"Friends? I don't know as I'd say that, given the difference in their ages. But I don't think Eddie has friends his own age, least I didn't ever see him with any."

"How did Melinda and Eddie meet?"

"Don't know. But he'd be over here, at least a part of pretty near every day in July and August, watching TV with Melinda or helping her with things she didn't really need help with—she had the chores pretty well in hand. Nice, polite boy. Didn't seem to know much, though."

I thought back to the tire-changing, but Pettengill said, "What do you mean, Oz?"

Finn shrugged. "It was like . . . like his daddy never showed him how to work things. Simple things, like basic tools and such. When I was his age, I could almost take apart a motor, but he didn't seem to have the hang of anything past a rake or a shovel."

Pettengill rubbed his chin.

I said, "Oz, how long has Melinda been gone?"

Finn looked at me steadily. "Some days now."

"When's the last time you saw her?"

He didn't have to think about it. "Thursday."

Very quietly, I said, "She told you she was leaving?"

Finn closed his eyes. "Not in so many words. She just acted kind of picky over her lunch—Velvetta, it was, good cheese on wheat bread—then told me there was something she had to do. Melinda was hoping to come back and see me afterwards, but she wasn't sure she was going to be able to."

"Did Melinda tell you what the something was?"

"No."

"She ask to use your car?"

He opened his eyes. "No. I suppose I could say she did, and maybe that would keep her out of some trouble." Finn looked to Pettengill. "But I've never lied to you, Kyle, and I'm not about to lie in front of you, either."

"I appreciate that, Oz."

I said, "It looks a lot like Melinda took your car and was driving Eddie south to Boston. Any reason you can think of for that?"

"None. I will say this. She knew where the keys were, and she sure used that car often enough to go to the grocery, get the things we needed. If I can, Kyle, I'd like not to have that Dodge of mine listed as stolen."

"Up to you to report it that way, Oz."

"Then it's not stolen, far as I'm concerned. It was a good machine, let somebody else get some use out of it."

I said, "Right now, it's just sitting near the bank of a channel in Boston."

Finn came back to me, eyes no longer hawkish but sad in the hound dog face. "What you were saying before, about a girl 'matching her description' being found dead by my car. You think it was Melinda, don't you?"

"I saw the girl who said she was Melinda driving your car, and I saw the body. For a lot of reasons, I can't be sure, but I think they were one and the same. If I can take something you know was hers back to Boston, maybe they can compare the fingerprints and be sure."

Finn shook his head, lids down again. "Go on if you want to, but I've listened to a lot of folks tell me things over the years, Mr. Cuddy, and you sound sure enough of what you say for me to believe you without that."

Pettengill said, "I wonder if it would be all right with you for us to take a look at her room?"

Without opening his eyes, Finn waved toward the staircase.

"Mind your head."

The stairs were narrow, the beam at the top a little low for somebody over five-eight or so. The second floor was stuffy and warmer by fifteen degrees than where we'd been.

As if reading my thoughts, Pettengill said behind me, "These old places, they don't have the roof insulation they might. Just right for what we see of spring and fall, but hot in summer and cold in winter."

I moved to the only doorway on the floor.

It could have been a cell in a convent.

The fleur-de-lis wallpaper was separating here and there, but somebody, probably Melinda, had tacked it down with some kind of paste where she could. The floor was pine, gouged and grooved by the feet of furniture and the shoes of people over the years. Like the living room, though, it was swept clean and polished, and the blanket on the bed was tugged down tight, military or hospital style, depending on your point of view. The closet was empty, just three hangers swinging on the single pole from the vacuum created by my opening the door. Nothing under the bed, not even dust balls. The one bureau had handles on three of its four drawers, but no clothes in any of them, just contact paper over the bottoms. The contact paper was fleur-de-lis, too, but in a slightly different pattern and almost new, as though someone recently had tried to match the wallpaper. There was nothing on the top of the bureau, not perfume or comb or even a penny of leftover change.

Pettengill had watched me opening and closing things. "Oz didn't tell us different, I never would've thought somebody was living in this room."

Hard to argue with him.

Crossing his arms, the chief leaned into the wall, moving his back around like a bear against a tree. "This would have been the master bedroom when Oz and his wife could make those stairs."

I shook my head. "Let's go down to the kitchen."

Old tin cabinets over Formica counters, the aluminum molding for protecting the edges long since gone. At the sink, gooseneck faucet, petaled handles, porcelain corroded around the drain. A Hostess donut box, empty on the counter next to a plastic dish holder. In the holder were a single plate, glass, knife, fork, and spoon drying, as though Finn took from the holder only the things needed for each meal, then washed them and put them back in the holder again to dry.

On the shelves inside the cabinets, some fine crystal glasses survived in twos and threes from what must once have been sets of six or eight, fast-food and gas-station promotional tumblers filling the gaps. All the glasses were turned right side up, like they'd already been dry when put away. I tented a handkerchief around the middle three fingers of my right hand, then dipped into three of the cheaper ones in front and brought them down onto the counter.

As I laid each into the donut box, Pettengill said, "You taking those for prints?"

"If you and Finn don't mind."

"I don't, and Oz told you the same."

"We'll check with him again on the way out."

"Anything else in here?"

I looked around at the yellowed linoleum and the rusty toaster and the old refrigerator that made me think of the handles on the doors of the last place I'd seen the girl I thought was Melinda.

"Not that I could tell you."

Pettengill said, "Oz?"

No response.

A little louder and a gentle hand on the shoulder. "Oz?"

His head lifted and his eyes opened, and for a second the smile came from the store-bought teeth, the young man inside looking forward to life again. Then Finn saw me and remembered, and the eyes focused, losing their brightness. "You get what you needed?"

I showed him the glasses in the box. "Okay if I take these?"

"Yes. I don't need them."

Pettengill and I thanked him, then turned to go. From behind us, Finn said, "Not fair."

I turned back. "I'm sorry?"

The old man looked up at me. "I've had myself a long life,

most of it happy with the love of a good woman to help. Life wasn't fair to Melinda. Short and unhappy."

I expected Pettengill just to nod again, but instead he said, "Never knew life to be fair, Oz. The days are good or bad, but fair somehow doesn't seem part of it."

The lower lip pouted out. "She deserved better. Girl with her spunk, she deserved better than she got. It turns out that body . . . is her, Mr. Cuddy, I'd appreciate your letting me know so I can at least arrange a decent funeral for her."

As we went through the unlocked front door, Oswald Finn said, "Lord, but I miss you, Melinda. I truly do."

Neither one of us made any move to go back in to him.

8

"WE GOING TO SEE EDDIE'S PARENTS NOW?"
Kyle Pettengill twisted in the passenger seat toward me. "Thought we might have some lunch first."
"Sounds good to me."
"Glad to hear it, since you're buying. Take this next right."
I did. "How about at least the name?"
"The name?"
"The last name of the parents."
Pettengill rubbed at his chin. "After we eat. Maybe."

It was a pub in the major block of the downtown on Main Street. I found a space two hundred feet from the front entrance, only about a dozen people stopping on the sidewalk to say hail to the chief. Lucky we hadn't parked any farther away.

Inside there was a burnished brass–railed bar and some half-back stools. Booths for couples and groups nestled under illuminated, stained-glass portraits of skiers doing cross-country, downhill, slalom, and moguls. The walls behind the portraits were dark wainscoting, all the way to the ceiling, where the chandeliers looked like giant Tiffany lamps. No ferns, no yuppies, just half a dozen porcelain pulls for draft beer and ales, only three of which I recognized.

Pettengill waved to a waitress, who called him by his first name, then aimed us toward a booth. Sitting on his side of it, he said, "You ought to try one of the taps, you like that sort of stuff. Best selection in the county."

"It won't bother you, my drinking?"

"Good for me, actually. Brings home that one with lunch isn't worth the ten with dinner that'd follow."

The waitress came right over with laminated menus. She reeled off the drafts, and I ordered a Catamount lager from Vermont. While I looked at the menu, Pettengill ordered a Dr. Pepper.

I said, "Made up your mind?"

"About what?"

"About what you're having."

"Don't need to. Always order the same thing here."

"Which is?"

"The French-dip roast beef and potato salad."

"Let me guess. The best in the county."

"It is."

When the waitress brought our drinks, we both ordered the beef. After she'd gone for the kitchen, I tried the beer.

Pettengill said, "How is it?"

"Just right."

"Told you."

I took another mouthful, then put down the mug. "I appreciate your taking me around like this."

"Might want to hold off on the thanks till after the next stop."

"Why is that?"

"Eddie's folks might not be as helpful as old Oz."

Like Old Oz had been a fountain of information. "That why you're kind of dancing me around them?"

"Partly."

"What's the other part?"

Pettengill sipped his soda. "You know much about being a small-town cop, Cuddy?"

"Some."

He nodded, like I'd agreed with what he was thinking. "Most of the time most of the days, it's almost embarrassing. I mean, the good citizens pay you to be there, but you're not really doing much. Answering phone calls that should be going to the electric company or the Fish and Game. Sometimes just talking with people who don't have anybody else to talk to while you've got your feet up on the desk and the sidearm sagging on your belt."

I said, "But then there are the other times some of the days."

Pettengill nodded again. "You ever faced a drawn gun?"

"Yes."

"Back when you were in uniform yourself?"

"And since."

Another nod. Pettengill was in love with them. "When I was going through the academy, one of the instructors told us something about facing a gun. He was an old state trooper, grizzly bear of a man, had some French-Canadian in his English. He says to us one class, 'I'm gonna tell you something, you never forget it. Somebody holds a gun on you, don't matter it's a man or a woman, you watch they eyes, now. If they use to guns, they shoot you without closing them. But if they ain't use to them, they gonna squeeze those eyes shut just before they shoot. They can't help it. They afraid of the noise more than they afraid of you. But if they know they guns, then they don't. They got use to the noise, and they don't think about it, and you gonna be dead. But if they close they eyes, that's when you move, and you ain't gonna have but the one chance, and you be sure you use that to kill them. Three bullets, chest.'"

"From what I ever learned about it, the instructor gave you good advice."

This time I thought Pettengill would nod, but he didn't. Instead he made little rings on the tabletop with the bottom of his soda glass. "Trooper said the last part just that way, 'Three bullets, chest,' like a doctor giving you a prescription for some kind of fancy pills."

I waited for Pettengill to get to it.

A sip of Dr. Pepper. "Couple years ago, when I was still drinking, these two subjects from Haverhill—specialized in robbing convenience stores, I later found out. These two decide to drive up the Interstate, hit a little store off it, just to extend their horizons some. Only the one behind the wheel took the Elton exit, and the distance was enough that they were pretty well out of patience by the time they got to the edge of town." Pettengill gestured southeast. "So they didn't just rob the seventeen-year-old working the cash register. When the take from the drawer wasn't much, it being only four in the afternoon, one of the guys—you don't need names, let's just call him the taller one—the taller one shot the kid. Just like that. Twice standing, twice on the floor. Left him there, lying in his own blood behind the counter."

More Dr. Pepper. "I was stopping off for some milk and bread after my shift. They were coming out the door, guns still in their hands, when I was closing the door to the cruiser. I look up at the first guy—the shorter of the two was in front—and I was lucky."

Pettengill watched me. I said, "Because the instructor was right."

A nod. "He was. The shorter guy brought his gun up and closed his eyes, and I dived and rolled against the cruiser and popped him with three in the chest as he got off one. Then his partner swung onto me, and I gave him the rest of the rounds in the cylinder the same way. Three bullets, chest."

That was the story, now for the point. Maybe.

Pettengill said, "Taller guy comes out first, I'm dead, because he probably wouldn't be closing his eyes before opening up. Three guys instead of two, and I'm dead again, because back then I was carrying just the revolver."

I let my eyes fall toward his waist, which I couldn't see through the table. "And now?"

"Nine mil, Sig Sauer. Enough for five of them, almost six, if they come in bunches."

I didn't say anything.

Pettengill played with his glass some more without drinking any. "You're a pretty fair listener, Cuddy."

"When I can learn something."

"What'd you learn from my carrying on like that?"

"I'm hoping you're going to tell me."

Almost a grin as the waitress arrived with our plates. The roast beef looked to be trimmed and lean, the bread fresh and home-baked, the salad from new red potatoes, the onion stock in a bowl big enough for easy dipping.

Pettengill waited until she was gone. "I wasn't sober that afternoon, I'd have been dead. Made me realize something. I liked the job a hell of a lot better than the booze. I came out of that a hero, but the next wrong thing I do, people will forget about the afternoon outside the convenience store and start remembering all the other things they don't like about me, and pretty soon the nephew of one of the town's elected officials is sitting in my chair with his feet up, talking to lonely people on my telephone."

"And therefore, while you're happy to help me if you can, you're not about to start a civil war here to do it."

"Like I said, a pretty fair listener."

We ate in silence for five minutes, politely dipping the receding edges of our French bread into our respective bowls of onion stock. Every part of the meal was what it should have been.

Pettengill was more proficient at the dipping part and finished one bite ahead of me. Wiping his lips with the napkin, he said, "Haldon."

"Haldon?"

"The last name of Eddie's parents. Polly and Thomas Haldon. You about done here?"

"Except for paying the check."

"They like cash fine, you want to just leave some on the table."

We drove two or three miles before turning into a gravel driveway that wound through scrub evergreens to a small and weathered saltbox Cape. A man was standing off to one side near a lean-to shed that seemed more weathered than the house. About thirty and slim, with short black hair, no mustache or beard. He was sweating, a long-handled maul resting over one shoulder, as though he'd been splitting firewood and stopped when he heard my engine. His work pants were green and his plain T-shirt white, the shirt looking clean except for the sweat stains.

Pettengill got out of the car first. "Thomas."

"Chief."

I closed the driver's side door, not bothering to lock it. "Mr. Haldon."

The man watched me, that steady, stony look you see in some country people. "Don't believe I know you."

Pettengill walked toward him. "This is John Cuddy, Thomas. A detective from Boston. He's working on a case, like to ask you some questions."

Haldon looked at Pettengill the same way he'd looked at me. "He police, too, Chief?"

"No, just private."

Haldon seemed to consider that. "Long as he's with you, we can talk to him. Wife's in the house. Let me just change into a shirt won't ruin her furniture."

Pettengill nodded. "We'll wait for you."

Haldon set the maul on top of a piece of firewood against the wall of the shed. Then he walked around his house, and I heard a screened door slap closed. Every move was deliberate, unhurried, as though he'd had the idea to go in himself and wasn't in any rush to get there.

I joined Pettengill. "Is the word 'standoffish'?"

The chief turned his head to spit onto the brown grass. "For Thomas, that was downright outgoing."

The living room had a dining area and kitchen separated from it by a half-wall. The living room floor was covered by a thick rug, BarcaLounger-knockoff furniture, and a coffee table displaying magazines on which the word "Christian" appeared as an adjective with some frequency. The walls were covered by needlework in cheap frames, homilies of home, hearth, and church stitched onto the fabric. There was no television set, no stereo, nothing beyond places to sit and things to read.

The dinner table had ten or twelve loaves of bread cooling on little racks over spread newspapers. The chairs were the kind that became popular a few years ago: natural stained seats with backs and legs painted white. Everything gave the impression of being new and stark. Including Polly Haldon.

She was about her husband's age and short, with narrow hips. The hair was barely past her earlobes and nearly straight, a mousy brown that seemed just to hang from her scalp. The glasses were plain black, but with an almost oriental cast to the corners at the temples, as though she were trying to inject something exotic into her appearance that wouldn't have been her fault. Mrs. Haldon already had asked us twice if we'd like tea and maybe some cookies when her husband, who had changed into a blue dress shirt, spoke to Pettengill.

"Chief, what's this about?"

Pettengill nodded in my direction, and Haldon's eyes followed his to me.

I said, "Mr. Haldon, is your son, Eddie, around?"

A stiffening. "My son. He can't have anything to do with your case."

"Could I speak to him?"

Haldon opened his mouth just enough to say, "No."

I looked toward Pettengill. No help from that quarter.

To Haldon, I said, "I have reason to believe your son was riding into Boston with a young woman named Melinda last Thursday."

Mrs. Haldon seemed to catch her breath. Her husband just set his jaw a little more.

I said, "Do either of you know anyone named Melinda?"

Haldon said, "What's her last name?"

"I don't know."

"Neither do we."

I looked to his wife. She was staring at me the way a rabbit does when it senses your presence and freezes, thinking and then just hoping you can't see it.

I said to her, "Mrs. Haldon—"

"When you're in this house, you will ask me your questions, not my wife."

I stared at Haldon. Just the stony look back.

Despite what he'd told me, his wife said, "Eddie's going to school."

Haldon turned and gave his wife the same look I'd been getting.

She withered. "Thomas, there's nothing wrong with telling them that." Polly Haldon engaged me. "Eddie wasn't doing well in that mainlining thing."

I didn't want to close her off. "Mainlining?"

"You know, when they take the children who are slow—"

"—our son is not slow, he's—"

"—and put him in with all the others. He just couldn't keep up, is all."

I said, "You mean 'mainstreaming,' maybe?"

"Whatever they call it, their system didn't work for Eddie."

"He has a disability?"

"Well . . ." The woman glanced toward her husband and rebounded like he'd body-blocked her. ". . . his mark, you see."

"Mrs. Haldon, I've met your son. That mark doesn't affect his brain."

"No, but it does affect his soul."

"Mrs.—"

'It's the Mark of Cain."

"Polly, that will do!"

I looked at Haldon, who obviously wasn't accustomed to having to raise his voice to be obeyed. "Where's your son now?"

Haldon said, "He's safe in the Hands of the Lord."

"Then you do know where he is?"

"That's our business, and none of yours."

"Have you even heard from him?"

Nothing.

"Do you know if he's with Lonnie Severn?"

Eddie's mother said, "There's no—"

"Woman, I won't be saying this again. That . . . will . . . do."

I tried her. "You're not worried about him?"

At first it seemed my question had broken through the wall Polly Haldon's husband was building around her. Then, "Why would I be worried?" She glanced again toward Eddie's father. "Our son's with Jesus. And learning more about Him every day."

An ecstatic smile lit up her face.

"Thanks for jumping in there, Chief."

"Couldn't see that it was my place to."

I slowed down for a curve, then geared up to fourth. "You realize they have no idea what's going on with their son."

"I realize nothing of the kind. You come to me with a story about helping some folks who are broken down along the Interstate. You tell me there's a corpse in the Boston morgue that might be one of them, account of some resemblance and Oz Finn's car being near the scene. You're not licensed here, so I take you around to the people who might know. Oz can't tell us this Melinda's last name, and he doesn't want to go official over his car. The Haldons believe their son is where they know he's safe, and they say he's getting religious instruction they approve of. Around here, that's as far as official inquiry's supposed to go."

"Chief, I know what I saw."

"And I'm not doubting that. But until the prints on Oz's kitchen glasses match up with the unidentified body in Boston, we don't even know the dead girl's this Melinda."

"Chief—"

"It isn't what you saw that's the problem, Cuddy, it's all these . . . inferences you're stacking, one on top of the other. And I'm sure not going to dial up a prosecutor and tell him a family that says they sent their boy away for religious school ought to be hounded by us until they tell you where and why."

I took the turn that led back to Elton's downtown. "That mean you want to be dropped off at your office?"

"Stop by the car wash first, see if they got that puke smell out of my cruiser."

"Guide me."

He outlined it, and for a mile or so we were both quiet.

Then, "Cuddy, if there was anything I could do for you, I would."

"How about directions to Lonnie Severn's trailer?"

Pettengill shifted in his seat. "I haven't seen Lonnie in town for a few days."

"I'd still like to talk with him."

Rubbing of chin. "If you thought Thomas Haldon was standoffish, you're not going to get any farther with Lonnie."

"I'd still like to try."

Pettengill nodded. "This road back northwest out of town. Be a big, weathered chicken barn on the right, all falling down. Biggest building you'll have seen since the Interstate. Take that right, and after a couple houses half a mile in, you'll see Lonnie's trailer on the left. It's shrouded some, so if you hit the turnout for a little stream on the right, you'll know you've gone too far."

"And if nobody's home?"

"Then I wouldn't know where he'd be." Pettengill shaved some of the sharpness off the next sentence. "Might try Reverend Vann Tucker. His church is this one here on the right."

We went by it too fast for me to see much.

"And that's Severn's church, too?"

"Don't know for sure. But when Lonnie found Jesus, Rev Tucker might have been the one showed him the way."

9

AFTER DROPPING PETTENGILL OFF AT THE CAR WASH, I FOUND the falling-down barn without much trouble, the old beams and posts looking like the bleached bones of a long-beached whale. I took the right and passed a couple of houses, somebody's dog running toward the Prelude, baying at me as I outdistanced it.

I clocked half a mile; without the odometer, I would have blown by the trailer on the left. Sliding by slowly instead, I picked up just the color and the fact that there was no vehicle in the rutted, sand-and-gravel driveway. I continued on to the turnout Kyle Pettengill had mentioned, maybe two hundred feet down and in sight, using it to reverse direction and come back to the place.

Parking on the side of the drive to avoid bottoming out on the crests of the ruts, I sat in the car. No one, animal or human, came out to greet me, though I could hear the closest neighbor's dog from back up the road, still howling once in a while.

The trailer was raised on cement blocks placed every five feet or so around its perimeter. It had a front door off-center to the right, and its metal siding had been painted a dull green that I didn't think came from the factory. There were two windows on my side, both small and neither open. The trailer seemed almost shuttered, like a lake house closed up for the winter.

After a few minutes, I got out of the Prelude and started walking toward the front door before noticing that the tire marks continued around to the back. I wondered why somebody with a driveway, even a rutted one, would park behind the place, but I decided still to begin with the front door. Its sill was a few inches above the stoop, which consisted of eight or ten uneven concrete blocks that held a rusting bucket and a couple of brushes, the kind you'd use scrubbing floors. I knocked on the aluminum door, its screen having too many holes in it to provide much barrier to insects. No answer. With the toe of my shoe I moved the bucket to the side to try the door. Locked.

Following the tire tracks behind the trailer, I saw them stop just short of the patio arrangement. Three folding chairs stood in the dirt around a piece of plywood laid over trestles of more concrete blocks, forming a makeshift picnic table. The chairs were aluminum-piped but not the lawn variety, the back of them stenciled with the name of a funeral home. All the chairs were rusty, but only one looked well used, and it was at the end of the plywood piece that had the most food stains on it. There was a homemade barbecue a few feet from the table, a filthy piece of iron grating serving as a grill between—surprise, surprise—more concrete blocks.

Next to the back door, a section of old, elbowed stovepipe came out and up from the wall, a crude patchwork of shingle and tape around the hole cut to accommodate it and a little coolie hat of tin crimped over it. Under the pipe was some ribbed camouflage cloth, the words PORTA ROOF on it. I pictured Severn during hunting season, putting the thing up against a tree like an umbrella and huddling under it with a rifle.

The back door wasn't favored with a stoop, so you'd have to swing yourself up to enter it like a tractor cab. I reached at chest level to try the handle. Also locked. I thought about breaking in, then decided to go back to the car and try another tack first.

The church was white clapboard on the outside, looking freshly painted. It rested on a foundation that somehow seemed older than the building it supported. The structure was blocky, and instead of a steeple, the top of the facade over the main entrance ended abruptly and horizontally, like a giant widow's walk on the home of a sea captain.

The chunky stones of the parking area crunched under my feet as I passed the sign with white plastic letters on a black velvet pushboard, advertising SUNDAY WORSHIP and announcing EVERYONE WELCOME. In more modest lettering underneath was REV. VANN TUCKER, PASTOR.

I opened the front door of the church. The interior was fairly dark, the woodwork fairly light. The center aisle felt wide for the proportions, perhaps twelve rows of pews to either side of it. No colorful decorations, even the window above the altar just plain glass.

A head appeared over the surface of the altar table, then a man stood up under the head. About five-ten, he was a little heavy, with cornsilk blond hair and wire-rimmed glasses. The white collar affixed to his shirt was reversed, but the sleeves were rolled up, and it was obvious that he was doing housecleaning.

"Can I help you in any way?"

"Reverend Tucker?"

"Yes." He adjusted his glasses and came down off the altar. I'd overestimated his height some. Once level with me, he was no more than five-six or so, with the tails of the shirt tucked into baggy beige jeans. He wiped his right hand on the jeans and extended it to me. "Vann Tucker."

We shook. "John Cuddy, Reverend."

"From Boston, by any chance?"

"The accent kind of gives it away."

"Oh, only some. More the way you're dressed. A little ... formal, perhaps, for Elton." As though reminded, formality crept into his voice as well. "Are you police of some kind?"

"Not for a while, but Chief Pettengill did suggest I might talk with you."

"About what?"

"A case I'm working on. Do you know a man named Lonnie Severn?"

Tucker sucked in some air before saying, "I do."

"I'd like to ask you a few questions about him."

Tucker looked around, as though perhaps we weren't the only ones in the small church. "Let's sit here. It's as good a place as any for the truth."

He led me to a pew. There was no kneeler to trip over or flip up, and the benches were all covered with burgundy cushions, about the only color in the building.

Tucker's glasses had slipped a bit as he sat, and he adjusted them again. "What are your questions?"

"It might help if you could tell me something about Severn generally."

"Generally. Very well. Generally, he used to be a destructive alcoholic. Would have cost him his job at the circuit factory if the computer company that owned it didn't decide to close the whole thing anyway. Then he found the strength to resist the addiction through the Lord, and as far as I know, Lonnie remains sober and seems to be prospering."

As far as he knew. "I take it that he's not a part of your congregation?"

"No. No, I do volunteer counseling for some of the civic and charitable organizations in the area. I suppose I shouldn't say 'volunteer,' since it's part of my job to do that sort of thing for the Church, but most of them—the organizations, I mean—are unfunded in this era of underbudgeted social services, and I met Lonnie through one of those efforts he turned to originally."

"Severn's not from around here, then?"

"No. His family's from the South somewhere, I think."

"Do you know where?"

"No, I'm sorry. He probably told me, but I've forgotten." Tucker's glasses slipped again. "He's lived in New England for quite some time, though. Boston area, then I think Manchester before coming up to us."

I thought about Mrs. Squires's license plates disappearing from the mall near there. "Reverend, would you know which church Severn does attend?"

"No. But not because . . . I don't think Lonnie 'attends church,' as I believe you mean the expression. I think he's turned more . . . fundamental?"

"Evangelists, you mean?"

"Not necessarily." Tucker looked troubled. "Forgive me, but it's very difficult discussing this without using technical religious terms."

"Whatever makes you feel more comfortable."

He pushed at his glasses again. "Perhaps this will help. Many of the churches in this area are Protestant rather than Roman Catholic. But many of our congregations, like this one, are relatively poor. Accordingly, the"—he motioned with his hand—"relatively 'no-frills' look here is only partly religious and mostly financial."

He looked at me hopefully. I said, "With you so far."

A judicious nod. "Well, then, I think you can understand that there are some . . . ministers who might preach more religiously and less financially about the values of simplicity."

I thought about the starkness of the Haldons' home and attitudes. "Go on."

"As far as I know, Lonnie found his way through the forest thanks to such a minister far from us."

"Do you have a name?"

"I'm sorry, no. But why don't you just ask Lonnie?"

"If I see him, I plan to. Do you know anything about this other minister?"

"No. Lonnie, when I saw him in town once, said that he'd been delivered by a 'preacher of prophesy,' thanks to someone in his family. Lonnie was very grateful to God for what He'd done for him."

"What the preacher had done?"

"Ah, no. What God had done. For Lonnie."

"Any idea where this other minister is from?"

Tucker's glasses started down his nose again. "Only the vaguest."

"Which is?"

"Somewhere south again, though I must tell you . . ." The troubled look returned. "Even that feels . . . off?"

"Off?"

"Yes. As though . . . as though I didn't really think it was the South."

"You felt Severn was lying to you?"

"Oh, no. No, not at all. More that . . . I just remember feeling that the church wasn't exactly in the South."

Not exactly making much headway here. "Reverend, do you know what Lonnie does for a living?"

"For a living?"

"Yes. How he's managed to afford the trailer and that new pickup even though he got laid off with everybody else from the computer factory?"

"No. No, I don't. Most people up here get by."

"Get by?"

The glasses slid once more. "I'm afraid that's rather a technical term, too. 'Getting by' means doing whatever seasonal work is available to hold off the creditors and put food on the table. Berry-picking, trapping, splitting and delivering firewood, and so forth."

"And Lonnie does those things."

"Most of the people do because most of them have to."

A wild shot. "Like Thomas and Polly Haldon?"

"Oh! Oh, my. Are they involved in this case of yours, too?"

"I think so. What can you tell me about them?"

"Not much, I'm afraid. I've virtually not seen them since they left."

"Left?"

"Left the congregation here."

I stopped. "The Haldons were part of this church?"

"For quite some time. At least, until the closing."

"The closing of the factory."

"Yes. Yes, I'm afraid that tested many people's faith, which is understandable. But the Haldons turned away from us, and now they seem . . . well, almost to avoid me."

This clearly wasn't easy for Tucker, and I didn't want to make it harder for him if I had a choice. "I spoke to them today, Reverend—"

"Oh! And how are they doing?"

" 'Getting by', if I'm using your phrase right. But what I was going to say is, they still seem awfully religious."

"I'm so glad."

"Mrs. Haldon gave me the impression that she was intensely concerned about Eddie's birthmark, though."

"Yes. Poor boy. Polly always has been very . . . sensitive about that."

"She called it 'the Mark of Cain.' "

"Oh!" Tucker got agitated. "Oh, my. She never mentioned anything about that to me."

"Reverend, what exactly is the 'Mark of Cain'?"

"Well, it comes from the Old Testament, the Book of Genesis. Cain killed his brother, Abel, and the Lord 'set a mark upon Cain' and exiled him."

"What kind of mark?"

"The Scripture is rather ambiguous about that. But through history, many people unfortunately interpreted all sorts of blemishes as the Mark of Cain. A sign of evil, even deviltry."

"A sign of Satan, you mean?"

Tucker grew somber. "I'm afraid so."

I shook that off. "Getting back to the Haldons, you wouldn't know where they may have turned, would you?"

"Turned? You mean, to what congregation?"

"Or minister."

"I'm sorry, no." Tucker hung his head, causing him to actually have to catch his glasses in midair as they came off. "You must think me not much of a pastor, Mr. Cuddy."

"Actually, I was thinking the opposite. When I was growing up, there was a priest I really admired. He never rushed a ceremony, always had an ear when you needed one. I get the feeling you're a lot like him."

"Thank you." In a very quiet voice. "Thank you so much for that."

As I stood to go, Tucker said, "By the way, how is Eddie?"

I looked down at him. "Eddie?"

"Yes. Didn't you meet him?"

"His parents said he was gone."

"Gone? You mean off to his new school?"

I sat back down. "You know something about that?"

"Only that Chris Kiernan told me he was leaving the system. But that was just last week, so I didn't think he'd already be gone."

"Who's Chris Kiernan?"

"Christine, actually. The principal at the Elton Elementary. Eddie's school."

I must be getting dim. Of course there'd be educational records here that would have to be sent on, wherever Eddie went. "Can you tell me how to get there?"

The school lay at the center of a semicircular driveway, orange pikes in the ground to tell the winter's snowplow where to curve its blade. A ball field with an iron-cage backstop and rubber, permanent bases off to the left, a parking area for teachers' cars off to the right. The building itself was two stories high, red brick and white trim, sporting a small white cupola on the roofline and a flagpole flying Old Glory. The entire effect was so reassuring it made you believe in the future of America again.

Up three steps and inside the entrance, the office marked PRINCIPAL stared me in the face. I walked to the windowed counter next to a doorway, and a woman so old she had to be a volunteer asked from a secretarial desk if she could help me.

"I'd like to see Christine Kiernan."

"And you are?"

"John Cuddy."

The woman seemed to assess me, then said, "Just one moment, please."

She got up and entered a second, open doorway behind

her. After ten seconds, she came back out and said, "This way, please."

I went through the doorway by the counter and past the secretary.

From behind her oak desk, Christine Kiernan rose to greet me. And rose and rose. She had to be nearly six-five, with long chestnut hair drawn back into a flowing ponytail and ruby earrings. The blouse was white with small teddy bears in various colors printed on it, a solid skirt beneath that picking up one of the teddy colors. Her face was long, the eyes high and sparkly, all coming together to form what my grandfather's generation would have called a handsome woman.

In a mellow voice, Kiernan said, "Mr. Cuddy?"

"Yes."

"Christine Kiernan." She made no move to shake hands. "Sit down, please."

I took one of the oak visitor's chairs, eminently comfortable even though it wasn't padded.

Kiernan folded her hands on the blotter in front of her, the big, tear-off kind that show the month in review. "What brings you here?"

"I'm a private investigator, looking into what may be the disappearance of one of your students."

A frown. "One of *my* students?"

"Or perhaps former students. Eddie Haldon."

The frown deepened. "Do you have some sort of identification?"

I took out the holder and passed it to her.

She looked up from reading it. "This says 'Commonwealth of Massachusetts.' "

"That's right."

"You're not licensed in New Hampshire, then."

"No, but if you'd like, call Kyle Pettengill about me. We had lunch together today."

Kiernan didn't seem convinced. Handing back the holder, she picked up the phone, dialing directly herself. Then, "Kyle, Chris at the Elementary. . . . No, I'm fine, how about you? . . .

Good, good. Kyle, I've got a gentleman sitting in front of me named John Cuddy. . . ." Kiernan laughed in spite of herself. "Yes, that's him. Kyle, what I want to know is . . . Yes, yes. . . . I see. . . . Right, well, I guess I will. . . . Thanks, Kyle, I'll do that, too. . . . Right, bye."

I said, "What made you laugh?"

"Something about the way Kyle described you."

"I don't suppose you'd want to share that with me."

"You can ask Kyle, tell him I don't mind if he doesn't."

"Okay."

Kiernan took a breath. "Mr. Cuddy, New Hampshire is a very . . . libertarian state. Do you know what I mean?"

"Macro version: minimal governmental intervention in the lives of its citizens. Micro version: you mind your business, and I'll mind mine."

She watched me. "Was that your way of telling me not to underestimate you?"

"It was my way of telling you what I thought 'libertarian' meant."

Kiernan nodded. "Then you can appreciate my position. School records are confidential unless the appropriate authorities jump through the appropriate hoops to get them, and the appropriate authorities—for our purposes, the police— aren't interested in jumping just now."

"Meaning you can't tell me if you sent Eddie's school records to a given address at the request of his parents."

She hesitated before answering. "Meaning I can't discuss Eddie, period, without parental permission."

"Which Pettengill told you I'm not likely to receive."

"Ever."

"Look, Ms. Kiernan, I do appreciate your position. But hear me out for a couple of minutes." I went through Melinda and Eddie with the flat tire on Oswald Finn's car, Severn in the blue truck, the body from the channel, and the Haldon's attitude when I spoke to them. "So, that's where I am. I think Eddie's in some kind of danger, or at least that his parents don't have a clue what's really going on with him. I need help here, and you're in a position to maybe give me some."

Kiernan did hear me out. It wasn't until I was finished that she stood and folded her arms, moving to the window behind her and looking at some jungle gym equipment and two bicycle racks.

Over her shoulder, she said, "Do you know how you get to be a principal, Mr. Cuddy?"

Pettengill had asked me such a similar question, I just said, "No."

"It starts in school, I think. As a student yourself, admiring the men and women who help you and the other students you see sometimes struggling and sometimes excelling. Then you do a stint during college as a student teacher, and you realize it's not as easy as it looked, but you get hooked and go into it and grade homework when you can barely keep your eyes open after dinner and into the night. You get up at dawn to prepare new assignments, and you cover administrative things like bus duty and lunch duty, and if you're halfway decent you get tenure because they can't find many others who are willing to do what you do for what they pay you to do it. Then at some point you lose a little of the fire, a little of the 'why' you teach, and you drift into administration. You keep your tenure, even though you know you don't really want to go back into the classroom. But you also know that it's the only thing you've ever done, the only thing you could fall back on."

Kiernan turned to me. "All of which would be lost if somebody ever told a parent you were leaking student information to a smiling Irishman from Boston."

"That what made you laugh on the telephone?"

She smiled herself, fought it, and then laughed again. "Kyle said I would kind of like you."

"But liking me doesn't include helping me."

Kiernan unfolded the arms, sat back down. "Can you promise me confidentiality?"

"I can promise you I won't tell anyone else you told me a thing."

"And how good is your promise?"

"Out on the road, when I was changing the tire? Eddie

asked me if I'd promise to go looking for him if anything ever happened to him."

Kiernan processed that. "And here you are."

"And here I am."

Squaring her shoulders, she said, "Ask your questions, and I'll answer the ones that I can."

"Eddie have any close friends?"

"Not that I'm aware of. I'd usually see him at recess, off by himself."

"You have any idea why?"

"Children can be cruel, Mr. Cuddy, especially to other children who are different."

"The birthmark."

A reluctant "Yes."

I said, "What do you know about Eddie's homelife?"

"Not much. We have regular parent-teacher conferences, and the Haldons attended theirs."

"Let me guess. Attended, but didn't really participate."

"The way Eddie's teacher phrased it for me, 'They answered my questions, but didn't have any for me.' "

"And that's unusual."

"For people like the Haldons, anyway, who have some education themselves. I had the impression that they tolerated the fact that Eddie had to come to school, but they didn't like it and weren't about to promote it."

"Eddie have any brothers or sisters?"

"No."

"Any problems in school?"

Another hesitation. "I've spoken with his teacher from last year and the one this year so far—and by the way, you are not to approach them."

"I won't."

"They need their jobs more than I do."

"Like I said."

Kiernan squared her shoulders again. "I had the impression that the parents kept him from doing his homework. That he had just enough ability to tread water in class, but that the

Haldons focused him entirely on religion, not any other aspect of life or learning."

"And they could get away with that?"

"L-I-B, E-R-T, A-R—"

"Okay, point taken. Anyone else around here I could talk to?"

She thought about it. "Nobody that comes to mind. The mother always worked 'in the home,' as they say, and I believe the father's been out of work since the computer factory closed. And my impression is that they've been as insular about most things as they have about Eddie's education."

"Last question, then. Did they have you forward his school records anywhere?"

Kiernan looked down at her blotter, as though she were trying to decide whether we could do lunch on the third Thursday of the month. "This one really could get me fired, Mr. Cuddy."

"Not through me it won't."

She didn't look up. "I got a call from Mr. Haldon. He said they were taking Eddie out of school because he got a 'scholarship' to a 'Christian Institute.' "

"He give you a name?"

"No. Just said that Eddie wouldn't be coming to school anymore as of last Friday."

The day after the tire incident. "And did Haldon ask you to forward Eddie's records anywhere?"

Kiernan finally looked up at me. "No, and that's what troubles me."

"How do you mean?"

"When he didn't ask me about the records, I asked him. The question seemed to . . . throw him a little. Then he said, 'Just send them to us.' "

"Like the need for the records was . . ."

"An afterthought."

I looked into Christine Kiernan's eyes. For such a poised woman, they seemed awfully small and scared.

*　　*　　*

Leaving the school, I drove out toward Lonnie Severn's place again. Turn at the falling barn, past the neighbor's baying hound. Going by the trailer, it still looked deserted, the driveway as empty as I'd left it. At the turnout, I pulled in, positioning the car in the shadow of overhanging trees and angling my outside mirror back at the driveway. Then I waited.

An hour, two, three. I noticed that the air outside the car was colder than in town, the foliage around me turned more to autumn. The leaves on the oaks were the color of rust, the maples more like blood, others I couldn't recognize ranging in yellows from flat to bright, with the ferns a ghostly pale.

Into the fourth hour, a kind of false dark settled over the car, that time of day in the fall when the sun isn't down but behind the trees, and you're tempted to flick your headlights on anyway. In the entire time I'd been sitting at the turnout, only two cars and one pickup had gone by, none of them containing Severn.

I'd had plenty of time to think about Eddie and Melinda, of what I'd seen at the Haldon house and been told at the church by Vann Tucker and at the school by Christine Kiernan. I made up my mind, gave it ten more minutes to change itself, then got out of the Prelude. After opening the trunk and putting the gloves Nancy bought me in my pocket, I walked to the trailer.

The old bucket was still where I'd toed it away from the front door. I knocked heavily on the jamb, anyway. Nothing. I used the glove to wipe off the knob I'd tried earlier and moved around the back.

Chairs, camouflage cloth, everything looking the way it had on my first visit that day. Pulling on the gloves, I reached up to the rear door's handle, then knocked once more before trying the handle, finding it still locked. I looked around, walked to one of the folding chairs, and brought it over to stand on. With the extra height, I could hold the handle at about my waist. I torqued it hard, got nothing. Again, the same. Third time was the charm, and with a shearing sound, the door came open for me.

I waited, still standing on the chair, for two minutes. I didn't expect an alarm, but I wanted to be sure nothing on two legs or four inside the trailer came over to check on the noise. It was quiet as a library.

In fact, when I went in, it looked like a library. Shelving, most of it as makeshift as the picnic table and barbecue, lined the walls. All the books caused the narrow, shoebox design of the interior to seem even narrower. I was surprised. On the highway, Severn hadn't struck me as the bookish type. Then I remembered Kyle Pettengill mentioning how, once off the booze, he had a lot of time to read.

Closing the door shut out most of the faint light, so I left it open until I could find a flashlight next to the kitchen sink. Muting the beam with some toilet paper from the galley-style bathroom, I took stock of the place.

I'd entered through the back door into a kitchen/dining area, the alcove for eating probably doubling as living room with the table folded away. Midships was the bathroom and a linen closet, the closet also crammed with books. Opposite end was the bedroom, with a double mattress wedged into space that looked laid out originally for narrow bunk berths. More books on shelving above and around the bed. The whole place had a dank sense to it, the air fetid, the sheets damp. Not so much a house closed up as a cellar closed in, not enough sunlight penetrating to dry it out.

I got to work.

A majority of the books, mostly paperbacks, were from publishers I'd heard of like Ballantine, Avon, and Fawcett, but plenty of the others carried the imprints of Bethany House, Polebridge, and more I didn't recognize. A few works by Charles "Chuck" Colson in his post-Watergate incarnation. As with the Haldons' coffee table, many of the titles had the word "Christian" in bold print.

There was a separate section of magazines and promotional literature, the mastheads reading "Home to Jesus," "Holy Temple of Him Resurrected," and so on. Many of the promos featured men and women in what looked like prom outfits. Sweating faces and big hair, microphones in their hands and choirs behind them as they were caught by the camera in dramatic turns. The captions under the photos identified the preachers as the Reverend this and Sister that, but what struck me was the sheer number of different organizations.

Then I got to a section of material that seemed to be more recent, specializing in "the Church of the Lord Vigilant," the Reverend Royel Wyeth and his "Lifemate," Sister Lutrice Wyeth. The newsletters read like a small-town paper with a decided "God Loves You" theme. Inspirational poems were interspersed with calendared events and requests for contributions toward various line items on a seemingly endless budget of good works. There were photos of the exterior of an office building, the interior of a television studio, a "Christian Community" of small white bungalows, a tent revival meeting, etc. Two things stood out, once you saw enough photos. There wasn't a person of color depicted in any one of them, and there was no shot of a school as such. If Lonnie Severn roamed widely within the Christian band on the spectrum, he seemed to be focusing lately on this particular signal. I took some samples with a mailing address in Florida called "Mercy Key," the telephone area code listed as 305.

The rest of the place held nothing but what you'd expect in the kitchen drawers and plastic cabinets and built-in bureaus of a bachelor living simply on a gravel road in a forest. The clothes were alternately wrinkled or torn, universally smelly. The dining utensils were mismatched and bent, the glasses few and smudged. No liquor, though, and no evidence that any had been around.

I stopped for a minute and thought about it. If I lived out here, I'd have myself a hidey-hole for really important things.

Poking and prying, fifteen minutes later I tried the tank behind the toilet. A bundle the size of a broken brick, wrapped in opaque brown plastic.

I fished it out and took off the elastic bands. After some unraveling, I got to the core. Cash. Hundreds of bills, heavily fifties. Roughly ten to fifteen thousand, an awful lot of money for an unemployed man who'd just bought a new truck. Nothing but cash in the bundle, though, no names or addresses or documents of any kind. I rewrapped the cash and replaced it.

After checking to see I'd put everything else back, I clicked off the flashlight to let my eyes readjust to the dark. I hadn't found much, and Florida was a long way away, but it was a start and more than I'd had before.

Taking the toilet paper off the lens, I put the flashlight itself back by the sink where I'd found it. Opening the back door and stepping onto the chair, I noticed it was now darker outside than it had been inside. By the time I registered the boots on the ground, something was making contact with my head, turning everything so much darker still that the stars behind my eyes really stood out by contrast.

10 _____

I THINK IT WAS THE BOUNCING RATHER THAN THE COUNTRY MUSIC that brought me around.

I was lying on my back in what felt like the bed of a pickup truck through a sleeping bag I was on rather than in. My mouth was gagged and taped, my hands also taped at the wrists behind me. My legs were tied, but with about eighteen inches of slack between them, as though I was meant to be able to walk hobbled. I still had the gloves on, the pads of my fingers not able to say whether it was electrician's tape or something else equally strong that someone had used on me.

There was a burlappy hood over my head that was drawn to my nose every time I inhaled. It didn't seem to be affected by any wind as we moved along, so I figured I was in the camper shell of Lonnie Severn's truck. The hood or the sleeping bag—or both—smelled of motor oil and urine. The music was coming from just above and beyond my head. I didn't feel we were going fast, more an erratic jolting and rocking, as though the truck was crawling slowly over a bad dirt road.

Then we turned to the right and stopped.

I heard a door open from where the music had died, then

a shift in weight and the thump of the door closing. What I guessed to be the camper's hatch opened past my feet, a male voice saying, "You awake in there?"

It sounded like the redhead from the tire-changing incident. Not quite as much southern accent now, as though he weren't trying to disguise his voice anymore.

Severn said, "You ain't awake, I'm gonna stick you about an inch deep with a knife till you are. So, if you're awake, you pound your right foot twice."

I pounded.

"Good. Now, I'm gonna pull you out by your shoe a little, then you're gonna have to play like a worm till you're all the way out and setting on this back gate. You follow me?"

I pounded twice.

"That's the idea. You clown around any, this knife'll go in more'n an inch. We understand each other?"

Again.

"Okeydokey. Now, just relax some."

Severn first tugged, then dragged my left foot out maybe three feet before stopping. With the taping, I couldn't have managed much of a windup for my right foot, so I didn't try anything.

Letting go of me, Severn said, "Reminds me of the time I had getting you in there. Like two hundred pounds of potatoes, all loosey-goosey. All right, boy, now it's your turn."

Using mostly my feet, I worked my way toward his voice. My skull banged against the top of the camper frame as my center of gravity carried me out and down. I ended up in an awkward sitting position on the gate.

"Your head all right?"

I pounded my foot once against what felt like packed earth.

"Sorry I can't let you rub it, make it better."

Severn said it easily, like he'd used the line before.

"All right now, we're gonna have you stand up. We're gonna be walking, but not far. You get an idea to run, you go ahead. I got both gun and knife, and depending on how far you get into the trees, I'll use one or the other. Move a little forward but bent over, so you don't hit your head again."

I did.

"All right, you should clear her now. Stand up and walk forward."

I started, stumbling and almost falling before I caught the cadence the foot tape would allow.

"You'll get used to it."

Again, like he'd done this before. I tried to push that thought away.

"A tad left now."

It seemed to be even ground, the smell of pine and peat coming through the burlap.

"Now a tad right. More. Good."

Another thirty-four paces, which I felt were important to count because I couldn't do anything else.

"Okeydokey, stop right there."

I stopped.

There was the sound and air swish of Severn moving by me out of reach, the other senses kicking in to offset the loss of sight. I heard footfalls on wooden steps, then the sound of a wooden door swinging open. Then more footfalls coming back down. Three steps, if he was taking them cleanly.

"All right, we're gonna climb three steps. You first. You're gonna have to be careful going up or the tape'll make you fall on your face."

Like he'd learned that from the mistakes of others, too. I felt myself sweating even though the air temperature through my clothes felt like the low fifties.

"Go on."

I moved slowly forward.

"First step's just ahead of you."

I lifted left, right to climb it, then repeated twice more.

"Stop."

Again him coming up and around and past me.

"Now walk to me, slow."

I did.

"Good."

Then he hit me again on the side of the head.

"Caught you on the way down this time."

I don't know what brought me around. Severn seemed sure I was conscious, so maybe I'd moaned or rolled my head.

"You might be wondering how come I hit you that once at the trailer and again here and you don't feel any blood sticking to that hood."

I hadn't been, but he was right.

"Used this nice little billy club a feller gave me. All padded with leather, so it don't leave a mark. Works pretty good though, wouldn't you say?"

I started to say something, stopping when I realized I wasn't gagged or taped at the mouth anymore.

"Come on, you can talk. Ought not to be able to move nothing, but you can talk."

He was right about the moving part. Now I was sitting down in some kind of wooden armchair, the spokes like vertical ribs against my back and shoulders. My ankles were tied or taped to the legs, my wrists the same to the arms. Severn had taken off my gloves, but the hood was still in place, some kind of light flickering through it. Then I caught the scent of woodsmoke and the occasional crackle of an open fire.

"That old bucket at the trailer. You don't know how many times I meant to move it out of the way, but just one of those things you never get around to? I was driving home—the back way, not past the chicken farm—and I see this little car sort of hiding in the turnout, and I say to myself, 'What kind of fool goes fishing in a dried-up stream at night?' Then I see it's got Massachusetts plates on it, so I stop and come over, and what do you know? That old bucket's not where I left it, and there's this little shining inside my trailer, like a lightning bug in a jar. And I say to myself, 'Lonnie, I believe you have yourself a burglar.' "

I couldn't think of anything that would make things better, and I didn't want to make things worse, so I stayed silent.

"After I—what would the police call it, 'apprehended'

you?—I figured it would be a lot easier to have our talk out here in this old hunting camp. You can't appreciate it, but we're in a nice, private spot about ten miles from the nearest humankind. And we're gonna talk about things till I'm plain sick of hearing your voice."

"Severn, Chief Pettengill knows I was looking for you."

"So what? I just tell the chief I wasn't home for a couple days, never did see you."

"He won't buy it."

"He don't got to buy it. He's just got to prove otherwise. I may not have learned much in this life, but I learned that much. And he won't be able to prove nothing."

"These tape marks'll make it clear that whatever happened to me wasn't any accident."

"Kind of—what would you call it, 'pessimistic'?—on your part. You got to have faith in the Lord Jesus our Savior, faith that you're gonna get through this night. That's what I have to do every night. Got to have enough faith to get through it without taking a drink. I don't, my life ain't nothing, account of the demon rum'll kill me. Life without the booze is hard, life with it's just plain impossible."

"Severn, you didn't go to all this trouble just to turn me loose at the end of it."

"Well, I guess you're right there." A pause. "Won't be no body, either. This camp's got a dry well about fifty feet in back. Fool who owned her originally dug himself a well seventy feet deep, when the water table drops to a hundred by the time the hunting season rolls around. Now, I ask you, what sense does that make? So it'll be some time before anybody notices you. Years maybe, if you're lucky. So to speak."

I tried to keep my voice even. "What do you want?"

"That's better. Cooperation'll make everything just that much easier. I see from your ID and wallet stuff in the truck that you're a private detective from Boston. Now, what were you doing at my trailer?"

"Looking to see what might have happened to Eddie Haldon."

Another pause. Then, "Why?"

"When I stopped to help change their tire, just before I saw you, I promised Eddie I'd look for him if he got in trouble."

A third pause, then a laugh, mean and long, not like the good-Christian, recovering-alcoholic, but one from the earlier time, a barroom "Let's have some fun with this feller" sound. Finishing, he said, "Why do you care where that boy's at?"

Even trapped in the chair, I felt a little hope. Severn's question implied that Eddie was still alive. "I told you. I promised him."

Severn didn't say anything, just moved away from me, a scuffing sound, as though he were on his knees. I heard him pick something up and scuff back. Then all the fires of hell melted through the back of my right hand, and I screamed from it, rocking in the armchair, nearly carrying it over backward. A smell floated up, one I'd known in Vietnam often enough and once recently in Boston, the smell of burning flesh.

Severn's voice floated up to me, too. He must have been kneeling in front of me, like a subject supplicating before the king on his throne. "That was just a taste, boy. Just a taste of the blade from the fire. Our Lord God has said that fire cleanses, fire purifies, fire makes our tongues want to praise the Glory of His name. In your case, it's gonna make you want to tell me the truth, and we're gonna toast you a little at a time till you do. Now, nobody works for no snot-nosed kid, so who hired you, and why'd you take those Church papers from my trailer?"

I tried to keep the fear and pain out of my voice, and thought I was about half successful. "I told you the truth. I made Eddie a promise. I'm not working for anyone on this."

I felt I was talking too much, and I forced myself to stop.

Severn scuffed away from me. I tried to flex my right hand, didn't like what I felt there.

The scuffing back. Other hand this time. I nearly levitated, the second application seeming worse than the first, including the smell.

Severn said, "I don't know why, but things seem to work faster if I plow new ground each time. At least till I run out of it. That one, it was only about half an inch into your flesh, but I thought I felt a little bone at the tippy-tip. Hard to tell, with you jumping like that. Beauty of the fire part, it don't just hurt going in, it closes the wound coming out. 'Cauterizes' it, I believe is the doctor word. Now, what sinner of Satan you working for, boy?"

I thought about bad times I'd had in the service and since, and even some of the good ones with Beth and Nancy, but I couldn't see anything to do about this one. Then I felt Severn's hands close on my wrists, the knife lying long axis to my left forearm in his right hand. He pulled himself up to a standing position, leaning in close to my face. His breath was horrible, even filtered through the burlap. His voice rumbled, glowing with pleasure.

"Boy, we can do this for a very long time, because the Lord Our God has taught me patience. . . ."

I remembered something.

"Patience that is eternal in His Name. . . ."

I tensed for it.

"Patience that is—"

As hard as I could, I whiplashed my head forward at his, the Coco-butt that Justo Vega and I had practiced a generation ago in a Saigon bar.

The impact hurt, enough to distract me from the pain and the smell from my hands. Through it I heard Severn grunt, then crumple and bang elbows and skull off my knees. Leaning forward, straining, I got the hood to the fingertips of my right hand and tugged it off.

There wasn't much light, but it still blinded me coming as it did from the fire in the black woodstove, its door open. Severn lay on his left side in front of me, kind of fetal position. The room was about twenty by fifteen, with a couple of cots and a card table and not much else that registered until I found the knife.

On the floor, between my taped legs.

If I rocked forward, I could fall forward and get the knife into one hand. Only problem was, I wouldn't be able to reach the other hand's tape with it. I started to strain upward with my wrists at the tape, trying to pull the arms of the chair from the seat. But whoever built it did a good job with bolts and glue, because nothing would come.

Severn groaned but didn't move.

Despite the tape at my ankles, I could stand up, maybe, and—

Severn groaned again, rolling over onto his back.

I rocked forward and up, crablike, and hopped back toward the wall as fast as I could, crashing into it. The chair's back splintered behind me, driving one spoke into me, just below the shoulder blade, leaving my wrists taped to the arms but now free of the seat, shards of chair dangling from them like bizarre charms on a bracelet.

Severn opened his eyes and shook his head, as though to clear it.

I moved forward, then back again faster, crashing the wall harder and feeling the spoke below my shoulder blade lever out. This time the rest of the chair went, my ankles carrying away parts of the wooden legs, the seat of the chair clattering to the floor behind me.

That's when Severn reached toward a rear pocket for what I expected to be a gun.

I charged him as he came up with it, a black semiautomatic. Swinging my left arm at the muzzle, I knocked a piece of chair against the barrel and away from me as a round went off, the metallic "krang" deafening in that small enclosure.

Severn punched me in the groin with his free hand, but he'd already gotten me used to pain, to moving through it. I brought my left knee up to drive into his stomach, but he saw it coming and caught just a glancing blow as he stepped back, trying to get enough away from me to use the gun effectively.

That's when I felt one of the dangling shards of chair fill my right hand like a rounded knife, and I lunged with it up and in, under the jaw.

Severn dropped the gun and went to his knees, the shard buried almost to his spine.

In the movies, that's when the bad guy obligingly keels

over, dead. Or the camera pans off to another part of the fight scene. But that doesn't often happen when you actually stab somebody. In real life, it can take some time to die.

Severn used both hands to yank at the shard. I helped him pull it out, the blood flooding down onto his shirt and frothing as he tried to breathe through it. And blubber through it.

"You killed me! . . . Oh, Jesus is my Savior. . . . Jesus is my Lord!"

"Severn—"

"Oh, my . . . Almighty God . . . you killed me! . . . You gone . . . and killed . . . me!"

"Severn, where's Eddie Haldon?"

He clasped his hands and raised them. "My Jesus . . . please . . . save . . . me!"

"Where did you take him?"

"Jesus . . . my . . ."

Severn began coughing up blood, cups and then pints of it. He seemed to hiccup twice, a strange sound given everything that preceded it, and looked up at me as he collapsed forward onto the floor.

I began trembling, then shuddering so badly I sat down before I fell down, too.

There was a lot of time to do little things and think.

First I used Severn's knife to cut the tape off my wrists and ankles. Then I found a shaving mirror on a milk crate one of the cots used as a night table. Contorting with it, I could just see the gouge from the chair spoke under my shoulder blade. Painful, but pretty superficial.

I was almost embarrassed to see the wounds on my hands. The right, the first one Severn did, was red and blistering, but only in a one-inch-square patch. The left one hurt deep, but showed only an inch-long stripe of blackened skin, like a charcoal slash. Effective torture without much visible damage, and I wondered where he'd learned it.

There was some antiseptic salve in a first-aid kit on a pantry shelf, and I used that on the burns. It helped a little. The rest of the camp was pretty rustic, except for the slaughter-house scene in the center of the room.

Severn's eyes were open, but I couldn't reach them to close the lids without wading through the draining lake of blood in front of him. The light from the woodstove flickered over his features. He'd gotten a haircut since I'd seen him on Route 93, and his skin also looked less tan, though I chalked that up to loss of blood. The jug-handled ears stuck out more with less hair around them, and the buck teeth had bitten through the lower lip as he went down.

Keeping my shoes out of the blood by walking up to the body from behind, I patted a bulging rear pocket that yielded a wallet. I went through what Lonnie Severn carried on him.

A fifty, two twenties, and a five in cash. A Red Cross donor card with blood type on it, New Hampshire driver's license, no credit cards. Some prayers in handwriting, and a poem of sorts in the same. The poem read,

> Better to take a life there or here,
> Than live the rest of yours in fear.

I drew in a breath, continued on. Social security card, calendar from a bank in Manchester, and a scrap of index card. The last had on it, in the same handwriting as the poem, what looked like names and telephone numbers:

> Rev. Royel off. 305-555-7500
> comp. 305-555-7550
> Axel 305-555-7591

I figured "off." meant office, "comp." probably company. "Axel" I couldn't do much with, but the "Rev. Royel" part sounded consistent, if not inviting, especially given the area code.

I put the index card scrap in one of my pockets and Severn's wallet in another. Sitting on the closer cot, I watched the fire instead of the body and went over what I knew.

Melinda gets wind—probably through Eddie—of his parents' plans to send him to some "Christian Institute." She's streetwise, and that doesn't feel right to her for some reason. Melinda also has "spunk," as Oswald Finn called it, so she takes the old Dodge Swinger and spirits Eddie away.

Severn pursues Melinda and Eddie down from New Hampshire. Spotting their car while I'm changing the tire, he hides his pickup farther south and follows them into Boston. Severn kills Melinda and leaves her to be found pretty easily, but there's no sign of Eddie. Given the way I was handled in the truck, Severn could have taken the boy somewhere. Maybe here and into the dry well, although the camp had the feel of not being used for a while before we arrived. Also, if Severn's coming back up here to do something with Eddie or to him, why not bring Melinda, too, rather than dump her body in Boston where it would be found?

No, more likely Severn takes Eddie to that "Christian Institute." In Elton, Eddie's parents say he's gone with their blessings, their old pastor and the boy's recent principal both feeling he was leaving the area. Severn has lots of stuff in his trailer on Rev. Wyeth's operation down in Florida and some telephone numbers from it in an otherwise thin wallet. Last Thursday to late Monday would be enough time to drive to Florida and back if he didn't do much else and lived on caffeine. And a working arrangement with the Church of the Lord Vigilant might explain the cache of cash and new truck.

Then I got around to me. Chief Pettengill knew I was looking for Severn, and I broke into the trailer before Severn sapped me and brought me here. My car's sitting two hundred feet from the home of the man I just killed. I don't have any idea where I am, other than Severn's saying we were ten miles from other people. Even if that was an exaggeration, I sure as hell can't find my way out to recognizable landmarks at night over the cowpath we bounced along to get here.

I lay back on the cot, the adrenaline fading fast. I didn't like the image of me explaining to Pettengill how all this came about. And I couldn't see him letting me out of the state to go looking for Eddie Haldon, especially fifteen hundred miles south. I didn't even know enough about New

Hampshire law enforcement to be sure how many shots Pettengill would get to call once he learned of Severn's death. At my hands. After I'd broken into the man's trailer.

No, I didn't like any of it, but I fell asleep thinking about it, all the same.

I awoke at close to first light, shivering since I hadn't pulled any blanket over me and the fire had gone out. I was pretty hungry, but not enough to raid whatever larder might have been left in the camp. I restarted the fire and went outside to look around while it caught.

The camp was in a small clearing, the navy blue GMC Sonoma parked in sight. I tried not to think about walking from the back of it to the cabin the night before. Instead I circled the building, nothing more to the place than a scaffold from which I guessed a deer would be hung while the hunter dressed it.

I followed a narrow path behind the camp until I came to the dry well. There was a thick, wooden cover on it, maybe three feet by three feet, which would take some lifting, but that was just fine.

I walked back to the camp and found my gloves. Then I went to the pickup again. The keys were in the ignition, my wallet, identification holder, and the Church papers on the passenger seat. In the back was the sleeping bag I'd lain on, forest green on the outside with a red liner showing elk leaping over rocks. I rolled up the bag and carried it under my arm.

Inside the camp itself, the fire was coming back nicely. I dragged Severn's body by the heels away from the browning blood, which looked shiny and sticky on the floor. Getting him into the bag, I zipped it closed before swinging Severn over my shoulder. He was lighter than I would have guessed.

Carrying him back to the dry well, I tried to think of what I could do about the blood in the camp and couldn't think of much. I'd seen a broom but not a water source, and no amount of scrubbing was going to do anything about the soak-through and staining.

At the dry well, I lifted the cover off with my gloved hands. I couldn't see down past ten feet from the mouth, so I dropped a small stone in the center. I'd counted to "five/one thousand" before it clinked at the bottom.

I slid Severn's sleeping bag and body in after the stone. There were some whispers and squeaks as the bag brushed the sides of the well on the way down. The thump, when it came, was dull, the well deep enough that no cloud of dust came up. I couldn't think of anything to say that would have sounded sincere, so I just put the cover back in place.

Inside the camp again, I fed the burlap hood, bits of broken chair, and tape into the woodstove, adding more logs so the stuff would burn as completely as possible. I thought about burning the floorboards to destroy the blood, but I wasn't sure I could keep the fire contained without water, and besides, it was one thing to vandalize the place, another to burn holes in it. Or burn it down, the much heavier smoke bringing the helpful or even just the curious. With luck, the people who owned the camp wouldn't return for years or want to know how their floor got stained when they did.

I wiped off everything else I'd touched without gloves on, then walked out to the truck. It started up and proved itself over the half mile or so of rocky track to a dirt road. I went right first, but the road gave out in front of two large, fallen trees that had a lot of undergrowth behind them. Turning around, I continued another three miles before hitting pavement, then another four miles before a road sign appeared with a state route number on it. The next intersection had junction signs for the same road that went through Elton. Following it, I got near enough to the town center to orient myself, then drove out again, finding the falling barn and Severn's trailer. I could just see my car, still at the turnout.

Parking the pickup in the driveway, I took the keys from the ignition. Walking around the back, it didn't seem as though anybody else had been by. I opened the sprung back door and climbed inside. Severn's wallet and key chain went on the kitchen counter, me barely remembering to take out each of the cards I'd handled and wipe them clean of any prints. Then I went to the bathroom and got his brick of money. I thought about taking all the Church of the Lord Vigilant literature, but decided it would leave even more of a gap in his shelf arrangement, a gap someone who knew him might spot even faster.

Then I walked back to the Prelude, got in, and let my breathing calm down while I thought things through again. Nothing more I could see doing.

I started up and drove south toward the Massachusetts line. I made myself get fifty miles from Elton before stopping for breakfast, which amounted to choking down an English muffin and some tea.

11 _____

D RIVING BACK INTO BOSTON, I LAID OUT A WAY TO COVER MY tracks and a mental list of what had to be done to move forward in finding Eddie. I stopped at the condo to clean up and change clothes. The only message on my telephone machine was from Nancy, calling the night before around eight, she said on the tape. I checked with my answering service. A message from Chief Kyle Pettengill, asking me to get in touch with him.

I dialed Nancy first. A secretary in the DA's office told me she was on trial and did I want to leave a message. I said yes, that I'd pick Nancy up by the front door of the courthouse building at six that night unless I heard back to the contrary.

I called Pettengill next and drew a female voice that sounded like it should still be home, nursing the flu. She said Pettengill was out, but would return my call as soon as possible. I told her I was just returning his, no rush, but that I'd probably be away for a while, and therefore not reachable. She said she'd tell him, and I figured I'd done what I could on that front.

After showering, I let my hair dry naturally while I performed an actual count on the money from Severn's toilet tank. It totalled $14,350, still a lot of cash for a man who'd just gotten a new pickup. The truck. I kicked myself for not checking the glove compartment for a registration, to see if he really owned it, and any paperwork that might have told me where it had been.

I put most of the bills in my own hidey-hole and the rest in a briefcase in packs of five hundred. Then I got into another suit and went down to the Prelude.

"Sneezer, how've you been?"

The man who looked at me through the crack in his door didn't seem all that happy to see me. From what I could see, given the length of the security chain, his hair was a little more shot with gray and his allergies no better than they had been. Sneezer always claimed it was the allergies that made him anorexic, an albino ant in clothes meant for a human being.

He started to say something, then sneezed. Three times, reflexively.

I said, "What is it, this time of year?"

During a reprieve in the sneezing jag, he said, "You don't got time to hear them all. What do you want?"

"To start with, I'd like to come in."

"Come in? You got any idea how many airborne particles get caught on your suit there? You're like a rat from the Black Plague."

"You want, Sneezer, I can strip naked out here in the hall, but that might start the neighbors wondering more about your business than they do already."

"Awright, awright. Let me get a mask on first, though."

I waited while the door closed, then after a bit heard the sound of the chain coming off, and the door opening. I stepped into the apartment, one of four on the third floor of a wooden mammoth in Somerville, the blue-collar town wedged between East Cambridge and Boston. Sneezer had lived there for at least five years I knew about, a virtual prisoner of his allergies.

Another jag, Sneezer first pulling the surgical mask away

from his face. Then he shook his head. "Geez, it's bad and getting worse, Cuddy."

"You ever thought of relocating?"

He just looked at me. "I can't afford to rent nowheres else around here but Somerville."

"I don't mean around here. I mean like Arizona, New Mexico maybe."

"Huh. You know what's happened out there?"

"No."

"The snowbirds, all these people from like the Midwest—Michigan, Ill-a-noise, wherever—these people, they get to the desert and they look around and say, 'Hey, it's warm and everything, but where's the trees and the lawns?' So they start planting away and draw down their fucking water to make Arizona look like Grand Rapids or wherever, and guess what?"

"They bring the pollen along with them."

"Right. That's exact-a-mundo right. Now the stupid fuckers have no water to drink, and the asthmatics and people like me are bug-fucked. Again."

"Sorry to hear it, Sneezer."

He rubbed a skeletal finger against his nose under the mask, the eyes above it runny and red. "So, what do you want?"

"I need a package."

"A package. A package of what?"

"Sneezer." I looked to the closed door behind him where a bedroom ought to be. Only the bed was against the wall of the living room where we were standing, unmade with a couple of throw pillows on it.

He looked with me, then back to me. "What is this, some kinda entrapment?"

"This is unofficial, Sneezer. I need enough fake ID to look good."

"Fake ID for you?"

"Right. Under the name 'John Francis.' "

"On the level?"

"On the level."

"It'd look better, I could stick a middle initial in there. Most people got them."

"Make it 'C.' "

"That's smart. Lots of people, they don't realize they're better off sticking close to their own names, so they don't get thrown off, somebody calls over to them."

"Thanks for reassuring me."

Sneezer seemed to draw back. "Only thing is, I don't give out no free-bies."

"Cash."

"How much?"

I said, "You tell me your price, I tell you if I'm willing to pay it."

"We talking foreign or domestic here?"

"Just domestic."

"Okay, without a passport, I can run you a set of driver's license, library, that kinda shit for seven hundred."

"Five."

"You just said—"

"Sneezer, I said I'd tell you if I was willing to pay your price, and now I'm telling you I'm not going seven, but I will go five."

The skeleton finger made another pass at the mask. "Six."

"Five."

"Five-fifty."

"Five."

"Geez, and people wonder why independent businessmen are going under."

"Five, and I want to wait for it."

"Wait for it? You got any idea—"

"Sneezer, you have all the blanks back there in the 'bedroom.' I go to the Registry of Motor Vehicles, they take ten minutes max, once you get to the head of the line, and they're all government employees. You're a professional."

He thought about something. "How long does the driver's have to stand up?"

"No more than a couple of weeks."

"That's good, account of the registry has this new format,

holograms like the credit cards, and it's going to be a bitch to get them—"

"Sneezer, the old format's fine."

"Okay. I can give you an old-format license, it'll still have a year, year and a half to go on it."

"Fine."

"Who's going to be looking at it?"

"Just travel people, rent-a-car or hotel."

Sneezer darkened a little. "Cops?"

"Maybe."

"In-state?"

"No."

"Where?"

"Far."

"Okay, they oughta think they're seeing what they've always seen, then, and far enough away, not that many of them. Social security?"

"I won't be using it."

ᴗkay. I'll just do one for window dressing, fill up the slots in the wallet there. You want some photos of loved ones, too?"

"Yeah, if they're nobody anyone would recognize."

"Hell, I'm not gonna give you Madonna or something, just shots from somebody else's wallet, you can give them any names you want. Talking about it, how'd you like some photo club or other shit like that, really look authentic."

"If it all comes under the five."

A squint. "I already agreed to that. You planning to get hurt on this thing?"

"Hopefully not."

"Okay. Then I can give you a dummy Blue Cross/Blue Shield, too. Everybody carries one of those, look funny without it. Only thing is, you can't try to use it, or it'll bounce like a pogo stick."

"You got anything else back there besides the driver's that can have a photo on it, in case somebody asks for two forms of ID?"

"How about a check-cashing card from a supermarket?"

"Nice touch. You can make the photos look different?"

"Cuddy, I got hats, I got wigs, I even got Groucho glasses and noses. For you, though, we just put a Red Sox cap on with one kind of lighting and take it off, comb your hair down with less lighting, you'll look years different, that's what you want."

"I want it to look real, not like a package."

Sneezer squinted at me again. "Hey, I'm a pro, remember? What're you trying to do, hurt my feelings here?"

"Yessir?"

"I'd like two thousand dollars in travelers checks, please."

The teller smiled at me through her Plexiglas window. "Do you have an account with us?"

"No, I don't."

"Then I'm sorry, Mr. . . . ?"

"Francis, John Francis."

"Then I'm sorry, Mr. Francis, but we can't issue the checks until your own check clears our—"

"This would be for cash."

"Cash?"

"That's right."

"There's a service charge of—"

"No problem."

She smiled. "Then I guess we have no problem, either. Can I just see two forms of photo ID?"

Smiling myself, I slid them under the window.

At a pay phone, I called long-distance directory assistance first, finding out that area code 305 covered south Florida, at least from Miami to Key West. Dialing directory assistance there, I got the Miami number I wanted, marshaling my coins to be sure I'd have enough as I pressed the buttons.

The voice that answered said, *"Las oficinas de Justo Vega,"* and then more I couldn't follow.

I shifted the receiver to my other ear. "I'm afraid I don't speak Spanish."

"Oh," said the woman's voice in lightly accented English. "That is all right. Can I help you?"

"I'd like to speak to Justo, please."

"May I tell him who is calling?"

"Tell him John Cuddy from Saigon."

"From . . . ?"

"Saigon."

"Vietnam?"

"Yes. On a pay phone."

"Please hold."

The next voice yanked me back, to the brittle clink of beer bottles on a bar and the dull clunk of black helmet liners on a desk top and the impossibly toylike sound of an M-16 the first time I heard one go off in Military Police Office Basic, all of us being trained in R.O.T.C. Basic with the older M-14s. "John, the hell you doing back in Vietnam?"

"I'm not, but I figured it was the easiest way to cut through the layers of insulation around a busy lawyer."

"Oh, man, you have not changed. Where you calling from?"

"A pay phone in Boston, but I'm going to be in Miami, probably sometime tomorrow night, and I wanted to talk with you about some things."

"So talk."

"Not over the phone."

A pause. "You got some kind of trouble, John?"

"Yes."

"Okay. I will have one of my men pick you up at the airport."

One of his men. "I have to rent a car, anyway, Justo. Just give me directions to your place."

"John, I . . . Believe me, it would be better for you, we have somebody come out, pick you up."

"Okay."

"You got your flight number and all with you there?"

"No. Can I call you with it tomorrow?"

"Tomorrow? Sure, sure. Just use this same number, leave the information with my secretary. We will have somebody at the gate in Miami to meet you, sign with your name on it and everything."

"Fine. Just one thing, Justo."

"Whatever you need."

"My flight will be out of Washington, D.C., and the name on your sign should be 'John Francis.' "

Another pause. "I understand."

And he said it as though he really did.

The short man hung up his phone and stood to shake hands. "Thank you for waiting, sir."

"No problem."

"My name's Bert."

"Bert, pleased to meet you. John Cuddy."

I sat in the chair next to his desk, posters on the wall behind him advertising the Caribbean and Cancún with well-oiled couples basking in the sun on colorful towels or walking hand-in-hand along the beach at sunset.

Bert said, "This time of year, just everybody's making their travel plans in advance for Thanksgiving."

"I understand."

"Is that what you need as well?"

"No, I'm going to be flying tomorrow."

"Tomorrow? Well, then, we'd better get started. Where are you heading?"

"Washington, D.C."

"Dulles or National?"

"Which airport, you mean?"

"Yes."

"Try National first."

"Okay. Time of day?"

"Early morning."

"All right. . . ." He clacked at his computer terminal. "Let's see. . . . We have two choices, three if you're going first-class."

I thought about it. John Francis might travel first-class, but John Cuddy wouldn't. "Coach."

"Coach it is, then. Let's see. . . . How about eight A.M., arriving Washington/National at 9:29, give or take."

"Give or take?"

"Busy airport."

"That'll be fine."

"One-way or round-trip?"

"Better make it one way. I'm not sure when I'll be heading back."

"Will that be a charge, then?"

"Yes." I handed him my own, real credit card.

He began processing things. "You traveling on business or pleasure?"

"I'm going to visit some people I used to know."

Bert frowned. "Used to know? Don't you still know them?"

I looked at him. "Not exactly."

"Hi, Nance."

She was waiting for me downstairs, just outside the Sheriff's Department metal detector. It was easier that way, in case I was carrying a gun. Which I was.

Nancy adjusted the shoulder strap of her briefcase on the saddle of her suit jacket and strode toward me.

"John, is everything all right?"

"Fine."

Her eyes searched mine, the smile a grim one. "Why don't we just get some take-out, go to your place."

"We had take-out last time. Wouldn't you like a real meal?"

"What I'd like is a real talk."

"I'm not going to be able to finesse this, huh?"

"No, you're not."

From a pay phone, I called Pizzeria Uno on Boylston Street. The deep-dish would be ready by the time we got there.

We walked south on Tremont, not talking with the crush of other people around us at commuter time. Once we hit the Boston Common and passed the Park Street Station, we lost most of the crowd. Continuing through the Common, people stretched out from natural gait far enough that we were basically walking by ourselves.

Nancy took my right hand in hers, and I jumped when she pressed it.

Letting go immediately, she said, "What's the matter?"

"Nothing. I got burned a little."

She looked down, then stopped and held my hand up by placing hers under my palm. "John, that's pretty nasty. What happened?"

"Just a burn, Nance."

"Like just a 'paper cut'?"

Our talk about the scars. I started walking again. "Come on. I'll tell you over dinner."

Nancy stood her ground. "I won't be able to eat dinner unless you tell me what happened, why I couldn't reach you last night."

I stopped. "All right."

She came up to me, and we fell back into step.

I said, "That case—or incident, I guess—from the tire changing."

"The woman in the Fort Point Channel."

"Yes."

"They're still not calling it homicide, John."

"I'm not surprised. But I traced the plates, and I have some glasses that might have her prints on them."

"Meaning you can identify her?"

"Only by a first name. We'd know the dead girl was a runaway named Melinda."

"Which is something you were already pretty sure of."

"Yes."

"Go on."

"Well, making a long story short, tracing the plates also led me to the little boy's family, who seem to be happy he's gone—"

"No."

"Yes. And I ended up with a guy who . . ."

Nancy took my arm, gingerly.

I said, "Don't worry. No damage other than . . . Well, other than a little burn on the left hand, too."

"John. . . ." A shake of the head. "No, tell it your way."

"As long as I tell it?"

She hugged my arm this time.

"I broke into the trailer of a guy named Severn, because it looked as though he was the only one who could steer me toward the little boy."

"Eddie."

"Eddie, right. Well, Severn caught me at it, knocked me out, and took me to a place for some . . . directed conversation."

Nancy's voice quavered a bit. "He . . . tortured you?"

"Yes."

"Oh, John. Have you seen a doctor?"

"No."

"Why—"

"Nance, I ended up having to kill the guy."

The hug on my arm got tighter. "I . . . I don't want to sound stupid about this, but . . . I could tell that."

"Tell it from what?"

"From the way you looked at me inside the door when you picked me up."

"How did I look?"

"Like you wanted to . . . spare me something. Like you wanted to put on a happy face and joke around like we do."

"Nothing wrong with that."

"Unless it's not sincere, and you don't deceive all that well, John."

"I hope only where you're concerned."

Nancy changed her tone. "Would it help for you to give me some details?"

"Severn was going to torture me till I told him something he wanted to hear, then he was going to kill me. When I broke free, he had a gun, and I had to take him."

"I know."

"You know?"

"That you had to take him, that you wouldn't have killed him otherwise."

"I wish I hadn't. And not just because of taking his life. Severn didn't get to tell me much about Eddie."

No response at first, then, "Do you think Eddie's still alive?"

"From something the guy let slip, yes. But all I have to go on is some stuff I found in his trailer, which leads me toward the Florida Keys."

"Florida."

"Yes."

Nancy didn't say anything else until we crossed Charles Street and entered the Public Garden. "You said before, you didn't go to a hospital."

"Right."

"Because that might have tipped the police about Severn being . . . gone?"

"Or at least have tied me to some violence when the chief up there knew I was trying to see the guy."

"Then the authorities don't know about what you had to do."

"I couldn't see how my explanation would cover it and still let me go after Eddie."

"And a promise is a promise."

"My only virtue."

Nancy kissed my shoulder. "Sometimes."

"More pizza?"

"I'm stuffed, John. Freeze it so you can nuke it."

"Doesn't make sense."

Nancy leaned over my coffee table, the glass of red wine making spot shadows on her face. "Why not?"

"Won't be around to eat it."

"Florida?"

"Eventually."

"All that way because this boy reminds you of someone from the service."

"Yes."

Nancy's eyes grew sad. "Someone you feel . . . badly about."

"That's right."

"Can you tell me?"

Leaning back, I closed my eyes and did.

When I was finished, Nancy didn't speak for a while. Then, "John, I understand."

"Good."

"But I want you at least to call me."

"That'll be hard, Nance."

"Why?"

"I'll have to use a pay phone, all coins so the call won't be traceable."

She worked on that. "When you can, if you can, I want to hear from you, John Francis Cuddy."

"Might be just the first part."

"What?"

"It may be a 'John Francis' you'll be hearing from."

A slow smile. "He'd be okay, too. When are you leaving?"

"Tomorrow, early A.M."

Nancy set down her glass, taking my left hand carefully into hers. "Well, then. We'd best be sure you get to bed soon enough to actually get some sleep afterward."

"I'd like that."

"The sleep?"

"More the 'beforeward' part."

Nancy ran her lips along my knuckles. "Me, too."

Afterward, we lay side by side, sheet and blanket over us, both our faces aimed at the ceiling, talking more to it than each other.

"John, you know I wanted you to tell me about what happened."

"I do."

"Even if it . . . compromises me a little as a prosecutor."

I didn't say anything.

She clucked her tongue off the roof of her mouth. "But I don't see how I'm conflicted."

"What do you mean?"

"The police here have a corpse, my jurisdiction if it's homicide. You have some glasses with 'Melinda's' prints on them, and Melinda may turn out to be the dead woman, but that wouldn't establish homicide."

"No, it wouldn't."

"If it was homicide down here, do you believe the man you had to kill in New Hampshire was the killer?"

"Yes."

"Proof of it?"

"Just my"—I thought of Chief Kyle Pettengill—"inferences."

"Any proof the other way?"

"You mean that it wasn't homicide?"

"No, I mean that it was homicide but not your guy who did it."

"Oh. No, no proof that anybody else was involved in Melinda's actual killing."

"Well, then, I don't see how what you've told me puts me in any conflict. If the dead woman is Melinda, and it was homicide but the killer himself is now dead, there'd be nobody for my office to prosecute."

"And there's no reason to open a file with no way of really closing it."

"Right."

"Nice, Nance."

"What do you mean, 'nice'?"

"The reasoning. Letting both of us off the hook after I told you what I didn't want to tell you but you wanted to hear."

Nancy shifted onto her side so that she would have been looking at me, though in the dark I couldn't see her face. "I was kind of hoping you did want to tell me."

I thought about it.

She said, "Like you would have told Beth."

"You're right. I did want to tell you. Or, more accurately, a part of me wanted to—what was the word you used on the walk, 'spare' you?"

"Right."

"Well, I guess a part of me did want to spare you, and another part of me wanted to ... I don't know, 'confess' it to you, I suppose."

"So somebody could 'absolve' you."

"The 'right' somebody, anyway, as you also once said."

"The right somebody prefers 'share' to 'confess.'"

I saw what she meant. "I'll try to work on that."

"Work on something else, too?"

"What?"

"Back when we were walking tonight, you said the family was happy to have Eddie gone."

"I think they see him as some kind of . . . Jesus, burden because of the birthmark."

"John, that's horrible, I know, but think about what that means for you."

"For me?"

"Yes. If the boy is still alive, and you do find him, what are you going to do with him?"

I hadn't thought about it.

Nancy said, "Based on what you've said, bringing Eddie back to his parents won't help him, and taking him to the authorities may mean some of your having to . . . Some of what happened in New Hampshire having to come out. Plus, most likely the authorities will give Eddie back to his parents or at best put him in a foster home."

"I still have to find him, first."

"Just be sure you've thought it through by then, okay?"

Nancy said the last as gently as she'd taken my hand at dinner, and I rolled toward her with a long, slow kiss.

"Hey"—a dreamy fringe around her voice—"remember, you've got an early flight."

"I'll sleep on the plane."

12 ═══════════

I DID. SLEEP ON THE PLANE, THAT IS.

The flight to Washington, D.C., boarded and departed Boston's Logan Airport on time. Our flight attendant, a heavyset woman in her thirties, was sitting diagonally across from me and my seatmate, a bald guy in his fifties. I looked out the portside window, the harbor islands shimmering in the early morning sun. As a kid, I went on field trips via the ferry to George's Island, the air ten degrees colder than in the city. We picnicked and played kickball, but more exciting was running through the ruins of the old fort there. The battlements guarded the entrance to one of the colonies' best ports, tracks from the cannon still evident as ruts in the stone ramparts.

The captain turned off the seat belt sign, and our flight attendant got up to get the beverage cart. After she went by our row, my seatmate tapped me on the forearm.

"Remember when 'wide-bodies' meant just the planes, not the stewardesses?"

I gave him a long look. "Nice talking to you," I said, and closed my eyes.

* * *

In Washington's National Airport, I got my two suitcases at the carousel, took off the luggage tags, and went up to the PURCHASE TICKETS HERE counter of another airline. The uniformed agent behind the computer smiled and asked if she could help.

"Yes. My name's John Francis. I need a flight to Miami, sometime this afternoon."

"One moment, please."

They had space on a flight leaving just after two. I thought that would give me enough time. "First-class, one way, please."

"Certainly, sir. Credit card?"

"I'll be paying cash. And could I have a couple of those luggage tags, too?"

"Help yourself."

The Miami ticket for John Francis in my coat pocket, I took a cab into D.C., the driver finding a chain place I remembered being near DuPont Circle. The desk clerk was very accommodating, imprinting two keys on his computer for me. He seemed happy that he could book John Cuddy into a room that early in the morning. So was I.

Upstairs, I unpacked one of the suitcases, the one with cooler weather clothes in it, hanging things up that needed to be hung and putting in drawers underwear, socks, and so forth. Then I took my other suitcase, still without a luggage tag, and brought it downstairs, leaving it and two dollars with the bell captain.

Outside, I got another cab and told the driver to take me to the center of Georgetown. I paid him "by the zone," and after he dropped me off, I went hunting. Fifteen minutes later, I found what I was looking for, behind the cash register in a T-shirt shop.

A stumpy kid whose eyes still appeared a little hungry, he wore a Hoyas basketball sweatshirt over grunge jeans. Before approaching him, I browsed until we were the only people in the store.

"You go to Georgetown?" I said.

"Yeah. Help you with something?"

"Maybe. How would you like to earn a hundred bucks?"

The kid gave me a tainted look. "I don't want any trouble."

"No trouble. And not even illegal. All I want you to do is keep going to a given hotel room over by DuPont Circle every evening and mess up the bedclothes."

"You what?"

"Maybe run some water on the soap, and splash a little on the towels, too."

The kid regarded me differently. "You want me to make it look like you're staying there."

"Right."

"When you're not."

"Right again."

"For a hundred bucks."

"Now. Another hundred when I come back to you here and tell you to stop."

"When'll that be?"

"Not sure. Maybe a week, maybe less or more. But you get to keep the hundred, no matter what."

"And I get the other hundred, no matter what."

"Uh-huh."

"And it's not illegal?"

I held out the duplicate computer card the happy clerk had given me. "Not as long as you have my key."

The kid turned it around in his head, then nodded. "Let's see the hundred."

I showed him two fifties. "What's your name?"

"Kevin."

"Pleased to meet you, Kevin."

He waited, then said, "I'm not supposed to know your name, right?"

"You must be Dean's List, smart as you are."

"Yeah," Kevin said, nodding. "My parents are real proud."

Outside the shop, the sky had clouded over, more covering the sun than threatening rain. Inside a drugstore, I used a pay phone to call Justo Vega's office, leaving word with his secretary on the flight number and arrival time for "John Francis." Then I went to a rotating display of sunglasses and picked out the biggest-lensed aviators they had.

The woman at the cash register smiled. "You must be thinking the sun's gonna come back out today."

"Yeah. Yeah, that's why I need them, all right."

The third Washington cabbie of the morning said, "This is it."

"You sure? I don't see it."

"Word of honor, Mac. It's over there, kind of built into the knoll, where all the people are walking. You might want to start with the cluster, depending."

"Depending on what?"

He lowered his voice. "On why you're here."

I paid the fare, got out, and went over to the cluster.

As I approached it, I could see that the bronzed statue was surrounded by lush, tended grass, like the greens of a golf course. Somehow I didn't expect that, maybe because most of the grass I saw in Vietnam was higher. And rougher.

The cluster itself is three soldiers, grunts in the bush, wearing fatigue uniforms, the trousers bloused into the tops of their boots. One is African-American, another is white, and the third is hard to tell, because he's got a boonie hat on. Which is just as well, that way you can use your imagination for who he'd be. The black has a towel around his neck and an M-16 in his left hand. The white isn't holding anything. The guy in the boonie hat, though, has a heavy M-60 machine gun across his shoulders and belts of ammo for it across his chest. None of them look glad to be there. The sculptor got that part right, too.

At the base of the cluster were mementos, a few miniature American flags but mostly little wreaths and bouquets of flowers. The flowers were all different sizes and colors, a lot like the grunts depicted in the statue and the hundreds of thousands of others they represent.

The cabbie was right about starting at the cluster. It let me work my way over to the Wall. Or, more accurately, let me work my way up to the Wall, even though it was on the same level as the cluster.

The beginning of the path to the Wall itself has steel gray cobblestones, maybe five inches square, the ones at the center of the path grouted, the ones to the sides with blades of the good grass growing up between them. A black sign has ghostbuster diagonal stripes through words and logos that prohibit food, drink, smoking, bicycles, and running.

I don't think they had to warn against the running part.

The people moved slowly along the path, as the cobblestones gave way to large pieces of slate. I was approaching the Wall from the west, the structure itself beginning as an acute angle with only a few names on it, then gradually growing taller, section by section, until it peaks in the middle. It then grows shorter again, like a compressed boomerang with its center point aiming upward, forming a sort of retaining wall for the knoll. The stone is black and glossy, I would have said marble until I heard someone else, reading from a guidebook, say granite. Small bunkerlike humps rise from the ground at six-foot intervals, footlights to illuminate the names at night. Over fifty-eight thousand names.

I decided to walk the length of the Wall once, just to get used to it a little. At the center there's wording that a lot of people stopped to read. It says that the names of the men and women who served and died or were reported missing "are inscribed in the order they were taken from us." Each name is chiseled into the stone, diamonds separating one from another like mini-tombstones. The listing of the lost begins with 1959 at the center, the highest point of the Wall, and then runs eastward as the Wall tapers, the sequence beginning again at the far, tapered section of the west Wall, where I had started.

As I oriented myself, an elderly couple was putting a question to one of the volunteers, who stood beside a park ranger. The volunteer was about my age and wore a ball cap, placket shirt, and blue jeans. He showed the couple how to take a rubbing using artist's graphite on paper against the name they wanted to carry away with them. The park ranger was in his early twenties, wearing green uniform pants, a brown uniform shirt, and a Smokey the Bear hat in yellow straw. The ranger answered another person's question, politely and pleasantly but just slightly bored.

I moved to the eastern end of the Wall, where the names I might recognize would be, almost having to kneel in order to read some of them. I reached out and touched the first names of the officers, the last names of the troopers, which is how I retained the ones I knew. I caught myself doing that touching, then felt self-conscious until I noticed most everyone else doing the same thing, at a different block, some on their knees, some standing but stooping, others up on tiptoe, depending on how tall they were and how high or low the name they were looking for happened to be. The names were hard, because they were real people to me, however long gone. But the hardest part wasn't the roll call in stone. It was the things left at the base of the Wall.

Small flags, like the ones at the cluster, just many more of them. Mostly American, here and there a Canadian maple leaf.

White carnations, identically wrapped but at distant panels, making me think that somebody nearby was turning a buck hucking them.

Elaborate, freestanding wreaths, with sashes and bows, names gilded onto the sashes. Other wreaths were more homemade, of twisted branches and wildflowers and some lace to bind the twigs, small tear-sized dark spots on the lace, names of soldiers or hometowns on cards tied loosely by bakery string.

A paper and wire violet with a yellow explanatory tag, like the ones men and women in American Legion hats will sell at the entrances to supermarkets on Memorial Day.

Unit patches. Americal, Big Red One, 173rd Airborne. Some baseball caps. First and Third Marines, 82nd Airborne, Seabees Can Do.

A baseball glove, the Andy Carey third baseman's model from back in the fifties, some unreadable autographs in blue ink.

Two packs of Camels, a torn page from a spiral notebook reading, "Owed you these, J. T."

A Special Forces green beret, old and faded and torn.

Album covers from the sixties. Richie Havens, the Doors, Joan Baez.

Triptych of photos showing Cobra helicopters, flying in formation over a rice paddy.

In laminate, a news article describing the supposed final judgment in the Agent Orange litigation, and how little each veteran in the class action was ever likely to receive.

The distinctive pie-plate of a World War I expeditionary force helmet, in chalk on it: "From Gramps to Susan. RIP."

A piece of needlework, a message stitched from the one who made it to the memory of the one it was made for.

Notes penned for the world to see, some literary and others barely literate, all in shaky hands. "Jim, Because of you, I'm alive today, Leroy." "Honey, I've never forgotten, Ellen." "We're retired in Fort Myers, now, but we stopped by because this might be the last time Dad can drive it." A few notes were sealed in envelopes with just a name written on the back, no address necessary.

Then I found the panel from the Tet Offensive, and I started recognizing more and more names due to the heavy street fighting around Saigon. Finally, I came to PFC Duquette's place in the stone, "Frenchy," as the other troopers had called him. Only that wasn't his real first name. It was "Edward."

I reached out, my fingertip feeling soft against the polished granite. I found myself tracing the letters to the left of Duquette. "On my way, Eddie. On my way."

I stood away from the Wall for a few minutes, swallowing hard. The people moved by, still so slowly, so quietly. No laughter, and no crying you could hear. The only noises were the shuffling of shoes and the tapping of canes and the ticking of wheelchairs and baby strollers, people at opposite ends of the spectrum, coming for the same purpose. To visit and remember.

I moved back to the center of the Wall, the mementos at its base the thickest, which made sense because the panels there were the highest, containing the most names. The sunlight was at an angle to the slabs, which made the black turn to copper and gold, reflections of trees and sky and passing mourners. A reflection in a mirror, perhaps the truest memorial of all. A memorial to what was wrong with our being in Vietnam. What was wrong with the United States then, too. The people who didn't understand, and who didn't welcome us back.

I noticed that the name of the last person killed in 1975 lay just eight vertical feet below the name of the first killed in 1959. They were separated only by roughly the same depth at which each of them, all of them, would have been laid to rest.

Nancy was right, I needed to come here, but that seemed as good a point as any to walk away.

Cabbing it back to the hotel, I told the driver to leave the meter running while I rousted the bell captain and reclaimed my suitcase. In the taxi again, I tied a "John Francis" luggage tag to the handle.

At National, I checked my bag and went to the gate an hour early. Waiting, I watched the anonymous progression of harried business people and leisurely retired people, happy married people and cheerful disabled people. One man of the married people constantly played the same practical joke. He had a twenty-dollar bill on a thin wire hooked to a remote device in his hand. He'd put the bill on the ground near an arrival gate, then when someone stooped to pick up the bill, he'd activate the remote and tease the twenty away, some of the passengers chasing the bill for three or four awkward steps. After one passenger screamed and clutched her heart when the bill danced away, the man's wife made him stop playing with it.

The first-class passengers got boarded quickly, "John Francis" at a window seat on the starboard side. I was barely settled before the flight attendant asked if "we" would like a cocktail before takeoff. I declined, but my seatmate on the aisle, a big, florid man in his forties, accepted readily.

After the first three gulps of his martini, he turned to me. "I always fly first-class. Know why?"

"Because you can afford it?"

"And because if I don't, my kids will."

I closed my eyes as he hailed the flight attendant for another round.

The captain's voice woke me up, announcing our approach to Miami International Airport and calling our attention to Fort Lauderdale below us. I looked out my window to the west and down.

The shoreline trailed into the water, the beaches appearing deserted, whitecaps on the aquamarine water. Then I realized that my perspective was off, that the whitecaps were the wakes of the bigger boats, the smaller ones just metallic specks in the late afternoon sun. I adjusted for the houses, even the condo towers surrounded by parking areas seeming too small, the roofs like square white dots in a hundred tipped dominoes, with the occasional square, clay-pot mansion. The black access roads to the smaller development houses looked way too wide. Then more whitecaps told me I had another bad perspective, the "access roads" being instead the intracoastal waterway system, man-made doglegs and diagonals that, from the air, didn't lead anyplace but into cul-de-sacs and dead-ends. I thought briefly of what this view would have been like fifty years ago. Look what they've done to my song, Ma.

Twenty steps into the muggy Jetway, my shirt was plastered to my skin, chilling me as I hit the air-conditioned arrival lounge. Justo Vega's "man" wasn't hard to spot. About six feet and slim, the black hair was balding front to back, the bandit mustache full. I put him around thirty in a designer short-sleeved shirt and some kind of shiny slacks that didn't use a belt to keep them up. He held a hand-printed piece of cardboard saying just FRANCIS on it.

Walking up to him, I said, "What if there was more than one 'Francis' on the flight?"

Bright, flashing eyes. "Then I ask you your first name."

It came out, "Den I ass chew chore furs name."

"Good answer. Call me John." I offered him my hand. "Be gentle, I burned myself a few days ago."

Quick, light grip. "Pepe. You got the luggage?"

"One suitcase."

"Let's get it."

"I need to make a call first."

"Phones over this way."

I reached them, Pepe lazing against an opposite wall, maintaining a discreet, disinterested distance. I was lifting the receiver of the first one before noticing it was good only for credit card calls. I replaced the receiver and found one that took coins, feeding a quarter into it. I dialed Nancy's home number, was told electronically to feed some more, and got her tape machine. After the beep, I said that I'd arrived safely in Florida and would call again when I could. Hanging up, I moved back over to Pepe.

He started down the corridor toward baggage claim before I did, walking like a sailor on liberty, long-strided and loose-hipped. Pulling even, I said, "Where are you from originally?"

"This is Miami, man. You got to ask?"

"Meaning Cuba."

"Hope you a little quicker with the bad guys."

"So far."

That got the beginning of a grin.

Carrying my bag through the parking garage, Pepe kept looking left and right and over and behind. The air was cooler than inside the Jetway, but not by much. When we reached a two-door Ford Escort, bright red, Pepe put my suitcase in the trunk. Then he lifted a flap in the carpet and took out a big, black semiautomatic.

I said, "Glock nine millimeter?"

"Is a Glock, but the ten mil, fifteen rounds in the mag. I come to the States, I want to buy American, but you do no got one with the punch and capacity, so I got to go German."

"Austrian."

"That's not Germany?"

"Not for a while, now."

"Huh."

He opened my door for me, then went around and got into the driver's seat, pulling his shirt from the front of his pants and sticking the Glock in his right-front waistband, cross-draw for a lefty. I noticed the car was a manual transmission.

As we started up, I said, "You like a stick shift?"

"What, the car?"

"Yes."

"No, but is safer."

"In traffic?"

"Kind of. You read the papers?"

"In Boston."

Pepe got us out of the garage and onto an access road. "Well, down here, you drive a little shitbox like this, stick-shift instead of the automatic, the bad guys, they do no think you tourist, so they do no try to jump you."

"Then why do you need the Glock?"

"Some of the bad guys, they do no care if you tourist or no."

I nodded. We took an entrance ramp for a highway.

He said, "Back last spring, when the jury let that cop off, Lozano?"

"Yes?"

"This whole road was block off. You could get on at the airport, and off at the hotels, but man, in between? Just cops everywhere, keep the airport people from getting off and the blacks from getting on."

I looked down at the deteriorated neighborhoods below and around us. "Rioting?"

"Not that time. But from before. Years ago."

Pepe glanced at me. "You gonna be driving around here after you see Mr. Vega, man?"

"Yes."

"You get bump by somebody behind you, or they wave at

you on the highway, yelling something about your tire or anything, you keep right on going, man. They try to ram you off the road, you ram them right back. Bad guys, man, you do no stop for them."

"Thanks for the advice."

"Just be sure you take it, huh? You need anything before we get to the house?"

"No, but maybe afterward."

"Like what?"

"Like a smaller cousin of what you took out of the trunk."

Pepe was thoughtful. "You ask Mr. Vega about the laws of Florida on that?"

"I'll still be wanting the cousin."

We got off the big highway. "How much smaller?"

"Thirty-eight revolver."

"Man, you living in the past."

"I feel comfortable with it."

"You never use anything bigger?"

"Just back when I knew Justo."

"The war?"

"One of them, anyway."

A real grin this time, as he turned his head to me briefly. "You all right, man. But I never try to buy a revolver down here, do no have an idea what the market is like."

"Try for a two-inch barrel, Smith & Wesson or Colt. No Saturday Night Specials."

"How many you want?"

I turned to him. "One ought to do it. A box of fifty rounds, too."

"Man, revolver, take you all day to fire off the fifty."

"Hopefully I won't need that many."

"Then why you want them?"

"I've been wrong before."

Pepe laughed.

I looked at him. "I hope you're a little quicker than this with the bad guys."

Pepe roared.

*   *   *

At the gate to the two-story coral-colored house, there was a sign next to an electronics box that read ARMED RESPONSE.

I said, "Who's the 'armed response?'"

"Me."

Pepe reached under the dash, and the gate came open. We drove in, and he reached under again, the gate closing behind us. He waited till it shut before continuing around the fountain to the front door. The fountain was of three cherubs in white porcelain, some irregular green stains on it. No water was flowing, none even sitting in the catch basin. There was thick shrubbery masking both the security fence and the sides of the house.

"You go in. I got to secure the car."

"Secure it?"

"Like to park it, man. Then a little 'home-shopping network' with the telephone."

"Don't get you."

"For your revolver."

"Can I advance you some cash?"

"Let me call around first. Go ahead."

I went up to the door—two massive, wooden doors actually, with carved panels in a geometric pattern—and knocked. One was opened immediately, as though someone had been waiting there for me. A petite Latino woman, in a uniform like a nurse or housemaid might wear. "Please to come in."

The entry hall faced onto a sweeping staircase to the second level, giving an airy, atrium affect to it. Tiles rather than carpeting on the floor, more geometry in the wall hangings between back windows showing a small sailboat moving along against a light chop. From the gate, I hadn't realized the house was waterfront.

The woman said, "Please to follow me."

She led me through the hall and under the staircase to a rear, French-doored area that gave onto a patio, the evening air pleasant now, the sun and humidity packing it in for the day. There was a lot of expensive-looking pipe furniture in white and flamingo pink arranged like a living room set. A man was standing and turned to us, waving me on as he spoke into a portable phone in his hand.

Justo Vega hadn't changed much. A little heavier, a little darker from year-round sunshine. Still the crooked smile, the dazzling white teeth, the shoulders that seemed to yaw like a boat at anchor on the sea, as though his body heard music inside independent of his head and always was moving to it. He wore slacks and one of those white cotton tennis sweaters with a V-neck in red and blue that I hadn't seen in years.

He pushed a button on the phone and came over to give me a bear hug. "John! John, it is great to see you again."

"Hope I wasn't interrupting anything."

"What, the phone? Nothing. Besides, down here, you want to talk confidential, you cannot use a cellular, it is just radio waves someone else can pick out of the air. No, you want to be secure, you must use a land line, you know it?"

Security, again. "So, how are you, Justo?"

"I am well, John. Very well. But not such a good host, I leave you standing on my patio for so long without offering a drink. What will you have?"

There was a tall, half-full drink with a lime section in it on the round table. "What are you having?"

"Gin and tonic."

"Could you make a vodka tonic?"

"Done."

The petite woman disappeared into the house while Justo patted a seat for me. The waterfront was more waterway, boats parked against the concrete sides of it like too-large trucks in too-small spaces.

I said, "Quite a place."

"For a poor immigrant, I have done well for myself."

He said it lightly. I motioned behind me. "Maid, your 'men.' "

"Man, actually. Pepe is the only 'house security.' We tend to say 'one of my men' down here so the person you are speaking to, or others listening in, believes you are somewhat . . . stronger?"

"Security that big a problem, Justo?"

He rolled his lower lip under his upper teeth for just a

heartbeat. "Worse than ever. Too much unemployment, too much drugs, too much immigration—though that is a hell of a thing for me to be saying, eh?"

I shrugged.

The maid came out with my drink and a fresh one for Justo, taking away the unfinished one he hadn't touched since I'd joined him. As she withdrew, he raised his glass, "To absent friends."

We clinked. "Funny you should say that. I just visited . . . I just went to the Wall."

A nod. "Your . . . first?"

"Yes. I can't see going back again, somehow."

"Me, too. I had business in D.C., I went out there, figure to see it quick, just so I would know what it really felt like. I was there almost two hours. You?"

"Not quite as long."

Vega fiddled with his drink. "You talk much to other vets, John? About being over there, I mean."

"When it comes up."

"Same here. I cannot really talk about it, still. Or ever, probably. Oh, the parties and the stupid stuff, the drinking bouts, sure. But not . . . not the war, itself."

"Remember the Coco-butt night?"

"The Coco . . . ? Oh, sure, sure, the wrestler thing. God, what a headache that gave me! Worse than any hangover."

"Came in handy, though. Just a while ago."

Justo looked at me strangely. "The drinking?"

"The Coco-butt."

"I don't get you."

"We 'secure' to talk here?"

Justo's look went from strange to wary, but he said only, "Yes."

I outlined for him what had happened in Boston and New Hampshire. He started shaking his head about the time I got to the hunting camp with Lonnie Severn.

"John, I am glad to my heart that you are all right. Truly. But I do not see . . . I am not sure how a Miami attorney can help you in this."

"I'm hoping you won't be able to."

"Now what are you saying?"

"Justo, I'll be trying to track the boy, Eddie, to a place called Mercy Key."

"Mercy."

"Yes. You know much about it?"

"I have driven through it. Not too far south along U.S. 1. Just below Key Largo, I think, and that is the most northerly of them all."

I downed some of my drink.

Justo joined me, then said, "So, what do you want me to do?"

"I'd like to leave my 'John Cuddy,' stuff here, and maybe some cash, then go to the rent-a-car place as 'John Francis.'"

"You will stay the night. It is . . . less safe to drive at night around the airport."

"Pepe gave me some tips."

"Heed them."

"I plan to."

"Anything else?"

"I may need legal help with what happens down there. I'm hoping I won't, but if it's necessary, you may be getting a call from either 'Cuddy' or 'Francis.'"

"And if I do, I handle it depending on which 'John' seems to be in trouble?"

"Right."

"So far I understand."

"So far."

A small, wise smile creased the corners of his mouth. "All this you could have arranged with a pay phone and Federal Express. What else?"

"Pepe said I might ask you about the Florida gun laws."

"Carrying a concealed weapon, you mean?"

"That's what I mean."

"To buy a gun, you need a Florida driver's license and must wait three days."

"Pepe suggested he could take care of that part for me."

Justo grunted out a laugh. "I told him to get you anything

you wanted. Pepe has not been in this country long, but he is resourceful." Serious again. "However, it is one thing to buy a gun, and another to carry it. In order to get 'John Cuddy' a license to carry concealed, it would be sixty to ninety days, after photograph and fingerprints and processing through the Secretary of State's Licensing Division up in Tallahassee. For 'John Francis,' impossible."

I thought of Sneezer back in Boston. "No . . . freelance license operations?"

"Not that would stand up to a police check, and why else would you want a 'license' except for that?"

"Okay." Picturing Pepe in the airport garage, I said, "How about if I keep a gun in my car?"

"The law says it must be 'securely encased.' Trunk is best, hide it under something."

"Glove compartment?"

"The law expressly says that is acceptable, even if you do not keep the compartment locked."

"Got it."

Justo grew somber. "John, one thing."

"Yes?"

"I have a wife—Alicia—and three children."

"Sorry, I should have asked."

A wave of the hand. "It is okay, they are off for this week and next, visiting Alicia's mother in Atlanta. Children, they are like kittens, they grow up so quickly, you want the grandmother to see them before that, and mine are only one, two-and-a-half, and four right now. But what I mean is . . ." He looked away. "You are still in the business, John. I am not. I have Pepe for security, but that is because I am well-off, a target not a player. I cannot have any violence come to visit me . . . my family here."

"I understand. How's married life treating you?"

"Oh"—lighter—"it is not so bad. I met my wife at the law school, you can believe it. She was still a student, I was guest lecturer to her Trial Practice class. We talked afterward, I felt a little funny, but Alicia persuaded me I was not like her teacher. She will be a pretty good lawyer, I think, once the children are of an age she can leave them during the day and not feel regret about it. How about you?"

"We never had any kids."

"But you got married?"

"Justo, I forgot you wouldn't have known. My wife died."

"Oh, John. I'm so sorry."

"No, don't be. It's actually a pretty good sign that I forgot you wouldn't have known. It means I'm looking forward instead of back, and I'm with—as a matter of fact, I'm with a lawyer, too. She's a prosecutor in Boston."

Justo used his glass to clink against mine without actually offering a toast. "You know, it is funny. If we stayed in the Army, we would be retired by now, half-salary pension, something like that."

"PX privileges."

"Even go to army doctors, we get sick. But I am glad we did not."

"You ever consider it?"

"No, not even close. Those days, it would have meant another tour in-country, minimum. But I must tell you, before I met Alicia, it was something I thought about. You see, I already had this house, 'the life,' you know it?"

"That's what prostitutes call their trade, 'the life.' "

"Yes, well, it is not so different for the lawyers, either. Legal whores, kind of. We charge for doing things others would find unpleasant, and we do not always enjoy our work. In fact, before I met Alicia, I was not living life so much as life was living me. And wearing me out, bad."

"But now?"

"The wife, and the children. John, you look into their eyes, and you see the face of God, and that is a very good thing."

I had a flash of Eddie Straw, saying good-bye to me at the edge of Route 93, and I wondered what face of God he was seeing.

"John, you okay?"

"Yeah, just drifting a little. Sorry."

"Hey, it has been a long day for you, we are going to

grill something special. What do you want for dinner? Steak, poultry, fish, we got it all fresh."

"Your choice. Whatever the house does best."

He picked up his phone, pushed a button, and after a buzzing noise said something into it, rapid-fire Spanish. He pushed the button again. "Kind of an intercom. Not cheap, but so convenient. She is going to bring out another round, too."

I hadn't noticed, but I'd drawn my drink down to ice. "Thanks, Justo."

He nodded. "Ask you a question?"

"I think you're entitled."

"No. I mean, not about you going down to Mercy Key or any of that. I mean, about . . . the Wall."

"Sure."

"What . . ." He cleared his throat. "What got to you the most?"

"The most."

"Yeah."

I didn't have to think about it. "The things people left there."

"Yeah," said Justo Vega, not bothering to clear his throat this time. "Yeah, me too."

13

S O, YOU ENJOY YOUR BREAKFAST WITH MR. VEGA?"

"Yes. He said it was a traditional Cuban meal. Eggs, ham, some peppers and onions, fried plantains."

Pepe rolled his shoulders a little as he turned the car onto another residential street. "Traditional, like the way things use to be?"

"I think so."

"Then that's right."

Pepe's tone made me look over at him. "How do you mean?"

A shrug. "Mr. Vega, he come here before the Revolution, he was just a kid. He remember things the way he see them, growing up. Not like that no more."

"In what way?"

"Aw, man, the government in the United States, it do no let the companies make the trade with Cuba. So, the government in Cuba, it make the trade with the Soviets, you know it? But the Soviets, they go down, Cuba go down with them."

"The economy, you mean?"

"Everything, I mean." Pepe glanced at me and grew quieter. "The people, they do no got pork, then no chicken. People losing the weight—eight, ten kilos—that's like twenty pounds, man. No gasoline, everybody riding bicycles down there now, no cars to worry about. They even got *los bueyes*—I don't know the English for it."

"Sorry, I don't speak Spanish."

"Big cows, kind of, with horns but real heavy, pull things on the farms?"

"Oxen, maybe?"

"Yeah. Yeah, 'oxen,' I hear Mr. Vega use that word, talking with somebody. No gasoline for the machines on the farm, the cities do no even got electricity half the time now. You got to wait on lines in the morning for bread, and rice, and sugar. They got great beaches, new hotels, and stores for the *turistas*, but everybody else, they got to—how you say it, *'resolviendo'*?"

"Resolve things?"

"When you like make the trade, stuff for stuff but no money."

Pepe got dark, even quieter. "When I am growing up in *Habana*, I hear the stories. How the Batistas, they make deals with the American gangsters, the Mafia, let the gangs come down, open the hotels, turn the Cuban men into slaves, the little girls into whores? Well, let me tell you, that happen again. The hotels and the stores, the *diplo-tiendas*, these are there for the rich *turistas* from Europe, but not the people. No, man, the people, they try to go in the stores, the policeman at the door say no. The little girls, they are on the street, trying to trade their ass for some hard money, a dinner of real food, not the—how you say it, the outside of the grapefruit?"

"The rind."

"The 'rind.' Yeah, that's what we doing, cooking the rind in spices, like Hamburger Helper, only there is no hamburger."

We got onto a highway. In a different tone, Pepe said, "See that building?"

He gestured toward an oddly shaped skyscraper with pink glass.

I said, "Yes."

"You got to drive back to us, you use that for your—land mark?"

"Landmark, right."

"It is just seven blocks south from Mr. Vega's house, they keep that pink glass all shiny with the spotlights, even at night."

"Thanks, I'll remember it." I looked back at Pepe. "You think Castro's in trouble?"

Another shrug. "The young people, they try to leave, these old boats of wood, man. Even this Air Force captain, he fly his plane to Key West."

"I thought that happened years ago."

"It did. This is the second one, I am talking about."

"And the rest of the people?"

"The old ones, they remember when they could no see a doctor, could no find good work, everything corrupt. They still support Fidel. And many of the middle people, too. But now you hear even the soldiers and the police talk in private about him, or make with the fingers. . . ." Pepe mimed a man stroking his beard. "Talking about him without saying his name, you know it?"

"I follow you."

"Well, they now having—not 'parade,' the . . . deh-mone-*stray*-tion?"

"Yes, demonstration."

"Yeah, well, the people, they now in the streets sometimes, thousands of them, man. They yelling, '*Libertad! Libertad!!*' louder each time. 'Freedom, Freedom.' "

"You think there could be another revolution?"

"I think maybe. Or Fidel figure out he can no stay in power, he step to the side, have somebody else talk with United States about letting the companies make the trade again." Pepe glanced at me, sharply. "He no do this, maybe we go back for our families, because a lot of people, they going to die. Starve to death, man."

I didn't want to push him on that. "Speaking of trading, you find anything for me last night?"

Pepe grinned and reached under the driver's seat of the Escort. "I wonder when you get around to that."

He handed me something heavy, wrapped in a towel. When I took the package from him, it felt like two independent pieces inside.

"You want to open that, make sure is okay for you?"

I looked around us on the road. "Here?"

"Be better than when you on line for the rent-a-car. Make them nervous, no?"

I leaned forward and laid the package on the floor mat. Unwrapping the towel, I saw a Smith & Wesson Detective's Special with a checkered grip and a box containing fifty rounds of thirty-eight cartridges. "Perfect."

"I did no fire the thing, man. Hope it gonna work."

"I hope it doesn't have to, but thanks." I found the serial number, still on the frame. "We have any idea where this came from?"

The head went left to right like a metronome. "I drive to the city, go in a bar. I talk to a guy, he know another guy. The guy I know go out for a while, I have a drink. The guy I know come back, he got what is between your feet."

"I was thinking about whether it's been used recently."

"Oh, you mean, like for a crime or something?"

"That's what I mean."

"Maybe, but I do no think so. This guy I know, he pretty good, that way."

It was the best I was likely to get. "Thanks, Pepe. What do I owe you?"

"Two-fifty, man."

I took out my wallet. "That's all?"

"Nobody want this kind no more, like I told you yesterday. Too old-fashion."

I counted out three-fifty and handed it to him. He used his right hand to flare the bills, then gave them back. "You got too much, there, man."

"A commission."

Emphatic shake of the head. "I work for Mr. Vega. I get

you the gun because he tell me to get what you want, and
you tell me you want the gun. Two-fifty."

I took out the extra hundred, handed him back the rest.

Sticking the money in his pocket, Pepe said, "You want
real good deal on a rent-a-car, I take you to this other guy
I know?"

"Thanks, but I need one from the airport."

"Okay." Pepe got serious. "You just be careful driving
now, John Francis, all you got is that old-fashion gun."

"Takes longer to rent the fucking car than it took the plane
to bring me here."

Pushing my suitcase, heavier with Pepe's towel-wrapped
items in it, I nodded politely, but the pudgy guy wearing the
Bermuda shorts and Hawaiian shirt on line in front of me
wasn't finished yet. "Two weeks a year I get vacation to get
outta the fucking city of New York, and I gotta waste a fucking hour of it on a line here."

I shook my head this time, hoping for a change of luck.
We were about twelve people from the front of the line, a
blazered employee directing the next person to one of the
twenty or so equally blazered agents behind the counters and
computers, like a huge bank with lots of tellers. After each
earlier element moved forward, our employee handed a six-
by-nine card to the third person in line.

When the pudgy guy finally got his, he turned around
again. "Oh, great, just great. The headlines, don't scare you
off, what do you suppose this does?"

The card had warnings to the rental company's "Valued
Clients." It used bold type and underlining to emphasize the
kinds of advice Pepe had already given me, the first one
being "If you are bumped from behind, continue on to the
next well-lighted, populated area." The refrain in each warning was *DO NOT STOP!*, the surrounding language sounding
like it was drafted less by the advertising agency and more
by the legal department.

"So," said the New Yorker, "What do you fucking think
of this?"

"I think they want you back again next year."

"You do?"

"Yeah, but I can't think why."

He gave me a dirty look, but got reached by the blazer and waddled off to the empty window. I got waved to one five over from him.

My agent turned out to be a pleasant woman in her twenties, a trace of the Old South in her voice. "Good morning, sir. Reservation?"

"No. But whatever you have will be fine."

A bright smile. "Boy, if I could only tell you how rarely we hear that."

The pudgy guy five windows over boomed out, "You gotta check *what?*"

We both glanced at him. My agent said, "New Yorkers, they don't like the fact that our computers can run their drivers' licenses, see if they're accident or ticket risks."

I tried to keep my voice steady. "You can do that now?"

"Uh-huh. License, please?"

I handed her the "John Francis" one. "Must make it better for the company."

"Oh, yes. We can access only a few registries. New York, Ohio—Florida, of course. You'd be surprised how many people who live here rent cars after flying from another part of the state."

"It's a big state, all right."

"Yessir. But, since yours is Massachusetts, there's no problem." The bright smile.

I returned it as she handed back "my" license, and the pudgy guy boomed, "You gotta be shitting me!" to his agent.

Her finger tapping the same button on the keyboard, I had the feeling my agent was scrolling as she glanced over to the New Yorker again and frowned. "Well, I'll tell you what. We've got a Sunbird, white-on-white convertible. I've driven one, and they are just the most fun. Would you like that?"

I didn't have to think about it. Every tourist's dream should be John Francis's as well. "Perfect."

"Great. Let me just print you—"

"Do you have any idea, you fucking spic, who you're talk-ing to here? I'll have your fucking job, your fucking house, you got one that isn't packed with your fucking kids—Hey, hey! Get your fucking hands off me!"

The three security guards had materialized out of nowhere, one on each of the pudgy guy's arms, the third talking into a radio. The radio guard's other hand hoisted the suitcase from five windows down as the entire quartet disappeared through a doorway that the radio man had to use a key to open.

My agent said, "Sorry about the disturbance, Mr. Francis."

"Happen often?"

A not-so-bright smile and a hush-now voice. "The party line is, 'almost never.' The truth is about twice a shift, more in season. These people come down from the cold for a vaca-tion, they don't like to be told they'll be taking buses or taxis everywhere they want to go."

She handed me the contract forms and a sheet of very specific directions. "Your Sunbird is in stall number C9, out the door and to the left. You'll be heading where, Mr. Francis?"

"The Keys."

The agent used a red pen to circle one paragraph of direc-tions on the front of the sheet and another on the back of the sheet. Turning it over to the front again, she said, "Just follow the streets as indicated until you see the ramp for Route 836 West. Route 836 will take you to the Florida Turnpike South, and from there you'll be fine."

"And until there?"

"You have our safety tips card?"

"Follow them as well as the directions."

The bright smile. "That's what I'd do."

Outside, the humid air hit me like a wet rag. I walked to Row C in the parking area and found stall #9, a freshly washed convertible in it. The trunk was small and shallow, but held the suitcase easily. The license plate had green let-tering on a white background with an orange cutout of the state superimposed in the middle. On my last visit to Florida, the word LEASE had been at the bottom of the plate, to let the locals know the car in front of them might do confusing things. Now there was just a county designation.

Getting behind the wheel, I tested all the bells and whistles, making sure everything worked. I'm not nuts about air-conditioning, so I undid the roof clamps at the windshield, pushing the button at the top of the frame and ignoring the suggestion about snapping the tonneau cover in place over the lowered canvas. Rereading the directions the agent had circled, I started out, both doors automatically locking as soon as I put the convertible in gear. I wondered if that was an-other security device, added especially for the Florida market.

The humid air began to feel cooler, even at slow speed. I made all the correct turns at traffic signals and street signs until Route 836. Stopped at a light before the ramp, I'd just put the directions in the glove compartment for the eventual return trip when I was bumped from behind, my head bounc-ing off the leather rest at the top of my seat. The unloaded revolver still in the trunk, I threw the gearshift into reverse, figuring to ram the car behind me as whoever it was got out to approach me, knock them off their feet. What I saw in the rearview mirror, though, was an elderly couple, him fat, her thin, both with their mouths open in terror and their hands up, showing me they were unarmed. I took a breath, nodded to them, and made the righthand turn for the 836 ramp.

I went about ten miles, getting onto the Florida Turnpike South. I saw some things on the side of the road that I didn't expect, like a broken, elaborate ceiling fan; half a refrigerator; and a highway patrol officer in a marked Mustang coupe with a rack of blue bubble lights that barely avoided over-hanging the door gutters. I didn't see some things I did ex-pect, like speed limit signs, everybody doing sixty-five while I dawdled along ten miles an hour slower, learning the Pon-tiac and watching for Mustang coupes. Then I started seeing some things I expected to see but didn't want to, the after-math of Hurricane Andrew.

Like everybody else, I'd caught the aerial news films and watched the victims being interviewed, mikes thrust in their anguished faces, but nothing really prepares you for being there. Tall trees broken halfway up the trunk like matchsticks. Whole apartment complexes, looking at first as though they were just under construction, until you remembered that carpentry crews don't put the roofs on last. Single-family homes in cookie-cutter developments, some roofless, too, others with plastic or tar paper held down with concrete blocks, a lucky few just missing patches of shingles, like a fish with some kind of scale disease. There were even signs outside lumberyards advertising themselves as HOME REPLACEMENT centers. The worst, though, was the stretch just before the Turnpike ended, the entire landscape flattened, not a tree or bush over six feet high left standing, like the hand of God had just swept everything off a table many miles wide.

Trying the radio to lighten things up, I couldn't get the "scan" button to work, and the local stations I found were either country western, salsa, or poor-taste DJs making fun of Canadians driving and old folks doing anything. The devastation of the landscape reappeared here and there on the two-lane road past the Turnpike, but after a few strip-city malls, the side views began looking very much like what I pictured the Everglades to be. Patchy grass islands; low, coffee-colored water in sloughs that showed no current; the nests of imposingly large birds that looked like ospreys, on the tops of utility poles overhead. Ten or so miles of that, and I passed a sign for a stagnant body of water called LAKE SURPRISE, then another sign that said KEY LARGO KEY.

The map I'd gotten at the rent-a-car agency showed Key Largo as the first, or most northeasterly, of the Keys, as Justo had said. The rest of the islands arced more or less southwesterly from there over more than a hundred miles of U.S. Route 1, the bay to the Everglades themselves to the north and west, the ocean to the south. A small sign on the shoulder showed "103" in vertical white numbering on a green background tacked to a short white post. Soon after, I saw "102" and so on, the mile markers getting lower as I drove south. I wondered if Key West's marker would be "0."

Key Largo seemed pretty developed, a lot of consumer

shops and hotels along both sides of the road. On the ocean side, there was a marquee by a shielded driveway, indicating that Kmart, Publix, and the public library were there, the last in the smallest print. I guessed people should be happy the library got any billing at all.

I passed some other curiosities, like a four-story building on a median strip at mile marker 99 that had one of its sides painted entirely as a tropical reef, with a diver and fish and the kinds of coral Caryn talked about in the scuba class. Mostly, though, the buildings were one or two stories, with flat roofs, probably for ease of installing and maintaining air-conditioning systems. The predominant construction looked like cinder block under stucco, maybe with reinforcing bars in the blocks against hurricane force winds. Or waves. Everything looked about six inches above sea level, though from the road there was no water visible on either the ocean or bay side. It was oppressively hot every time I stopped for a traffic light, but there was a certain brightness to the air, as though you'd just taken off sunglasses.

At the south end of Key Largo was a bridge rising over what a sign called MERCY CREEK. Crossing the bridge, I saw MERCY KEY MARINA painted in large red letters on the aquamarine walls of a hangarlike building. Then another sign identifying the next land mass as MERCY KEY.

On the map, Mercy looked like most of the other Keys. Longer than it was wide, the island tapered like a loin lambchop for seven miles southward before another creek separated it from Plantation Key. But that was on the map. From the road, you could see that Mercy Key was higher than Key Largo, fifteen, even twenty feet of elevation seeming pretty constant from the glimpses of water both oceanward and bayward. What's more, there was far less development, and a kind of restraint about what there was, especially after the median strip, now all trees and shrubs, resumed to separate north- and southbound traffic. I passed only three motels that seemed of any size, most names suggesting instead small motor courts or trailer parks. Two thirds of the way down the island, there was a road to the right with an arrow saying TENT GROUND.

As the median strip narrowed and ended, I crossed over the bridge to Plantation Key, another marina directly on my right. The median strip never started up again, Plantation appearing more developed than Mercy, a kind of suburban shopping center feel to it. Further on, I crossed a few more causeways, seeing a sign for ISLAMORADA that was either a Key or a town, I couldn't tell which, and seemed like a part of the New Jersey shore transplanted, bars and restaurants and neon intact. When I reached mile marker 80, I made a U-turn.

I hadn't seen anything of the Church of the Lord Vigilant, and I thought I'd best find it before choosing a place to stay. Driving back north through Plantation and over the bridge to Mercy, I realized why I'd missed the Church. First, it was on the north side of the road, hidden by the forested median while I was driving south. Second, it wasn't a church. Or at least, it didn't look like one. What it looked like was the office complex from the newsletter photos I'd seen in Lonnie Severn's trailer.

I just drove by, noting the mile marker near it for future reference. The complex itself was two stories high, with the typical white stucco finish. There was some navy blue trim around the narrow, vertical windows, the kind that colonists used to notch into the walls of their forts for shooting outward without getting shot themselves. The rest of the place didn't look defensive, though, with several cars parked comfortably in the shade of spreading, full-leafed trees, the colorful bushes in reds, purples, and oranges planted tastefully as border lines.

Continuing north, I pulled into the broad drive of the first large motel I saw, figuring anonymity might be an asset. However, the ocean-side place was a little too classy as I walked through it, markers for POOL and SHUFFLEBOARD and VILLAS 101 THROUGH 111, enthusiastic employees popping out from behind booths and desks before I'd gotten a hundred feet across the grounds and ten feet inside the main building. I politely took a few of their brochures, saying they were for some friends back in Scarsdale, and returned to my car.

There weren't any other big places heading north, and I crossed onto Key Largo and went another five miles before deciding I didn't want to be that far away from the Church offices. Turning south again, I went back over Mercy Creek, past the marina, and stopped in the first large hotel I came to on the bay side. It was called MERCY LODGE on the cathedral gates at the edge of Route 1, but inside seemed a lot more low-key than the first place. No one bothered me as I parked the car in one of the many unlabeled spaces. I walked over to the registration area, a central building that had buffed marble floors, a paneled counter, and ceiling fans with wooden paddles turning just enough to ruffle the leaves on the miniature palm and rubber trees in the lobby. The place tried for historical dyslexia, wanting you to believe it had been built in 1909 instead of 1990, and as a result I kind of liked it.

The clerk behind the counter was slim, in his twenties, and had a nametag that said CLARK on it. Clark the Clerk. "Yessir?"

Clark's Adam's apple bobbed under the white, open-collared Brooks Brothers sport shirt with the little ewe on the left breast. He was awfully wan for someone who worked in South Florida, the pale blond hairs on his arms darker than the skin they grew from. His hair was blond, too, and cut short, studious rather than athletic, the eyes crossing just a wee bit as he focused on me.

I said, "I wonder if you have a room available?"

"Sure do. How long will you be staying with us?"

Already reeling me in, not wanting the out-of-season fish to get away. "Indefinite. Cash deposit."

Clark seemed pleased. "Let me just get you to sign in here, Mr. . . . ?"

"Francis, John Francis."

"I'm Clark, Mr. Francis, just like the nametag says. What kind of room will you be wanting?"

Another employee came around a corner, using a carpet sweeper on the tiles for no reason I could think of. It made a sound like a studded snow tire spinning on icy pavement. "Single room, king- or queen-sized bed if you have it."

"No problem. I can give you first or second floor."

"Any reason I'd want one over the other?"

Clark glanced around conspiratorially. "Well, the second floor has less bugs, flying and crawling, but it's also farther from the pool, and neither one's going to have a great view on account of the hammock."

"The hammock?"

"Yessir. The trees. Or glade of them, I guess you'd call it. They grow right down to the water, and except for our beach area on the bay, we can't cut them back. Environmentalists."

He said the last neutrally, but I had the sense he didn't agree with them on a business-generation basis.

"So, what'll it be, first or second?"

I decided I liked the idea of being nearer the ground than farther from the bugs. "First."

Clark gave me the same approving smile he would have regardless of my choice. "Well, then. Let me get you the key—uh, only one key?"

"Probably."

He tried to wink, but it came off artificially. "One for now, then."

Clark ducked under the counter a moment, then came back with the kind of envelope that companies paying their workers in cash used to have for payrolls. Into it he put a metal key and what he called a courtesy card that would allow me to sign for drinks at the pool or the bay-side bar, when it was open.

"Why would it be closed, Clark?"

"Because we aren't half full up, and it's kind of hard to keep somebody down there for nothing."

"But the pool one stays open?"

"That's right. Most of our off-season guests are from Germany, and they seem to like the pool more than the bay."

Again neutral, but I had the feeling he agreed with the viewpoint this time. "Where's my room?"

"Uh, the . . . deposit?"

I took out some more of Lonnie Severn's fifties.

The diagram Clark gave me didn't exactly qualify as a map, but it allowed me to find my way to Room 139. Mercy Lodge was configured like a squared-off horseshoe, the open end facing the bay. Registration, restaurant, and indoor bar formed the center of the horseshoe, the south wing housing rooms 101 to 130 (and 201 to 230 above them), the north wing 131 to 160 (231 to 260 above).

I left the Sunbird in another unlabeled slot, moving to the door of Room 139. I could hear an ice machine gnashing and clanking in the enclosed staircase that led upward outside Room 140. Setting down my suitcase, I walked over to the noise. A soda machine stood next to the ice-maker, but there was plenty of space for someone to wait and come up behind a guest approaching doors 138 to 142. I decided I'd best watch my back arriving home late.

The key turned easily in the lock, the door opening onto a reception area with double sinks nicely sheltered from both the doorway and the bathroom by a half-wall. Beyond the wall was the sleeping area, a queen-sized bed in the middle of it. Two chairs and a little table nestled on the right side of two sliding-glass doors. The doors gave onto a four-by-twelve balcony with two strap-woven lawn chairs, no table. When I slid open the glass doors, I could see over the pick-eted railing to some guano-splattered boulders forming a rip-rap wall and leading down into the hammock.

The trees themselves were what I'd guess was there before we were. Rough bark and scraggly limbs and small leaves, all packed densely together with lots of saplings shooting toward the sky and some kind of moss hanging from the branches. Look a little closer, though, and you could see vines encircling some of the trees and small bushes trying to get a toehold in the rocks. Closer still, and some kind of spider that looked like a crab with a black, pointy shell was spinning an orblike web at eye level to me. A ground squirrel suddenly scampered over the closest rocks and behind one of the larger trees.

I went back inside the room. Unpacking the suitcase, I slipped the Detective's Special and ammunition inside a zippered pocket for the time being. Then I took the rest of the cash from Lonnie Severn's toilet tank and thought about where to put it. The travelers checks would carry fine, but I didn't fancy having that kind of cash on me or in the hotel's safe, and you never know where the maid staff might poke. Then I thought about the squirrel.

Moving back to the balcony, I stopped and listened a moment. Hearing nothing, I hopped over the rail onto the rock wall and stopped again. Still nothing, and only the two rooms on either side of mine could see me where I was. Nobody seemed to be looking onto the hammock.

I dropped down the wall to its base. No evidence of a gardener's care. I found a nice cleft between two of the boulders, then shoved the plastic-wrapped cache into it. Measuring up, the cleft was between the second and third pickets on my balcony rail. I stuffed some dirt into the cleft and worried the dirt until it looked smooth and natural. Then I climbed back up the wall and over the rail.

Sitting in one of the balcony chairs, I thought about what my next move should be. It would be nice to get an introduction to the Church as "John Francis," reasonably wealthy tourist and world-weary potential convert. However, I didn't know anybody who could do that, and I didn't see it happening quickly enough to help me. Before barging into the Church's offices, I at least could establish Mr. Francis as a good tourist.

I changed into swimming trunks, T-shirt, and old running shoes. Taking my room key and courtesy card, I headed toward the pool.

The pool turned out to be on the other side of the parking area, near the tennis court. When I reached the water itself, all but one lounge chair already were taken, the sides of the pool filled with men in bikini trunks and beer guts, the

women wearing female versions that flattered them not at all.
The air was soggy from the smell of coconut oil, even with
an eight-foot waterfall that looked so artificial the only natural
thing about it was that the water fell downward. The single
empty lounge was next to a woman with brassy blond hair
and a figure twenty years past the thong suit she wore. I got
a nice smile, then a frown as I turned away.

The beach area was about a quarter-mile walk down a path
through the hammock that had me swatting at only two mosquitoes, the breeze from the milky, turquoise bay keeping the
bugs off the beach. The sandy waterfront was nearly deserted,
plenty of chairs in sun and shade available. There was a
thatched-roof bar, unstaffed as Clark had predicted, and a
thatched-roof water-sports area with one sleepy-looking attendant in sunglasses, orange laces on the earpieces trailing
down the back of his neck. I got a towel from him by showing
my courtesy card, then spread towel and T-shirt on a chair.
Leaving the key and card in my running shoes, I went for
a swim.

The bay deepened only gradually, and as I walked out to
knee height I realized the sand had to have been trucked in
and dumped, the floor of the bay feeling marly once I was
ten feet from the water's edge. At mid-thigh, I dived forward,
the water refreshing after all the driving. Swimming first
toward an L-shaped wharf on my left, I did some imposed
laps back and forth, south to north, over and over as exercise.
The bay was very saline, but the wind from the north kept
the few people out of the water, so it was like having a
choppy but limitless pool to myself.

Back on shore, I noticed most everyone was coupled up,
which was fine except that it made me a sore thumb. I lay
down on the lounge to drip-dry, watching the bay.

It was hard not to notice the watercraft. Two windsurfers,
keeping track of each other through the plastic windows in
their sails. Farther out, a guy and a girl, him sitting on a
Wave Runner, her standing on a Jet Ski, doing flashy maneu-
vers more for our benefit than their own, I thought. Still farther, a catamaran with HOBIE on the sail, only one hull in

the water, the woman who held the tiller extension riding so far hiked out over the other hull that she looked at first like a special effect.

Then a Para-Sailer crossed my cone of vision, the man "taking off" from a platform on the stern of the tow boat, a helper playing out line as the guy rose. After some headway was achieved, though, the driver cut back on the throttle, the guy in the chute descending and shifting from a paratrooper position in the harness to a trapeze artist's, hanging upside down by the crook of his knees. When the boat slowed down enough, he almost did a handstand on the water's surface. Then he righted himself and the boat took off, a yellow and tangerine streak in the water, the parachute a double blossom in the same colors, a three-hundred-foot line holding him at a forty-five degree angle to the surface, about one-hundred-fifty feet in the air.

But the watercraft were really just man-made camouflage. The bay was like the hammock that way: If you looked long enough, you saw other things. Seagulls and terns, sure, but also what appeared to be turkey vultures, circling high above, their wide black wings having separate white feathers at the ends, like slightly spread fingers. A bird that I thought was a heron, with zigzagged neck and a strangely graceful way of flapping its wings. In the water itself, some kind of duck, with gray and white feathers and a red beak. The duck would paddle alongside the beach, neatly moving around the few waders, sticking its head vigorously under the water while its tail wagged on top, reminding me of Nancy's cat trying to push his way under her blanket.

I was almost the only person still on the beach for sunset. A flaming pink globe, bigger than it seems up north but somehow easier to look at, settled toward the horizon past the L-shaped wharf. The surrounding sky shaded from purple to soft pink, lots of grays at the edges. White buoys in the water looked dark against the glary surface, with boat canopies and light poles and hammock trees silhouetted against the backdrop of low clouds. A couple sat at the side of the wharf next to a post, the man leaning his head into the post, the woman leaning her head into his shoulder as two pelicans necked on the circular platform at the top of the post itself. I thought about Beth, and times like these that we'd had, and Nancy, and times like these that we hadn't yet had, but I hoped would.

The mosquitoes surged as soon as the sun disappeared, and I realized I was keeping the kid at the water-sports hut. I dropped off the towel with a three-dollar tip, him thanking me profusely and hoping I'd be back the next day.

In the room, I showered and shaved, noticing that the bath towels smelled like apples. Putting on a Lacoste-style shirt and khaki slacks, I used Pepe's towel to wipe the Detective's Special and cartridges of any predecessors' prints and loaded six, being careful to wipe the bullets again as I slid them into the cylinder. I wrapped the towel around the gun and went down to the Pontiac. Locking the covered weapon in the trunk, I decided to leave the canvas top down and drove south to a break in the median. Crossing over to the north-bound lanes, I passed the Church's offices at normal speed. Lights were on and cars still there.

I continued north onto Key Largo, turning left about half-way through and stopping for dinner at a place on the bay side. It was expensive-looking, with a white-stone parking lot and planted rows of banyanlike trees, Christmas lights strung in the branches. I walked through a narrow corridor of tropical garden with an incongruous pay phone moored to a post. Past an indoor restaurant was an open-walled, roofed-over outside bar.

From the bar area, the place fell away to a concrete slip holding a twenty-foot-wide, sixty-foot-long boat. The sides of the slip were broad enough to be dance floors, which is exactly how a few brave souls were using them, moving awkwardly to a string band's reggae beat though it felt too early to be dancing, even on vacation. Every time the band finished a song, the tourists seated at tables under umbrellas applauded politely, as polite tourists will, their way of saying they sure appreciate your effort, but it would be just fine, too, if you took a break and didn't come back for a couple of hours.

I sat at the bar on a low-backed stool. The bartender, a tall, pretty blond woman with a prominent engagement ring and wedding band, asked what I'd have.

"You have splits of chardonnay?"

"Half bottles?"

"Yes."

"No, but the house stuff by the glass is Fetzer and isn't bad."

"Let me try that, then. And a dinner menu, please."

She poured a generous six ounces of wine from a 1.5 liter bottle, put the menu in front of me, and took off for a while. It didn't take long to understand why.

Across the bar from me were two couples—Chicago area, from "dah Bears" routine the men were going through. Then they switched over to debating liqueurs.

Husband Number One: "Drambuie's the class of that crowd, no question."

Husband Number Two: "You kidding? You ever had B & B?"

Wife Number One chipped in with, "Or how about that real nice scotch, Courvoisier?"

H-1 turned to her. "That's not scotch, for chrissake."

W-1: "It's not?"

H-1: "Hell, no. It's whiskey."

As I sipped my wine, I wasn't sure I could take any more of them than the bartender could.

When she returned, I ordered a small Caesar salad and a grouper dish. Then H-1 asked her if she could find the Chicago/Atlanta game on the television mounted over her head and toward the restaurant.

She said, "The Cubs and the Braves are playing tonight?"

"Baseball?" H-1 looked stricken, turning first to his buddy for support, then back to her. "Blondie, I don't wanta watch no baseball. I wanta watch the Bulls against the Hawks on WGN. That's Channel 39 down here."

"I'm sorry, sir. I didn't think it was basketball season yet."

"It isn't. They're supposed to be doing a replay of a game with Michael against Dominique."

The bartender just said, "Oh," but there was a world of scorn under it. Using a remote device beside the cash register, she brought the TV up and on to 39 in green fluorescence on the lower right part of the screen. Sure enough, opening tip-off.

H-1: "There, see what I told you?"

H-2: "C'mon, Scotty, shoot the ball. What do you think he passed it to you for?"

W-1: "Which one's Scotty?"

The Caesar salad came out with some warm rolls in a little covered basket. The salad was good, the rolls great.

As the game progressed, H-1 zoned out on it while H-2 maintained a steady patter on basketball and whatever else seemed to occur to him, W-1 occasionally asking a stupid question and W-2 just staring into her frothy pink drink.

When my grouper arrived, done Lorenzo-style with crab-meat and peppered rice, I asked the bartender where the locals hung out. Leaning on her elbows, she said softly, "What, you don't think those folks are natives?"

I smiled. "Primitive, but not natives."

Good smile back. "Well, when my husband and I can get a sitter, we go over to ocean side." As I started eating, she named three places, with approximate mile markers. I liked the way she'd told me she was unavailable without telling me.

The bartender gestured toward my plate. "How's the grouper?"

"Great."

"It's all fresh down here. Try the yellowtail before you leave. I think it's the best."

"Jesus Christ, freaking Dominique, he has to come to life against us?"

I said, "Another question?"

"Sure."

"How come all the local places are on the ocean side?"

"They're not. But it's usually cheaper over there."

"Why?"

She tossed her head back over her shoulder, roughly west/southwest. "No sunsets to charge for."

I decided to take a chance. "You know anything about the big church down here?"

A puzzled look. "Church?"

"The Church of the Lord Vigilant, I think it's called."

"I'm not much for organized religion, but they have an office on Route 1, maybe five, six miles south on the ocean side. That's about all I—"

"Hey, Blondie, you suppose we could get another round over here before half-time?"

"You bet"—that same scorn in it but a good-bye smile to me.

I enjoyed the rest of the dinner and suffered through the rest of the first half. I decided to pay up by travelers check before "Ho" made another bonehead play or "Bill, that freaking reject" missed another block-out. The bartender stayed inside the restaurant as much as possible, but I'd already decided she wouldn't be much help to me. As I left, H-1 returned to the general conversation, which had moved on to great traffic tie-ups on the "Dan Ryan," which I took to be an expressway of some kind.

I stopped at the pay phone in the garden corridor and tried Nancy's home number again. The phone rang four times, and I was about to hang up when a breathy "Hello?" came over the wire.

"Am I interrupting anything?"

"Oh, John. No, no, I was just on the second landing when I heard the phone."

"Get my message yesterday from the airport?"

"Thanks, I did. Are you still in Miami?"

"No, the Keys now. I'm okay, but nothing much has happened yet."

"Is that good news?"

"Probably not. I'm going to rattle some cages tomorrow."

"Be careful the things in the cages don't bite you through the bars."

A couple walked by, leaving the restaurant. We exchanged smiles.

"John, are you still there?"

"Yes. I'm in kind of a public place, but I wanted you to know something."

"What?"

"I miss you."

"Good." A pause. "I miss you to pieces already."

"Nance, if anything goes wrong down here, I'll be trying to reach a friend in Miami. Justo Vega."

"Coco-butt."

"Right." I gave her his numbers. "If you don't hear from me again by a week from tonight, you might give him a call."

Another pause. "I'm sure he's a nice man, but I hope I won't have to."

"Me, too."

It wasn't until I was in the parking lot, sitting on a dewy driver's seat and making a mental note to raise the top next time, that I realized that Wife Number Two, the one with the pink drink, hadn't said anything in the hour-plus I'd been with them. Not one word.

14

THE NEXT MORNING WAS FRIDAY, AND I SLEPT IN, FEELING that air-conditioning dryness in my throat and lungs. When I went to the glass door, I noticed something. There were no screens on the doorway, so you could open it to go on the balcony, but not keep it open at night because of the bugs. I watched a gecko move up the side wall near the railing, stalking something, and wondered if the no-screen design was a security device to encourage guests to keep the balcony doors, accessible to an intruder, locked.

When I showered, the towels, which hadn't yet been changed, still smelled like apples. After drying off, I dressed pretty much as I had the night before, hoping to make a good impression on the Church.

Taking the gun back to the trunk and driving south with the top down, the heavy, humid air was almost a relief to my throat. I stopped at a place that advertised breakfast twenty-four hours a day. Inside, I was the only one at the counter, the waitress asking if I wanted coffee, me going for tea instead, her asking where I was from.

"Boston. And you?"

"Miami, all my forty years until the Hurricane."

"Andrew?"

"That's the one, though I've seen hurricanes before, and mister, believe me, this was more a huge tornado."

She set down my tea in a heavy porcelain mug and laid a menu beside it.

I said, "Driving here from Miami, I saw the countryside. Incredible."

"I know somebody living in Homestead—that's the part got worst hit?—they said it was the Hounds of Hell and the Four Horsemen of the Apocalypse all rolled into one. Me, my house got wrecked, and I kind of figured, 'This is Mother Nature, serving me an eviction notice.' "

"So you live down here now?"

"Yes. I like the reef—protection from the hurricanes?—and the small-town atmosphere. Miami's ... well, let's just say it isn't what it used to be. But down here, the prices! I mean, twenty-five years ago, we'd come to the Keys on a lark, the waterfront property on Mercy could be had for five thousand dollars. Five. Now, forget it."

"That because of the Church?"

"The church?"

"Of the Lord Vigilant. Has it driven up the prices any?"

"Wouldn't know. Haven't followed it much. What'll you have?"

I looked at the menu. "What do you recommend?"

"Well, you have a big day ahead of you, I'd try the Jamaican Breakfast. It's got chunks of dolphin—the fish, not the porpoise things—grilled with olives, peppers, and onions. Fried plantain and toast, two eggs any way though I'd suggest scrambled."

"All that please, and orange juice."

"You got it."

She yelled "Raúl," and a short man sporting homemade tattoos came out and went to work on the grill with a spatula, scraping and spreading and flipping. I had some tea while the waitress squeezed oranges on an ornate, bulbous machine that was designed like a 1954 Cadillac. Pouring the juice into a glass, she added crushed ice to chill it.

The juice and the Jamaican Breakfast arrived at about the same time. Aside from the olives, which were a little strong, it was a fine way to start what turned out to be a long day, if not a big one.

I figured to drive past the Church offices, then, if everything looked good, turn around and come back, going inside to introduce myself. Two vehicles parked in front slowed me down, leading me to pull into a convenience store lot north of the offices and adjust my rearview mirror to watch the entrance. One of the vehicles was a white Chevy Caprice with green and gold racing stripes down the flanks and a gold star with MONROE COUNTY SHERIFF'S OFFICE on the driver's side door. As an out-of-state investigator, the first thing John Cuddy would do is visit the local force, like I had with Chief Kyle Pettengill up in New Hampshire. As John Francis, tourist and potential convert, I wasn't interested in making the acquaintance of any Keys' officers, especially with the unlicensed weapon in my trunk.

The second vehicle that made me wait was a navy blue GMC Sonoma pickup with camper body, identical to the one Lonnie Severn had been driving.

After five minutes, a tall young man came out of the building. He wore green uniform pants and a gray uniform shirt, his right hand lightly slapping a black baseball cap against his thigh rather than putting it on his head. He climbed into the cruiser, started up, and drove by me, paying no attention at all to my car.

I decided to give it ten more minutes.

At eight more minutes, a huge man with a smallish head came through the same entrance. He almost had to duck under the doorframe and wore a white long-sleeved shirt over white pants. Folding himself into the pickup, he started north as well, ignoring me even as I fell comfortably into the light traffic behind him. The truck had Georgia plates on it.

At the first opportunity, he turned left and across the median, me following. He seemed a very cautious driver, waiting until no traffic was heading south before pulling into the

left-hand lane and immediately signaling to edge over into
the right, slower lane. I did the same.

We drove south a while, then he put his signal on for the
arrow marked TENT GROUND that I'd seen the day before.
I gave him a little more room before turning myself.

The side road was dusty, a rooster tail kicked up by the
truck allowing me to keep it in sight without having to hug
its bumper. We passed a few slapdash shacks, mangy dogs
scrounging in the yards, then a jumbo circus tent with no
walls in the middle of a large, grassy field that was empty
but had the feel of an occasional parking lot. Since the pickup
kept going, so did I.

There was suddenly no more dust in front of me, and I
could see the truck moving up a short causeway to what
looked like a smaller Key ahead. I stopped at the side of the
road just before the causeway and got out, ostensibly to admire the view of the bay. A clear sign, navy blue on white,
said LITTLE MERCY KEY—PRIVATE PROPERTY—NO
TRESPASSING, PLEASE. I thought the "please" seemed
cutesy.

The pickup continued over the causeway and onto the
smaller Key. It stopped at what looked to be a gate, some
figures moving around it as the truck started again and slid
from sight due to the contour of the road.

I admired the view some more, then followed again.

Coming up and over the causeway, the gate was visible
against high, white walls behind it, as though the gate and
the mesh fence it was part of were an enclosure. To the right
of the gate was a guardhouse, two men standing by it. There
was concertina wire across the top of the gate and fence, like
a secret research base off in the desert somewhere.

The two men held up their hands as I got closer. They
were in their twenties, both wearing white long-sleeved shirts
and white pants, just like the big guy. They had braided,
navy blue string ties and white bolos in the shape of a cross
at their collar buttons. No weapons I could see, but each
guard wore a left-ear insert with wire running under the

neckline. Both were clean-cut, brown-haired, and stern, the Sons of the Pioneers as White Muslims.

I stopped the convertible, and each walked to a front door. The one on my side said, "Sorry, sir, this is private property."

I said, "Doesn't it belong to the Church?"

The one at the passenger door said, "And what church would that be, sir?"

I turned to him. "Why, the Reverend Wyeth's. The Church of the Lord Vigilant."

My guy said, "Sir, if you have business with the Church, its offices are on the Overseas Highway."

I turned back to him. "The what?"

"Route 1. North." He gave me the mile marker.

I said, "Well, thanks very much. Maybe I'll be seeing you again later."

In unison, they said, "Have yourself a very blessed day, now."

I shifted into reverse, wheeled around, and started toward the causeway.

In front of the white and navy office building, I left the Sunbird in a space marked VISITORS, AND WELCOME, TOO! Probably the same sign-maker as out by the causeway. The small brass plaque at the entrance said:

THE CHURCH OF THE LORD VIGILANT
WORLD HEADQUARTERS
THE REVEREND ROYEL WYETH, YOUR PASTOR

I opened the door onto a reception area that would have fit any corporate office I'd ever visited, except for the artwork on the walls. Christ Driving the Moneylenders from the Temple, the Last Supper, the Crucifixion. In fact, several depictions of the Crucifixion, but none of the Reverend. I thought of the "no false, graven images" passage from the Bible.

The woman behind the desk had a headset as well, this one more like a pilot's. She was in her early thirties, the hair worn short and curly. Her long fingers whisked over the buttons on her console, a pianist who had mastered a particularly difficult concerto, nodding at me while she said into the mouthpiece, "Certainly, ma'am, I'll connect you, and have yourself a very blessed day, now.... Why, thank you! I will, too."

No security in white square-dancing outfits anywhere in sight. There were fliers next to her on the desk, and I took one. It advertised a "Worship" that Friday evening on the "Tent Ground" at five o'clock. That seemed kind of early, but then I didn't know much about the industry.

The receptionist played a few more chords on the switchboard before looking up at me. "May I help you, sir?"

"Yes. I'd very much like to see the pastor."

"The ...? Oh, Reverend Wyeth."

"Right. I'd like to make a contribution to the Church."

"Oh, bless you, sir." She reached under her desk. "We have these handy envelopes for just that purpose."

"Actually, it's a rather large contribution I had in mind."

"Rather large?"

"Yes. A little much for an anonymous envelope, if you get my point."

"Yessir, I surely do. I'll call upstairs for you. Your name, please?"

"John Francis."

"Well, Mr. Francis, my name's Urlene. You just have yourself a seat, now, and get real comfy, and I won't be a moment."

If I heard another sentence like that one, she'd be having to bring me an insulin shot to ward off the diabetes. I took a white leather chair in an arrangement under the Last Supper. The chair was a bit on the stiff side of "comfy." Off to the right, behind the reception desk, was what looked to be a gift shop. It had bumper stickers and T-shirts, bookmarks and CDs, coffee mugs and trivets. At the distance, the only things I could make out were the shirts. They had simple legends like REJOICE and PRAISE WORSHIP, as well as more elaborate ones like DON'T GET CAUGHT DEAD WITHOUT JESUS. My favorite was a face of the crown-of-thorns Christ with DYING TO MEET YOU, intended, I guessed, as a birthday gift for that terminally ill friend who has everything.

Urlene said, "Mr. Francis?"

"Yes?"

"I'm just as sorry as I can be, but the Reverend is engaged right now and simply cannot be disturbed."

"How about Mrs. Wyeth, then?"

Something moved behind the woman's eyes, but she still sounded the same. "Uh, well now, generally, when the Reverend is engaged, Sister Lutrice is engaged with him."

Urlene said it without the slightest hint of double meaning.

I shrugged. "That's too bad. It was to be a very large contribution."

She got the tense of my sentence. "Well now, you just sit tight for another teeny moment, and I'll see what I can do."

After a second internal phone conference, it turned out that what Urlene could do was get another woman to come down and lead me upstairs. This woman, a near carbon copy of the receptionist in appearance, was a little more concise in demeanor and didn't bother to introduce herself.

"We'll just go down this hallway, Mr. Francis."

She walked in front of me along a corridor toward a staircase. On one side of the corridor was a thick door leading into a small television studio, the arrangement of chairs and table for interviewing, the color of the leather more maize, probably as an allowance for the klieg lights that would turn anything white into a radioactive glare. On the other side of the corridor was an equally thick door, an internal window showing a four-sided table and as many radio microphones spreading in an octopus rig from a central, piped cable, a hand-printed sign saying:

WHILE ON THE AIR
*SPEAK 2 TO 3 INCHES AWAY FROM THE MICROPHONE!
*DO NOT TOUCH OR TAP MICROPHONE!
*ENJOY THE SHOW AND HAVE A VERY BLESSED DAY!

My guide said, "Mr. Francis?"

"Sorry." I caught up to her at the base of the staircase with a white carpet runner on it.

She forgave me. "We'll be going upstairs, now."

I followed her, getting the feeling that a lot of the people she guided needed the constant reassurance.

At the top of the stairs were two office doors on the same side of a corridor shorter than the first floor, as though one of the offices had taken part of the second's hallspace. Six people, all women around thirty, were working at desks and computer terminals in an open area. My guide knocked at one door, nodded once tersely, and opened it for me with a practiced smile, not coming in herself.

The woman inside the office was already standing behind a blond wood desk with stacks of correspondence and a space-age telephone on it. About forty-five and trying hard to look ten years younger, she wore stage makeup and a navy blue gingham dress from the Daughter Nell collection that went well with her frosted hair and fluttery blue eyes. I had the feeling some of the makeup was coordinated with the dress, too, but I couldn't tell you why. There was a modest wedding band on her left ring finger, only pinpoint diamonds in her earlobes. She had the smile of a small creature who fed on smaller ones.

"Well, Brother John Francis. So nice to meet you!"

"Mrs. Wyeth, the pleasure is all mine."

"Sister Lutrice, please. We're all family here, Brother John."

She came from behind the desk, shapely legs but a strange way of walking, almost prancing like a majorette twirling a baton. At ten feet, I realized the dress helped to hide full breasts, and at hand-shaking distance, the face seemed drawn and tight, too many nips and tucks by the plastic surgeon's scalpel.

Wyeth took my hand, nails against the palm, one making a nice trail across it as she withdrew her own hand. "Urlene tells me you're giving the Church a very large donation, and I can't tell you how pleased the Reverend and I are to receive it."

Only they hadn't, yet. "Well, as I explained to Urlene, since it is a rather large donation, I didn't want to simply leave it in an envelope."

I thought there was a flicker at "rather large," as though Wyeth were lowering her sights a little and the candlepower of her smile with them. We both sat down, me in a white leather chair that came from the same place as the arrangement downstairs, she in the mate to it, a high-back swivel model.

She said, "Well, now, Brother John. Exactly how much are you contributing to the Cause of Christ?"

"I guess before I settle on a figure, I want to have a better sense of what the Church does."

Some theatricality, but not much, went into, "Why, what it does is the work of the Lord! That's all we do, all we're dedicated to doing."

"I was sort of hoping I could see some more . . . tangible examples of that work, Sister Lutrice."

"Tangible."

"Yes."

"Well, you came by the studios downstairs, where we broadcast the Message of Jesus to all who would watch and listen."

"I suppose I was leaning more toward your facility on Little Mercy Key."

The frost spread from the hairdo to the mouth. "I'm afraid the Compound is off-limits to all but members of the Church."

I thought about the phone number in Lonnie Severn's wallet for "Comp." and figured it might stand for "Compound."

Something about me made Wyeth suddenly warm back up. "However, Brother John, I will be doing a television spot this afternoon, and taping a radio interview with a marvelous Christian children's author after that. Maybe I can arrange for you to see those, sort of a one-man studio audience?"

"Sounds exciting, but I really had more of a tour in mind."

The frost came back into the voice. "Well, I'm afraid that won't be possible just yet. Of course, once we have your contribution and you become a member, almost anything is possible."

The way Wyeth ended her sentence, I had the feeling she was referring back to the nail across the palm, and she smiled as I was thinking it.

I said, "Lots of ways to solicit contributions to all kinds of causes."

Frost turned to ice. "Yes, well, I'm sure you may wish to think over your intentions, Brother John, and perhaps get back to us?"

I stood up. "The Reverend won't be in on the tapings, then?"

"I beg your pardon?"

"Your husband, the pastor. He doesn't do the TV and radio stuff?"

"Not today's," Wyeth said, turning to a stack of correspondence on her desk and pressing a button to get Brother John escorted the very blessed hell out of her office.

Back in the car, I decided that I hadn't handled things very well with Sister Lutrice, but that there probably wasn't a way to handle it well. The primary skill of a phony is to spot another one. "John Francis" wasn't going to be fooling her, though by the same taken she wasn't going to be fooling me.

Not holding a lot of hope for the tent meeting that evening, I figured I'd have to find some other way to check out Little Mercy Key. From what I'd seen so far, that way would probably have to be by water.

I continued north to Key Largo, asking around at several marinas about renting a boat. It took about three minutes for the people at each yard to realize I didn't have a clue about how to navigate the waters and that they therefore might not be seeing their boats again. After two hours of that, I was hungry, so I stopped at a place on the median strip for a crabmeat salad.

After lunch, I drove south on Route 1, hitting the Mercy Key Marina. I thought since it was relatively close to Little

Mercy, the navigation wouldn't be that much of a problem, and if it was, I might even be able to just row past it.

I pulled into the parking area. There was nobody around with anything that looked like a boatyard uniform, but a wiry man of sixty or so stood at the fish sink, cleaning one of three speckled, flashy fish, the body shape of a mackerel and about twenty inches long. Approaching him, I couldn't see his hands through the tough work gloves, but the liver spots on the backs of his forearms made me push his age northward, especially since the black hair ended in snowy white side-burns. About my height, he was wearing wraparound sun-glasses, which made his eyes impossible to read. He also had an avid audience, five pelicans that were mostly brown and a heron about three feet tall with a snaky neck, white feathers, and black legs.

I stopped a respectable distance away as he used the fillet knife. "Nice catch."

He moved his head toward me, then back to what he was doing. "Thank you." The voice was gravelly but command-ing, like he'd once used it, maybe had to overuse it, bark-ing orders.

Thinking of a Legal Seafoods market case back in Boston, I said, "Those weakfish?"

The knife worked on the skin of the fish he was filleting. "No. These are speckled trout. Mouths are the same, though."

"The mouths?"

Again the look, the sunglasses blocking any reading of his eyes. "Why they're called 'weakfish' back north. The mouth is like tissue paper, hook tears right through it, you're not careful bringing them in."

Tossing some of the entrails from the fish to the big white bird, he made sure it had some before he scattered the rest for the pelicans, hopping and yapping as they shoveled the stuff with their front-end-loader beaks. He gave the impres-sion of a man who didn't talk much but didn't mind talking.

I said, "Why'd you do that?"

"Do what?"

"Toss the food first to the heron?"

"Egret. Great egret, technically."

"I thought it might be a heron."

"Herons have yellow bills and yellow legs. What's that one got?"

I looked at it. "Yellow beak—"

"—bill—"

"—and black legs. That makes it an egret, huh?"

"Every time. You don't give the egret its food first, he'll go after the pelicans. And not just the food, either. I once saw an egret like that drive its bill clean into the skull of a pelican, most vicious thrust I've seen outside of . . . in a long time. Like a dart through a melon." Flinging some skin in slices to the birds in the same order as before, he seemed to decide he'd been a little pedantic with me. "Howard Greenspan, by the way."

"John Francis."

Half smile. "Sorry about not shaking."

"Looks like you've got your hands full."

"Best to clean them soon as possible." A visored look. "You a fisherman, John?"

"Not really. I have the impression you are, though."

"All my life."

"From the Keys originally?"

"No, but my wife and I have been down here twenty years now, and we go after them day and night."

"Where do you fish?"

"Out back."

"I'm sorry?"

Greenspan pointed with the knife toward where I thought the mainland would be. " 'Out back' means the back country, the little mangrove islands north toward the Everglades." He pointed the knife the other way. "Between the main Keys and the reef, we call that the 'patches,' kind of reef fishing, but still pretty calm. Beyond the reef and into the ocean proper, we call that 'outside.' "

"Bigger water."

"And bigger fish, that's your preference. Don't taste any better, though."

"You ever available for hire, Howard?"

Again the visored look, with a little frown. "Don't hire for anything, anymore."

I was losing him and didn't want to. "What did you do before retiring?"

"Some soldiering, some business things. You?"

"The same."

Greenspan looked over again, but didn't follow up.

I said, "How much soldiering?"

He started on the next fish. "Marines, twenty-four years' worth."

"Beginning?"

"Just after Pearl through early 'sixty-six." A pause that might have been a hesitation, might have been my imagination. "You?"

"Army, late sixties."

"Late, you say?"

"Went in mid 'sixty-six. Discharged a captain, 'sixty-eight."

A nod, then nothing but, "Colonel, myself."

"Decide that trying for thirty just wasn't worth it?"

Another look, and I didn't think he was going to say anything until, "Kind of."

I let that part drop and took a chance that his last name implied no connection to Wyeth's church. "So, you fish the back country. That mean all around these Keys?"

"More up north, like I said. The Bob Keys, Manatee."

"What kind of boat?"

Greenspan gestured with his head this time. "That one there."

I looked past the black modular docking to a couple of boats about twenty feet long. They looked identical, same length, color, and tall bridge area amidships, even the same 150-horsepower engines. Except the near one had a blue bubble light on top of its bridge and the words FLORIDA MARINE PATROL stenciled on the hull.

I said, "The police boat?"

"No. The one next to her."

"They brother and sister?"

A gruff, gravelly laugh, the kind you heard bucking up spirits in foxholes. "Kind of, actually. The Marine Patrol bought both of them—Aquasport 19s—then ran out of budget to run them. They've got money to put gasoline in their black-and-cream cars, but not their boats. Now I ask you, what sense does that make for a 'Marine' Patrol?"

"Not much. So, you bought it from them?"

"Auction. They took back the lights, but everything else on it made for a good deal. The engine's more than you'd need for fishing, but it comes in handy running before a storm."

"You ever fish the Keys around here?"

I'd kind of asked him that once, and Greenspan looked at me. "Like where?"

"Oh, like Little Mercy?"

Back to the trout. "Not very good fishing around there, though you'll see plenty trying late afternoon, on the way in."

"How about the island itself?"

"Wouldn't know."

"Why not?"

This time a look with a set to the jaw, neck cords out some. "Because it's private property."

Getting off that, I said, "You mentioned fishing at night. Is that dangerous?"

Starting on the third fish, Greenspan seemed to think about whether he was going to keep the conversation going. It was ten seconds before he said, "Not if you know where the cuts are."

"The cuts?"

"The passes. Channels, kind of, between the mangrove islands or through the shoals. You know where they are, you're fine any time of day. You don't, you'll run aground in ten minutes, have to hop out and do an African Queen to get her off the sand."

"And you know where the cuts are."

"I've learned. Takes a while."

"Could you show me where the ones are between here and Little Mercy?"

"Could, but don't intend to."

"Why not?"

He looked up and spoke slowly. "Because you need to get there by water, you've no cause for being there. Private property, like I said."

Thinking I should change the subject, I motioned toward his boat. "Anybody ever mistake you for the law, Howard?"

"Once in a while."

"Drug smugglers?"

"Not so much here. More of them down toward Key West."

"But if you were mistaken by them, it would be kind of dangerous for you, no?"

A last visored look as he put the fillets from the third fish in a red Coleman cooler next to the sink and took off the gloves. "Something I learned a long time ago. Never known it to be wrong. There're only three questions that matter, and they all have to do with dying."

"What are they, Howard?"

He held up fingers on his right hand. "When. How. And how well."

Slipping the knife into a sheath on his belt, Greenspan hoisted the cooler and walked steadily toward the marina building.

Back at the hotel, I stopped in the lobby and checked with Clark. I didn't expect John Francis to have any messages, and Clark didn't surprise me. He had on a burgundy Brooks shirt today, as did all the other staff members I saw, as though there were seven Lodge-issued colors, one for each day of the week.

I played tourist again for a couple of hours at the beach, grateful that my girlfriend in the thong bikini apparently preferred concrete to sand. Then I went back to the room and showered off, noticing that the towels today smelled like peaches. Thinking of the tent meeting and mosquitoes, I put on a long-sleeved dress shirt, loose-fitting Docker slacks, and black socks before heading out to the Pontiac.

*   *   *

The parking situation on the field was handled in a very low-key but efficient way by more clean-cut young men in white outfits, though these were typically teenagers. The process would have reminded you of parking outside a college football stadium, except that there was no charge, which surprised me a little. I got out of the Sunbird, remembered to put the roof up against the dew, and joined the swelling throngs entering the tent area.

There was no charge to get in there, either. Someone had set up folding chairs in long rows with one center aisle, over six hundred seats by the sample count I made. The front of the tent itself was a tabernacle in white and gold raised two feet off ground level, everything looking as though it could be broken down and shipped on a pickup truck. Which made me look around until I spotted the huge man with the small head, who seemed to be coordinating security with the sheriff's deputy I'd seen leaving the Church offices just before him that morning. No sign of the Reverend Royel Wyeth or even the devoted Sister Lutrice.

I went to take a seat on an aisle, but was beaten to it by an older man with a crabbed left hand. Figuring he might be part of an act to follow, I moved to another row and picked a chair one away from a plump, modestly dressed woman with rosy cheeks despite the temperature, which still felt close to ninety. Holding a leather handbag in her lap, the woman smiled at me. I sat down, and I wouldn't have blamed her for laughing at me.

I'd nearly fallen over in the folding chair, it being set on a kind of rounded gravel that gave when I put weight into it. Catching myself, I said, "Excuse me."

"Oh, that's all right. Happens to everyone their first time here for Worship."

Sensing I might have a mentor, I said, "Why don't they just have grass under the tent, like outside?"

The smug smile of an avid mentor. "Well, two reasons. One, the grass won't grow without sunlight, and this tent's up year-round."

"Good point. What's the other reason?"

"Snakes."

"Snakes?"

"Yes. They live in the grass, but don't like to come over the stones. Too exposed, I imagine. We've only got a few poisonous kinds on the Keys, but it wouldn't do to have people jumping up from their chairs at the wrong time during the Worship, would it?"

"Sure wouldn't."

Young, white-outfitted men and women began moving down the center aisle passing collection baskets. Their counterparts on the outside tent-flap aisles kept the baskets moving briskly through the crowd.

To my mentor, I said, "You come to these . . . to the tent here often?"

"Oh, whenever I can. Live Worship is really the best way to see any Prophet, and the Reverend Royel sits at the Right Hand of the Savior in my book. The Good Book, that is."

We laughed together at her joke. "How about Sister Lutrice?"

"Just to the right of the Reverend."

The basket for our row reached her. I was stunned when she dropped a hundred into it, but I managed to do the same with two of Lonnie Severn's fifties. Passing the basket, I said, "I was a little surprised there was no fee charged."

"What do you mean, to get in the tent here?"

"Or to park."

"Oh my gracious, they *charge* for parking where you're from?"

"For major events."

"Well, not here. No, the Reverend Royel depends on the generosity of his flock for that."

I tried to notice the contributions out of the corner of my eye. Most bills going in were twenties or higher, even from some folks whose clothes suggested they didn't clear that in a day. Based on what I saw, the members of Wyeth's flock were generous to the point of impoverishing themselves.

The place had filled up, and the plump woman graciously moved a seat toward me a second before I would have had

to move toward her. The air inside the tent was approaching
the level of a steam bath, my damp shirt clinging to my chest
and back.

"Cozy," I said.

"Oh, you're lucky you got here as early as you did. There'll
be standing room only when the Worship starts. In fact—"

Her next words, if any, were drowned out by the roar of
the previously sedate crowd, leaping to its collective feet as
I spotted just the top of Royel Wyeth's big hair move across
the tabernacle toward a low altar. So far I'd seen only the
small, still photos in Lonnie Severn's pamphlets. Once the
crowd was back in its seats, I began to appreciate just what
the plump woman had meant.

Lutrice Wyeth was resplendent in a navy blue gown, tasteful as a bridal dress and much less revealing. Royel Wyeth
wore a suit the same color as his wife's dress, but with a
white starched shirt and boloed string tie, like his parking
attendants and security guards. Wyeth himself wasn't that
tall, and I suspected that, unlike Chief Pettengill in New
Hampshire, the Reverend just might take advantage of some
orthopedic help in the height department. But after a master-
ful, if somewhat stagy, introduction and benediction by Sister
Lutrice, the floor was yielded to her husband, who lived up
to every aspect of his billing.

The eyes under the pomaded, silvery hair engaged you,
even twelve rows back. His face was full and a little flushed,
beads of perspiration twinkling under the strong lights on
him. But he'd learned the trick of focusing on a different
face for each sentence, so that face would stay glued to him
throughout the performance, afraid to be later caught not
looking. His hands moved as though they were fine instru-
ments, accompanying his speech as featured soloist. And
what a speech. His voice was rolling thunder, exhorting each
of us to examine his or her life anew.

"... And the Lord God has said this unto us, to each and
every *one* of us, Sisters and Brothers, that we must look *in*-
ward as well as *out*-ward, that we must search out that which
is in us and *good*, but drive out that which is in us and *e-vil*.

That we must do this daily, indeed, *hour*-ly, so His Greater
Glory might have a vessel, a *worth*-y vessel, to do His Holy
Work here on earth, that we might en-*joy* His Kingdom in
Heaven, when *each* of us is called Home to be with Him."

Royel Wyeth came down off the altar, jumped down, in
fact, as light on his feet as a dancer, as balanced as a stunt
man. He moved along the center aisle, the gathered straining
forward and sideways to be near him, but never leaving their
seats or even reaching out to touch him. Instead, they let him
come to them, and he did, a tilt toward this man, a hand on
this woman's shoulder, a pat on this little girl's or boy's head
as he continued the presentation.

"And how might we *do* that work, ful-*fill* the Holy Mission
that only He can design and permit us to execute to the best
of our abilities? By opening our *hearts*, Sisters and Brothers,
and our *pocket*-books as well. There is no need of money in
God's Heaven, but much need of it here on His Earth. There
are heathen to con-*vert*, and heretics to de-*nounce*, and most
of all Satan to re-*sist*, Satan with his temptations, Satan with
his lurid glances, his sweet-sounding sins, and his eternal
mort-gage on the souls that dare follow his path. The Mark
of Cain is the secret, dear Brothers and Sisters, the Mark of
Cain will *tell* us what more needs be done, once we have un-
lock-ed its secrets and *plumb*-ed the depths of those agents of
Satan among us."

I thought about New Hampshire, Polly Haldon mentioning
the Mark of Cain, Reverend Vann Tucker describing it from
the Bible. As Wyeth made his way back toward the tabernacle, another round of collection basketing took place. If anything, the contributions this time were twice what they'd been
the time before, and believe it or not, I could understand why.

You weren't there, so the best I can do is this: Burt Lancaster was magnificent as Elmer Gantry, but since you'd already
known Lancaster as a star by the time he played that role, you
couldn't entirely divorce yourself from thinking you were
watching a great actor in the part of his career. Now take
Johnny Weissmuller as Tarzan, or Sean Connery as James
Bond. If you're like me, you never saw those actors as any-

thing before they played those characters. As a result, for me, Tarzan was Weissmuller and Bond, Connery, rather than the other way around. Well, Royel Wyeth wasn't just *an* evangelist, he was *the* evangelist, and if it weren't for three annoying details, I might have given him some of my own money. The three details were that I was pretty sure he'd had something to do with Melinda's death and Eddie Haldon's disappearance, very sure he'd had more than something to do with my having to kill Lonnie Severn, and damned sure he was crazy. Sincere, and perhaps the greatest stage presence I'd ever seen live, but absolutely stark, raving nuts.

I sensed the crazy part when he hit the Mark of Cain section of the speech. I thought it was the only aspect of the presentation that seemed out of phase. I watched Lutrice Wyeth, seeing her drawn-tight eye corners wobble just a little, the best she could do for wincing and covering it. The Reverend Royel Wyeth was effective, but only because he believed every word he said. In spades and to the bone.

"And so, Sisters and Brothers, after you have *open*-ed yourselves to Him, He can *open* himself to you. The Lord Jesus can come *down* off that cross of wood, *down* off that Mercy Tree on which he *died* so that we might *live*, so that we might *pros*-per and sing *prais*-es to His Name. *A*-men, I say. *A*-men to you all."

Wyeth finished the tirade just as he reached the altar, the crowd jumping to its feet again. I joined them.

My mentor nudged me in the ribs. I had to bend down so she could yell in my ear. "Oh, isn't he just wonderful?"

I nodded and yelled into hers. "There's a lot of Ronald Reagan in that man."

She continued applauding wildly. "Oh, I couldn't agree more!"

I expected to have trouble predicting the end of the show, but after we all sat down once more and both Wyeths and some of the collection basket folks began an *a capella* version of "Jesus, the Cross I Bear," I counted out a wad of twenty fifties. While the hymn's last note hung in the air, I got up in a crouching way and edged past my mentor, who seemed shocked. I was on a crouching run toward the front and the exiting Wyeths before the deputy and the man with the small head converged on me. The deputy was strong, but the huge man was a mountain. I cried out, "Reverend, Reverend Royel!"

There was enough in my voice to make him turn. Wyeth saw the wad of money in my hand, now fanned so he could appreciate the denominations.

"Reverend, I just want the Church to have this money, and these men won't let me give it to you."

He stared at me. Into me. Then, "Cody."

The man with the small head grunted something.

Wyeth said, "Cody," with a little more juice behind it.

Cody turned his small head. Wyeth said, "You and Deputy Billups let this good man through."

Another grunt.

"Let him *through*."

Lutrice tried to say something to her husband, but Wyeth just held up one hand as a silencer, reaching for my "donation" with the other as Cody and Deputy Billups loosened but didn't release their grip.

Taking the money, Wyeth looked at it, then back to me. "I hope you don't believe this buys you *any*-thing but the Lord's Gratitude."

"It's the Church's money, Reverend."

Wyeth seemed to hear the sincerity, if not the irony, in my voice. Nodding, he said, "Then the humble shall be exalted. You will take supper with me now?"

Lutrice started to protest, but the hand rose again, and she didn't seem to want to challenge him, at least not in public.

"I'd love to, Reverend," I said.

"Then so ye shall." As almost an aside to his wife, he added, "There is *al*-ways room at the Lord's Table for a just man."

Given the look I got from Sister Lutrice, I hoped she'd be far away from the Lord's Kitchen.

*   *   *

We walked to a pony tent set in a small copse of trees and flowers that looked tended rather than natural. The scent of some kind of bug spray filled the air, and a few flying insects vaporized on the blue lights that intermingled with lanterns hung from tent posts. A large picnic table was flanked by benches, a navy and white checkered tablecloth over it. Pitchers of what looked like Hawaiian Punch and iced tea stood in tandem with baskets of biscuits and tubs of butter. The sound and smell of sizzling chicken came from three of those bubble-top barbecues staffed by women wearing JESUS LOVES ME . . . AND YOU, TOO! aprons over their white outfits.

We sat the way my plump mentor thought of us: Royel Wyeth at the head of the table, Sister Lutrice at his right hand, me at his left. Cody and Deputy Billups sat respectively next to Lutrice and me. Some white outfits, including the concise woman who'd escorted me to and from Lutrice's office, filled up the rest of the benches. No one spoke except the Reverend, there apparently being no conversation worth having except his.

He said to me, "And your *name*, Good Christian?"

"Francis. John Francis."

"You seem a bit warm in that shirt, Brother John. From what part of this *fine* country do you hail?"

"Boston."

"Boston. Home to *Cot*-ton Mather, *In*-crease Mather, and many others who spread the Word of God. Tell me, John, have you ever visited the city of Salem?"

"Yes, Reverend."

"And is it as . . . *dramatic* as the Christian Histories would have us believe?"

I looked to Lutrice, who looked coldly back. To Wyeth, I said, "Dramatic?"

He regarded me strangely. "Yes. The witch trials."

I gave it a beat. "I'm not sure any of the public buildings involved in the trials are still standing, but there is a museum about that era."

"Yes. Well, mu-*se*-ums never quite capture the . . . *es*-sence of an event, do they?"

"I guess not, Reverend."

"Of course not. In order to *feel* His power, His *Maj*-esty, in order to experience it, one must be where such events oc-curred. A certain spirit continues to per-*vade* such places."

"Yes, Reverend."

"Ah, a Good *Pil*-grim, John, a *Good* Pilgrim you are. Lutrice, would you do the honor of pouring John a beverage while the good sisters serve our meal?"

Very evenly, Lutrice said to me, "Punch or iced tea, John?"

"Iced tea, please."

Before she finished with the pitcher, the three aproned women were dishing out chicken parts, potato salad, and coleslaw. When all at the table were served, the women set down their platters and bowls and bowed their heads.

Royel Wyeth then bowed his head, eyes closed. Everyone else at the table did the same, except for Lutrice and me, keeping our eyes open and on each other.

Wyeth intoned, "Oh, Lord, we *thank* Thee for providing this bounty, for *nour*-ishing our bodies and pre-*serv*-ing our souls for the fight against Satan and *all* his minions. For these gifts we are grateful unto Thee, and hope to *live* in the bosom of Thy Love forever and ever."

Everyone at the table said "*A*-men."

The food was old-fashioned good, but bland. No spices I could taste. Checking around the table, I didn't see even salt and pepper.

Royel Wyeth said, "And so, John the *Pil*-grim, what brings you to us?"

"Well," I said around a bite of chicken wing, "I'd read about the Church in some pamphlets, and I was very impressed by how . . . fundamentally you seemed to be attacking problems."

"Yes. 'Attack' is a fine word for it, too. One must be ever *vig*-ilant, and *vig*-ilance often requires action. Tell me, John, were you ever in our armed forces?"

"The Army, but a long time ago."

"I've often feared that as we make our young men good warriors, we ex-*pose* them to unfortunate and unnecessary temptation."

"Absolutely right, Reverend."

We went back and forth on that for a while as the aproned women circulated again, clearing the table and setting a generous slice of yellow pie in place of the dinner plates. No coffee, though, and no smell of any brewing.

I said, "Lemon pie, Reverend?"

A shake of the head, the pomaded hair staying firmly at attention. "Key *lime* pie, John. A staple of the area."

I said, "I don't usually eat dinner this early, but it's almost refreshing."

"Yes, John. The Good Lord never *meant* for man to stay awake past the sun. The man who goes to *bed* with the sun can *rise* with it, begin the Good Lord's work earlier than most. It is also important to have the tent meetings here *earl*-ier on Fridays rather than later. Can you guess why?"

I felt a little like a nephew being bounced on a pompous uncle's knee, but I said, "No. Why, Reverend?"

"In order that our flock, most of whom are *paid* on Friday, do not have the temp-*ta*-tions of the night competing for what would be, and should be, their do-*na*-tions to the work of the Lord."

Good opening. "About those donations, Reverend. I wonder if you could tell me what sort of projects I'm helping to support?"

Lutrice gave a stagy look to the watch on her wrist. "Oh, my, Royel! We will have to hurry to make that satellite hookup."

Wyeth patted her hand lightly without looking at her. "Patience, my dear, *pa*-tience. Our efforts take many forms, John. There is the *spread*-ing of our Lord's Word, of course, through the pamphlets, as you've read, and our radio and television *broad*-casts, as Sister Lutrice is reminding me. We also have the Compound."

"The Compound?"

"Yes. A *spir*-itual community where good Christian families, members of our Church from all over this fine country, can spend their vacations, a spiritual *res*-pite from the temptations of the secular world in which they must *strug*-gle to remain as God means them to be."

"I'd love to see that, Reverend."

"Royel, honey, we really must—"

"I'm afraid you cannot, John. No, no, you first must go through a screening process, to be sure you're pre-*par*-ed to join our Church and to be sure it may re-*ceive* you."

No time for that. "Any other projects, Reverend?"

"Yes." The eyes began to glow, the same fervor that electrified the audience in the tent and probably the viewing audience in front of their TVs. "We've established the *first* Center for the Study of *Sin*, an institute whose *sole* mission is the investigation of and research into sin."

I thought, "The Sinstitute," but kept it to myself.

Wyeth was on a roll now. "How Satan in-*sid*-iously inserts sin into every good soul's life, Pilgrim John. How his minions, especially—"

Lutrice said, "Royel, I really must in-*sist*. We can speak to Pilgrim John at another time, but the satellite hookup simply can-*not* be postponed or we'll lose it and *all* the money we've paid for it."

Either her mimicking his way of accentuating words or the mention of money broke through to her husband. With a decisive nod of his head, Wyeth rose and everyone else did as well, me slower than the others.

The pastor shook my hand firmly, regarded me solemnly. "I hope our breaking *bread* together at the Lord's Table has *help*-ed you see the path you must follow to His Grace."

"I think it has, Reverend."

Lutrice told Cody to personally escort me back to my car so I wouldn't get "lost in the crowd."

Actually, there wasn't much crowd left to get lost in. My car was one of the dozen or so still in the parking lot, small clutches of the flock gathered at their bumpers and tailgates, speaking to each other and laughing quietly.

I walked with Cody next to me, wondering if Lutrice had passed some code word to him and also wondering where I'd try to hit him if she had.

For distraction, I said, "Cody, you been with the Church long?"

A grunt that I realized was his voice. "Four years."

"Do you like it?"

"The Church is my life."

"What'd you do before that?"

"Ten to fifteen at Raiford."

I looked at him. He said, "I was a sinner, an armed robber. I almost drown-did in sin. The Reverend showed me the path, the path to the Lord. He done that for lots of folks. He could do that for you, too, you let him."

We reached my Sunbird. "Thanks, Cody. I'll think about it."

He said, "No, you won't."

Then Cody turned and walked back toward the pony tent, the big body bouncing along, the small head seeming a distortion on top of the broad shoulders.

15

L EAVING THE TENT GROUND LOT, I TOOK A RIGHT TOWARD
Route 1. Driving, I tried to see how I could learn more
about the Church from the Church, and I couldn't see
a way, now that Lutrice Wyeth would close the gates against
me. Given what wasn't served at the picnic table, though, there
was another kind of place where I might get information about
the underside of the Wyeths and their organization.

After changing into a clean, short-sleeved shirt at the
Lodge, I started with the local haunts I'd gotten from the
bartender at dinner the night before. The first was on Mercy
Key, located one flight up in a wooded, almost treehouse
effect that tried hard for Hemingway and came off as *Gilligan's Island*. Stuffed plastic fish, some four and five feet long,
hung at angles to a thatched wall behind the elliptical bar
itself. The windows were just cuts through rough-planked
paneling, the stools barely sittable. Given that it was the off-
season, the place was nearly empty, even on a Friday night.

The bartender was a guy in his twenties, doing his best to
convince a couple of women in their thirties that they hadn't
made a mistake by coming to the Keys for their vacation.

Over in the corner, two men were talking fishing, each not exactly nursing what looked like triple-scotch-rocks in front of them.

The bartender, wearing a washed-out parrot shirt and khaki shorts, came over and asked me what I was having.

"Draft beer?"

"Don't have any. Miller, Miller Lite, Bud, Bud Light."

"Miller Lite, then."

"Glass?"

"Not if it's already in a bottle."

It was.

After using an opener to pop the twist-off, he went back to his vacationers. The two fishermen, both sunburned on the tops of their hands, forearms, and ears, were waxing eloquent over the fighting abilities of dolphin versus shark.

About halfway through my beer, the two women, who'd been stealing glances at me that I didn't return, settled their tab and clumped out of the place. The fishermen ordered another round, one turning out to be triple bourbon instead of scotch. After the bartender finished with their order, he strolled over to me.

"Another?"

"I don't think so. Planning on going over to the Church after this."

"The church?"

"Church of the Lord Vigilant. Friend of mine told me it was something I ought to look into. Know much about it?"

"Not too religious, myself."

"I mean, you heard anything I ought to know about, I'm thinking of joining up?"

The keep's face turned a little, a deer that's caught something in the wind it didn't recognize but still didn't quite like. "Maybe you should ask your friend."

"My friend?"

"The one who told you about the church, remember?"

He went over to compare stories with the fishermen. A few minutes later, I left a five on the bar and slid off my stool.

*   *   *

Thinking I might be asking a bit too close to the subject, I drove north for a while. The second place I tried was a restaurant called the Padd-Thai on Key Largo. Located in a pastel-colored mall, it had a sign out front advertising a live blues band.

Inside, I was a little early for the entertainment, a Melissa Etheridge tape adding a nice touch to the dark room and kidney-shaped bar. The bar was set a rational distance from the bandstand and separated from one eating area by a garden wall and from another by French doors like the ones at Justo Vega's house. I sat on a high-backed rattan stool, about ten other patrons scattered on the same around the railing.

At one end of the bar enclosure, there was a woman who looked Thai taking a Pilsner beer glass from an overhead rack and putting first ice cubes, then ice water into it. She used a swizzle stick to vigorously stir the contents like a cocktail, then poured out the ice and water before pouring a Coors into it. After she served the beer to another guy, she came over to me.

"You like a menu?"

"Just a drink, thanks."

"What kind?"

"That depends."

A nice smile. "On what?"

"On why you were doing the routine with the ice and water there."

"Routine?"

"Yes. If you're frosting the glass, why not just put it in the freezer for a while?"

"Oh, I get you. I do that for two reason. One, the glass is too delicate for that. Two, I prepare glass like this, even if there is just a little soap from dishwasher, water wash it out so head of beer not ruin."

"Then a Coors, please."

"Right away."

She duplicated the routine, came back with my beer.

I laid a twenty on the bar. "My name's John, by the way."

"I am Dang. My husband and me, we own this place."

"Up in Boston, the Thai restaurants have a dish called pad Thai."

"We, too."

"But they spell it P-A-D."

"P-A-D mean the fried noodles. P-A-D-D mean the fan, like to make yourself cool?"

"Good name for a restaurant down here."

Dang took the bill. "Especially in summer and now."

"When does the band start?"

"About ten. They very good, you like the blues."

"I do."

She rang into the register, returning my change.

Trying to keep the conversation going, I said, "Are you from Thailand, originally?"

"Yes. Near Laos, northeast part of Thailand."

"You speak Laotian, then, too?"

She addressed me but scanned the bar professionally, to see if anybody else needed anything. "I speak Laotian, Thai, study English in school, too, but hard to speak it."

"Why is that?"

"I come to United States in 1974, I am thirteen, but my stepfather is Air Force, Homestead AFB."

For "Air Force Base." I said, "What first struck you about the States?"

"Struck me? How . . . alien everything is. I cannot give direction to cabdriver, I cannot buy thing in store. I know only formal English, not idiom. I don't understand what people say to me. They say, 'Get out of here,' I don't know they mean, 'You're kidding,' I think they want me to leave them right now. Excuse me."

A woman across from me had raised her hand. As Dang served her a white wine, I got a nice smile from the woman. I smiled back but didn't move over.

Dang took care of another customer, then returned to me. "I think she maybe like you."

"Not in the market. Actually I'm thinking of joining one of the churches around here."

"Doesn't mean you cannot talk to a lady. You talking to me."

"But you're married, and safe. This church—the Church of the Lord Vigilant—you know anything about it?"

A steady look from the brown eyes. "They do not drink, so I do not see them."

"Heard anything about them?"

"No. They mind their own business."

Dang moved away from me to the far end of the bar. I drank only half the Coors, figuring to save my liver for what was looking to be a long season.

Thinking now I might be aiming a little high, I stopped in a dive partially hidden by a grove of trees. There were as many motorcycles in the lot as pickup trucks, and only a handful of passenger cars, none of them looking touristy.

Inside, a four-man rock-a-billy band in the corner was wailing out a number about the virtues of killing cops. To the right was a pool table, a bunch of guys holding cues and dressed in black biker leather, sleeves cut off for the warmer weather. Most of the stools were taken, six couples dancing awkwardly to the music. There was enough cigarette smoke in the air to mask a battalion-size maneuver. All white, about half the men and a quarter of the women looked as though they'd done hard time.

I waited for someone leaving the bar to push his money toward the keep. He was a pale man with a deadpan face in a blue, pocketed T-shirt, tattoos on both forearms and one bicep.

As I moved into the bar, I caught some of the conversations to my left and right. Leftie was regaling his companion, a woman in biker gear, with his "most recent" appearance before the grand jury. Rightie was saying, "I'm telling you, there's so many goddam *cubano* spics in that Miami town, it's gotten so's I get a nigger waiting on me in a place, I wanta kiss his thick black lips, just account of he can speak English, you know?"

Seeing some long-necked Budweisers around me, I ordered one.

The bartender opened it on a device screwed into the sink between us, then set it in front of me. Over the music he yelled, "Deuce."

I gave him a five, he came back with three in change just as the band was between songs.

I said, "Thanks. How's it going?"

"Next couple on the dance floor hits the beat'll be the first, but otherwise fair to middling. You?"

I took a sip of the beer. "Good."

One of the bikers at the pool table suddenly butt-ended another with a cue. The receiver held up a hand, meaning no more. The keep saw all this with me, didn't even twitch.

I said, "Friendly discussion."

He looked at me. "Nothing worth shedding blood over, anyways."

"That kind of thing, always makes me feel a little religious."

The deadpan look. "Religious."

"Yeah. I hear there's this outfit down on Mercy, what's the name—oh, yeah. The Church of the Lord Vigilant."

The band struck up some chords, then seemed to need a readjustment of equipment.

The keep leaned into me, lowering his voice. "You got a badge?"

"If I did, I sure wouldn't show it after that last song."

The keep nodded, then picked up my beer and poured it slowly into the sink. Setting the bottle down very deliberately in front of me, he said, "No refunds."

"The conversation was worth the money, only just barely."

"Don't hurry back."

I tried two other places up and down the Overseas Highway without any better luck. It seemed nobody wanted to talk about the Church, the Reverend Royel, or the Dragon Lady from *Hee-Haw*. Then I stopped at a smaller place with a tree-ringed, gravel parking lot off a side street on the ocean side, the name PINKY'S in the same color neon lit over the door.

Inside, the linoleum was old, peanuts and popcorn in wicker baskets on the bar. There was the smell of fried fish coming from somewhere in back, but it looked like the kind of joint where the bar tabs would be bigger than the dinner bills. Trophies for what seemed to be softball lined a shelf under the small, ceiling-mounted television, and taxidermy on plaques labeled SNOOK, TARPON, and BONEFISH looked as though they actually might once have been alive.

A foursome of guys shared a bucket of beer at a corner table, all working stiffs to look at them. A bearded white, a bald white, a tall African-American, and a short Latino. At the far end of the bar, a solo white guy in his late twenties hunched over a mug, drawing on a cigarette and staring morosely into his beer. In the center of the bar, a middle-aged tourist couple was listening intently to the bartender, a woman also on the kind side of thirty with natural blond hair, a healthy tan, and a bare midriff showing the kind of abdominals you get only by working out hard and keep only by working out harder.

The bartender was gamely, even enthusiastically advising the tourists on other places they might hit. "If you like blues, the Padd-Thai up around mile marker 103 has a great band, Jimmy Hawkins and the Cyclones. You want just nice music, there's these two brothers up at Snapper's, they do great guitar duets and a just hilarious redneck routine."

The couple glanced at each other. "We don't know, Donna . . ."—stretching out the first syllable like it was "Dawn."

"Oh, it's not what you might think. No racist stuff or anything. More like, 'You might be a redneck if your front porch collapses, and it kills more than three dogs.' "

The couple laughed.

"Or, 'You might be a redneck if your family tree doesn't branch.' "

Bigger laugh.

Donna said, "I don't want to spoil it for you, but they got

a million more." Confidentially, "You want something a little raunchier, there's 'Big Dick and the Extenders' down at Islamorada, around mile marker 82 or so. They perform in a bar called Woody's, gray place that's got this old-time wood-sided station wagon pasted on the front of it. Big Dick himself is like a three-hundred-pound Indian—American Indian, I mean—and he insults the people in the audience like Don Rickles, then gets them to come up with him and tell everybody their favorite dirty jokes. It's a hoot."

The couple asked for a napkin to take down the names and the mile markers. While they were doing that, Donna looked carefully at the morose guy, then came over to me. Her hair was drawn up into a ponytail on the side of her head, like a *Flintstones* cartoon character. "What can I get you?"

"Draft?"

"Killian's Irish Red, Coors, Bud."

"Killian's fresh?"

"Tapped it two hours ago myself."

"Great."

She smiled, gauging something, then came back with the ale. "Boston, right?"

"Good ear."

"When we moved to Virginia, a Welcome Wagon of the neighborhood women came over to us. One of them was from Boston and sounded just like you."

"It's an accent you can pick out, once you've heard it."

The middle-aged couple said, "Thanks, Donna," and left a five on the counter.

She said, "Hey, thank you a lot! Y'all have a nice time in the Keys, now."

I said, "By the way, Donna, my name's John."

She extended her hand, giving mine a firm, slightly more than friendly shake. "John, pleased to meet you. But my name's not D-O-N-N-A, it's D-A-W-N-A."

"Sorry."

"Don't be. It's a mistake everybody makes."

"I have to confess, I can't tell where you're from."

"Here, originally. A true conk, and there aren't many of us left."

"Conk?"

"C-O-N-C-H, from the shell, only it's pronounced 'conk,' like a rap in the head."

The morose guy called out, "How about another beer here before you get a rap in the head?"

Dawna glared at him. The quartet in the corner shut up, then continued their own conversation more quietly.

She said, "Jay, don't you start now."

"I'm not starting anything. I'm ordering another beer."

"I told you when you sat down, it was two and out. That's number two, and you're out."

He got up and moved toward us. Dawna reached for something under the bar. Jay ignored me and lunged across for her. Bad idea on both counts.

I stomped my right heel from the rung of my stool into his left instep. He howled and brought his booted foot up to hug it, like you do when you stub a toe. I grabbed his left boot, and he had to hop on the good foot to keep his balance. I led him that way out the door and into the parking lot.

Jay said, "The fuck you think you're doing, man?"

"Probably getting you out of harm's way."

I let go of his boot, Jay catching his balance on the uneven stones, but limping.

He said, "You broke my fucking foot, man."

"No, it'll go away after a while. Maybe you should go away, too."

"Fuck you, man."

Favoring his left side, Jay moved to an old Buick with a lot of primer and a shot suspension system. I was back in Pinky's before I heard more than saw his car wheeling out of the lot, spritzing gravel against the side of the building.

Dawna was standing at the end of the bar, her right hand holding a sawed-off bat handle and slapping it into her palm like a patrol officer with a nightstick. On a level floor with me, she stood about five-seven in sneakers and blue jeans with pockets a different shade of blue than the pants. Then she waved the bat at the receding sound of the Buick's engine. "That his cruiser?"

Great, a cop. "Cruiser?"

"Yeah, we call old oil-burners like Jay's 'Keys Cruisers.' "

"Then, yes, it was his. He have a gun that you know of?"

A smile, gleaming teeth against the tan. "Kind of late to be asking about that, isn't it?"

I smiled back. "Kind of."

A male voice echoed, as though from a kitchen. "Dawna! Order up."

She said, "Don't go 'way," then went behind the bar and through a doorway out of sight.

As I sat back on my stool, I could overhear the four guys in the corner talking. The bearded white said, "The motherfucker bombed that hundred-story building in New York, he oughta be shot for the motherfucker he is."

The tall black said, "You got that right."

The bald white guy said, "Only one fucker we fucked with enough to do that."

The tall black said, "Saddam Hussein. He the baddest, man."

White beard: "Yeah, I didn't really hate the guy till he fucked with the environment over there."

The short Latino said, "The environment?"

Bald white: "Yeah. The oil fires and all those seals and birds."

Short Latino: "Seals and birds? I thought he fucked those Kuwait sheik guys?"

Bald white: "Yeah, but nobody ever cared about it till he killed those animals, man."

Tall black: "You got that right, too. Nobody gives a fuck about no sand niggers. You fuck up some seals, though, the whole world be down on your case."

White beard: "You know, this was all foretold."

Short Latino: "What you saying, man?"

White beard: "This philosopher, Notra Damus. He, like, predicted all this shit."

Short Latino: "Notra . . . ?"

White beard: "Damus, man. Notra Damus, like the football school. Back in 1560, he predicted all this."

Bald white: "All what?"

White beard: "All this"—belch—"conflagration."

Short Latino: "Confla . . . ?"

White beard: "Conflagration, Luis. The world's like a fire-ball. He predicted all this shit in four hundred quatrains, like seventy percent of it's come true."

Short Latino: "Quatrains?"

White beard: "Yeah."

Short Latino: "Man, I, like, didn't know they even had trains back then."

White beard: "What?"

Short Latino: "I thought they was still in stagecoaches."

White beard: "Hey, Luis?"

Short Latino: "Yeah?"

White beard: "You're a disgrace to your race, man."

Short Latino: "Hey, fuck you, okay?"

Bald white: "Yeah, and the stagecoach you rode in on."

They all started laughing good-naturedly as Dawna brought their food on a tray and distributed the plates without having to ask who'd ordered what. Then she came back behind the bar and over to me.

"By the way, thank you a lot for what you did. My last name's Adair."

"Dawna Adair."

"Yeah, a lot of people say it fast, think I'm 'Dawn' even instead of 'Dawna.' What's yours?"

"Francis, John Francis."

The gleamy smile and a wink. "I remembered the 'John' part. You down here on vacation?"

"Kind of."

"Where're you staying?"

"Mercy Lodge."

A sour face. "Kind of stuffy, isn't it?"

"A little."

"You ought to have a local show you the sights."

"Actually, I was hoping somebody could tell me something about one of the local sights."

"Which one's that?"

"The Church of the Lord Vigilant."

The tan seemed to wane a bit. "You don't look the type."

"To do what?"

"To join the Church."

"That could be my problem. I haven't been able to get anybody to tell me about it."

The sound of boots coming through the door made both of us turn around, but it was a bunch of six or seven guys I didn't recognize. She did.

"Hey, Dawna, how's it going?"

"Great. You guys?"

"Can't complain."

Adair said, "You do, your friends get sad and your enemies get happy."

Three or four laughs. "Hey, that's pretty good."

"Sit down, be right with you."

They took stools at the end that Jay had occupied.

Adair leaned over to me. "I'm going to be pretty busy from here on out, Friday night and all."

"I understand."

She looked at me steadily. "But I get off at two."

John Francis said, "For some . . . sightseeing?"

"If you're interested."

"Should I come on in?"

A shake of the head. "Just as soon meet you in the parking lot, so these boys don't get any ideas of their own."

"Two o'clock."

Adair turned her face so "the boys" couldn't see it, then winked at me again before going down to them.

I drove north once more to the Padd-Thai, thinking about how I was going to handle my "late date" with Dawna. I made up my mind, leaving the convertible in a parking lot three times as full as when I'd been there earlier. Owner or not, Dang must have finished her shift or switched to some other task, because a young guy in a Prince John beard was scurrying around inside the kidney-shaped bar enclosure, waiting on what was now a full house except for one empty rattan stool, which I took.

The band was onstage but between songs, each of them sipping different-colored liquids. There were four of them, Jimmy Hawkins on lead guitar backed up by a bass guitar, drummer, and keyboard. Hawkins had Charles Manson hair and a thousand-yard stare, but when the group launched into the unplugged, ballad version of Eric Clapton's "Layla," you could hear a pin drop in the place. After a roaring ovation, the bartender took my order for a Coors and served it in a glass, going through Dang's routine with the ice and water first.

I sat through two more sets, the band able to mix music from the Rolling Stones to the Allman Brothers to Muddy Waters awfully well and sound awfully good doing it. During the third, closing set, Hawkins let another guy from the crowd come up onstage and use his equipment to do a couple of songs with the group. The other guy was good, and after the second song, he laid the guitar reverentially on its stand. From the audience, Hawkins yelled out, "Hey, man, don't worry, you can't hurt that. Hell, I surf with it."

The bartender went around for last call, but I passed and made my way back out to the Sunbird.

I eased into the tree-ringed lot of Pinky's, the white gravel crunching under the tires, only two other cars and a pickup truck still there. The neon sign went off as I put the car in park. Then I remembered Dawna Adair's comment about the other boys getting "ideas." Driving out again and onto the side street, I positioned the car so I could see between the trees. That way, if she weren't the next person out, that person wouldn't see me.

A few minutes later, Adair came through the door. The night air was cool, especially so close to the ocean, and she'd pulled a rugby jersey on over the midriff top, a tote-style handbag slung from her shoulder. When Dawna looked around the lot, I could see her take a breath, then kick a stone in front of her shoe, like a disappointed kid kicking a tin can. She crossed her arms, shook her head, and started across the lot, but away from the three vehicles. I got out of the convertible without closing the door.

Adair was about halfway through the lot when a figure rose up from under one of the trees at its edge. As he hit the moonlit gravel, Dawna stopped cold and started fumbling in her bag as she backed up. He was staggering, but boxing her in, like a quarter horse will a skittish steer.

It was Jay, the morose guy I'd thrown out earlier. And he was carrying a long-necked beer bottle in his right hand, the fingers holding the neck for hitting rather than drinking.

With no time to go to the trunk for my gun, I was moving through the tree line as he closed on her.

Adair was about to speak when I said, "Jay."

He turned, eyes raging at something inside more than at me, I thought. "You motherfucker, I'm going to do you good."

Dawna had a little spray can in her hand, but I waved her off.

Then Jay took two slyly quick steps toward me, reached down the hand holding the long-neck, and smashed the beverage part against the lot, giving him a handle and wicked cutting edges as he came for me. Fast.

I tried to relax, the way I'd been taught in a sawdust pit a generation ago by a sergeant who'd spent his career instructing military police officers in unarmed defense. I let my left foot slide back and my right foot forward, pointing at Jay. Slightly cupping both hands, I brought them up, elbows in and at the width of the shoulders, forearms forty-five degrees to the ground, right hand a little forward of the left. If Jay knew what he was doing, he'd think I was a leftie and might move the wrong way first. If he didn't know how to use the bottle, I'd be able to tell soon enough to switch positions.

He knew something.

Slashing high with the forehand first, Jay missed, then came in low with the backhand. He caught and tore open my pants above the left knee but he didn't get the leg itself. His momentum combined with the alcohol made him follow through too much, opening his left arm, the one without the bottle in it, to me.

I sidekicked at the elbow with the ball of my right foot, feeling something give as I connected.

Jay bawled out in pain, dropping the bottle so his right hand could reach for his left arm. "You broke my fucking elbow, man. You broke it!"

"Hyperextended or dislocated, Jay. I were you, I'd get me to a hospital while medical care can still help."

"Fuck you, man! And fuck you, Dawna, you fucking bitch."

He got to his feet, staggering away and onto the side street.

I walked over to Adair, who was still holding the spray can. "Mace?"

She handed it to me. "Yes."

The can felt full as I gave it back to her. "I should have let you use it, but I didn't think he'd break the bottle over your refusing to serve him in there."

Dawna put the Mace in her bag. "Well, I guess it goes a little deeper than that."

"How deep?"

"Jay's kind of my ex-fiancé."

I just looked at her.

Adair returned it steadily. "So, this mean the date's off?"

"I'd like to think about it."

"How about while you're doing that, I sew up your pants, at least?"

"I don't have a needle and thread."

"I do." The gleamy smile. "At my place."

16

ACTUALLY, WALKING TO WORK IS USUALLY FUN, EXCEPT FOR tonight, of course. Uh, take a right ... here."

I did. We passed some houses on stilts, I assumed as a precaution against storm flooding, even with Mercy Key's higher elevation.

Adair said, "You see, you get to kind of organize your mind on the way in, and then you get to blow off steam on the way home. Plus, it helps keep those unwanted pounds from showing."

"You don't look as though you have a problem there."

"Thanks, but really the food goes right from my lips to my hips. If I didn't do five aerobics classes a week—including three step ones?—I'd be a blimp inside a month. How about you?"

"Me?"

"Yeah. You're not old, but I don't see many men your age in your kind of shape. What do you do?"

"Some jogging, stationary bike, StairMaster."

"They did a run down here last December, called it the 'Key to Shining Key Ultramarathon' because they went along U.S. 1 from Largo all the way to Key West."

"That's something like a hundred miles, right?"

"Uh-huh. And it was a hot day for that time of year, into the eighties." Dawna stopped. "You do Nautilus, too, right?"

"How'd you know that?"

"Your arms." She reached over with her left hand, the index finger very slowly and lightly tracing the bicep, then down the forearm, then up the tricep again. "Free weights'll give you either a body-builder look or a beer-truck look. You don't get that nice, long muscle definition like you've got without using the Nautilus." A low, purring quality came into her voice. "Uh-oh, now I'm giving you goosebumps, maybe I better stop?"

We came to a T-intersection. "Which way from here?"

"Left, then two blocks and a right."

After the left, I went two blocks but didn't see anything.

"Okay, the right is just ... there."

I pulled into a narrow driveway with a couple of old stumps as posts subtly marking its entrance.

Adair said, "Home sweet home."

It was a smallish place of gray, weathered wood, the moonlight showing multicolored, volleyball-sized fishing floats strung across the front of the house like cranberries on a Christmas spruce. Two stories, the first having no apparent doorway, the second an abruptly slanting roof. Nice trees and flowering bushes were planted all around, a topless Jeep Wrangler parked on scrub grass off to the side.

I said, "Everything but a dog to greet us."

"Tough to have a dog here, John. With no frost to kill them, you have fleas year-round." Dawna swept her hand at the building. "You're looking at an authentic conch cottage. Well, actually it's more like a cigar-maker's house."

Putting the Sunbird's floor-shift into park, I said, "Don't get you."

"Come on in, and I'll show you." Adair reached over with her left hand, briefly covering my right and giving it a squeeze. I jumped a little.

She said, "What's the matter?"

"Just burned it some, couple days ago."

The low purr. "In that case, I'll be gentle."

Dawna took a while getting out of the car and walking to the side of the house. I followed her.

"There's no front door, because everybody comes to the dining room to get in."

"The dining room?"

We reached the back of the house. Another sweeping gesture. "The dining room."

It was a covered patio, the floor laid in wide, weathered planking, the ceiling just the underside of the roof above it. The furniture was rattan, like the stools at the Padd-Thai, except for a solid wood table and a similar swing with cushions, sort of a love seat suspended on chains secured to a beam by what looked like blackened railroad spikes.

"Nice," I said.

"Oh, John, you don't know how good it can be to have your meals outdoors, any kind of weather. When we lived in Virginia, we had the change of seasons, and I liked that, too. But down here . . . I don't know. There's oodles of bugs, but I just love it."

"What makes it a cigar-maker's house?"

"My grandpa got the idea for it when he visited Key West. A lot of the Cuban tobacco people moved there a long time ago to make cigars. He was really struck by the look of their houses, and when he got finished working for Mr. Flagler's railroad, he built this place to retire to."

"Mr. Flagler's railroad?"

"Yes. Mr. Flagler was an oil man, built the line from the mainland all the way down to Key West. But the railroad got destroyed in the hurricane of 1935. Two-hundred-mile-an-hour winds, eighteen-foot tidal wave—"

"Eighteen feet?"

"Yessir. That's how this Key got its name."

"Mercy, you mean?"

"Right. Used to have an Indian name. When the storm came up, the railroad sent a train down the line to try and rescue some workers, but everything except the engine car got washed away. The people who made it to here, though, they lived through the storm, because parts of Mercy are, like, twenty feet above sea level, highest ground in all the Keys."

"And so the survivors renamed the place 'Mercy.' "

"Uh-huh. Also did some fancy construction. Come on, I'll show you."

Adair slid open a pocket door in the patio wall of the house. We entered a small kitchen, and a beetlelike thing that looked like a cockroach on steroids skittered across the floor in front of us.

"What the hell was that?" I said.

"Palmetto bug. You don't want to step on them, the air'll smell like spoiled almonds for days."

Past the kitchen was a living room area, with throw pillows and sectional furniture and a ceiling fan. The ceiling over the living room was an atrium, plants hung from the exposed beams.

"This is really nice, Dawna."

A wink. "Wait'll you see the upstairs."

I followed her toward a narrow staircase, like one to an attic. I thought Adair was accentuating her hip movements a little on the steps, but that may just have been me.

We crested at a half loft, more plants hanging from staunch collar ties spaced only three feet apart, again secured to the angled roof beams by railroad spikes. The spike motif continued with the wall-covering bookcases, the spikes being laid at the diagonal in right-angle bookends. The books themselves included some Danielle Steeles and Sidney Sheldons, but many by Joyce Carol Oates, John Edgar Wideman, and even Brontë and Dickens, what looked like grammar school awards of some kind here and there. Only one window, at the back over a small table with a hurricane lamp on it.

I said, "Very nice."

Dawna had moved to her bed, a brass curlicue painted white, sitting on it. "And built to last. Grandpa saw what happened to the houses on the other Keys from the hurricane, so he gathered up as many of the railroad spikes as he could find—said to me, 'I helped build that damn railroad, girl, seems to me I can unbuild it as well'—and he used only Dade

County pine. It's a kind of wood, when it gets older, the resin hardens as it dries. I tried to have that window there enlarged so I could fit an air conditioner? Forget it. Jay broke five saw blades before he quit."

"Your ex-fiancé."

"Uh-huh. I think he has some kind of complex."

"I believe you could say that."

Adair reached down to pull her jersey up and over her head, the midriff top riding north with it a bit as the neck cleared the top of her head. "I mean, when we were together, he was kind of a funny mixture, you know? One minute he'd be so confident, a girl'd tell him she has a boyfriend, Jay figures she's just letting him know she's not a lesbian. Other times, he'd be real insecure, like on account of his name."

"His name?"

"Yeah. He once said to me, 'It's just not much of a name, Dawna. It's, like, just one syllable. Only a letter, really, 'J.' '"

Somehow Jay didn't strike me as the type to use the word "syllable" in a sentence. "How long were you two together?"

"Not so long."

"But long enough to get engaged."

Adair reclined so her elbows were resting on the bed, like a woman sunning on the beach and propping herself up to take a look around. "That's the one downside of the Keys, John."

"What is?"

"The kind of person who's attracted here. Not exactly bums, but kind of . . . misfits? People who didn't like who they were or what they did or how they lived somewhere else, so they come down here for vacation or something, and the Keys kind of . . . speak to them, capture them somehow."

"Poetic."

A frown. "You're making fun of me."

"No. I was serious."

She cocked her head, enough like Nancy does that I noticed it. "You are serious, aren't you?"

"Yes."

In the purry voice, Dawna said, "You're gonna have to take those off, you know."

"What?"

"Your Dockers, there. You're going to have to take them off for me to sew them."

"And wear what in the meantime?"

"Oh, no, don't tell me. You're one of those guys who doesn't believe in underwear?"

"I believe in underwear."

"Well, then there won't be anything for me to see, will there?"

Kicking out of my shoes, I undid the belt buckle and took off the pants.

Adair said, "Solid all over."

I tossed the Dockers to her, but she made no attempt to catch them, just letting them fall onto her legs. When I didn't do anything, Dawna leaned over to her night table, taking out one of those miniature sewing kits some hotels give you for free in the room.

Using her lips to stiffen the thread toward the eye of a needle, she said, "How come you're so interested in the Church of the Lord Vigilant?"

I'd been debating how much to tell her, and given how poorly I'd done with my lies, I decided to try the truth.

Adair stopped sewing about halfway through my story. When I finished, she went back to the tear in the pants, but worked more slowly.

Dawna said, "You're serious about all that?"

"I am."

"And you think this Eddie is with the Church somehow?"

"Yes."

"Well, I don't know much that can help you. I was there only the once."

"There?"

"On Little Mercy. Little Mercy Key, I mean. That's where they have the Compound."

"How did you happen to be there?"

"I knew this other bartender, Mack. I was kind of helping

him—sisterlike—through his divorce. He was from Wisconsin, originally, and he didn't have any real friends down here. Mack kind of caught the religious fever, I guess you'd call it. At least, that's what he called it, a 'fever.' Anyway, he started going to meetings at that tent ground on the way to Little Mercy."

"I went to one, too."

"You did?"

"To get a look at Reverend Wyeth."

"He is a trip and a half, isn't he?"

"Very effective preacher, though."

"Mack said that's what sold him on the idea at the beginning, that this reverend really seemed to be . . . genuine, maybe? But then, when Mack brought me to the Compound—kind of as a guest, to see it?—it was really weird."

"How long ago was this?"

"Gee, maybe a year, on account of Mack's been down on Key West since last Thanksgiving."

"What's it like?"

"The Compound, you mean?"

"Yes."

"Well, it's . . . weird, like I said. There's this security gate you have to go through, like for an Air Force base or something. And there are these guards, they don't look like guards, they look like they're all dressed up to go country dancing, but they're guards all right. And once you're inside, all the people are dressed the same."

"The same?"

"Like the guards. And the buildings are white, too, with, like, navy blue trim. They're just tiny places, all in neat rows like beach cottages only no frills. And whole families live in them, 'on vacation,' Mack said, but it seemed to me that it was all kind of . . . artificial, like they'd built this little make-believe town for the people to playact in for a week or two a year."

"Did you see anything called the Center for the Study of Sin?"

"No. Well, I mean, I did *see* it, I suppose, on account of

it's, like, part of the Compound, but ... I'm not explaining this too well, am I?"

"You're doing fine."

Adair seemed to concentrate. "The Compound itself is like I said, rows and rows of these tiny 'vacation' houses, but they also have a dining hall for everybody, and a little office building—the big one's on the Overseas, ocean side."

"I've been there."

"Okay, where was ... Oh, yeah. And at the back of the Compound, there's like this other wall, and the infirmary kind of butts into it, and Mack said the Center place was beyond that."

"Beyond the infirmary."

"And the wall."

I thought about it. Why wall off the Center, and why have it be attached to the infirmary?

"Dawna, did you see anything else while you were there?"

"Yeah, some people who I didn't know were members."

"Members?"

"Of the Church. I mean, everybody's dressed the same, it's kind of hard not to notice the one thing that's different, and that's the faces. I saw maybe five people from around here who I didn't know were part of the Church, and it really surprised me."

"Anything else?"

"I don't think so."

"How about a man about thirty, with reddish hair and kind of jug-handle ears?"

More concentration. "Could have been, I guess, but I don't remember specifically. I was there only the once, and then for just maybe an hour or so, but I don't remember him. Who is he?"

"I think he's the one who took Eddie up in Boston." I stopped. "You know, you're the first person I've talked to who's been willing to discuss the Church at all."

"Kind of close-mouthed about things, you mean?"

"Yes."

"Well, that's the Keys, John. Like I said before, lots of people are here—and real glad to be here—because things didn't work out so well elsewhere. You go to a place like Alabama Jacks up on Card Sound Road some Sunday afternoon, you can see them all partying together. Rednecks and swamp rats, bikers and square dancers. They all dress different and talk different and think different, but they tolerate each other. People kind of live their own lives here, minding their own business about personal stuff and expecting you to mind yours."

Thinking of Kyle Pettengill and Christine Kiernan describing New Hampshire, I said, mostly to myself, "Libertarian."

Adair nodded. "Kind of, but even more libertine."

I just stared at her.

She said, "Now what's the matter?"

"Nothing."

Dawna put my pants aside, then her hands on her hips. "You were thinking, 'How does this airhead barmaid know those words, much less that there's a difference between them?' Weren't you?"

"Not after looking at your books."

She softened. "I love my books. And you see the awards over there? Those are for spelling bees. I was the champion, almost. I got as far as I did not because my mother or father was that smart and taught me, but because every time I missed a word, I went and looked it up. Like with 'libertine,' and I found 'libertarian' first in the dictionary. People who love to read love words, John, it's just that a lot of us don't go around flaunting it."

"Or maybe get much chance to even show it."

Her turn to stare at me. "You understand what I mean, don't you?"

"That you end up for a while with guys like Jay because the other kind are hard to find."

Adair came off the bed slowly, moving toward me in a way that was only technically a walk. Putting her hands on my shoulders, she began to knead them, the fingers strong and penetrating.

In the purry voice, she said, "After what Jay tried in the

parking lot there, I'm a little scared. Would you stay here with me tonight?"

"Only with some ground rules."

Dawna left me, bounding over to the night table. Opening the sewing kit drawer, this time she came out with what looked like a three-inch-square version of a 1940s gold cigarette case.

Adair said, "Safety first, right?"

"What's that?"

"This?" She looked at it, then to me. "It's a Condom Caddy, of course."

"A what?"

"A Condom Caddy." Dawna flicked a latch on it. "You've never seen one before?"

"I don't get around much."

"Oh, John. These are *the* thing. A girlfriend of mine gave it to me for my thirt—as a present. See, it holds three. These are the Stealth ones."

"Stealth?"

"Yeah, you know, like the bomber. 'Nobody Can Even See You Coming'?"

"Dawna—"

"If you don't like these, I've got some other kinds, too, or we could use whatever you've—"

"Dawna, it's not that."

"What's not?"

"What I meant about ground rules. I'm committed to somebody else, back in Boston."

"Committed. You mean, like, not married but kind of?"

"Fair description."

Adair dropped her hands to her side. "You're serious about that, too, huh?"

"Yes. But if I weren't, you wouldn't be able to keep me away with a whip, a chair, and a gun."

"Well, thank you a lot."

"I mean it. You're terrific."

Brusquely, but not unfriendly. "Yeah, well. I'd still like you to stay, if that's okay with the 'ground rules.'"

"Sure."

"The downstairs'd probably be cooler for you. I can turn on the ceiling fan, and the sectional stuff's pretty comfortable."

"It'll be fine."

Adair went to the bed. "Here, let me give you a pillow."

"Dawna, I don't need—"

"John, for God's sake, take the pillow, okay?"

"Okay."

At the bed, she seemed to remember my Dockers. "And here, don't forget your pants." Tossing them to me, backhand.

Adair was right about it being cool in the living room. After I went out to the car and brought my gun inside, I stripped down to just briefs, the sectional furniture not quite a box spring but not bad. Dawna had left a nightlight burning for me so I could find the stairs to the bathroom if I needed to. I was planning on not needing to.

The window near my head was screened and opened, the night sounds of a billion insects and a few larger creatures coming through it like nature's unfinished symphony. More dozing than quite asleep yet under the sheet, I came bolt upright with the sound of a quiet footfall on the staircase, my hand closing on the butt of the Detective's Special.

Adair's voice said, "I was kind of hoping to sneak up on you."

"Not a smart idea, given the reason you wanted me here."

"Depends on which of the reasons we're talking about."

As she approached the sectional, the light near the stairs made her figure show through the shorty nightgown. Dawna had let down her hair, a wave of musky perfume reaching me before she did.

The purry voice said, "I thought I'd give you a chance to change your mind."

"With a few more arguments in your favor?"

Adair kneeled down. "And even more where they came from."

I said, "It's your house, so we play by your rules. But if my ground rule isn't one of them, then I have to leave."

"In the morning."

"Now."

A sigh. "God, somebody in Boston's an awful lucky girl."

"I keep reminding her of that."

Adair stood and walked toward the staircase. Turning back to me on the first step, she said, "You wouldn't happen to have a younger brother, would you?"

"The 'younger' part hurts a little, Dawna."

"Oh, don't be so sensitive."

When I heard the brass bed creak upstairs, I rolled over and tried to fall back to sleep.

17 ═══════════════

A DAIR SAID, "UP AND DRESSED ALREADY, HUH?"

"Yes."

"Your eyes are all bloodshot."

"I didn't get much sleep."

"The sectional wasn't comfortable?"

"You know that's not the reason."

"Good. That makes me feel a lot better."

"Dawna, you're a small person."

"How about I treat to breakfast?"

"What do you have?"

"Nothing, but there's this great place over on ocean side you should see. I'll have to do some errands after that, so we'll take both cars."

"Fine."

"Wait till you see the road."

The gun safely back in the trunk, my Sunbird lurched over the ruts in the dirt road as I followed Adair's Jeep from a convenience store where she'd picked up a newspaper. The road petered out at the parking lot of another waterfront place in a grove of scraggly trees. It was a one-story, windowless, rough-planked structure, with the same wood used for a solid fence eight feet high. There was no sign indicating the name or even that it was a restaurant, but the smell of burning grease was heavy in the air as I came to a stop. We were two of maybe a dozen vehicles, mostly pickup trucks, in the lot. I didn't notice any navy blue GMCs, though.

Dawna got out of her Jeep carrying the paper, a long-form like the *New York Times*, under her arm.

I said, "This'll be worth the trip?"

A wink. "Best breakfast in the Keys."

I nodded toward the newspaper. "But not the best conversation?"

"Habit. Every time I eat breakfast out, I have to read the *Miami Herald*. Drove Jay nuts. Come on."

She walked me around back to a patio with a bar, already serving drinks, under a thatched half roof shored up like a mine shaft with posts that weren't quite perpendicular. There were tables for two and four in the enclosure formed by the high fence, the furniture apparently acquired one piece at a time from different junkyards. Most of the clientele looked like people out of work.

Adair gave me a gleamy smile. "Welcome to Pedro's."

We took a table in the corner under the branches of a tree whose trunk was on the other side of the fence. A waitress in shorts and a Key Largo sweatshirt came over immediately with menus, a steaming pot of coffee, and two ceramic mugs the size of beer steins.

Dawna said, "Thank you a lot," and the waitress filled hers. I said, "Tea, if you have it," and the waitress was back immediately with a large decanter of hot water and two bags.

When she left, I said, "Great service."

"Most of the people who come in here need to take on fuel for a long day ahead. She was kind of relaxed for Pedro's."

"You plan to live on the Keys forever, Dawna?"

A shrug during a gulp of coffee. "Probably. The two years my mom and I were in Virginia, there was just enough change of the seasons for me to like it, the way I said last night. But the Keys are where I want to be. The reef offshore for snorkeling and scuba, the sunsets . . ."

"That what brought you back?"

"No, my mom brought me back. My dad was kind of . . . well, today I guess the word would be 'abusive,' and it wasn't till after he died—he went out drunk into a storm, stupid—that my mom felt comfortable coming back. And by then, my grandpa was sick, so we kind of moved into that house. When she—my mom—died, I got it, mortgage-free."

"So you can live here relatively cheaply, but do you really want to stay?"

"How do you mean?"

"If the prospects are all . . ."

"Guys like Jay, you mean?"

"Yes."

"Oh, there're others, and pretty soon I'll be at the age where my best 'prospects' are older men looking for a well-conditioned girl who isn't so young she doesn't know anything."

"That's not the most optimistic outlook I've ever heard."

"No, but it's realistic. And most of the people are pretty nice, even if"—Adair lowered her voice—"they are kind of misfits, like I said last night." Keeping her voice low, but putting the purr into it, she said, "Speaking of last night, you have some second thoughts after I went back upstairs?"

"And third and fourth thoughts. They still stopped at the same point, though."

Looking at the menu, Dawna said in a normal voice, "Too bad."

The waitress came back for our orders. Adair went for one of just about everything. I said to the waitress, "French toast, please."

"Bacon or sausage?"

"You have a recommendation?"

"Don't matter. They're both terrible for you."

"The sausage, then."

"Good choice. Drink?"

"Orange juice, big glass."

"Only kind we have."

She gathered the menus and left us. Dawna said, "Service is fast, but . . ."

"Reminds me of a place back home called Durgin Park. It's in the old North Market Building by Fanueil Hall."

"I've never been to Boston."

"Well, Durgin Park is big, and popular, especially with the tourists, who'll wait in line for an hour to sit at long communal tables with people they don't know, sharing bowls of vegetables family-style while their waitress serves them the way a drill sergeant treats recruits at boot camp."

"Why do you suppose people get off on being treated poorly?"

"I don't know. Given what you tolerate from Jay, though, I'd guess you might have some thoughts on the subject."

Adair smiled. "I guess the word is 'touché,' huh?"

"Just because your dad was abusive doesn't mean you have to put up with somebody like that."

"Maybe I just hope he'll go away."

"You contacted the authorities about it?"

"Why?"

"To get, I don't know, a restraining order or something against him."

"Not how it works down here, John."

Dawna opened her paper, which I took for a "case-closed" sign. The waitress brought our orders, and we ate pretty much in silence for five minutes or so.

Then Adair folded over the paper and sighed. "I'm sorry. You're just trying to be helpful, and I want you to be more than that, and I'm not being fair."

"Forget it." I took another bite of French toast. "You thought of anything else about the Church since last night?"

"Not that—uh-oh."

When I looked up from my plate, Dawna was looking over my shoulder. As I turned in the chair, she said, "I didn't think he'd come over here. I'm sorry."

Jay was standing in the doorway to the patio, a soft cast on his left elbow, a husky guy to one side and a fat guy to the other, all three dressed in work jeans and T-shirts. No weapons in sight, more like they just stumbled on us rather than came hunting.

I looked back to Adair. "Probably recognized your Jeep in the lot."

"What are we gonna do?"

"Borrow your paper?"

"What?"

"Can I have your *Herald*?"

A confused expression. "Sure."

Taking the paper, I began to roll it longways as I stood to face Jay and his friends. The rest of the patrons, getting the general drift of the situation, rose from their tables and moved toward the bar.

Jay said, "Gonna be a little different this time, fucker," and came forward, each friend circling so they'd have me from three directions. Nobody showing knives or worse yet.

I waited till Jay was ten feet away and the two flanking friends were twelve or so to either side of me. Then, holding the rolled-up paper like a riot baton, I went forward quickly at Jay, feinting first to his face, then driving the butt end of the paper between his stomach and breastbone. There was a loud whoosh of foul air from his mouth as he doubled over.

The husky guy got to me first, and I drove the top end of the paper into his face, maybe breaking his nose, then kicked him in the shins. I jumped back toward Dawna, the blade of a buck knife in the fat guy's right hand slashing through open air where my chest had been. I tripped him, the momentum carrying him into the husky guy, both of them now on the floor near where Jay was vomiting.

As the fat guy tried to get up, I dropped the paper and straddled his back, grabbing his hair with my left hand and pulling upward hard. He cried out and struggled to get the blade to what was hurting him. I caught his right wrist in my right hand and twisted it till he dropped the knife, then brought the edge of my hand down hard on the muscles between his neck and right shoulder, causing him to slump. By this time, Jay was scrabbling toward the knife, and I stepped on his hand, hard enough to make him scream about it. When I turned back to the husky guy, he was still on the floor, one hand to his bloody nose and the other up in Roberto Duran's *no más* pose.

I was picking up the knife just as two deputies in gray shirts and dark green pants but no headgear came through the patio doorway. One was Billups, the deputy providing security at the Wyeths' tent meeting. The other was a slim black male, who was about to draw his sidearm, some kind of nine millimeter.

I dropped the knife. "Glad to see you."

Billups took two seconds to survey the scene. "Who started this?"

Without hesitation, Dawna Adair pointed to me and said, "He did."

I looked at her. "Thank you a lot."

18 ────────────

D EPUTY BILLUPS'S LAST NAME WAS ON THE BRASS TAG OVER
his right breast, a five-cornered star over his left. Billups recited my rights, handcuffing my wrists back-to-
back just above the tailbone. After checking my pockets and
finding the car keys, he tossed them to the black deputy,
whose nametag read SHERMAN. Then Billups took me outside Pedro's as the scattered patrons returned to their break-
fasts.

I said, "It was self-defense. The other witnesses will back
me on that."

"Deputy Sherman'll be taking their statements."

There were two white cruisers with the Sheriff's Office
green over gold racing stripes along their sides, red and blue
bubble lights on the roof. One was a Ford Crown Victoria,
the other a Chevrolet Caprice. Billups marched me over to
the Caprice, easing my head pàst the doorframe as he put
me in the backseat. The hot air was stifling, the conditioning
not reaching past the taxicab Plexiglas shield to the front.
Sitting awkwardly, I could see a side-handled billy club, an
elaborate radio, and a pump shotgun mounted barrel-up on
the passenger's side of the radio.

Billups got into the vehicle, skimming a black mesh ball cap across the seat. After starting the engine, he keyed the mike, speaking in normal English instead of radio code to "Dispatch" about bringing me into the "Station." We drove out the dirt road, Billups taking it easy on the ruts and shock absorbers.

On Route 1, he drove steadily, no siren or lights, to a building I hadn't noticed Thursday on my scouting trip. At the road edge of the parking area, there was a sign hanging from a pipe frame that displayed the sheriff's name over MONROE COUNTY. The station itself was a one-story fortress, a public version of the Church's office building, even down to the nice flowering shrubs.

Billups brought me through a glass door toward a counter area with a small plaque saying DISTRICT VI—MERCY STATION. Beyond the counter were SAY NO TO DRUGS posters and women in civilian clothes staffing desks. We turned left past a framed POLICE OFFICER'S PRAYER into a short corridor with detention cells maybe eight feet wide and ten feet deep. He stopped at a cell with a steel sink, seatless hopper, and stand-up shower on one wall and a wooden bench, like you'd find in a sauna, on the other.

I said, "Am I going to be here long?"

Billups took off the cuffs. "Law says up to eight hours." No smile.

About one of those hours later, he came back for me. "On your feet."

We went from the corridor into what seemed to be a squad room, outside windows on two of the four walls, a central table and folding chairs for eight or ten. A small television set was screwed into a ceiling corner, like the one at Pinky's. Next to a bulletin board with personnel information on it stood a honeycomb of mailboxes, last names under them. Past the honeycomb was a rack of manila folders, labeled WARRANTS and REPORTS and then some form numbers that made no sense to me.

A sideboard held a computer, the officer sitting at it turning toward me. He wore sergeant's stripes on his gray shirt and a dour look on his tanned face, the eyes brown and flat. About my age and beefy, he used his feet to pedal the swivel chair over to the table. As Billups guided me to one of the folding chairs, Deputy Sherman came through the door, closing it behind him.

The sergeant said, "My name's Tidyman, Mr. Francis. Whit Tidyman. And I'm doing my best here to decide if we should be booking you or making our apologies."

I didn't say anything.

Tidyman pursed his lips. "You aren't interested in helping us decide which?"

Nodding toward the deputies behind me, I said, "Billups pulled me—"

Tidyman said, "Deputy Billups, I think you mean."

I liked that he'd stand up for his officers. "Deputy Billups pulled me out of the restaurant before his partner could find out that I was the one who got assaulted."

Tidyman said, "My road deputies here didn't go double to Pedro's, Mr. Francis. They responded separately in two vehicles, and it was just pure luck they got to the scene at the same time and didn't step into a hornet's nest when they did. Deputy Billups pulled out of there the one combatant he didn't know, and I credit him for that. Now, you've been read your rights, and you can talk or not, but I'd like to resolve this now if we can, before I have to go and get formal on you. So, what happened?"

Seemed reasonable, especially if it meant "John Francis" wouldn't be fingerprinted. I told him about the incident with Jay in Pinky's parking lot the night before and the three of them coming for me on the patio that morning. Tidyman let me finish.

He looked up at his deputies and back to me. "You stayed the night at Ms. Adair's place, then."

"I did."

When Tidyman realized that was the extent of my answer, he said, "And you're just a little burned that she didn't back your play with my deputies at Pedro's, aren't you?"

"Probably."

"Within ten minutes of Deputy Billups pulling you out of there, Ms. Adair was on the phone to me here, saying you'd helped her last night and were just in the wrong place at the wrong time this morning."

"Why didn't she tell that to your men?"

"In front of her horse's ass 'ex-fiancé' and his friends? Dawna Adair has to live on Mercy Key. You're just a tourist, right?"

Slipping the question, I said, "You don't have some kind of Domestic Violence unit here?"

"We do. Got an Abuse Hotline down on Key West, though that's mostly for children and the elderly. We also have a Domestic Abuse Shelter on Plantation, Family Resource Center right close by. But those good folks have to get triggered by something, and this here is the first time I've heard there was anything off about what old Jay was doing. Whereabouts are you from, anyway?"

Nice change of gears. "The accent doesn't give it away?"

Tidyman pursed his lips again. "Whyn't you just sort of answer me straight, Mr. Francis, we'll get along a lot better."

I looked at him. A lot of iron under the beef. "Boston."

"Boston. What's the weather like up there now?"

"The weather?"

"Yes."

"Warm days, cooler nights. I'd have to make some calls for the barometric pressure and humidity."

Tidyman grinned. "You've a—what's the word, 'jocular'?— way about you, Mr. Francis. What I was wondering was, why you'd be visiting the Keys this time of year, the weather's still so nice back where you're from?"

"I had a yen to see this part of Florida."

"A yen. And your employer?"

"My employer."

"Yes. The boss didn't mind your taking off like that?"

"I'm kind of my own boss."

"What business?"

"Dawna's backing up my story with you by phone the reason I haven't been booked?"

Tidyman paused. "That, and my wanting to wait for Deputy Sherman to come in and tell me what all he got from the witnesses who were treated to a little floor show with their breakfast."

"And what did they say?"

"I answered your question, how about you answering mine?"

"My business."

"Yes."

"Self-employed, got laid off by the recession."

"Laid off from where?"

"From the few customers who turned to me."

"For what?"

"Consulting."

"On what?"

"Various things."

"Give me some examples."

"What did the customers at Pedro's tell Deputy Sherman?"

Tidyman leaned back in the chair, rocking on the swivel post like an old man on his porch. "That you nearly beat three men to death."

"Not even close."

"With a roll-up newspaper."

"The pen is mightier than the sword."

"I'm wondering where you learned that."

"The saying?"

"The trick with the paper."

"Saw it happen in a bar once."

"Lots of hardcases learn that trick while they're jailing, keep some of the other boys in line."

"Not in this case."

"We got to cap the hardcases out sometimes—release them early because we're over capacity for the facility, even the new one down on Stock Island. They take what they learned inside, use it on the outside."

I nodded in sympathy.

Tidyman said, "You ever in the service, Mr. Francis?"

"For a while."

"Overseas?"

"Yes."

"Southeast Asia?"

"Here and there."

Tidyman came forward in the chair, forearms having a tough time finding a comfortable rest on the tabletop. "Did an inventory of your wallet. Lots of ID, lots of cash and travelers checks, but no credit cards."

"Never a borrower nor a lender be."

The pursed lips. "You're kind of a hard man to pin down to anything, Mr. Francis."

"Maybe because I didn't do anything you can hold me for."

"Oh, I wouldn't say that. Deputy Sherman also did an inventory of your vehicle outside Pedro's."

Shit. "It's a rental. I hope he was gentle."

Tidyman nodded to Sherman, who came forward with a plastic baggie containing the revolver from my trunk. Tidyman took the baggie and dangled it a safe distance from me. "You wouldn't happen to have a permit for this, now would you?"

"No, I wouldn't."

He waited for more. I didn't give him any.

"We had somebody put a bullet through one of our courtrooms on Plantation a couple years ago, the building behind our Spottswood Station. You go up to Courtroom A, you can still see the hole, keeps us alert." Tidyman made the baggie swing like a pendulum. "How do you suppose the law in Florida looks upon this sort of thing, Mr. Francis?"

"What, frightened tourists still trying to bring their dollars here to spend and having a personal weapon locked in the trunk?"

"A loaded weapon?"

"The only kind there is, and it was securely encased."

Tidyman lowered the baggie. "You wouldn't happen to have had any law training, now, would you?"

He had a good ear. I said, "Some."

Nodding, the sergeant handed the baggie back to Sherman. "Deputy Billups tells me you had a forceful way of contributing to one of our local churches."

"I wanted to be sure the money went to a good cause."

"That what brought you down to Mercy?"

"Like I said, I had some time—"

"I mean to Mercy Key in particular."

Tidyman's voice had a burr in it, the iron coming through the beef. I said, "Could we speak privately?"

He seemed to weigh things. "Deputies, would you excuse us?"

Billups and Sherman left without a word.

When the door was closed again, Tidyman said, "What makes you think they can't hear us now?"

"Four walls to this room, Sergeant. Two border the outside world, one the detention cells, and the fourth I don't know about. But I'd be real surprised if the union let you drill holes to monitor what goes on between your officers in the squad room."

Tidyman grinned again. "We don't have a union, but you're right. The politics wouldn't let that happen. You've been in, haven't you?"

"In?"

"Come on, Francis. It's one thing to be evasive, another to play dumb. In law enforcement."

I wondered what happened to the "Mr." before my last name. "Just military."

"When you were in 'for a while,' 'here and there.' "

"Right."

Tidyman did the rocking routine again. "All right, nobody 'here' but us chickens. Now, what's on your mind?"

"I'm thinking of joining the Church."

"What, the . . . Reverend Wyeth's?"

"Yes."

"You don't strike me as the type they're looking for."

"Maybe I'm looking for them. Can you tell me anything about it?"

"The Church, you mean?"

"Yes."

Tidyman played with the points of his star. "The Church of the Lord Vigilant is an institution down here, Francis. The Reverend seems to run it with a pretty tight hand, that wife of his maybe tighter. But the Church and its members spend a lot of good money on Mercy, buying heavy from local people who can use the trade. A real shot in the arm, especially after all the problems Andrew brought."

"The hurricane."

"Right."

"So the Church pours its coffers into the local economy, and nobody bothers it."

"No reason to bother it, unless you can give me one."

"Not yet."

Tidyman stopped rocking. "Somehow, I don't think we're talking about your new—what would you call it, 'vocation'?"

"Or vacation, which is what I'm—"

"You going to cut the shit and tell me what you're really here for?"

The burr was back, with a vengeance. "Like I said, not yet."

Sergeant Whit Tidyman pursed his lips, mellowing the voice. "Don't wait too long, now. Things have a way of spoiling fast in this climate, you don't keep your eye on them."

"Do I get my gun back?"

"Francis, you're lucky to be getting your car back."

19

DEPUTY SHERMAN TOOK ME TO PEDRO'S IN HIS CROWN VICTO-ria to pick up the convertible. He had even less to say than Billups had on the ride to the station, but he returned my keys and stayed long enough to be sure my car was functional.

I drove first to Mercy Lodge. At the registration desk, a female version of Clark, in a yellow shirt today, checked her computer and said a Ms. Adair wanted John Francis to call her at home, leaving the number. I went to my room, shooed a gecko out of the tub, and took a long, hot shower to wash the smell of jail off me. I didn't have the air-conditioner throat, since I'd slept at Dawna's house under the ceiling fan and fresh air the night before, but when I dried off, the towel had a scent of banana rather than apple or peach. I wondered if the different scents had to do with intentional additives, like the different colors of the staff shirts, or just came from whatever was in the laundresses' lunch that day.

I wanted to see Adair in person, but after what happened at breakfast, I thought twice about having another meal with her. Instead I headed north, stopping at a place called Mrs.

Mac's Kitchen. From the outside, it looked like a small bungalow at the beach, with an old screened door at the entrance
and jalousied glass on the windows. Inside there was a Formica counter with bar stools that were ancient in the Year
One. Some booths were arranged around the windows, wait-
resses in shorts and T-shirts calling half the customers by
first name.

I took a stool at the counter, and a waitress wearing jack-
o'-lantern earrings handed me a sunset-covered spiral binder.
I asked her about the earrings.

"I'm just trying them out, for this Halloween party I'm
going to next month? But when I walked through the parking
lot, the wind come up, and these things started whistling like
a little kid on the top of a pop bottle."

As I looked at the menu, she recommended the beer of the
month, which turned out to be a British ale. At $1.50, I went
for it and the Basic Burger at $2.50 more.

Nursing the ale, I looked around the place. Collar ties like
the ones in Dawna's loft held old-fashioned beer bottles and
cans in a museum display. Tacked on the walls above the
windows were license plates from everywhere down through
the years. The oldest I could see was, by coincidence, a " '59
Mass," white letters on a maroon background, reminding me
of my dad's car from that vintage. Before the burger even
arrived, I was glad I'd stopped there.

"Oh, I called you."
"I got the message. Can I come in?"
Dawna Adair slid the pocket door all the way open. "Sure."
I followed her back into the living room, each of us taking
a different piece of sectional furniture.
She said, "Look, I'm really sorry."
"I know."
"No, really. You helped me out, and then I let you down.
But I just couldn't—"
"Dawna, I've had some time to think about it, and it's
okay. Sergeant Tidyman told me you called him and got me
off the hook. I don't want to butt into your life any more

than I have already, but you might want to contact somebody official about Jay."

A vigorous nod. "Whit—that's the sergeant's first name, Whit?—told me the same thing, and he said he was going to have a talk himself with Jay. If that doesn't work, though, I'm going to have to put my ex-fiancé out of my misery."

I grinned, and she laughed, and things eased up from there.

"So, John, you never got to finish breakfast this morning. I have some tunafish . . . ?"

"I've eaten, thanks. I need something else."

"What?"

"An introduction to your friend."

"My friend?"

"Mack, the bartender."

"Mack? Why?"

"I'm thinking he can tell me more about the Church, and especially the Compound on Little Mercy."

"Oh, I don't know." Adair gnawed on a fingernail. "I don't think he'd want to talk about that."

"Why not?"

"It'd bring back a time in his life that wasn't so easy, you know?"

"The divorce."

"And everything that went along with it."

"Dawna, I really need help if I'm going to find the boy I'm looking for, and I can't just crash through the gate."

More gnawing.

Quietly, I said, "And after this morning at Pedro's, I can't very well turn to the Sheriff's Office."

Adair worried a different nail, then gave me another nod, less vigorous this time. "Last I heard, he was working a bar in Key West called the Far Horizon. But if he's not there anymore, just ask around to the other bartenders. We keep track of each other pretty well in a kind of informal way, so if he's still on the Key, somebody'll know."

"A last name would help."

"Olsen. With an 'E,' not a second 'O.' " The spelling bee

champ managed a wink. "Tell him you know me, and I owe you a favor."

"Will that make him cooperate?"

"It should. He owes me enough of them."

"Dawna, thanks."

"Hey," she said, resting her hands on her thighs. "That's what friends are for, right?"

Crossing the bridge to Plantation Key, I started the long drive south, the Saturday afternoon traffic allowing the Sunbird to do an erratic forty on the road. The little green-and-white mile markers told me how much farther it was to Key West, which my rent-a-car map said actually would be mile marker (or "MM") #0. After Plantation Key, I got onto Windley Key, then Upper Matecumbe, which featured to my left the THEATER OF THE SEA and a horrible conglomeration of semi-high-rise places called HOLIDAY ISLE. A few miles later, I saw on my right the bar Woody's that Dawna had mentioned to the middle-aged couple, although the marquee more discreetly identified the group playing there as "Big Richard and the Extenders." After that, I hit MM #80 and went over a bridge to Lower Matecumbe Key.

The pattern of bridge after bridge, Key after Key, repeated itself. Long Key to Grassy Key to Crawl Key at MM #60. Then onto Vaca Key, passing through a place called Marathon, which I remembered from sports fishing articles and which made Holiday Isle look tasteful by comparison. A causeway at Pigeon Key took me onto the Seven Mile Bridge, a truly spectacular sequence with turquoise water blinding in the afternoon sunshine. An older structure ran parallel with the Seven Mile to the north, supported by what looked like compressed, concrete milk jugs. People were bicycling and jogging along the older one, which I assumed was the railroad bridge. In the early part of the century, they built them to last.

I hit MM #40 near the end of the Seven Mile and went onto and through Bahia Honda Key and its state park. Between there and MM #20 I drove over more islands than I can name, but signs on Big Pine warned me to be cautious of the 'Key Deer,' a group of four even showing themselves, almost skipping alongside the road, causing a traffic jam as tourists piled out of their cars to snap a shot with little Donnie or Ruthie in it to provide perspective on the two-to-three-foot-tall creatures. After the jam, I passed through Sugarloaf, Saddlebunch, and Boca Chica Keys, finally crossing the Boca Chica Channel onto Stock Island, a desolate spot that I remembered Whit Tidyman mentioning as the site of a detention facility. Then over a final, short bridge and I'd reached Key West itself.

I wasn't quite prepared for what I first saw. I had an image of Key West as kind of a small village at the end of the chain of islands. In fact, it's a pretty big island itself, with large hotels and wide perimeter highways. After some accidental turns and glances at my map, I maneuvered the Sunbird down narrower streets and got a parking space near a graveyard that seemed at the edge of the downtown district, which looked a little more like what I expected. Wooden cottages, the facades having upper stories hanging over lower ones like beetlebrowed faces, the latticework painted in pastels. Plenty of flowering trees, though palms and bougainvilleas were the only ones I could identify. The graveyard had stone monuments and mostly flat slabs, many cracked and crooked as though frost-heaved, which I couldn't understand.

I came upon a main foot-traffic drag called Duval Street, whose principal establishments seemed to be T-shirt shops and bars, many of the latter on the second floor, people sitting at outdoor tables or just leaning out windows or over railings, watching the parade of humanity go by. I walked up to a panhandler whose sign read, WHY LIE? I JUST WANT AN-OTHER BEER.

I said, "You know a bar called the Far Horizon?"

"No problem. Three blocks down, on the right. And you have yourself a fine sunset, now."

"Sunset?" I said, laying a five into his hand.

"Hey, man! Thanks. Wait a minute, you never seen sunset here?"

"No."

"Be sure you do, over by Mallory Square."

"And where's that?"

"Another three blocks past your bar."

"Thanks."

He fluttered the five at me. "No problem."

The Far Horizon turned out to be a street-level joint with a couple of taps and a blender that had every color of the rainbow coating its clear plastic sides. A half-dozen patrons, in pairs, leaned elbows on the bar tended by a woman in her forties with a blue ribbon in her hair like a prize poodle. I walked up to her.

"Mack around?"

She looked at me blankly. "Mack who?"

"Mack Olsen. A friend of mine from Mercy named Dawna Adair asked me to look him up."

She smiled. "Mack's not on till eight tonight."

"That be a good time to catch him?"

"Between then and ten. After that, it gets pretty hairy around here."

"Thanks."

"Who should I say is looking for him?"

"Just tell him Dawna's friend, John."

"John. You have a good night."

"Thanks. I'll try."

Wandering farther up the street, I started paying more attention to the people around me. Some tourists, but mostly folks with long hair, often my age. More than a few black-leather bikers and clean-cut college kids and deeply tanned yachters. Gay couples strolled hand-in-hand, cars cruised by slowly, everybody carrying open containers of booze, the cops on foot patrol smiling and joshing with the people as they passed. No problem.

There was a lot of laughing and jeering coming from a bar called Sloppy Joe's. A sign by the door imposed a two-dollar cover charge, but the management didn't seem to mind people just sticking their heads in the open windows to listen, so I joined them for a minute.

The place was packed, a guitarist up on stage wearing the
outfit of baseball cap, shirt, and jeans that the Beach Boys
affected in their later years. A banner above his head had the
name PAT DAILEY on it, young guys in red with SECURITY
on their backs located around the stage. Dailey's act seemed
to consist of one part cheerleading, one part ranting mono-
logue, and two parts bawdy songs, the crowd joining in for
choruses of "I'd Have to Be Drunk to Do That," "I Could Be
Your Father," and so on. I stayed long enough to decide the
man wasn't just a good guitarist but also a genius at involv-
ing the audience, trading insults with them and threatening
to leave the stage, the crowd erupting after each threat with
a not-quite-spontaneous refrain of "Stay, Just a Little Bit
Longer." He would.

Getting hungry, I moved toward where the panhandler had
told me Mallory Square was. I found it, but my watch told
me it was a bit early for sunset, my stomach adding that the
long drive counseled an early dinner. I found a place on Front
Street called the Hog's Breath Saloon (motto: "Hog's Breath
is Better than No Breath at All"). In an open-air dining area,
I sat on white resin furniture and had a great plate of mixed
seafood with a couple of Jamaican Red Stripe beers in the
squatty brown bottles. From a counter near the bar I bought
Nancy a T-shirt with a boar's head, and the bar's motto, on
it. Before I was able to elbow my way slowly toward the
door, three different tables of tourists asked me to take their
group portraits with thirty-five-millimeter automatic cameras.

Back on the street, the crowd was swelling toward the
water. I joined them and ended up on a pier with hundreds
of spectators and dozens of peddlers hawking everything
from ice cream to youth elixirs. The best, though, were the
performers.

Against a backdrop of honky-tonk harbor and tethered
drug-enforcement blimps, I watched a couple of men playing
the bagpipes in full Scottish regalia except for white tank tops
showing off heavily developed upper bodies. Another guy,
the "Evel Knievel of the Dairy Bar," astounded his audience
with "stupid egg tricks." Down the line past him was a man

who balanced things on his head, from a snow tire to an inverted bicycle to a grocery cart, for a finale tossing the tire and bike into the cart and balancing the whole shebang by clenching one rung of the cart in his teeth. The best, though, was a man screaming gibberish in English with a German or French accent, it was literally impossible to tell which. The gibberish was aimed at a group of house cats, sitting on red-padded pedestals supported by umbrella sticks, like lions and tigers in a circus act. The man would scream at the cats, and they would do tricks like opening the latches of a cage or dancing a pirouette, all to the amazement of the fairly generous crowd. And, oh yeah, the sunset was beautiful, too.

As I walked away from the pier, I began to think I'd have to spend significant time on Key West to get the hang of it.

"Mack?"

A man swabbing the bar top of the Far Horizon lifted the wet rag and looked up at me. He was stocky, with hammy forearms and that honey tan some blonds get. His handlebar mustache stretched almost from ear to ear beneath piercing blue eyes and very faint eyebrows.

"You Dawna's friend?"

An accent that sounded northern Midwest, and I remembered Adair saying he was from Wisconsin. "Yes, John Francis."

Olsen dried his hands on a different towel before shaking. "What can I do for you?"

I looked around. It was about nine, not as many people in the place as when I'd stopped there earlier. Maybe they weren't back from sunset yet. "It'd be a help if you could tell me what you know about the Church of the Lord Vigilant."

You could see the shutters come down, like a pawnshop locking up for the night. "No, thanks." He went back to the swabbing.

"I'm trying to find a missing boy. I think he may be in the Compound on Little Mercy Key, and I need some information about it from somebody who's been on the inside."

"Something wrong with your ears, pal?"

"Dawna said I should tell you that she owes me a favor."

Olsen stopped with the rag again. Closing his eyes, he shook his head, then opened them to look at me. "That the truth?"

I took a chance. "You know it is."

A grim smile, then a lighter one. "Yeah. Yeah, that's Dawna, all right. Back when I was living on Mercy, she helped me through a pretty rough patch. When I asked her what I could do for payback, she said, 'Hey, just help somebody else sometime, huh?'" He tossed the rag into a sink. "Okay, what do you want to know?"

"How did you come to the Church?"

"I was living in Milwaukee. Married, but no kids, and the marriage itself was heading into the toilet. I hated the winters, didn't know why until I got to Key West and somebody told me about S.A.D."

"What's that?"

"'Seasonal Affective Disorder.' Up in Milwaukee, we'd have weeks where it'd be dark, all day long. Turns out I've got to have sunlight, otherwise I'm real tired, even mean, during the winter. I'd put on weight, then be mad about it, always on the edge of depression even though I was sleeping ten, twelve hours a night, you know?"

"And coming down here cured it?"

"Yeah, but you wanted to know how I got started with the Church, right?"

"Right."

"Well, that's how. You see, the marriage was breaking up, and I saw this circular for Reverend Wyeth's church, and it sounded real good. I'm sure I was just kind of subconsciously wanting to come down to the sunshine, but the circular gave me a reason to do it, so I left my wife—we didn't have much of anything going, tell you the truth, even without the S.A.D.—and I moved to Miami first, make some money after her lawyer took me for all of mine. After a month or so, I got to feeling better, but I didn't know why, so I thought I should still check out the Church. I went down to Mercy Key with some cash in my pocket and started going to the tent meetings. By now, I was feeling better and better every day."

"But because of the sunshine, not the Church."

"Right, right. Also, I think, because the pace on Mercy was just a lot slower. But at the time, I didn't know that the religion stuff wasn't really the reason I was feeling better. Not until I started getting deeper into the Church and noticing things."

"What kind of things?"

A pair of women down the bar signaled for another round. To me, Olsen said, "Hold on a minute." He got their drinks, served them, and came back to me.

I said, "You started noticing things?"

"Yeah. Like the Church was taking in a lot of money. Hell, the tent meetings alone must have grossed thousands a night, and the TV and radio? Millions, I'm guessing. But I didn't see where it was going."

"What do you mean?"

"Well, you visit the Compound, and it's just okay. I mean, everything's new and all, but the features are kind of . . . spartan?"

I thought that might have been one of Dawna's words.

Olsen said, "I worked construction back in Milwaukee when I wasn't tending bar—got me into the sunlight in the good weather was probably why I liked it, but I didn't know that then, of course. Anyway, I worked construction, and all the stuff in the Compound is bottom of the line. Faucets, light fixtures, even the structural things. And the food in the dining hall—Wyeth called that 'the Table of the Lord'—was real simple and cheap. Even the infirmary was just like a first-aid station, not a real hospital."

"Why would they need a real hospital, though?"

"I don't know, except that Wyeth kept going on in his sermons about how we had to be 'independent of the heathen secular world around us'—his way of saying it. We had to 'resist the Devil's temptations made through his minions,' and so on. But in the Compound itself, you'd see things, and once I was over my own depression from the S.A.D., I was kind of able to look at the Church separate from what I thought it was doing for me, and I could see what it was starting to do to me."

"To you?"

"Yeah. Like all of us in the Compound being expected to tithe twenty-five percent of our income to the Church."

"Twenty-five percent?"

"And this from a lot of folks can barely pay their taxes as it is. Because you don't really get to live in the Compound full-time. It's more a place they bring you for—I don't know, kind of a 'booster shot' of religion, like they used to give us as kids against polio?"

"I remember."

"Well, that's what it felt like. And I started noticing the other people around me, how they were acting."

"Which was?"

"Artificial. Strange. Dawna saw it right off, soon as she was with me there on a visit. Like everybody's being too polite because they're afraid that if they're not, they won't fit in, and the Reverend'll ask them to leave."

An old-timer at the end of the bar called for another draft. Olsen drew it, then came back to me, grinning.

"Something strike you funny?"

"Kind of. I was just thinking about the Reverend's show."

"Television?"

"No. The live kind, in the tent."

"I went to one of them."

"He still have everybody sing, 'Jesus, the Cross I Bear'?"

"The people in the white shirts, anyway."

A grunt. "First time I heard that, I didn't have a hymnbook in front of me. I kept trying to figure out why they were singing about 'Jesus, the Cross-eyed Bear.' "

I laughed. "You ever hear about something called the Center for the Study of Sin?"

Another grunt. "The 'Sinstitute'?"

Having thought the same thing the first time I heard the phrase, I just looked at him.

Mack said, "That's supposed to be where a lot of the money's being spent—the money the Church gets, I mean, from donations and so forth. But I got to tell you, I never saw anybody who looked like a scholar coming out of there."

"Out of where?"

"The Center. It's kind of tucked behind the infirmary. Or at least it was supposed to be. I never saw the inside of it, and I don't know of anybody who did."

"The Center exists for the study of sin, but nobody goes inside it for classes or anything?"

"Uh-unh. Well, except for the Reverend and Sister Lutrice—she's his wife?"

"We've met."

"Well, I'm sure they must go in there. But aside from them, all I ever saw were guards." Olsen paused for effect. "Armed guards."

I thought of the guys in white outfits who'd stopped me. "You mean the people at the gates?"

"Nossir. I mean the thugs—that's the only word for them—the thugs that guard the Center. One guy, real big, but with this little itty-bitty head."

"Cody."

"Right, Cody was his name. And this other guy, had Howdy-Doody ears and red hair, what was his . . . ?"

I said, "Lonnie Severn."

"Severn, yeah that sounds right, but I'm not positive. I kind of stayed away from them."

"Why?"

"Well, first, they didn't really mix with us, the members of the Church, I mean. They kind of stayed separate, but even if they didn't, they would have—I don't know, seemed separate, somehow. Also, by the time I was getting this sense of them, I was starting to pull away from the Church, especially after . . ."

Olsen stopped. I said, "After what?"

He looked around, but nobody needed a drink. Even though there wasn't a patron within ten feet of us, Mack began to whisper. "The red-haired guy, this Severn, he came up to me once. Said, 'You're a bartender, right?' I said to

him, 'No, but I used to be, before I found Jesus.' And he kind
of—I don't know, smirked at that, which I thought was real
odd, I mean since he made his salary off the Church. And
he said, 'You tended up in Miami, though, right?' and I said
I did, and he said, 'You meet any high-class whores up there?
I don't mean streetwalkers, now, I mean good, clean call girls,
got their own places.' "

"Where was this, Mack?"

"Right when we're in the Compound, just outside the dining hall. And I asked Severn why, and he said, 'Never you
mind. Just give me a name and a number.' And—well, I did
know a couple, you know, for the richer conventioneers,
wanting to party but being a little afraid of the 'consequences'
of what they might bring back home to momma? So I gave
Severn the name and number of this beautiful—and I mean
stunning—woman, gets five hundred the hour, and he says
no problem. And, well, that's what convinced me."

"Convinced you?"

"To leave the Church. So I just kind of dropped out, but
they don't like you doing that, so they kept after me, and I
moved down here."

"They don't come to Key West?"

"Are you kidding? With the bars and the gays and the—I
don't know, just the feel of this place, the Rev and Lutrice
would bomb us if the Air Force'd lend them a plane."

I thought about it. "Can you give me the name of this
woman in Miami?"

Olsen watched me. "You want to talk with her, too?"

"Yes."

"Why?"

"I won't know that till I talk with her."

He twisted the end of the right mustache. "I'd have to set
it up, make it look like you were a customer for her."

"And I'd expect to pay you a . . . broker's commission."

Olsen nodded. "You want me to use your real name with
her?"

"John Francis."

He watched me some more, then nodded. "As good as any, I guess. One thing, though."

"Yes?"

"You see her, even just to talk, it's still five hundred net to her."

"Understood."

Olsen went up and down the bar quickly, filling a couple of orders, then disappeared through a doorway. A few minutes later, he was back out and coming over to me with a slip of paper in his hand.

"She's expecting you tomorrow at three o'clock. This is her name and address."

I looked down at the paper. Just the first name, 'Zoe,' with a street and apartment number.

I said, "I don't know Miami all that well."

"I'll write you out some directions."

"While you're at it?"

"Yeah?"

"Draw me a diagram of the Compound, too."

"The Compound?"

"Especially the infirmary and the Sinstitute area."

Olsen looked at me. "Hope Dawna owes you a big favor."

"There'll be a cartographer's commission in it."

"A what?"

"Never mind."

Rather than drive back to Mercy Key that night, I decided to stay over at a small motel on Roosevelt Boulevard. After taking a shower, I realized that the towel didn't smell like any kind of fruit, which reminded me that I was wasting a lot of Lonnie Severn's money on my room at Mercy Lodge.

20

EVEN WITH MACK OLSEN'S DIRECTIONS TO ZOE'S PLACE IN Miami, I figured it might take me a while to find it, so on the drive back north that Sunday, I stopped for lunch. It was a restaurant on the bay-side just south of Mercy Key that advertised waterfront, shaded dining.

A nice young woman in a buttoned-down salmon shirt and shorts led me to a table on a roofed, screenless deck cantilevered over one of the canals to the bay. A couple of the red-beaked ducks were swimming below me, some gulls tacking and wheeling in the wind. The waitress brought a menu with a wine list, and before she moved on, I ordered a half bottle of sauvignon blanc.

The table to my left was empty, the one to my right and behind my chair shared by a man and three women, all in their high sixties or low seventies. The women wore sundresses, the man cruise-wear pants a funny shade of green and an almost matching golf shirt. He was holding forth about the India/Burma theater during World War II.

"And the water, they had to truck it in from a lake thirty-five miles away. From the looks of that water, I'm right glad I never got to see the lake."

Appreciative laughs from everyone, the woman I thought might be his wife cuffing him good-naturedly on the arm.

"But, because they had to truck it to us, we got only a gallon a day per man. I'm embarrassed to tell you, I didn't have a bath for six months, and neither did anybody else."

Sympathetic murmurs.

"And the butter, or what they called butter anyway, it came in a can, and you couldn't spread it with a regular knife. Had to use a bayonet, if you can believe it, and you can. And then, once you got it spread, you had to turn the bread upside down to eat it. Know why?"

A chorus of "No, why?" even from his wife, who I thought probably did know but didn't want to spoil a favorite punch line.

The man said, "Because the butter was like glue, and if you ate the bread right side up, everything would stick to the roof of your mouth, even without bridgework up there."

Tittering and nodding.

The man was gaining momentum. "And the meat? Hah, we were told one night we'd finally have fresh meat, and know what? It turned out to be water buffalo, tasted like somebody'd cut up an old shoe into the pot."

The best reaction he'd gotten. You began to realize the guy was doing a great job of being male partner to all three women, a role that he probably hadn't sought but was playing well. I was sorry Nancy wasn't there to see it with me.

"Sir?" said my waitress.

"Oh, sorry. Daydreaming."

"That's all right, that's what the Keys are for. This is your wine, right?"

"Right."

She popped the cork and poured as I read the menu. "You really serve alligator meat here?"

"Yes, but if you've never tried it before, I'd do the appetizer instead of the entrée."

"Appetizer, then, and the amberjack with green salad." I glanced again at the menu. "The smoked amberjack."

"Only way we can make it."

"I don't follow you."

"You have to smoke amberjack to prepare it right. Any other way's poison, only we don't usually mention that."

"I'll still give it a try."

"Bring you some rolls?"

"Please."

The wine was chilled just right, letting the flinty flavor come through. The sun, bright on the water, dimmed enough under the roof not to need sunglasses. A gentle breeze luffed the napkin without blowing it away. Very nice.

I noticed a tall, white bird that looked like the egret at Mercy Key Marina, the day I spoke with Howard Greenspan while he was cleaning his fish. This bird stalked the shallows, peering through the reeds like Spielberg's dinosaurs around trees in *Jurassic Park*. I'd read an article about how some scientists believe that the dinosaurs never really died out but evolved into birds the way we did from apes. You watch one of the big ones hunting, and you can believe it, as the older guy at the next table might say.

The rolls and the alligator dish arrived at the same time. The meat was deep-fried and served with cayenned mustard sauce. It was enough like chewy veal that I was glad the waitress had suggested just the appetizer portion.

The egret had reached the far end of the decking when my amberjack was ready. It was a fillet, browned on the surface from the smoking, cut into sections about a finger's width and length. I tried one. Excellent, and not quite like anything else I'd ever tasted.

I was working on the green salad as the foursome behind me settled up with our waitress. Suddenly I heard and felt a whooping of wings, and the egret, all three feet of him, was landing on the empty table to my left. He had black legs and black, splayed toes, the plumes draping off his back so very long and detailed they seemed to have been pasted on from another species. The bird turned its head this way and that, almost sniffing the air as it watched me. This close, I could see a greenish mask across its eyes, the bill six inches long.

Then the bird jumped onto my table. Remembering

Greenspan's comment about the pelican skull, I didn't move as the egret struck with its head like a snake at my plate. A cross section of amberjack in its bill, the big bird paused long enough to eye me, then whooped off and across the canal to the opposite shore.

The man behind me said, "I've been all over this world of ours, and that's one of the five oddest things I've ever seen, you can believe it."

My waitress said, "Would you like a new meal?"

"No, thanks."

"You sure? No telling where that beak's been."

"Really, it's okay."

I finished my lunch, even savoring it a bit more after the egret than before, thinking Key West wasn't the only place down here that would take me a while to learn.

Following Mack's directions faithfully, I still got a little turned around in Miami, probably from some road construction that looked as though it might have been done since the last time he'd been up there. It was almost three when I found the apartment house, twenty stories of white brick and aquamarine panels overlooking part of the intracoastal waterway. I was a little surprised when the sign at the semicircular drive advertised it as a condominium complex.

Leaving the Pontiac in a visitor's space, I walked into the lobby. Security consisted of a man about fifty in a white uniform shirt. The potbelly was visible and the wheeze audible when he stood from behind a high-front desk. "Help you?"

Mack had said to ask for the apartment by number, so I did.

The guard looked me up and down, nodded, and picked up a telephone, hitting what I figured to be three buttons on a console out of sight behind his desk, probably next to a couple of television monitors. After the time it takes for two rings, he said, "Expecting somebody? . . . Yeah. . . . Okay."

The guard replaced the receiver. "You can go on up. Elevators are over there."

I walked across the lobby to them as a video camera swung

with my walk. Inside, I pressed the floor I wanted, another camera's lens peeking at me through a small hole in the car's ceiling.

When the doors opened, there were two signs, one pointing left with twelve hyphenated units listed, its twin to the right. I walked right, a door opening for me before I had to knock.

Mack Olsen had used the word "stunning," and it fit. The woman looking out at me had the most radiant violet eyes I've ever seen. They were set the right distance apart in a heart-shaped face framed by crow-black hair in bangs and two exotic flips at the front of her neck. The lips seemed to swell, especially when she shook her head for effect. Zoe was somewhere between twenty-five and forty, skin tone a shade darker than tan against a sheer white blouse and red pantaloon pants with tassles, like a harem dancer's.

"Yes?"

It sounded stupid in my head, but I said, "Mack Olsen told me he'd arranged an appointment."

The eyelids closed over the violet, not a blink but a slow-motion sequence as her left hand, with violet nails, just brushed at the hairs on the top of my right wrist. "I'm glad he did. My name's Zoe, sugar."

"John."

She didn't laugh at the pun on the term for a customer. Or maybe she just didn't notice that sort of thing anymore. "Come on in, John."

The living room of the condo was tastefully decorated but had an arid quality to it, like it had been the model for brokers showing the units. Lots of pastel leather and brass-on-glass, tall windows giving a partial water view, wall-to-wall carpeting deep enough to sink into and gray enough not to show the dirt.

Zoe turned slowly at the couch, tapping it with a nail while saying, "Care to start with a drink, John?"

I figured she might be like any salesperson, having to repeat a customer's name frequently at the beginning of a pitch in order not to forget it by the end. "No, thanks."

Zoe frowned, sinking into the love seat across the coffee table while I took the couch. "What's going on?"

I said, "I don't get you."

"Mack calls me yesterday with this 'urgent' request for a Sunday matinee, and I was free, so what the hell. But you're not in a hurry. You're not even nervous, and you're not so bad-looking you couldn't do well enough on the straight wherever you're staying. You feel like cop, but you're not from Vice, because they wouldn't go to the trouble of driving a hundred-fifty miles to Key West and twisting Mack's arm into giving me up. So, what's going on?"

I was impressed. "Intuition play a big part in your business?"

"In any business. What's going on?"

"I need to talk with you. I'll pay your hourly rate for it."

A small smile that showed wrinkles at one corner of her mouth. "My hourly rate?"

"Mack mentioned five hundred."

"Let's see it, sugar, just so it doesn't intrude on our conversation later."

I took out ten fifties and passed the bills to her.

Counting them, she said, "You know, you'd be surprised how many guys just want to talk, nowadays."

"I'm sorry?"

"The clients. The old days, a condom was something they remember as a kid moving from their old wallet to the new one they got at Christmas or Hanukkah, and they loved my M & M routine."

Zoe stopped, so I said, "M & M?"

"Yeah, you know, like the candy ad? 'Melts in your mouth, not in your hand.' "

I nodded.

She said, "But now, a lot of them are scared shitless of AIDS, so they set something like this up, then spend most of the time asking me just to kind of talk to them, maybe touch them here and there the way they don't get—or don't get off on—back home. And it's not just dirty talk, either. Some of them want to know whether I am or not."

"Am or not what?"

"Part black. Or lesbian." The eyelids went to half-mast. "How about you, sugar?"

"I'm neither."

The smile again. "All right. So you're not so interested in me. What do you want to talk about?"

"A couple of questions about your situation here. Confidential?"

"You mean, do I have television cameras or hidden mikes running on you?"

"Yes, but more how confidential would somebody think their visit here would be."

Zoe drew her legs up under her, rolling her shoulders a bit against the back of the love seat. "You're not from Miami, but you a cop from anywhere?"

"No."

"You realize that if you are, even Internal Revenue, anything you try to stick me with goes up the entrapment chimney?"

"If I'm not a cop, I probably don't know that, but it doesn't matter to me one way or the other."

The smile, intriguing when she wasn't just putting it on. "Pretty confidential, then."

"This place, you mean."

"And coming to see me. There's the cameras in the lobby and on the elevator, but that's it. I don't do any off-the-street stuff, just referrals. And the guy I rent from here takes cash and is real happy about it."

"How about the doorman downstairs?"

"Leo? Ex-prison guard from Jersey. I saw him break a guy's arm once, nearly took it off at the shoulder."

"And he's on your payroll?"

"I'm not big enough for employees. Let's just say he's a security consultant."

I thought about my talk with Sergeant Whit Tidyman and smiled.

Zoe said, "You have a nice smile, John."

"Likewise. I want to talk with you about a referral Mack sent your way."

"I don't talk with one customer about another."

"Confidentiality."

"Right. It's, like, a rule of mine."

I said, "There's a good reason you should make an exception here."

"Which is?"

"I think the customer's involved in the disappearance of a little boy."

A disgusted look. "I don't do perverts. Not if I can spot them, anyway, and I usually can."

"I'm not sure sex has anything to do with the little boy being taken. I just need to find out anything I can use toward finding Eddie and bringing him back."

"Eddie." Zoe played with a tassle at her ankles. "Will any of this come back on me?"

"No."

"How do I know that?"

"I promise."

A cynical laugh. "Yeah, right."

"It's why I'm down here, looking for him."

"What is?"

"A promise. I promised Eddie I'd try to find him."

"You promised the kid you'd look for him before he was even gone?"

"That's right."

"And you always keep your promises?"

An image of PFC Duquette from the Tet Offensive entered my mind. "For a while, now."

Zoe stared at me. "It was kind of unfair, using the kid's first name to sucker me in like that."

"It wasn't intentional."

She broke off the stare, went back to the tassle. "Okay. Which client?"

"The Reverend Royel Wyeth."

Zoe threw her head back and laughed, almost a shriek.

I said, "What's the matter?"

"Mack said he sent the Reverend to me?"

I thought about it. "Not exactly. Mack said it was one of his men."

"Yeah, well, that it was. But it wasn't the Reverend who came to see me, sugar."

"It wasn't."

"Uh-unh. It was Mrs. Reverend."

"Mrs. . . . Lutrice?"

"Yeah. Oh, she didn't call herself that, and when I answered the door, it wasn't her in front of me, but this kind of creepy, redheaded guy."

"You get his name?"

"We weren't introduced. He just came in first, looked around, then went back out into the hall, and brought her in. She was wearing a wig—or another wig, maybe, I never did think what you see on television was her real hair."

"You watch their show?"

"I'd seen it, channel-surfing with the remote. You have a little toot on from the nose candy, some of these TV evangelists are a caution. Even some of the sixties sitcoms, for that matter."

"So you're sure it was Lutrice Wyeth."

"Positive."

"What can you tell me?"

The smile and half-mast expression. "Anything you want to know, sugar."

"What was your impression of her?"

"Of her. Well, you know how most women are interested in romance, and men are interested in sex?"

"All right."

"No, really. In order to get romance, women learn to kind of tolerate sex, and in order to get sex, men learn how to fake romance."

"Go on."

"Well, Sister Lutrice, she wasn't interested in romance, or touchy-feely, or anything. She's no lesbian, either."

"You're sure of that?"

"I can be. No, she showed all the classic signs."

"Of what?"

"Of a woman whose husband has the dead meat."

"Impotent?"

"You'd be amazed how many of these women come to us . . . 'therapists.' I think maybe it's because they're afraid of AIDS, too. You know, it's easier for a woman to get it from a man on account of the fire-hose effect."

"Okay, I follow you."

Zoe stopped.

I said, "What's the matter?"

"You're really not getting off on this, are you?"

"On what?"

"You're here in my place—well, my office, kind of. I'm guessing you figured out I don't exactly live here."

"I got that impression."

"Yeah, well, the impression I'm getting is you aren't asking me these questions because they excite you. You're asking them because you really might need the answers."

"That's right."

She shook her head and took a breath. "Anyway, Sister Lutrice wasn't interested in romance, or tenderness. She wanted to be used, hard. Not abused, just . . . vigorous?"

I nodded.

Zoe said, "I had the feeling she might have kept the Reverend on a pretty short leash in a lot of ways, and this was her way of kicking back without giving him . . ." The lidded smile. "I almost said, 'without giving him his head.' "

I nodded again.

"Anyway, after a few routines with a few devices that I'm guessing you wouldn't be interested in hearing about in great detail, Sister Lutrice went off to use the shower, and I was thinking of joining her—she still had some time on the meter, and she has great juggies, those aren't fake—when the red-headed guy comes in the bedroom. He's been in the living room all this time, sampling my scotch."

"Your scotch?"

"Yes."

"You sure."

"It was on his breath."

"And when was this?"

"Last year sometime."

I thought about it. Maybe Severn fell off the wagon down here, but got back on up north.

"Sugar, you okay?"

"Yes. What about the redhead?"

"Well, he comes in the bedroom, saunters in, like, and just watches me. That's what I mean by creepy. He didn't make a move, didn't say a word, just watched me. I heard the shower stop, and I called out to Lutrice—I didn't want to hit the panic button."

"The panic button?"

"There're a couple of them around the unit, wired into Leo's panel downstairs. If I have a problem up here—"

"Got it. So, you didn't call Leo."

"No. But Lutrice came out, wrapped in a towel, and said to me, 'I've really had enough, honey, and I'm all cleaned up—' Then she saw the redhead. And she said, 'It's paid for up to the hour, honey,' but she was looking at the redhead this time, not at me."

"And he took advantage of it."

"With a condom. He didn't like it, but I told him no way otherwise, and Lutrice told him, too. Almost like she was kind of relieved to hear me insist on it?"

"And then?"

"And then she watched."

"Watched."

"Yeah, and I had the feeling she got off again, too, because she went back into the bathroom afterwards."

"With the redhead?"

"Oh, no. No, that . . ." A puzzled look crossed the violet eyes. "I'm not sure just how to say this, but I got the feeling she couldn't think of him as kind of . . . doing anything with her directly. It was more that he was one of the help, driving her to the restaurant and maybe not sitting to eat with her but getting some of the dessert she couldn't finish on her own?"

"Lutrice say anything about the Church or her husband?"

"No. No, like I said, with the wig and all, she was trying real hard not to let on who she was, like driving all the way up here for . . . the kicking back."

"And that was the only time you saw her?"

"Right."

"I'm not sure you can tell this, but did you think she'd visited any other . . ."

"Therapists like me?"

"Yes."

"Why would she, after having me?"

"Maybe before you, I mean."

"Not that she mentioned. And the way she moved in bed here, she wanted it so bad that it was a while before I was doing anything really . . . special to her."

I nodded again.

Zoe said, "I'll tell you this, though. I'd bet I know why she hasn't been back."

"And that is?"

"She's found herself a . . . stand-up guy?"

I found myself wondering who that might be. Deputy Billups maybe, providing more than security? "Anything else you can think of that might help me?"

The slow blink. "Oh, lots of things, sugar."

"Thanks anyway."

"You sure? Still got half an hour on the meter."

I said, "What I've gotten so far is worth the money."

"Where were you when I was twenty-two?"

"That would depend on when you were twenty-two."

The slow smile. "Just get out of here, before I make a fool of myself."

Actually, Zoe hadn't told me a lot that was worth much. I couldn't see where Severn being off the wagon was any leverage if Lutrice obviously knew about it, and besides, he was dead now. Also, I couldn't use Lutrice's frolic as leverage with her or the Reverend without Lutrice being tipped that I'd gotten the information from Zoe. That left me with the "stand-up guy" possibility, which looked pretty thin.

It had been a long drive up to Miami, and it figured to be an even longer drive back to Mercy Key. I thought of a way that the trip wouldn't be a complete waste.

"Hey, how you doing, John Francis?"

"I'm doing well, Pepe."

He stood on the house side of the gate, taking a little box from his pants pocket and aiming it at the lock. "You find us all right, eh?"

"The funny pink skyscraper is a good landmark."

The gate swung open. "I told you. Mr. Vega, he not home yet. You want to come in, wait for him?"

"No, thanks. Actually, I wanted to see you."

"Me? How come?"

I moved closer to him. "I need another gun."

"Another gun?"

"Yeah."

"What happen to the last one I got you, man?"

"Let's just say I broke it."

"Broke it?"

"Yeah."

Pepe scratched the side of his head with the remote device. "Gonna take me a couple hours, set it up."

"I'd rather not wait inside."

"Uh-unh. I rather not, too. Tell you what, there's this nice sports bar a mile from here, got all the cable. Watch yourself some Sunday Night Football, I get you what you need."

"Football doesn't start till eight, Pepe."

"So?"

"I need the gun before that."

"Before?"

"Yes. Another revolver, with a calf holster this time, if your friend has one."

"You sure?"

"About what?"

"Another revolver. I mean, you do no have such good luck with the last one."

"Revolver, Pepe."

"Okay, okay. Hey, man, it's pretty hard to break a gun, no?"

"But not impossible."

"When you was a kid, you this tough on toys, too?"

"Pepe?"

"Yeah?"

"How do I get to the sports bar?"

21

DRIVING SOUTH ALONG THE FLORIDA TURNPIKE FROM MIAMI to the Keys, the new revolver—a snubby Colt—felt snug in its holster against my left calf. I thought about going to the hotel first to clean up. Then I decided it would be pretty late after that to find Dawna if she wasn't at work, and I wanted to thank her for the lead to Mack Olsen and Zoe, however little help they'd been. Maybe she'd even have something else, or somebody else, I could try. I stayed on U.S. 1 through Key Largo down to Mercy and on to Pinky's.

Parking in the tree-ringed lot, I was relieved not to see Jay's old car. Inside the door of the place, two of the blue-collar guys I remembered from my first visit were in the corner, the bald white one and the tall black one, sitting in the same chairs. They eyed me as I came in, the white guy even nodding in wary recognition. I nodded back, then walked up to the bar.

A middle-aged man in shorts and a T-shirt was coming through the doorway to the kitchen with a towel over his shoulder. "Hi, what'll you have?"

"I was looking for Dawna."

A neutral expression. "Dawna?"

I could understand that. "Dawna Adair. I met her here a couple of nights ago."

Before the keep could answer for himself, the bald white guy in the corner said, "That boy's all right, Charley. He's the one threw Jay out last Friday."

The keep looked to him, then back to me. "Dawna's off tonight. Probably home, seeing it's Sunday and all."

"Thanks."

As I left, the tall black guy burst out laughing in a locker-room way at something the bald white guy had muttered.

Turning in at her driveway, there were no lights visible from the front of the cigar-maker's house. However, there was a faint glow in the foliage at the back, probably from the loft window, and the Wrangler was parked at the edge of the driveway, the hood cool in the evening air. I walked around the house, stopping at the pocket door to the dining patio, which was open. I knocked on it anyway. Nothing.

"Dawna?"

No answer.

"Dawna, it's John Francis."

The same again.

From the open door, I could see inside the house. Adair's tote bag sat on the kitchen counter, a key ring next to it. A little louder, I said, "Dawna?"

The house was quiet, except for the noises of insects, most outside the kitchen, but some buzzing around the fluorescent light on the range. Given the bugs, who would leave a door open at night down here?

I moved through the kitchen into the living room area and stopped. Nothing. I crossed to the staircase, going up one step at a time and on the outside, so as not to make the floorboards creak. No worry there. The Dade County pine apparently didn't warp, either.

The bedroom loft was shadowed, the only light coming from the hurricane lamp on the small table at the window. I went to the window, the view overlooking the roof of the dining patio and the backyard. I didn't see anything, the one sound beyond the insects that occasional drip you hear from an air conditioner.

Then I remembered. Adair had said the Dade County pine was too hard to saw through, so Jay had given up trying to put in her air-conditioner. I turned toward the dripping sound and looked up. Into a nightmare.

They'd crucified her.

Dawna hung over the bed, her blood hitting the sheet the dripping sound I'd heard. Her wrists had been nailed to the collar ties near the roofline, another tie being used as the base for nailing her feet. The nails were three of the blackened railroad spikes, probably from some of the bookends. White adhesive tape was over her mouth, her eyes open, a deep stab wound on her right side that might have gotten a lung. She wore just a T-shirt and shorts, red drops also falling from her nostrils, as though she'd drowned, coughing up her own blood. Hours ago.

Out loud, I said, "Dawna, I'm so sorry."

I caught myself about to gag, and stopped it. After swallowing a few times, I thought about where this put me. I'd been seen minutes ago at Adair's place of work, asking for her and being recognized as somebody she knew and maybe even mentioned by name to someone else. The Sheriff's Office hadn't fingerprinted me after the breakfast incident at Pedro's, and the checkered handle of the revolver Deputy Sherman had taken from the trunk of my rent-a-car wouldn't give up a latent even if they thought to try the cartridges as well. But I had touched things here on Friday night, and now it was a crime scene that would be gone over carefully by technicians. Latents from Dawna's house might be matched eventually with my prints on file, either from the service or from my licensing as a private investigator in Boston, both identifying me as the definite John Cuddy, not a vague John Francis.

Moving slowly around the bed, I tried to remember where I'd been on my first visit. Adair reclining on the bed, us talking, me going back downstairs to sleep. I didn't think I'd touched any smooth surfaces on the second floor except the bathroom faucets.

I went into the small, tiled room, using a clean washrag as a wipe-cloth. Then I went downstairs.

I couldn't hope to get all the hairs that might have fallen out of my head, or the other faint forensic stuff, but I used the wipe-cloth on everything else. Edge of table, light switch, the kitchen counter. I tried to remember whether I'd handled anything in the kitchen, then noticed Dawna's tote bag again. Pinky's parking lot on Friday night, the cannister of Mace. I opened the bag to find it.

And found the note instead.

It was on simple white paper, written in a shaky, feminine hand with a Flair-style pen. It read,

To whom it may consern,
   I am real afraid that John Francis, a man I met, is trying to disscredit the Church of the Lord Vigilant. I am afraid he will do something to put me in perel of my life because he is sick or something. If anything happens to me, please see to it that this note goes to the Sheriff's Office.
                                                        Dawn Adair

I closed my eyes. The spelling bee champion, knowing she was going to die, intentionally misspelling three words and then even her own first name, putting the lie to what the note seemed to be saying about me.

Pocketing the paper, I risked that whoever had been to the house was staking it out and even now calling me in anonymously. I ran that risk to walk back through the living room and back up the stairs.

Next to the bed, I looked up at Dawna, into the eyes that wouldn't ever look at anything again. And I made her a promise, too.

22

I GOT OUT OF THE HOUSE, INTO THE CAR, AND DOWN THE driveway to the road. No one stopped me on the way to Route 1. I turned north, realizing I'd have to go back to the hotel, wipe down the surfaces that the maid wouldn't have cleaned for sure. I took a left and went through the median, carefully keeping ten miles below the speed limit until the turn for Mercy Lodge.

I drove very slowly through the lot, not seeing anyone suspicious or official. I parked a ways from the building and killed the engine, sitting in the dark and quiet for a while, watching and listening. Nobody.

Crossing to the lobby, I didn't see anyone behind the desk, so I cut through to the back door that gave onto the horseshoe. There was no one around on the bay side either, a few voices drifting down here and there from the upper-floor balconies.

Approaching #139, I checked the area by the soda machine before going to my door. Nobody.

Inside the room, I thought about packing hurriedly, then decided it might look better when they came for me if it appeared as though I might be coming back there. I went to work with a clean facecloth, taking only about ten minutes to sweep the place. After another minute to look around, I used the facecloth to toggle the light switch, then tossed the cloth toward the sinks as the door was closing from the spring.

Retracing my steps, I went back into the empty lobby. I'd almost reached the door to the parking lot when I heard, "Oh, Mr. Francis?"

I stopped, heart pounding, and turned. It was just Clark, who might have been bending over behind the front desk but now was standing, his arms sticking out from under a tangerine polo shirt.

I tried to breathe normally. "Yes, Clark?"

"I took a message for you."

I went over to the desk. "Thanks."

"Uh, I'm afraid the printer's down, so I'll have to read it off the screen for you." He laid his hand on top of the monitor facing him.

I said, "The printer's down, but the computer's up and running?"

The eyes crossed slightly. "Right. Just a second."

He clacked some keys, then peered hard at the screen I couldn't see. "Dawn called. Said you should come over to her house right away."

"Dawn." I stared at him until he looked from the screen to me.

Clark seemed worried. "Something wrong?"

I said, "When did you get that call, Clark?"

"Oh, not more than twenty minutes ago."

I gave it a beat. "So you'd say she's still expecting me?"

"Yessir. She sounded like she really wanted to see you, too."

"Thanks, Clark."

"Happy to help."

I walked as evenly as I could to the Sunbird, then started up and drove out to the highway and southward. I took the only route I knew past the bar and toward Adair's house, which I hoped was the only way there was to get to it. Reaching the T-intersection, I pulled the car into a driveway just past it and still two blocks from hers. The darkened house I'd chosen was up on stilts, the windows shuttered. I backed into the shadows under the raised living area, getting out of the car and walking to the road end of the driveway. Looking toward the house, I couldn't tell my car was there.

Some thick bushes bordered the driveway. I settled down behind one of them and waited for the trap to close.

Six minutes later by my watch, the first Sheriff's Office vehicle went flying toward Dawna's house. It was a Chevy Caprice like the one Deputy Billups had used to bring me into the substation, siren off but bubble lights throwing dazzling blasts of red and blue against the trees. Thirty seconds after that, a second cruiser, this one a Crown Victoria, roared past, again lights but no siren, and Sergeant Whit Tidyman behind the wheel, no collar to his shirt, as there would be if he was in uniform. I got a good enough look to identify him thanks to the headlights from the unmarked sedan behind him, two men in the front seat, following close on. Five minutes later came a cream and orange ambulance, siren wailing now.

I waited another half hour before a second unmarked sedan blew by, trailing behind it a white minivan, the words CRIME SCENE stenciled on its doors. I didn't know what the protocol was on the Keys, but I was hoping that pretty soon some of the uniforms would be leaving. I moved back to my car, and forty minutes later, I was proved right.

I let Tidyman's Crown Vic get a little past my adopted driveway, then started the Sunbird and drove out and behind it. Enough cars were on the road that I didn't think he'd spot me. As we went north on Route 1, I figured it was even money that Tidyman would head south to the substation or, because he was out of uniform, on to his house. I got lucky: He continued north, away from the substation. Then I thought about my doing a similar drive a few hours before, back to the hotel, and remembered I'd left Lonnie Severn's money in the riprap wall below my balcony. A legacy to the squirrels, but too late to worry about it now.

The cruiser eased off Route 1 onto a parallel access road before Tidyman turned again, a residential street. I kept going on the access road, driving for two minutes before doubling back and taking the turn he had. The Crown Vic was easy to spot, parked inside the enclosure made by a solid stucco fence about three feet high, the pattern molded into the fence resembling wainscotting from an English pub. The house beyond the fence was of similar construction, some short palm trees like tilted bowling pins around it.

I stayed on the road past the fence and watched for another boarded-up house. There was one five doors down, also on stilts, and I repeated the hiding of the car under the overhanging structure. Then I walked back.

A mailbox was bolted to the top of the stucco fence. The stick-on letters formed TIDYMAN.

I moved down the narrow driveway, keeping the cruiser between me and the small house. Tidyman had left his vehicle sprawled in the center of the gravel, as though he weren't expecting anybody else to come visiting. There was a shed just about the size of a station wagon off to the side.

Watching the front of the house between the palms, I saw a light shining from a big window. Then another light came on through a high, square opening that I took to be a bathroom window.

Drawing the Colt from its calf holster, I moved quickly to the front door. When I heard the sound of a flushing toilet, I tried the door. Unlocked. I slipped inside a compact living room and flattened against the wall near an interior archway.

Footsteps, and then Tidyman went by me, wearing old chino pants and a T-shirt, no place for a firearm except in a calf holster of his own.

I said to his back, "Hold it right there, Sergeant."

He stiffened but didn't turn around, and his voice was steady. "I suppose I got to assume you're armed."

"You already found one, remember?"

"Actually, Deputy Sherman found it, and it was locked in

your car as I recollect, but I suppose you having another is
still a good bet."

"The percentage one, anyway."

"Your play, then."

"Pull up your pant legs, high to the knees."

"I'm not carrying."

"Humor me."

He did. No weapons or even holster marks on the skin.

I said, "Don't surprise me with one in the chair cushion or
anything, huh?"

"You can always leave me standing."

There was a bare rocking chair in a nonwindowed corner
of the room. "Walk to the rocker and have a seat."

Tidyman moved easily, but straight to it, no attempt at a
detour. He didn't turn until he was lowering himself into it.
"Looks like the percentage bet paid off."

"They usually do, which is what makes them—"

"—the percentage bet. Now what?"

I watched him. Tidyman was good, very good to be this
steady under the circumstances. I began to feel some optimism.

Lowering the revolver a little, but not much, I said, "I was
set up."

"Never met a killer yet who wasn't."

"I didn't kill Dawna Adair."

"You expect to convince me of that at the point of a gun?"

"A captive audience tends to pay better attention."

Tidyman crossed his arms, slowly. "Go ahead."

"First, I don't think anybody could have put Adair up there
by himself. She was a strong young woman, and the condi-
tion of the body says she was alive when they did her."

No response.

"I think that lets Jay off the hook, since he has a bad arm
thanks to me, and his friends looked like a brawl was about
the peak of their violence curve."

Still nothing.

"Second, I decide to kill her, I'm not going to do it that

dramatically and obviously in a house you knew I'd stayed in, so my prints would be all over it."

Like talking to a statue.

"Third, they tried to get Dawna to tie me to it, but they botched that part, too."

Tidyman finally blinked. "Tie you to it? How?"

"Before I show you, I need an answer to a question. A straight answer."

"Maybe."

"Did anybody on your team show unusual interest in anything at the house?"

Tidyman was blinking rapidly now. "Interest?"

"Yes."

"Well . . ." He seemed to look inside himself. "Deputy Billups, he kept trying to bring me back to the kitchen."

"And her tote bag, right?"

Tidyman stiffened. "Boy, you realize that's the second way you've admitted to being at the scene?"

"I was there, all right. A better question is, how did I know somebody—Billups—wanted you to look in the bag?"

A shake of the head.

I reached into my pocket, took out the note. "I don't think they'd have been stupid enough to handle this without gloves, but you'll see, it doesn't affect the thing itself."

I crossed to Tidyman, then sailed the note the last four feet to him, backing up as he caught it.

"Read what it says."

He looked down, reading, then stopping himself, going back over it. Then another shake of the head. "Misspelled words here."

"Three of them."

"And even her own . . ."

"That's right. Spelling bee champion, leaving an important clue to who might hurt her, and she misspells—"

Tidyman said, "All right, all right. I get your point. But how did you know all this?"

"Dawna had helped me out with some people to see. Never

mind just who. I decided to thank her before driving back to the Lodge. Good thing, too."

Tidyman shook his head again, this time like he had a crick in his neck. "I don't get you."

"I tried the bar where Adair worked first. A guy in Pinky's recognized me from when I handled Jay on Friday. I asked the barkeep about Dawna."

"So? You could've been trying to set up some kind of alibi."

"Could have, but wasn't. The point is, Charley the barkeep told me she was probably home, so I stopped by there and found her before getting back to the Lodge for my message."

"Your message?"

"Yeah. As I'm crossing the lobby, the clerk—a guy who knows me by sight—spots me, says I got a message from 'Dawn' not twenty minutes before."

" 'Dawn,' he said?"

"That's right. And he claims to have taken the message himself. Only he says the printer's down, so he has to read it off the screen to me."

Tidyman caught up. "Instead of handing it to you."

"Right."

"And you figure Adair was dead before 'Dawn's' message came in for you."

"Right again."

He pursed his lips. "You figure this—the hotel guy, you know his name?"

I liked that Tidyman didn't, and relaxed a little. "Yeah. Clark."

"You figure this Clark is in on the setup you're trying to sell me?"

"And maybe made the anonymous call to your station."

"You know about that, too, do you?"

"I guessed."

Tidyman gave me the dour expression. "And just how am I supposed to check all this?"

"Easy. Call Clark and see."

"Call him?"

"Right. I'll work the buttons, just so we don't have the problem of your dialing some rapid-response force by accident. When you get Clark on the line, just ask him to ring my room."

"Probably already have a deputy there, though."

"Fine. Just ask Clark if he got any messages for me. He'll deny it."

"He will?"

"Sure. That's how he and whoever's in on it will cover themselves. Clark'll say, 'Never was any message from any 'Dawn,' Sarge, and the computer and printer have been fine all night.' That way, when I'm caught at the house after you get the 'anonymous' call about me, I look like a killer making up a story about a supposed 'message' with no hard copy of it from the Lodge's printer to show you."

Pursing his lips again, Tidyman thought about it. "Make the call."

There was a phone next to the small sofa. The line was long enough to reach to the rocking chair. I dialed the Lodge, got a ring, and passed the receiver, keeping the muzzle of my gun at respect distance from Tidyman.

He held the receiver to his ear. "Hello, this is Sergeant Whit Tidyman of the Sheriff's Office. Who've I got? . . . Well, Clark, let me ask you a question. Any deputies still there? . . . You let them in? Good. Now, I have another question. Did this John Francis get any telephone calls today? . . . That's right. . . ." A frown. "He did not? No messages at all, you sure of that? . . . Well, we're trying to track him, see maybe where he went, like to somebody might have tried to reach him. . . . And your message system, that's been working all right? . . . So there's no chance he got a message you wouldn't know about. . . . No, you did just fine telling my deputy that. . . . No, just sit tight and help out if you're asked. . . . Yes, thanks and take care now."

Tidyman set down the phone.

"See?"

Looking up thoughtfully at me, he said, "Clark—Clark the Clerk, you notice that?"

"I did."

"Clark, he's damn sure you didn't get any messages from anybody."

"Now do you believe me?"

Tidyman said, "Could be Clark says you didn't get any messages because you didn't. The whole message business might be just something you made up."

"And I called your station anonymously, to let you know somebody should run out to Dawna's house, too?"

"Yeah."

"But then why come to you, right?"

Tidyman didn't respond.

"And why not just shoot you now, since you didn't fall for my story."

Still silence.

I said, "After all, the state of Florida can execute me only once."

Tidyman nodded his head, slowly. "Oh, somebody's gonna fry for this, all right. But I'm getting the feeling it isn't gonna be you."

I lowered the revolver to my thigh. "You believe me."

A glacial sigh. "I wished I didn't. But Billups, he's been acting peculiar for a while now. Missing his shifts, kind of going off on his own. Even angling for special duties, like providing security for the Reverend's tent meetings, when I'd have thought that'd be the most God-awful assignment a deputy could draw. Besides, you're right that it'd take two strong men to do what I saw at Adair's house tonight. How about you tell me now what you wouldn't back the first time I had you in to the station?"

Holstering my gun, I told him about Eddie Haldon and Melinda up in Boston, but left out the part about Lonnie Severn and the hunting camp. Tidyman shook his head, like a child overwhelmed at first, then getting a grip by focusing on details. When I'd finished, he said, "Jee-zus. Kidnapping, murder, and what all else?"

"That's part of the problem, Sergeant. I don't know what else."

"Long's we're in this so deep, how about you call me Whit?"

"And I'm John."

"For real?"

"For real. So, Whit, where do we go from here?"

Another sigh. "Well, I don't know. Ordinarily, I'd take you into protective custody, but if Billups is part of this, then maybe that's not such a good idea."

"I'm also a little worried about anything official getting back to the Church."

Tidyman looked reflective. "Account of they might do something to the boy?"

"Get rid of evidence before somebody came searching it out."

A nod. "Tell you what, then. Where's your car?"

"About five doors down, under a house."

"Under . . . ? Oh, I get you. Can it be seen?"

"Not at night. Tomorrow, I'd guess so."

"All right. Let's you bring it around to behind my shed here, so we don't have a road deputy spotting it and calling in the plate."

"How about after that?"

"You said one of the people you talked to gave you a layout of the Compound?"

"Yes."

"Well, I've been there, too. Only twice, but enough so's I can picture that infirmary place and the wall behind it. Let's get some sleep, then work it out in the morning."

"Work what out?"

Tidyman looked up at me with the dour face and hard eyes. "Getting us inside so we can do some good for the boy and some bad for the Church."

23 _____

H OW'D YOU SLEEP?"
    I remembered Dawna Adair asking me roughly the
same question after I'd spent the night on her living
room furniture. "Pretty well."

"Sorry there's no guest room, but I'm a bachelor, so nobody
really comes to visit."

"It was fine, Whit."

"I walked out to the road this morning, see if I could spot
your car behind my shed in the light. Can't."

"Good."

"There's some sliced bread in the freezer. You can put it
right in the toaster, and pour yourself some orange juice for
breakfast."

"Good again."

"Sorry I don't have none of that Pierre water like the Lodge
probably does."

I guessed he meant Perrier. "Don't worry about it, Whit."

"I've got to go into the station for a bit over what happened
last night." Tidyman pulled on his face, making it longer.
"What size you wear?"

"In what?"

"Shirt and pants."

I told him. He wrote it down on a scrap of paper, then put the paper in a pocket as he fished keys from it. "I'm gonna go down to the clothes store, too, get you some things to wear."

I took out my wallet. "Don't be too elaborate."

"Save your money. This'll go in as a county expense."

"For a change of clothes?"

"Wait'll you see the clothes."

I spent part of that Monday morning watching a news broadcast out of Miami cover the tail end of Dawna's death, the camera crew not making it to the scene until after most of the forensic work was done and her body removed from the house. The Sheriff's Office spokeswoman said there were no details available about the killer's methods, but that a suspect was being actively sought.

Tidyman came through the door without knocking, and he saw me with my hand going up my pant leg toward the calf holster. "Sorry there, son. Just not used to having somebody in the house." He set down a bag showing the name of a store I'd never heard of. "Here, try these on."

I opened the bag and shook out the contents. A Florida Marlins baseball cap and some plastic, wraparound sunglasses, but also a white shirt, white pants, and a blue string tie with bolo. "The Compound uniform."

"Go on, try them."

I went to the bathroom to change. The pants were a little tight around the thighs, but the shirt was perfect.

Back in the living room, Tidyman was hanging up the phone. "Just one of the boys from S.H.I.T."

"From what?"

"Special Homicide Investigative Team. What we uniforms call the Homicide Unit down on Marathon." He asked me to turn around once. "Good fit."

"You'll have to help me with the string tie."

"And you're gonna be wearing the ball cap and the shades as we drive out there. Best way there is to alter your appearance, short-term."

"How short-term are we talking about?"

"We'll decide when we get there."

The cruiser bounced some as we started over the causeway to Little Mercy Key.

Tidyman said, "Now remember, keep your head down. Once we get to the infirmary building, you're kind of on your own."

"Got it."

"I'll be waiting outside, motor running."

"And if I can't find Eddie?"

"Then try to look around enough to make a good affidavit for a warrant so we can go in, fast and official, sometime later today."

"And if I get challenged?"

"Fight your way out." He looked down at my left leg. "Really can't see the calf rig at all."

"Good."

His cruiser got to the gate and I tipped my chin to my chest, my hand to my forehead.

Tidyman pressed a button to lower his window. "Got one of yours, went sick in a store out on the Overseas."

"You want us to take him in, sir?"

"No. I got him this far, might as well provide door-to-door service. The infirmary still at the end of your main street in there?"

"Yessir. Should we call ahead for you?"

"No. We'll be there before they can pick up the phone. That is, if you boys'll be so kind as to open the gate for me."

"Right away, sir."

I heard the gate as Tidyman sent his window back up. Then we were off again and making a hard left pretty quickly.

"Not exactly the Emerald City, is it?"

I tilted my head up. The streets seemed to be a simple grid, running off the main—and apparently exactly central—drag we were on. The houses were as Dawna and Mack had described them: small, plain bungalows of white stucco and blue trim, only a little landscaping. There were men, women, and children, all dressed the way I was. Adults seemed to greet each other with a wave and some words as they walked. In fact, we were the only vehicle except for a half dozen of the navy blue GMC pickups, some with camper shells, some without. Most of the people stopped to stare at us as we went by.

"Whit?"

"Yeah?"

"Open my window so I can hear what they're saying."

He did. I heard a smattering of "Have a very blessed day" followed by "Praise Him" or "Praise Jesus."

Tidyman said, "This one in front of us is the infirmary."

I eyed it carefully. A bigger version of the small bunga-lows, as though the architect had just quadrupled all the measurements.

I said, "Any last suggestions?"

"Yeah. Once you're inside, take off the shades and don't use any cuss words."

I smiled at him as the cruiser came to a stop. I got out, holding my belly.

Inside the door, another clean-cut, guardlike guy stood up behind a desk with nothing on it. "What's the problem, Brother?"

"Sick . . . pain . . ."

"I don't believe I know you. What's your—"

"Please, my stomach . . . doctor?"

He looked at me strangely. "Let's go to one of the nurse rooms."

"Praise Jesus."

The man took my left elbow gently, bringing me down an empty, sterile corridor to a small examining room without anything in the way of modern equipment in it. "Wait here, Brother, and I'll get someone."

"Have a . . . very blessed . . . day."

I waited only until I heard his heels on the floor outside fading, then got up and opened the door. Looking left and right, I saw nobody, so I went out and farther down the corridor, where it ended at a T-intersection. There were no

signs on which way to go, but to my left there was a big,
NO ADMITTANCE on the door that looked promising.

I eased the handle on the door, risking an alarm going off,
but none did, at least not that I could hear. On the other side
of the door, the corridor tapered down, then ended at a second door, which had no signs on it. I tried that handle. Also
unlocked and again no alarm. Going through it, I was in a
small, pebbly courtyard with a raised concrete platform, almost like a small stage, in the center of it. The walls of the
courtyard were high, twelve feet at least, with no windows
and only two doors, one to what appeared to be a double
version of the bungalow plan on the far side. I ran low across
the courtyard.

As I reached the bungalow door, a voice sounded off behind me, near where the platform would be. "Well, I'll be
goddammed. The Good Samaritan."

It was like hearing a ghost instead of seeing one.

Turning slowly, I faced Cody, his small head against the
stock of an M-16, sighting in on me, a silencer over the muzzle. Next to him was the ghost, the red hair still shaggy under
the Atlanta Braves cap and over the jug-handle ears, the tan
still in place.

Another silenced M-16 rested in the crook of the redhead's
left arm. "After we go see Big Guy, Samaritan, I got a couple
questions to ask you about my brother, Lonnie."

24

THE REDHEAD SPREAD-EAGLED ME AGAINST THE WALL, FRISK-
ing for the gun, which he found with no problem. "All
right, inside."

Cody grunted. "Axel, you going to go first, or me?"

The redhead took his weapon. "You first, Code. He gives
you any trouble, snap his neck for him."

Cody said to me, "Clear enough?"

"Yes."

We entered the double bungalow, a smell of antiseptic and
stale urine hanging in the air. There was a tiny foyer, just big
enough for a desk with an old rotary telephone that had a
lock through the 9-hole. A second door past the desk opened,
and Clark from Mercy Lodge came through it. He was wearing Compound white-on-whites now, though.

The crossed eyes. "Mr. Francis."

"Clark."

He sat at the desk with the locked telephone as we went
by it to the door he'd come through.

Axel Severn said, "Inside again, Samaritan."

I opened the door, the mixture of antiseptic and urine
stronger now. It was a short corridor ending in another T.

282

Severn said, "Now down and to the left."

We moved past the T, and I saw a third door. Cody reached past me to knock twice, quite politely. The commanding voice from the other side said, "Bring the *in*-fidel to us."

The knob disappeared in Cody's hand as he turned it and pushed.

The room was about twelve feet by fifteen. There were three straight-back armchairs, but one was reinforced at the joints with steel elbows and bolted to the floor. That chair had leather straps for wrists and ankles, an improved version of Lonnie's setup at the hunting camp in New Hampshire.

Royel Wyeth sat in one of the straight-back chairs, a pad and pencil in front of him on a small writing table with a single drawer. He wore a white shirt and maybe the same blue suit. Lutrice Wyeth sat in another chair, a different gingham outfit on, her eyes glittering with spiritual anticipation or chemical enhancement.

The Reverend said, "Sit down."

I said to Cody, "After you," and Severn rapped me in the right kidney with the butt of his rifle.

I buckled but didn't fall as Cody shoved me toward and into the bolted chair. He said, "You want me to strap him, Reverend?"

"No." Wyeth turned his gaze on me, the madness crackling behind his eyes like the logs in Lonnie's woodstove. "I wish to question him in a *nat*-ural state, for he appears not to be one of them himself."

I started to say, "One of what?" when there was another polite knock on the door.

Wyeth's eyes never left me. "Come."

The door opened, and Sergeant Whit Tidyman joined us, still armed and not under guard. "Severn, you get his hide-away gun?"

"Calf holster."

Tidyman looked at me. "You check for other weapons, too?"

"A course I did, even though I figured maybe you dressed him up to come here."

Wyeth said, "Ax-*el*, no im-*per*-tinence."

"Sorry."

Tidyman said, "Reverend, with your permission?"

"Yes, Whit."

The sergeant pointed. "All right, Francis, assume the position, that wall."

I stood up. "Not Billups, huh? You."

Tidyman used two hands to spin and push me against the wall. He did a much more thorough pat-down than Severn had, but didn't find anything else.

"Clean, Reverend."

Severn said, "I already told you that."

Tidyman used a pinch come-along hold on my elbow to move me back to the bolted chair and sit me into it. Then he went up to Severn, bumping him back a step with his chest. "Don't you ever . . . ever mouth off to me again, boy, you hear?"

Wyeth simply said, "Whit," and Tidyman backed away, Severn grinning a little.

The Reverend looked at Tidyman and said, "Report, please."

"His rent-a-car's behind my shed, so I don't think anybody'll spot it for a while. We can move it tonight to wherever makes sense, wipe it clean of prints so nobody can trace him, whoever he is. The deputies who tossed his room at the Lodge found some literature on the Church, which would have been a big help if Severn here hadn't turned a simple killing into *Friday the Thirteenth: Mercy Key*."

"Cody and me was just trying to make it—"

I filed that as Tidyman interrupted Severn with, "You even messed up the note."

"We made her set down and write it. She was glad to."

"The woman intentionally misspelled things on it."

"So what do you think I am, a schoolteacher?"

Tidyman said, "Including her name?"

Severn seemed about to say something else, then shut up.

Wyeth said to Tidyman, "I take it you still believe the official case is not *sal*-vageable, then?"

A shake of the dour face. "No. I realized when Francis here came to see me last night that we couldn't send it through the system anymore. Too many loose ends. We'll have to deal with him here."

A resolute nod from the Reverend, who turned to me and picked up his pencil. "Very well, I want you others to be *wit*-ness to this session, in the event that they have others like him doing their *bid*-ding now."

I said, "Who's they?"

A thunderous "I ask the questions here!"

I didn't say anything back, and Wyeth spoke to me more normally, sounding almost hurt. "When first we met, I thought I saw *some*-thing solid, *some*-thing Christian inside you. When we broke bread at the Lord's Table, I thought you seemed a man who under-*stood*. Now I see that you have instead been in their em-*ploy* in some way. What evil is it they wish you to do?"

I looked to Tidyman, but got nothing from his expression. I'd told him already; it wouldn't hurt any more to tell the madman as well. "Reverend, I came looking for Eddie Haldon, the boy that Axel here kidnapped in Boston."

Wyeth laughed, a smug, hearty sound. "Surely you know by now, that is just their *earth*-ly disguise."

"Disguise?"

"Yes, of course. As the Bible tells us, however, there is one thing they cannot hide from us. All their evil, all their temp-*ta*-tions, these they can shield from the eyes of man in the image of God. But what they can-*not* hide from us is the Mark."

I said, "You mean Eddie's birthmark?"

"The Mark of *Cain!*" The madness blazed through his eyes. "The Good Book tells us of the Mark, but not in detail. I alone have been chosen by the Lord Our God, *priv*-ileged to study those who bear it, to *learn* from them what we need to know. They are discovered as foundlings in the nests of my flock and brought to me here. Oh, and they are clever, as well. *Sly* in their ways, seemingly so *in*-nocent at first. It is only after weeks, sometimes months, of exami-*na*-tion, of inqui-*si*-tion, that their true natures surface, that the truth most foul finally *spews* forth from their mouths."

I looked first at Lutrice, then Tidyman. "He tortures little kids in this room."

Because I'd stopped with Tidyman, the back of Wyeth's left hand caught me from the blind side. "Not children! No, *change*-lings. Earthly husks, cocoons of Satan for growing his minions and then using them to cor-*rupt* all that is good around them. It is only I who can reveal the masquer-*ade*, and in doing so, gather the information that will one day permit us to *tri*-umph in Glory over the Unclean One."

I said, "I want to see Eddie."

Tidyman said, "Not a chance. Reverend—"

"I make the decisions here!"

Wyeth barely glanced at Tidyman, but Lutrice and the sergeant exchanged looks that carried clear messages. Hers was "Let's take our clothes off," and Tidyman's was "He won't be around forever." I thought of Zoe's "stand-up guy" remark.

Wyeth fixed me with the television stare. "The blasphemer wishes to see how we *deal* with the minions of Satan, he shall see. Bind him."

They led me down the hall opposite the interrogation room, my hands tied behind me by a strap Cody took off the bolted chair. Royel Wyeth carried a flashlight kept in the drawer of his writing table. Axel Severn used a key ring from his pants pocket to open a door.

At first, my eyes didn't adjust well, the taint of disinfectant and urine stinging them. No windows at all, the only light in the room creeping in from the dim corridor. I could make out bunk beds, eight of them, in four tiered pairings. Then a movement in one of the bunks, and I realized I was looking at something out of Romania before they put the Ceaușescus up against a wall.

Five boys, three of the beds empty. Heads shaved, they seemed to be held in by straps like the ones on the bolted chair. A single toilet in the corner of the room, next to a sink. The holding cell at the sheriff's substation was palatial by comparison.

Wyeth said, "Clark, aided by Cody, tries to look after their needs as best he can when he's not on duty at the Lodge, but they often *soil* themselves just to foul their bedding. Their *na*-ture, I've come to learn."

He clicked on the flashlight, shining it in the face of a boy perhaps two years older than Eddie. "Behold, the Mark of Cain."

This boy clamped his eyes shut, making the strawberry mark on his forehead seem to curl down one cheek. The beam of the light was wide enough that I could see bruising or scarring on the boy's arms, probably how Lonnie Severn had learned what he'd done to me with the knife in the hunting camp.

Quietly, I said, "Eddie?"

"I'm here. Over here!"

He was in the bottom bunk of a pair with no boy on top. Wyeth shined the light toward him. Thinner, bruised, scared.

Eddie said, "You kept your promise."

I found myself hoping that'd be worth something to him. "Stay strong, Eddie. It's not as bad as it looks."

Severn butt-ended me in the stomach this time, and I doubled over.

Axel said, "That's right, Ed-*die*. It's worse than it looks."

Lutrice said, "Royel, honey, don't you think we could take that one tonight?"

Wyeth shook his head. "No." He swung the light back to the older boy. "The ceremony proceeds as determined."

"But Royel—"

"I will brook no argument on this point, Lutrice. I have not yet *learn*-ed all I can from the younger one, and it is the older one's time, as each will have *his* time come." Wyeth turned to me. "As will *yours*."

Back in the interrogation room, I was sitting in the bolted chair, strapped to its arms and legs at wrists and ankles. Cody watched me from one of the straight-backs, the M-16 lying across his lap. When I'd asked him a question, he didn't answer, so I'd stopped asking. Then someone in the corridor knocked, not so politely.

Cody shifted the weapon to port arms, walked to the door, and opened it. Lutrice Wyeth came in.

To Cody, she said, "Leave us alone."

"You sure you—"

"Leave us a-*lone.*"

He looked at me, then came over to tug on each strap. Taking the rifle, Cody closed the door behind him.

Lutrice crossed her arms under her breasts, making them fill and rise under the gingham dress. "Well, now. What are we going to do with you?"

I said, "How can you let this go on?"

"Honey, right now you're just the fly in the ointment, but—"

"I don't mean me. I mean your husband's obsession, the . . . inquisition. Those are innocent kids."

She canted her head sideways, as though she were trying to remember something. "He didn't always have the obse..."

"Well, he has it now, and he's nuts..But you're not. Why don't you stop it, get him some help?"

"Twenty million reasons, honey."

"With dollar signs in front of them?"

"You just have no idea what a money machine that Royel is. And the amazing part, the absolutely miraculous part to me is, he means it. The man is not one percent bogus. With a lot of the competition, you can see the strings move when they talk, like a bad puppet show? Well, not with Royel. Nossir, in person or on the air, he is absolutely the real thing, and the flock can feel it, and they just about want to smother him with money." Sister Lutrice looked at me coyly. "Why, I bet even you can feel it."

"I can see his power. What I can't see is why you let it take this insane twist."

"I didn't *let* it do anything. Royel is a very forceful man." The coy look again as she sashayed across my line of vision. "But only in some ways."

Thinking back to what Zoe had told me, I wasn't about to raise it after what Axel Severn and Cody had done to Dawna. "You'd have to keep it close to the vest."

"Huh?"

"This part of the operation, the Sinstitute."

"You'd better not let Royel hear you say that. He hates—"

"Probably only Tidyman, Severn, Cody, Clark from the Lodge, your husband, and you. Pretty tough to keep a lid on it if word got spread any wider."

"Why, that's very clever of you. Maybe you do have a little of the . . . devil in you?"

"Which means the people out in the Compound, the real flock, don't know the truth about this Mark of Cain bullshit. They may hear that madman preaching on it, but for the most part they're good people, thinking they've found kind of a spiritual Disneyland, when really they're just your buffer against the outside world stumbling on this part of the operation."

"Disney World."

"What?"

"Disney World. Disneyland's out in California. This is Florida."

I just stared at her.

Lutrice said, "You know, you're wasting our time together."

I didn't answer.

Now she canted her head to the door. "Nobody's listening out there. I guarantee it. And this room's real soundproof. Take my word on that, too."

I said, "The parents. How do you fool them?"

A frown. "We don't. Not really, I mean. We have stringers out there, like Lonnie—Axel's brother?—even Axel, when things are slow here. They find the boys, we pay them a bounty for each one they bring in. Would you believe Royel insists that it be three thousand dollars? We wouldn't have to go half that for trash like the Severns, but . . . Anyway, we tell the parents the boys are going to a study center, and that's it."

"That's it? The parents never follow up?"

"Uh-unh. But you got to remember, that's not so surprising

now. The families are some of the true believers, and they'll truly believe just about anything Royel tells them. So, if the boys are still needed for 'educational' reasons down here, just a personal letter from 'The Reverend Wyeth' is all it takes. Plus, I think the boys are an embarrassment for a lot of the parents, and they feel like probably they're better off without the boys being a burden around home anymore."

I thought about the impression I'd had in the Haldons' house, finding myself sick to be agreeing with her. "But when the boys never—"

"I don't see why you are *so* interested in them. Maybe Royel's right. Maybe you do have the devil in you." The coy look and a milkmaid bend at the waist. "How about you put a little of your devil in me?"

"Your husband wouldn't mind?"

"Never crosses his mind."

"What about Whit Tidyman?"

The coy look got frosty. "Smart isn't always such a good thing to be, honey."

"Tidyman the new Royel?"

Her features screwed up. "He is not! I'm the new Royel, or I will be, once I get to be more and more of the show, TV-wise. That's the future, whether Royel likes it or not. Cable and satellite hookups, not tent shows in parking lots with skeeters and snakes." The frosty look melted. "So, how about it? They say your last experience is your most . . . powerful one."

"Thanks, but I haven't got a hundred on me."

Lutrice seethed.

I said, "Oh, did I aim too high?"

"Axel's gonna have a real good time with you."

"Lutrice, let me tell you something. He was anyway."

Straightening herself up, Wyeth smoothed out the dress and shook the hair until it fell just so. Then she went to the door.

I decided to ask again the question she'd cut off. "Lutrice?"

"Too late."

"Lutrice, you said before that your husband didn't always have this obsession. How did it start?"

She stopped, then turned back toward me. "I wish I knew

to tell you, honey, and that's the God's honest truth. Royel, he was always hung up on the Bible, and when things started going wrong for him down there—his little thingie, I mean, when it just started to go flip-flop instead of work right? Well, he remembered he'd been talking to these choirboys the day before, down here on a tour, like, without their parents, and Royel'd given each of them a hug. One of the boys—they were from Georgia, I believe, maybe Alabama—anyway, no matter. This one boy had the mark on his face, the strawberry kind, and Royel was reading the Scriptures that night, trying to figure out why he'd 'failed in his husbandly duty,' you might say. Well, Royel hits on that passage about the Mark of Cain, and he convinces himself that the boy practiced some kind of deviltry on him. So Royel goes and gets that boy out of his bed and brings him here—that chair, but it wasn't all bolted down and strapped like it is now. Royel talked to that boy all night long. 'Inquisitioned' him, you might say. And the boy—well, he must have been awful scared, and he just just up and died of shock, I guess."

"He died?"

"Yes, and that left me with a pretty mess, too, I'll tell you. But Cody and Axel were around to help with the body, and I was able to smooth it over with the parents—I came up with a story about him drowning, some money changed hands. I told you the parents just don't care sometimes, and the authorities never did get called into it. Even after all that, though, Royel's thingie didn't start working right again, and he decided he needed to do things more . . . ceremoniously, like. So Cody and Axel bolted and strapped that chair you're in, and Royel started inquisitioning till it turned into an obsession, like you said."

"And you all went along with it."

"For the money, honey. The root of all evil, but we did need Royel for that."

"You let him just 'inquisition' innocent boys to death."

"Well, not exactly."

"What do you mean?"

"Royel, he got it into his head after that first one that just asking them questions and so on in that chair wasn't really enough."

"Enough for what?"

"Enough for purifying them, to release their Immortal Souls from the bonds of Satan."

I shook my head. "What the hell are you talking about, Lutrice? What happens to the boys?"

She opened the door and walked through it, turning back with just her head in the opening. "Haven't you guessed? The same thing that purified Our Savior. The Mercy Tree."

As the door closed, I said, "Sweet Jesus, no."

I'm not sure how much later it was when Cody and Severn came to get me. First they stuffed a hankerchief in my mouth and taped it closed with adhesive. Then they strapped my hands behind my back and marched me into the corridor.

The Reverend and Lutrice, in long black robes, were outside the door to the bunk room. They carried black books like members of an adult choir, reading softly from them, almost a chant. Then Clark came out of the bunk room, his hands on the shoulders of the older boy whose face had been lit by Wyeth's flash beam.

The older boy wore just a wrapped towel as loincloth. His mouth was taped like mine, his eyes dull rather than wide with terror. He was struggling to walk.

Royel Wyeth interrupted his chant, turning to me. "They are too *weak* to actually carry the Cross, and our *mod*-est platform in the courtyard is a poor Calvary, but it serves us *and* the way of the Lord well."

I broke away from Cody and knocked Severn against the wall, trying to reach Clark and free the boy. At least give him a chance to run for the courtyard and maybe through the infirmary to the main part of the Compound. But somebody tripped me, and my hands bound, I went down hard, somebody else clubbing at the back of my head. Feeling myself slipping under, I prayed that the older boy would soon find a kinder place than Little Mercy Key.

25

W HEN MY EYES OPENED, IT WAS NIGHTTIME. I WAS LYING on my right side, the smell of motor oil and salt air in my nose. Through the headache, I didn't remember anything after the scene in the corridor outside the bunk room.

Now there was vibration everywhere, rattling my right elbow, hip, and kneecap. From where I was, in some bilge water back near the engine, I could see Axel Severn standing at the helm of the boat, maybe a twenty-footer. Cody stood next to him, seeming tense, watching where we were going at what felt like thirty miles an hour. The M-16s were stowed in racks for fishing rods under the portside gunwale.

Someone had removed the tape and gag from my mouth, which I took to be a sign that nobody would hear any noise I made. I was in some kind of dark jumpsuit, like an airplane mechanic might wear, but it felt as though they'd just pulled it on over the white church outfit. My ankles were strapped together, my hands tied the same way, but in front of me, not behind my back. At first, it didn't register.

Over the motor whine, I heard Cody say, "He's coming around."

Severn called to me. "What we're gonna do, Samaritan, we're gonna tie a tow rope to that strap there on your hands, then we're gonna slit a couple of your foot veins. We toss you over the side, you'll stand out real nice against the water and sky in those black overalls. No telling what'll come in on the blood trail, start nibbling at your bottom end till your top end tells me what I want to know."

"Maybe I can save you the trouble. What's on your mind?"

"Where's my brother at?"

"Who's your brother?"

Axel shouted over his shoulder. "You know goddam well who he is! Lonnie give me a call down here a week ago, left a message on my telephone machine saying somebody from Massachusetts broke into his trailer. Said he'd call me back, but he never did. You was with the girl and the little retard on the highway north of Boston, then I see you sneaking around the Compound. Now, where's Lonnie at?"

"I couldn't tell you."

Cody said, "Might be you will." He nudged Severn. "Let's try him over by Steamboat Key. I caught me a real nice black-tip just south of her."

Axel yelled to me, "Blacktip's a shark." Then to Cody, "How big?"

"Almost five feet," said Cody.

"Big enough for what we want."

I tuned out the banter. Looking around me, I didn't see anything I'd be able to use except the rifles, and they were a long crawl away, assuming I could get to them before Cody or Severn got to me.

My watch was still on my wrist, but I couldn't see its luminous face under the cuff of the jumpsuit. Above us, the night sky was about half clouded over, the moon gone but lots of stars shining, a brilliant carpet of them with the only ambient light coming from the gauges on the dash in front of Axel. The boat veered, and now we were bouncing through the chop, the vibration from the engine yielding to the steady battering against the hull.

I said, "Killing me isn't going to end this."

Severn laughed, a barroom sound reminding me of his brother. "Maybe not, but like they say with those lawyer jokes, it's a start."

Suddenly, Cody jumped and pointed, moving to the side of the boat. "I'll be. . . . Haven't seen that in years!"

"They're all over the goddam bay!"

"Just like Flipper, zigzagging around the bow and everything. You know, Ax, the scientists say they're like the closest thing to humans."

"They're just fish, Cody."

"Are not. They're like us, have babies and everything. There must be twenty of them, Ax. Be careful you don't hit none."

"You can't hit a goddam dolphin, he knows your boat's there."

"Well, be careful anyway."

Cody, who hadn't blanched at crucifying a woman and a boy, being concerned about . . . I shook my head, then pictured the mammals, playful and rollicking in a heavy chop. The best cover I could hope to have right now.

Taking a deep breath, I drew my feet to my chest. Using my palms on the rough floorboard to right myself, I stood up and pitched forward over the starboard side.

Hitting the water at that speed, my whole body felt as though it had just undergone the mother of all enemas. The wind got knocked out of my lungs, and I surfaced as the engine wound down. The water was warm, the surroundings seeming to be just small islands, maybe two or three hundred yards away, with heavy growths of low trees, stark against the lights of what I took to be larger Keys, many miles away. The boat, several hundred feet farther along, began a banking turn to come back for me, Severn and Cody yelling at each other.

The waterlogged clothes were dragging me down, which was almost a blessing. I took a breath and dived under, my bound ankles forcing me to do the dolphin kick I'd hated but learned in the scuba class. Then something bumped me, and something else from another direction bumped me again.

Out of air, I came back up. The boat was past me, idling, the chop rising and falling against the hull. Axel and Cody, weapons in their hands, were walking around inside the cockpit, sweeping the area with their hands cupped at their eyebrows, as though that would help them see better.

"—don't have a flashlight on this boat?"

"Cody, you want to shut up and try to spot this goddam asshole?"

Then I was bumped again and turned to look at a smiling face with small, pointed teeth and an eye in the side of its head. It pushed itself at me, and I felt its skin. Silky, alive in an alien way I can't describe. Looking toward the boat, I realized that what seemed to be all chop was partly the backs of dolphins, slate gray with blowholes behind the head as they arched through and out of the water, their dorsal fins small and hydrodynamic, their flat tails slipping into the water more than slapping the surface.

Severn started turning toward me, and I dove as I heard his weapon fire. I'm not sure how deep the water was, but I touched bottom fairly quickly. A sludgy, marly texture, with sharp pieces of something mixed in, like broken glass in mud. I kicked along the bottom as far as I could, my lungs screaming for air as I broached this time, maybe forty degrees off where I'd been.

"—can't shoot at them, Ax!"

"Get the fuck . . . off me, you . . . asshole!"

Blinking the salty water from my eyes, I watched the two men struggling in the boat, Cody having dropped his weapon somewhere, bear-hugging Severn so he couldn't use his, though another few rounds got touched off into the air, making that distinctive popping noise.

Then I heard the dolphins chittering, spent air coming from their holes like somebody opening a shaken bottle of soda. They were milling around the boat, on my side of it now, and I got bumped hard by one of them from behind. I took another breath and went under again.

I kicked with everything I had, away from the sound of the propellers idling in the water. I felt that dimness associated with blacking out, and swallowed some more salty water as I came up. Sixty yards away, Cody was holding Axel against the dash, yelling at him.

Then both their heads turned away from me, Cody pointing first. They seemed to take another fast look near where I'd last been, Severn saying, "I still can't see him," Cody adding, "He was all tied up, Ax, he's already drown-did."

By then Severn was at the helm, giving the engine a lot of throttle. It soon grew quieter around me, the dolphins just circling and bumping once in a while. Some of them seemed fascinated by how close they could come without touching me, almost like a Sioux warrior charging on a pony, counting coup with a stick.

As Axel's boat faded into the night, the sound of another engine came over the water, getting louder and stronger. The dolphins didn't seem to mind, but they did move off a little, in the direction of the oncoming boat rather than away from it.

The jumpsuit and other clothes were more of a drag now, forcing me to lie low in the water and drown-proof. The motor noise was getting progressively louder, seeming to home in on the last position of Severn and Cody near me. As the new boat moved through a gap in the islands, it stood against the lights of the distant horizon, a tall superstructure amidships. In fact, it looked a lot like the Marine Patrol boat Howard Greenspan had pointed out at the Mercy Key basin.

I tried to think things through. Unmolested, I could probably reach one of the small, treed islands and get at least my ankles, and maybe my hands, unstrapped. Even if I could get my hands free as well, though, I was too far from the inhabited Keys to swim for them. That meant I'd have to sit on the small island till I saw a fishing boat go by. Which might not be the next day, since presumably where Axel and Cody had lost me wasn't exactly a popular spot. I had no food, but more importantly, no fresh water. If I wanted to live, turning myself in to some authority other than Whit Tidyman's Sheriff's Office and getting off a quick call to Justo Vega in Miami seemed the better bet.

The new boat was approaching now, bow toward me from three or four hundred yards. It wasn't showing lights or sounding sirens. Maybe I was in a smuggling channel, and they figured Severn and Cody for drug-runners who might make another try.

When the boat was about a hundred yards off, a searchlight came on. As it swept the surface, I could see strobe shots of the dolphins, crisscrossing through the beam. The boat slowed to idle, swinging broadside to me now.

Then a woman's voice said, "Howard, I don't see any wounded ones."

A man's voice said, "If any got hit, there'd be a couple of them around it. Watch for a grouping, not individuals."

I recognized the man's voice, even without the woman naming him.

Calling out, my own voice cracked a little. "Hey, Howard? Howard! Over here."

Solemnly, the woman said, "Howard, if one of these creatures can talk, I'll never question you again."

In a command voice, Greenspan shouted, "Who's out there?"

"John Francis. I met you at the marina last week."

"You're in the water?"

"Afraid so."

After a couple of seconds, the boat's engines revved up. "Keep talking. We'll come on you real slow."

26

DORIS GREENSPAN SAID, "THEY'RE CALLED BOTTLE-NOSED dolphins."

I nodded, huddled in a woolen blanket on the deck of their boat, behind the cockpit area to be out of the wind, as Howard stood in front of the captain's chair, racing us toward the Mercy Key Marina. He'd introduced me to his wife—a short woman with deep blue eyes, pixie-cut gray hair, and a ready smile—as he'd pulled the blanket from a storage locker under the gunwale.

Doris sat on the seat next to me, her head only two feet above mine, speaking loudly. "The young males, they enter what the scientists call alliances, kind of street gangs in the water, hanging out together for years, doing synchronized swimming—"

Over the motor whining from the stern, Howard said, "Sweetheart?"

"Yes?"

"This may not be the best time to tell John all this."

"Oh. I'm sorry." She lowered her voice. "John, am I boring you?"

I shook my head no, then couldn't stop shaking for a minute.

Doris said, "I wish we had another blanket."

"That's okay. I'll be fine." I brought a hand out from under the blanket to gesture at an old military-issue forty-five caliber on the seat next to Howard. "That come with the boat?"

He heard part of my question, because he turned to us, Doris pointing to the weapon. Howard said, "No, in fact it's illegal even to carry one into the back country. But out here after sundown, you never know who you might run into, and that one served me well in the past."

I said, "And the night scope?"

Howard hefted the oblong tube, then stowed it under the dash in front of him. "Got it surplus, this gun shop down here. Found it's good for spotting things at a distance in the dark." He half turned this time. "Like tonight, for instance."

"Pretty brave to come over the way you did."

Doris said to me, "We thought they were shooting the dolphins. There're so few of them left now, you have to be really lucky to see a big pod anymore." She raised her voice. "Howard? That's real skinny water up there."

"Yes, sweetheart."

I said, "Skinny water?"

Doris came back to me, lowering her voice again. "Shallow. Don't worry, though, we'll get you in safe and sound and then to the Sheriff's Office."

I shook my head. "No good."

"What do you mean, no good? You have to report this, and you'd be from now till New Year's trying to raise the Park Rangers or Marine Patrol, this time of night."

"I mean, we can't go to the Sheriff's Office."

Doris stared at me, then said, "You're in some kind of trouble with the law?"

"You could say that."

She stared some more, then raised her voice again. "Howard, be sure to stay to the flag side going through the cut."

"Yes, sweetheart."

I looked at her. Before I could say anything, she said, "I'll tell you about the flags another time. Rest now. You can explain, if you want to, when we get to the house."

Reaching the deserted marina, Howard docked the boat with some help from Doris on the mooring lines. He started to talk about calling ahead to the Sheriff's substation, his wife cutting him off, then saying we'd discuss it at the house after they got me into some dry clothes. Howard looked at us, but didn't say anything.

Once the boat was secured, we walked to a Lincoln Town Car, me getting in the backseat, Howard and Doris the front. Working together, it took them a minute to get the heat going.

She said, "The air-conditioning, that's a breeze, but the heat, we don't use that much. . . . There, feel anything yet?"

"Not yet."

"You will."

Howard didn't say a word on the drive to the house, which turned out to be in a small, planned development on the ocean side. We drove in under a gate that was unlocked and unattended.

Doris turned in her seat toward me. "This is one of the three ways into the park, but we keep the other two locked after nine. Half the people here are in bed by then, and almost everybody's home."

I said, "Retirement community?"

"Yes. We spotted it twenty years ago, bought the winter after that. Have to be fifty or over to live here, but they allow some flexibility there, depending."

"Depending?"

"On who the owner might remarry."

"I see."

The streets were narrow, the houses small but sprightly in their lamppost and door lights. About half were one-stories on slabs, the other half on stilts. Howard turned into a driveway by a white one-story with a carport. The interior lights in the houses on either side and across the street were off.

Under the carport's roof, he slowed and stopped, killing the engine. "We all get out, the security lights will come on."

I said, "Movement sensitive?"

"Anything bigger than a ground squirrel. I'll go first, turn them off."

He did. Doris said, "Okay, let's get you inside."

There was a five-step stoop up to the kitchen level of the house. She said, "When the developer set it here, he said it'd be high enough for the storms, and so far, he's been right."

"Set it here?"

We walked from the kitchen into the dining area of a squarish living room, a sun porch beyond it. "This is a mobile home."

I said, "You're kidding?"

"No. Well, actually, it's two mobile homes, kind of welded together without the tall back walls. Howard can give you the details, if you're interested."

From the hallway past the kitchen, his voice said, "These should fit you. They're extra large."

Smiling, I took the long-sleeved T-shirt and sweatpants from him. "You just happened to have my size lying around?"

He said, "I used to be heavier," and showed me where the bathroom was, laying out a towel for me.

"Feeling better?"

Howard had a drink in his hand, whiskey or scotch from the color of it around the cubes.

I said, "Much better. Just a 'thanks' isn't really enough, but I mean it."

"Drink?"

"Vodka, if you have any."

"We do. Mixer?"

"Tonight just on the rocks, I think."

As Howard moved to a cabinet in the dining area, Doris

called out from the kitchen. "You'll have some dessert with us?"

"Dessert?" The clock on the wall read 12:40 A.M.

"Of course dessert. When we go night fishing, we have dinner first, but then reward ourselves with dessert afterwards, even if most people wouldn't think sweets'd go too well with booze. Sit at the table." She came through the doorway with a tray of what looked like Italian pastries as Howard handed me the vodka-rocks in an old-fashioned glass. "Sit, sit."

The table was an ellipse that fit the dining area perfectly. On the server behind Howard at one end of the table were tasteful knickknacks, including painted decoys of the red-beaked ducks I'd seen. "What are those?"

"Common gallinules," said Doris. "Antique wood, but you can buy hollow plastic ones now so lifelike, you'd swear the real thing was sitting on your lawn."

Above the decoys hung a beautiful painting of large pink birds in flight. I waved my glass at it. "And those. Not flamingos, are they?"

Doris said, "Uh-unh. Roseate spoonbills. When we first got down here, you'd see them every trip into the back country. Now?" A hopeless shrug. "Howard got the painting for me at this wonderful man's gallery. The artist displays right by his studio. The painting was too expensive, but it was a special occasion, right, Howard?"

A warm smile from him, but for her, not my, benefit. "Yes, sweetheart."

Doris asked me for my choice, the pastries already cut in halves so I could taste more than one. I took separate pieces of two cakes.

She waited for me to nod my approval of the flavors. "So, how come you were out there in the bay and Colonel Greenspan here had to go in like George Patton?"

"Sweetheart, Patton drove tanks, not boats."

"So George Custer then, and don't tell me he rode horses, we both know that already."

It seemed an odd thing for her to say, but she came back to me and said, "So?"

The cake was good, not to mention the first food I'd had since breakfast at Whit Tidyman's house, but I put down my fork and picked up my drink. "I'm not sure how much of this you should be hearing."

In the command voice, Howard said, "Why don't you tell us everything, and then like good old folks, we can forget the bad parts."

I stopped, then nodded. "Sorry. I wasn't trying to insult you after the way you came to the rescue like the cavalry."

I thought Doris winced at the word 'cavalry,' which seemed even odder to me after the Custer remark. "I'm a private investigator from Boston. I came down here looking for a little boy with a birthmark."

Doris said, "Birthmark?"

"Yes. A strawberry one on his face."

"Oh, the port wine stain, like Gorbachev."

I looked at her. "Yes, only more noticeable."

She said, "My sister in New York, she was a nurse at this hospital there. They can pretty much cure that, now."

"Cure it?"

"Yes. Some kind of laser, I think."

Howard said, "Sweetheart?"

"Yes?"

"Let the man tell us his story."

"Oh, right. Sorry, John."

"That's okay. Like I said, I was looking for this boy. I thought he'd been taken, kind of kidnapped into a radical religious group."

Howard said, "Back at the marina a few days ago, you asked me about Little Mercy Key—the Church of the Lord Vigilant?"

"That's the one."

Doris said, "That's the one what?"

I told them about what had happened to Dawna Adair, then about what I'd seen that day in the bunk room and, briefly, what I thought had happened in the courtyard.

Doris's hand went to her mouth and stayed there until I was finished. "My God, no."

"I'm afraid so."

Howard had finished his two halves of pastry, pushing the empty plate to the side, more for something to do, I thought, than to gain any space. "We heard about the Adair girl on the news, but they didn't give any details. That's pretty . . . strong, John."

"I know it's hard to believe, but—"

Howard said, "I believe you."

I turned toward him.

He said, "I've watched that Reverend Wyeth on television. Not because I'm interested in religion so much, or his in particular. Just because he had his operation here on Mercy, and I thought I should know something about him. I didn't much like what I saw. And heard."

"What do you mean?"

"He reminded me of the newsreels from the thirties. We'd see them in the movie theaters, Saturday afternoons. The ones from Berlin."

I said, "Not exactly, but close. That where the forty-five came from?"

"No. I was in the South Pacific. First Marines."

"Guadalcanal?"

Howard paused, then nodded, his eyes growing sad. "Got there in 'forty-two. Seven August. Did demolition work, mostly. I was a green lieutenant, my men greener. They had old, bolt-action Springfields. Even so, the Japanese couldn't beat us, but the malaria nearly did. When the Army first landed to relieve us in October, I could have kissed them. Americal Division, with the new-for-then M-1s." He looked up at me, his eyes suddenly sadder. "When we talked at the boatyard last week . . . You were in Vietnam?"

"One tour."

Doris said, "When?"

"Late sixties, mostly Saigon as an MP."

She looked down at her dessert. "I thought it might have been earlier."

"Earlier?"

In the command voice, Howard said, "Our son, Mike, was in the first of the Seventh."

"The Ia Drang Valley?"

"Yes."

Now the Custer remark and cavalry reaction made sense. The first battalion of the Seventh Cavalry was part of the First Cavalry Division (Airmobile). Renamed in the States after Custer's regiment before shipping over, the unit was in the initial major battle in 1965 between American combat troops and North Vietnamese regulars.

Howard folded his hands in front of him on the tablecloth, then spoke to them quietly. "Mike wanted to serve, but not in the Marines, because I was still on active duty, and he didn't want anybody to think he was getting a break because of being a colonel's son. So he went into the Army before college, figured he'd see some of the world before settling down to his studies." Howard looked up at me. "Mike was going to be a writer. He would have been a good one, too, from the letters he sent us." The eyes were back to the hands. "From Fort Benning, about how his airmobile—they called it 'air assault' then—about how his training was going, the sounds of the helicopter blades reminding him of his mother saying 'Whup, whup, whup' whenever as a little boy he'd hold something fragile. Mike wrote letters from his troop ship, too, as they sailed through the Panama Canal. And from Vietnam itself, how proud he was to be going into combat with 'three-war men,' meaning sergeants who'd served in my war and Korea beforehand."

Howard settled in his chair, his shoulders a little straighter. "It was Sunday, fourteen November, nineteen-hundred-sixty-five. Ia means 'river' in one of the languages over there. I got that from the book his battalion commander wrote with that war correspondent. We Were Soldiers Once . . . and Young. You read it?"

"No, I haven't."

"You might want to." An abrupt nod. "Mike's company commander wrote me a letter afterwards. I still remember the second paragraph. 'Your son was wounded twice in the battle. Despite his injuries, he was able during a lull in the fighting to guide three other casualties from his platoon back through the elephant grass to the landing zone, nearly carrying one of the men. As a chopper arrived near a termite hill, Mike tried to get one of his wounded friends onto his feet. Your son was shot from behind and killed instantly. He was a fine soldier and one of my best men. I shall miss him.' "

Howard looked back at me. "The news itself came from an Army lieutenant driving up to my office, olive drab sedan. I saw him out my window, and I knew. In my war, the news came by telegram, and I remember Doris telling me when I got back that wives and parents wouldn't answer the door if a knock came when they weren't expecting anybody. Later I heard that was how a lot of the Ia Drang families got their news, too. From Western Union, delivered by a cabdriver."

A shake of the head. "But when I saw that lieutenant come up the path . . . I retired the next year. I thought Mike's company commander might come to visit Doris and me. We tried to do that in 'forty-six, if we could, but I guess he had a lot of boys' folks to visit. Or maybe he was killed later himself, I don't know."

Howard's expression suddenly changed, and he stood. "Excuse me."

Doris watched him leave the room. I heard a door close, then the muffled sounds of someone vomiting.

I said, "I'm really sorry."

"Don't be. It's not so bad for us to remember Mike from time to time with somebody else, especially somebody who was there, too."

"Yes, but I'm sorry about Howard being . . . sick over it."

Doris moved her tongue around inside her mouth before saying. "It's not from Mike. Howard always does that."

"Always?"

"Throws up. It's the cancer."

I didn't say anything.

"Stomach. By the time we found out what was making him sick, it was too late for anything that would cure it, and he didn't want to go through what he'd seen with other people down here, the chemo and the radiation and all. So, he loses weight and toughs it out. It should be okay for a while yet, and he's had a good life, too, longer than what most of his friends from the Marines had."

"My wife died of cancer, brain cancer."

A stricken look. "But . . . so young?"

"A few years ago."

"Years. That's what I'll have, John. Howard's seventy-five? I'm only seventy, and fit as a fiddle. Ten good years left for me, the way I'm feeling. I won't stay here, I like the change of season too much, without Howard and the boat and the fishing with him to keep me on the Keys. But what am I going to do with them, the ten years? I ask you."

Doris Greenspan shook her head.

When he came back into the dining area, Howard said, "I can tell by your face that Doris told you."

"What, you wanted John to think he was gonna get sick from my desserts, too?"

The warm smile for her as he retook his chair. Then to me, the sound of command again in his voice. "All right, from what you told us, we can't go to the Sheriff's Office about the Church. How about the Highway Patrol or the F.B.I.?"

"By now Tidyman's sent them something with 'John Francis' on it. You think they'd believe a fugitive killer?"

Doris said, "C.I.A.?"

Her husband said, "They aren't supposed to do anything domestic."

"So, I.R.S.?"

"Sweetheart—"

"Howard, I don't know what initials we should be going to, but I do know we can't let these monsters get away with killing babies."

He looked at me. I said, "Doris, as soon as any kind of formal complaint was lodged, even hinted at, Wyeth's people would sidestep him and just dispose of the evidence."

She said, "What evidence?"

"The children themselves."

Closing her eyes, Doris shook her head again.

Howard folded his hands. "And even if we could persuade some agency on the quiet, none of them, state or federal, would go into a religious compound fast and hard after what happened to the A.T.F. in Waco."

I said, "I think you're right."

Doris opened her eyes, looking from one of us to the other. "So that means we can't do anything?"

Howard gave her the warm smile. "I didn't say that, sweetheart."

27

"I FEEL SILLY."

Over the barely idling engine, Doris said, "You're dressed fine for a tourist going fishing, John."

From under the front brim of the pith helmet, I glanced down through the lenses of the amber, wraparound sunglasses to the old Hawaiian shirt and yellow cruise pants Howard had lent me for the day.

"Besides," she said, "the idea is nobody should recognize you, right?"

"Right."

"So who's going to know you in that getup?"

Doris had a point. We were heading out from the marina on the mainland side of Mercy Key, moving slowly with no wake through what seemed to be a man-made canal with occasional concrete sidewalls, houses built no more than twenty feet back from the walls. The long-needled pine trees each had three or four pelicans perched in them, an occasional white egret on a television antenna. As we passed one pine, a pelican turned its back on us and let loose.

Doris said, "Usually they just fly off the branches and shit in the boats."

The water was muddy, small stands of trees trailing into the water along the few stretches of shoreline without walls. Many of the houses had large metal crutches and slings bolted into the concrete at the water's edge.

I motioned at the slings. "What are they for?"

Howard said, "Boats. Keeps them cleaner if you can sling them up like ... that one."

I followed his index finger to a twenty-eight-footer slung fore and aft about three feet over the water. The name stenciled on the bow was NAFKA.

Doris said, "In Yiddish, that means 'prostitute.' "

"That boat would cost a lot more than a prostitute, sweetheart."

"Like you'd know."

Howard gave her the warm smile. Near the left shore, a broad, scarred back rolled slowly at the surface.

I said, "What was that?"

Doris said, "Manatee. Sea cows."

It looked like it'd been flogged.

"Propellers," she said. "The boats are fast, the manatee aren't."

"You'd think they'd learn to avoid them."

Doris shook her head. "The manatee have small brains and less sense."

"I meant the boaters."

She looked at me. "Same difference." Then to Howard, "Shouldn't we check the marine forecast?"

"Good idea, sweetheart."

Doris flipped a switch on the dashboard, and the staticky voice of someone used to reading reports out loud came over a small speaker. Almost immediately he mentioned Florida Bay, predicting clear skies all day, with winds from the northeast and a light chop in the morning, calming down to flat by early afternoon.

"Good day for fishing," said Doris.

"Among other things," said Howard.

At the mouth of the canal, we entered the bay itself, the water getting cleaner almost immediately. When the color reached a deep aquamarine, Howard goosed the engine, the hull starting to bounce over the surface the way we had coming in the night before.

I didn't see any other boats. "We have the place to ourselves."

Doris said, "Lots of people prefer to fish the patches or out front."

"The patches are out to the reef?"

"Right. On the ocean side, the patches of sand or sea grass between the key and the reef, which is about three miles offshore."

"You can get there from the bay side?"

"Yes, by going through one of the creeks that separate the main Keys."

"You ever fish 'out front,' Doris?"

"Beyond the reef? Not usually. Big-game water for marlin, sailfish, that kind of thing."

"What are we after?"

Howard said, "Speckled trout, we can find any."

"The kind I saw you cleaning last week?"

"Right." He banked us north.

I said, "Isn't Little Mercy south of here?"

Howard nodded. "Better chance of a mullet mud off Little Mercy in the afternoon. Be more boats then, too, so we won't stand out as much, somebody's looking from the Key."

"What's a 'mullet mud'?"

Doris said, "When the mullet—the bait fish—feed on the bottom, they stir it up. The water gets milky-looking. That attracts the bigger fish, and the fishermen."

We rode for five minutes or so, still no other boats in sight. Then I noticed the water going from aquamarine toward white toward brownish dead ahead. As we got closer to the brownish, I thought I could see what looked like a dozen or so egrets walking, the water no more than three or four inches up their legs.

I said, "How much of a draft does this boat have?"

Howard noticed where I was looking. "About ten inches if I tilt the motor, but do you see those flags?"

Maybe a hundred yards in front of the bow was a line of what looked like flags for golf holes. "Yes."

"Well, that's what's called a 'cut.' "

"Those channels through the real shallow places you told me about at the marina."

"The same."

"How deep is the channel?"

Doris said, "Not very. The rangers used to blast through them a couple times a day to blow the encroaching sand back with their props, but the budget problems mean fewer patrols and narrower cuts. We have a depth-finder, but you're better off going by the poem."

"The poem?"

She said, "The conchs use it—'conch' is the slang for a native-born Keys-person. It used to be derogatory, I think, but now they seem to take pride in it."

"What's their poem say?"

"It uses water color to tell you depth. 'Brown, run aground; white, you might; green, nice and clean; blue, sail on through.' "

"Catchy."

"It can save your day, if not your life."

As we got near the flags, I could see they were just wooden pennants tacked near the tops of wooden posts, small birds like terns standing on every fourth post or so.

Howard said, "Just be sure you always stay to the flag side as you move through the cut."

As we approached each of the posts with a bird on it, the creature would eye us, then fly away. The wading birds, some of them gray or blue as well as white, ignored us.

As we entered deeper water on the other side of the cut, I said, "They seem pretty tame compared to the little ones."

Doris snorted. "The few that are left."

"How do you mean?"

"When Howard and I first started coming down here twenty years ago, the fishing was spectacular, and on both sides of every cut you'd see hundreds, even thousands of birds. Now there are maybe a tenth of the fish and a twentieth of the birds."

"Why?"

"Combination of things. The water for Florida Bay comes down from Lake Okeechobee through the Everglades and into the bay. Between the lake and the 'glades, there're sugar cane and vegetable farms that use fertilizers. When the rain runs off the fields, it carries phosphate into the water."

"And that's bad?"

"Standing alone, not terrible. The problem is, with all the residential development the last forty or fifty years, too much of the fresh water is being drained off to houses before it gets to us. That means too much phosphate, which causes algae blooms, and too little fresh water, which makes the bay too saline. You probably noticed last night, the water's saltier than the ocean, made you buoyant, too."

"And that affects the birds and the fish?"

"It affects everything. The sea grass is dying, coming up in . . . there! Just look over there."

I could see what appeared to be a manatee carcass, rocking slowly and lifelessly under the surface. "Dead?"

"Dead sea grass. Whole clump of it. When the sea grass dies, the little crustaceans and the mullet that live in it die, too. When they go, the bigger fish and the birds lose their food supply, and they're gone. At the rate of deterioration we've seen the last three, four years, pretty soon the bay's going to be dead."

Howard said, "Kind of glad I won't be around for that."

Doris didn't say anything. About five minutes later, though, she pointed off the port side. "Howard, I see a mud."

"I don't."

"Ten o'clock from the bow, about four hundred yards out."

"Got it. Good eyes, sweetheart."

He banked the boat again, slowing as we neared and circled a milky area shaped like an amoeba and maybe two hundred yards at the widest diameter. Moving upwind, Howard said, "Depth-finder shows four feet. String John up, sweetheart, and we'll drift through once, see how they treat us."

Doris got a fishing rod and reel outfit from under the gunwale and tied an odd-looking one-inch piece of metal to the end of the monofilament line. The piece of metal was attached to an odder-looking wooden thing about six inches long, sort of a concave bobber in red, white, and green. There was a matching metal thing on the other end of it, then line running from the second metal thing to a split-shot sinker and finally a hook.

I said, "What's all that?"

She said, "A popper rig. The big thing's a popper, the little metal gizmos the swivels that keep the line from getting all twisted and kinked as we drift. The split-shot takes the bait down from the gulls or terns that sometimes swoop for it when you're not paying attention."

"What's the bait?"

Doris smiled and took a small aquarium dip net toward the stern. She opened a box at the waterline and scooped up what looked like a giant shrimp, maybe as long as the popper. Taking the shrimp between the thumb and middle finger of her other hand, she set down the net and then used the thumb and index finger of her free hand to twist off the shrimp's tail.

"Why did you do that?"

Doris said, "Two reasons. First, there's a spike in there that can give you a nasty sting. Second, this releases a kind of shrimp odor into the water, so be sure not to let your shrimp go under before you present it to the fish."

"Present it?"

"Like, cast it out." She used the free hand to insert my hook up through the tail area and out again near the tummy. "See that little black spot inside the shrimp?"

"Yes."

"That's the vital organs. Have to be sure to miss those, or you kill the thing."

Doris swung the rig in a sidearm cast, gently sailing the popper and shrimp maybe thirty feet out, then handed the rod to me. The popper was bobbing in the light chop. "You just let it sit there, but maybe three times a minute, give it a tug, so the thing actually pops."

"That doesn't scare the fish?"

"No. It excites them, makes them think other fish are feeding. Now, you feel a bite, set the hook right away—meaning, yank back sharply on the rod—but just once, because the trout have tender, almost tissue-paper mouths."

As she turned to bait up her own pole, I saw my popper angling away into the water, but didn't feel anything, so I didn't do anything.

Howard said, "Might want to hook your fish before he's gone."

I yanked. Didn't feel anything still, and the popper came back to the surface. "I think it was just a mullet, trying to steal the bait."

"Not likely. Mullets are vegetarians. Probably not a trout, though. They're pretty aggressive about taking what they want. Better bring in your line, see if you still have shrimp."

I reeled in until I could see the hook. Bare. "Sorry."

"Nothing to be sorry about. You'll do better next time."

Next time was about ten minutes later, as we got near the end of the drift through the milky water. Neither Doris nor Howard had had any action. As I saw my popper disappear, I also felt a vicious vibration, and struck back. A strong run, zizzing line off the reel, then a silvery, almost dainty fish two feet long came out of the water, tail-walking across the surface before diving again and doing the same.

I said, "A trout?"

Doris said, "Ladyfish. Kind of a petite tarpon. Fun to catch, but can't eat them."

I got the fish close to the boat before it tail-walked again, throwing the hook.

Howard said, "Don't worry about that. Saves me having to take her off."

Doris said, "With a tarpon, they call that 'putting one in the air.' Fun, huh?"

I had to admit it was. Howard cranked up the motor.

"You going to head up and drift back again?"

He shook his head. "No. Our experience is, you find trout on a drift, it's worth staking out. Otherwise, look for a new mud."

Doris stowed the fishing gear, and Howard moved us another five minutes, roughly northeast.

I said, "Aren't we getting kind of far from Little Mercy?"

"Not really," said Doris. "We'll have the wind behind us this afternoon, and even without it, our boat will do twenty knots. Plus, there's less algae east of here."

I looked around. "I don't see any."

She pointed. "See how that water over there looks cloudy instead of milky?"

"Kind of."

"Algae bloom." A heaviness crept into her voice. "They're everywhere now."

Doris spotted another mullet mud, and we went to it. After rigging and drifting a minute, Howard had a strike, and another fish slugged it out on the surface, but didn't jump or tail-walk.

Doris said, "Trout. Keeper, for sure."

Howard brought the fish alongside while pulling a glove on his left hand. Lifting the fish with the rod, he grabbed it at the gills, the back in the crotch of his thumb and forefinger. "About twenty inches."

The fish was even more beautiful than the ones I'd seen him cleaning, white with speckles from the midline up toward the dorsal fin, an iridescence about the scales that danced in the light. Howard put it into the large red Coleman cooler, now bracketed into the deck near the bow. Then he lifted a long pole with one sharp end and one forked end from along the top of the starboard gunwale, taking a rope with him toward the bow. After lashing the rope to a cleat, Howard sent the pole over the side, sharp end down, and began working the shaft forcefully, as though he were digging a posthole into the bottom. Then he lashed the rope around the shaft, letting the rope slip and tighten till it didn't slip any more.

I said, "And that's 'staking out'?"

Howard said, "Right."

"That pole just sticking in there will hold this big boat here?"

"Better than an anchor. The point works its way into the mud and marl on the bottom. Once the pole sets, it's even harder to get the thing back out."

Doris rigged me up again, and I cast sideways. The sun was playing with the water, some large birds with that Z-neck flying over the small Keys to the right.

"Are those heron?"

Doris nodded. "Great blues. They live up north through the summer, then come down here when they feel the chill. Like a lot of people."

A pair of hawklike birds circled in the air, riding the wind currents. They reminded me of something I'd seen in Maine and on the power poles driving down from Miami. "And those. Osprey?"

Doris said, "Yes. They nest on the little islands, usually in the highest tree they can find. Mate for life."

"Silly notion," said Howard, but with the warm smile on his lips.

We seemed to be in a good spot, as first Doris, then Howard, then I had fish on. Doris brought in a trout about twelve inches, which got thrown back. Howard had a longer, bull-dogging fight from his. Lifting it alongside but not into the boat, he said, "Bonnethead."

The thing looked prehistoric, a flared head like a protractor, high dorsal fin. "A shark?"

"Cousin of the hammerhead. Tough customer, but no good for the table."

Mine turned out to be a catfish that fought well, still struggling on the hook as I swung it up. Then it grunted, like Cody, startling me.

"Weird, huh?" said Doris, as Howard took the hook out with a gadget that looked like a surgeon's forceps.

After we rebaited, Howard caught another keeper trout,

then Doris did as well. After the fish were put in the cooler, she said, "How about some lunch?"

I looked at my watch. One P.M. "I can't believe it's so late already."

"Time has a tendency to get away from you out here."

Doris opened a smaller cooler. Smoked turkey sandwiches on six-grain bread, bean sprouts and lettuce for garnish, and some fruit drink packets that were ice cold and great for the mouth and throat.

I said, "How do you keep these packets so cold?"

"Freezer. Then I put them in the cooler at the house before we leave. That way, they keep the sandwiches cold like ice packs, but melt just enough through the morning that they're drinkable by lunch."

After a couple of bites of my sandwich, I looked over at the pole holding us. "Why is the top end forked like that?"

Howard took a gulp of fruit juice. "So you could stand up and pole the boat along, fork end down without sticking into the bottom. Guides here will build a platform over their stern, a kind of crow's nest for spotting tailing bonefish or tarpon out on the flats."

"The flats?"

"Just offshore on the reef side of the Keys. The guide'll stand on the platform, watch for tails, then pole the boat along, so as not to scare the fish by starting up the motor to move toward them."

A formation of four pelicans flew just above the surface, like torpedo planes coming in under radar. The wingspans were five feet or more, the bodies looking a lot more graceful in the air than on land or in trees. They passed one of the smaller islands, a few forlorn bushes sticking up through the water.

I said, "How do they survive?"

Doris said, "The pelicans?"

"No, the bushes. How can they grow in salt water like that?"

"They're mangrove trees. They're what make the islands."

"Make them?"

"Yes. You're seeing their roots, those knobby knees coming
out of the water. The tree as it grows kind of 'walks' its roots
out further and further each year, making soil by holding onto it
as its root system expands."

"That's amazing."

A shrug. "That's nature, John."

Finishing lunch, I watched Howard, but he seemed all
right, not at all ready to be sick as he'd been after dessert the
night before. Putting the plastic and used drink packets away,
Howard said, "We have three keepers. That's six fillets, just
right for the three of us for dinner. Even when the fishing
was better, we always had kind of a rule that when we got
enough for the table, we'd stop fishing."

I said, "Fine with me. I've had a good time. And besides,
there are other things to do."

"Yes," he said, "there are."

Doris again didn't say anything, then suddenly jumped up
from her seat. "Oh, Howard, look!"

About a hundred feet in the air and two hundred feet out,
a pair of big pink birds flew from one Key toward another.

I said, "Roseate spoonbills?"

Howard went up to Doris, putting his arm around her
shoulder as her arm snaked around his waist. She said, "First
time we've seen any in years."

He cleared his throat. "This has been as good a day as we
used to have back then," and from the way her shoulder
hunched, he must have given her a squeeze on it.

In the low command voice, Howard said, "Coming up to
port."

He didn't have to tell me. You could see the high walls of
the Compound on the higher ground of Little Mercy from a
mile away. The walls around the courtyard of the Center for
the Study of Sin were behind the infirmary as we approached,
our boat staying well off. We were no longer the only one
navigating through the bay, and I could see what Howard
had meant by our not standing out.

"I don't see the boat that I was on last night."

"Neither do I."

Some people were staked out, a few drifted, a few others must have been anchored because they didn't seem to drift but weren't staked out, either. Everybody was fishing, nobody catching fish.

I looked past the boats, the bay flat and mirrorlike, the sky the same color as the water. The horizon disappeared, the more southerly Keys seeming to float in the air.

"That's one hell of an optical illusion," I said.

Doris smiled. "When it's smooth like this, it's as if the Keys were the clouds."

"And hard to see the horizon."

From the helm, Howard said, "Kind of optimistic, isn't it?"

I turned to him. "How do you mean?"

"Well, maybe not being able to see the horizon means you're not limited by reaching it."

Doris stopped smiling.

As we got closer to Little Mercy, the shoreline became clearer. Fairly bare, only a few stands of trees here and there near the water's edge. No real beach, just some parts that were a more gradual slope to the water and some driftwood piled up at its edge.

I said, "Not much cover."

Howard shook his head. "There used to be. Bastards cut down a lot of the natural hammock. Not supposed to, of course, but by the time the Marine Patrol noticed what was going on, most of the trees were gone."

"What does that driftwood say about the current here?"

"About what you'd think. Things tend to wash up on Little Mercy."

I looked away from the Key to the north and west. An industrious clatch of mangroves had formed a small island maybe a hundred feet long across a half mile of open water from Little Mercy itself.

Without my saying anything, Howard turned the helm toward the small island. "Sweetheart, remember when we used to be able to catch snook down here?"

"Long time ago, Howard."

I recalled the name from the taxidermy wall at Pinky's. "Snook?"

He said, "Great game fish. And the best eating. Near fished out now, though the tourist brochures would have you believe otherwise."

I watched the small island, more specifically the water around it. Green to almost blue.

I said, "What was that poem again?"

Howard smiled. "Don't worry. My memory was deep channels around here, and it's proving correct."

Fifty yards off the island, Howard turned, beginning to circle it. On the far side, the mangroves got thickest in the middle, so dense we couldn't see Little Mercy at all through them. I looked over at Howard.

He grinned at me. "I think so."

Doris looked from one of us to the other. "You mind telling me what you two are thinking?"

I said, "You and Howard can hide with the boat here, after you drop me off near Little Mercy. Then you'll pick us up out in the channel afterward."

Doris said, "Us?"

Howard shook his head again. "You can't go in alone and hope to get out with four boys."

"I'm not going to bring all of them out."

Doris said, "You can't leave the others to . . . them."

"I'm not going to. But Eddie's the only one I'm taking out."

Howard shook his head some more. "I don't get it."

"Me neither," said Doris.

I explained it to them.

Howard turned toward Doris, who said, "I can handle the boat by myself."

I looked at both of them. "This is my fight. You're already risking a lot as it is, your boat gets spotted."

Doris said, "It got 'spotted,' if it did, last night already. Besides, Howard's still right. You need somebody else to manage the diversion, and probably to help out with the people you're dealing with."

"Helping out may mean killing somebody."

Doris and Howard exchanged glances, then just looked back at me evenly. I was thinking, no wonder we won your war.

Howard said, "We'd have to make a long swim. A commando dinghy would be better for coming back with the boy, but too easy to spot coming in and too hard to hide for sure in the hammock that's left on Little Mercy."

I said, "Scuba?"

"You know how to dive?"

"I know how, but I doubt they'd rent me any equipment because I'm not certified yet."

Howard thought about it. "No. No, the bottom shoals up too much by Little Mercy itself. Last fifty yards, we'd be in only two feet of water, struggling with all that gear."

I said, "You have a better idea?"

"I believe so."

We'd almost completed the circle of the small island to head for the marina when Howard pointed. "Sweetheart, see that fin?"

"No."

He turned to me. "Rig up, quick."

I did, as Howard maneuvered the boat slowly toward the island.

Doris looked at the depth-finder. "Three and a half under the stern."

I said, "Ready."

Howard pointed. "Cast out that way, far as you can."

I did, maybe seventy feet.

Howard said, "Good. Get ready."

The strike nearly took me over the side. I set the hook into something that felt like a log, then it was up and out of the water, a big, bronzed hulk like a dolphin.

Doris said, "Blacktip shark, maybe four feet long."

I thought about Cody, mentioning blacktips the night before.

Howard said, "They're the only shark I ever saw jump like that."

I felt as though I had a runaway freight at the end of the singing line, the boat starting to turn and drag behind him. Then the fish came up again.

Doris said, "Bigger than I thought."

Howard said, "Close to five feet. John, keep a tight line, but don't try to horse him."

"How will we land him?"

"We won't. Once you get him tired and close on, we'll cut off the line. Hook'll fall out or rot in a couple of days."

The shark made a turn, heading away from the boat and the island, then jumped again and the line went slack. I tried to keep a little-boy sound out of my voice as I said, "Lost him."

Howard clucked his tongue. "Reel in."

When the popper appeared, there was less line past it and no hook.

Howard said, "That's what I thought. You didn't lose him. He swallowed your shrimp, and on one of his turns, his teeth just severed the line. Need to use wire leader, you plan on actually fishing for shark."

"I don't," thinking of going from Axel Severn's boat into the water the night before.

In the living room, Howard said, "John, I still think it's a good idea for you to stay here while I do the shopping. Let's just go over the list, okay?"

"Okay."

He tilted half-glasses on his nose. "Mask, fins, and snorkel. You can use mine, Doris's will fit me well enough, now."

She didn't follow up.

I said, "Does that mean that once we reach shore we're barefoot?"

"No. Ours are power fins, so we'll be wearing wet-suit booties under them."

"Good. Inflatable life vests?"

"Check. We have those, too, for you and me, though the shorty wet suits ought to be more than we need in that saline bay water. I'll get a child-size vest for the boy."

"The two plastic decoys?"

"Check."

"How about rope?"

"There's some in my workroom."

"Knives?"

"We have calf knives for snorkeling. I'll sharpen them up."

"All right."

Howard went on. "The gun shop where I got the night scope will sell me what I need for the diversion out the back door, no questions asked. While I'm getting that stuff, what kind of weapon do you want?"

"Something the water won't bother."

"We'll have to wrap any firearms to waterproof them, anyway. I have my forty-five from the service. Doris shouldn't need anything on the boat."

She just sat there.

I said, "In that case, get me a four-inch revolver."

"Not an automatic?"

First Pepe, now Howard. "Thirty-eight over a three-fifty-seven."

"Okay." He went back to the list. "You're sure about this boom box thing?"

"Yes. The smallest one they have, but the sport kind that's water-resistant. It has to be able to record and be turned up loud."

Howard grinned. "I'll tell the clerk I'm hard of hearing. Just the one tape?"

"It's all we'll have time for."

His eyes moved back up the list. "That everything, then?"

"I think so."

Howard folded the paper and put it in his shirt pocket as he stood. The warm smile. "Coming with me, sweetheart?"

She smiled back. "No, I have to get that trout all nice and seasoned for dinner."

"Okay."

After his car was out of the driveway, Doris stared at me. "You heard him, right?"

"Heard him?"

"The way he sounded. The last time he sounded that way was when we visited the Holocaust Museum in Washington. Howard and I went there after we saw the Wall."

I nodded, thinking of my own trip there.

"We found Mike's name on the Wall, Panel 3-East, and then Howard said we should go to the museum, it wasn't that far. So we did. You're supposed to order tickets in advance, but it was sunny outside, not so many people wanted to go in and ruin a nice day visiting with horrors. And so they took us.

"And everything we saw, John, was a horror. The replica of Daniel's House, the kind of place where the Jews and others lived. An office bridge with the names of the towns they were taken from, towns that got wiped out by their being taken. Replicas of the cattle cars they were moved in and the camps they were moved to. The worst for me was the room of shoes."

"Shoes?"

"Shoes, piled up in heaps on both sides of the walkway in between. Thousands and thousands of shoes the Nazis took off the victims before they killed them. And I broke down there, John, broke down and cried at all the shoes, all the children's shoes that the monsters were saving for somebody else to use. But Howard? He was like he was tonight, kind of even-keeled, planning our time there to be sure we'd see everything. The only time he showed anything was when we got to the rooms with the soldiers, our soldiers, liberating the camps. And he stood there and cried, John. But as much for the soldiers as the victims, because he'd been in the South Pacific and hadn't seen the war in Europe, what the Nazis did to the children there." Her voice suddenly changed. "You're going to get my husband killed tonight."

"Not if I can help it, Doris."

She shook her head. "No. No, you don't understand. What I'm saying, John, is Howard never quite forgave himself for living through the war. I know that sounds stupid, but he never quite did. He's been glad for our life together, glad we had Mike to raise, even after we lost him. But Howard always

thought he himself would die a hero, like so many of his
friends did when he was spared."

"Doris—"

"Let me finish here. Even his son died a hero. Not in Howard's war, but in yours. Do you see?"

"Doris, all I can do—"

"—is see that my Howard dies well."

I stared at her, thinking back to Howard's three questions
the first time I'd met him.

She said, "You saw Howard on the bay today, heard him.
Making little asides about his cancer, that comment about the
horizon and optimism. We had a good day together, John.
The best we had in years, like he said. Howard doesn't want
to go out with twelve tubes sticking out of him and some
bag to pee in. What you heard on the water was his way of
dealing with that, his way of telling me he's not going to
have so many more good days. You got us into this, you owe
him that much, okay, John? You owe it to my Howard that
he dies well."

Doris dropped her eyes to the floor, nodding once, more
to herself than to me, I thought. Then she stood up and
walked into the kitchen.

28

K IND OF WISH WE'D DONE A TRIAL RUN WITH ALL OF THIS."
I said, "Howard, there isn't that kind of time."
"Agreed."

"Plus, somebody sees us practicing, they might be able to identify your boat."

"Same."

We were under way, heading south from the Mercy Key Marina toward the channel to Little Mercy, the only boat on the water under a hazy quarter-moon. Doris sat on the fish cooler in the bow while Howard stood at the helm, me next to him. He and I were wearing the lightweight shorty wet suits, throat-to-belly zippers in the front to easily access what we'd carry against our chests. The suits were black, so they'd help on land, too, though they'd also make us hot after a while.

In a locker next to the dashboard were the weapons, waterproof plastic around them and taped tightly. The boom box, a recorded cassette already inside it, was wrapped the same way. The plastic gallinule decoys, holes cut for our eyes and snorkel spouts, lay on the deck nearby with the three deflated life vests.

Howard lowered his voice, though with the wind coming past her ears, Doris probably couldn't have heard him anyway. "How are you getting out of this afterward?"

I said, "If I can make Miami, I'm all set."

"But the Sheriff's Office has your name, right?"

"They have *a* name. John Francis."

Howard nodded. "And you have real—what, 'credentials,' I guess—in Miami?"

"And a friend to help me get north again."

"*A* friend?"

I grinned. "Another friend."

"That's better."

I didn't ask Howard how he planned to get out, and if he noticed I didn't, he gave no indication of it.

Doris said, "Are you sure you have everything?"

"Positive, sweetheart."

"You look awfully good in that outfit. Like Lloyd Bridges used to on his TV show, remember?"

I tried to give them some privacy, but the boat was too small for me to move very far off.

Howard said to her in a businesslike voice, "You can get behind that island without running lights?"

"After seeing it again today? Piece of cake."

I looked to Little Mercy, a mile from where we were now. The whole Key seemed dark, my watch showing one A.M. As we got to the half-mile point, a faint glow was visible behind the courtyard walls.

Howard took a compass reading on the shoreline near the courtyard. "You figure everybody's asleep?"

"It would help."

We got our gear and moved to the starboard side of the boat, me slinging the boom box over my shoulder on a double layer of Howard's electrical tape, him responsible for the lariat-looped rope and his "diversion" materiel. I climbed over the side first, holding on to the ladder as the slow-moving boat dragged me through the water. I heard Doris say, "Good-bye, Howard," as he came over to join me. We adjusted masks and snorkels, then the decoys over them. Doris looking down at us, Howard and I both let go of the boat and began to kick slowly, the fins never breaking the surface, the current and perhaps their own webbed feet just carrying two lazing gallinules toward Little Mercy Key.

We avoided lobster pot floats and the trailing lines to the pots themselves on the bottom. Nothing big swam near us as far as I could tell. After about fifteen minutes, the bottom started to shoal up, and I had to be careful not to splash my fins on the surface. Another five minutes and we were less swimming than crawling along the bottom, the shoreline of Little Mercy Key fifty feet ahead, a small stand of mangrove at the water's edge and the wall two hundred feet farther up the slope.

We moved on hands and knees quietly, using the stand of trees to protect us from the courtyard wall and anybody walking outside it. No sounds other than our own, and they were minimal.

On shore, we took off the hollow decoys and masks, waiting for our breathing to normalize without the snorkels in our mouths. Listening some more, hearing nothing. Then we unzipped the wet suits, taking out the weapons, which we unwrapped before the boom box. I'd just laid my revolver, a Dan Wesson .38, on top of the waterproof wrap when, from the other side of the trees, a voice grunted in exasperation. Cody's.

"Come on, Ax, this here is stupid."

"Cody, don't you be getting on me, now."

"But I'm the one's gonna get eaten alive out here by the skeeters, and you know it."

"I also know you're the one who wouldn't let me keep shooting till we knew that goddam asshole was dead."

"And what if you did? Those Marine Patrol people would've had us for supper."

"But we'd know the bastard was dead."

"Ax, he'd have to be dead, wouldn't he? I mean, otherwise, he'd have told them what we did, and we'd have the whole damn police force of the state of Florida down on us."

Severn said, "Who told Big Guy and Lutrice we drowned that asshole—who still probably killed my brother—and fed him to the sharks?"

"Well, hell, Ax, what was I supposed to tell them?"

"Cody, look. We said we killed him, and the sharks ate him. Even if he was dead when the Marine Patrol got there, what if they didn't see him, and didn't wait for him to float up to the surface?"

"I don't get you."

"It wouldn't exactly do to have him come washing up on the shore here, now, would it?"

"Oh, Ax, by now the creatures must've eaten him all up."

"Yeah, well, the way the current works, he'll be here if they didn't. He shows up, you just haul him in and come get me. I'm taking the key to the door back, too, just in case you get any ideas of quitting early."

I heard the squeaking of sneaker against sand, getting quieter as nothing else was said except for Cody's muttering, then a slumping sound as I suspect he sat down on the sand to keep watch.

Howard beckoned me to put my ear against his mouth. "We . . . cannot . . . get . . . past . . . him."

I shook my head.

Howard took out his knife, jabbing the point toward Cody.

I shook my head again, pushing my bootied foot into the sand, then pointing to my ear to show him we'd sound to Cody like Severn's sneakers had sounded to us.

Howard nodded, then shrugged.

I held up a finger. He watched me. I tapped my chest and used my hand to pantomime the dolphin-kick, then patted my black shorty suit.

Another nod.

Then I held up my snorkel and mask, pantomiming the dead man's float.

Howard pointed to my knife, then used his own to angle up steeply toward my heart from below, wrenching his hand to the right.

My turn to nod.

He thumbed me on my way.

I moved back very slowly on hands and knees into the water, the stand of trees still providing cover from Cody. When the water got two feet deep, I lay down. Drooling into my mask and rubbing the saliva over the glass, I put it on, taking the snorkel tube off the left-side strap and adjusting it down on the right, so its blowhole would be high enough to just break the water and provide me air without sticking up much above my ear.

Then I slid the diving knife from its sheath on the inside of my left calf and began to float, wriggling my feet just enough to bring me across Cody's cone of vision. I kept floating, hoping the wet suit would look enough like the dark jumpsuit they'd dressed me in for Cody to think—

"My God Almighty! It can't be. . . ."

I could hear Cody come thumping down toward the water. Could hear him, but dared not turn to see him.

Conversationally, he said, "Ax, you are a prophet, you are."

I still lay there. Hanging in the water that way, my arms out to the sides and my feet close together, made me think of Dawna, hanging over her bed. It helped to focus me.

I heard Cody set down his rifle, heard him sloshing out through the water, felt him grab me by the left arm and lift me.

"Hey, this ain't no jump—"

I drove the blade of the knife under his breastbone and up through his heart, wrenching my hand to the right. Cody made a deep, hacking sound, his hand on my arm jerking violently, the dying eyes rolling back into the small head before me.

Then I rode his body down into the shallows.

Tearing the mask off my face, I took a few deep breaths through the nose, fighting off the hyperventilation that the adrenaline triggered. Cody's body shuddered under me on the bottom before becoming still. By then, Howard was crouching on the shoreline, picking up Cody's rifle and sig-

naling me to drag the corpse through the water toward the
shadow of the trees. I did, and Howard joined me there.

He whispered, "You think the other one will be back?"

"Eventually. I don't see how this changes the rest of the
plan, though."

"Except to improve our odds." Howard hefted the M-16.
"Not sure I'm comfortable with this. Never used one when
it counted."

"Keep it anyway." I unzipped the wet suit, sticking the
revolver inside and sliding the sling for the boom box over
my head so the machine rode between my shoulder blades.
"Let's go."

We moved upslope toward the wall, two hundred feet
away.

On the outside, the top of the wall was still about twelve
feet off the ground. I moved around quietly till I found the
door that Severn mentioned, which I remembered from the
interior of the courtyard on my first visit to it. I listened, then
tried the handle. Locked, as Severn told Cody it would be.

I came back to Howard. "You'll have to give me a boost."

He made a stirrup of his hands, and I stepped onto them
and pushed up with my other leg as he heaved me toward
the top. I got a purchase with my right hand and enough
fingers of my left to do a pull-up, pausing at the top to look
into the empty, now peaceful courtyard, a low-wattage light
on by the doorway to the double-bungalow.

I got an elbow up, then levered myself higher to get the
other palm and elbow up, too. Sidesaddling lengthwise onto
the flat, foot-thick surface, I motioned to Howard, who tossed
me the free end of the rope he'd secured at the bottom. I
waved to him, Howard waving back and disappearing along
the wall into the darkness.

I lowered my end of the rope into the courtyard, then rap-
peled down it to ground level, about twenty feet from the
raised crucifixion platform. Drawing the revolver, I moved to
the exterior door in the wall. If it could be opened from my
side without a key, I planned to carry Eddie through it. If it
couldn't, I'd be rappeling back up the rope with him over

my shoulder in a fireman's carry. The door was locked, but only by an interior deadbolt. I turned the latch, and the door cracked open on its own.

Leaving the door that way, I moved back toward the interior entrance to the double-bungalow, where Clark or Axel, or both, might be sitting inside at the telephone desk. I set up on the blind side of the door, then waited for Howard's diversion. It didn't take long.

The first explosion made the walls shake, as did the second and third. The door in front of me burst open, Clark the Clerk pausing to close it. I sapped him behind the ear with the butt of the revolver, and he sank first to his knees, then to the ground on his side. I thought it was a good sign that he wanted to close the door, that there might not be anyone else inside but the boys.

I was through the door and past the desk when the next explosion quaked through the building, probably breaking any glass in the windows had there been any windows in the walls. As I got near the bunk room, the corridor light let me see the back of Royel Wyeth filling the doorway, roaring at the boys, demanding to know which of them was responsible for the attack on his Church.

I slugged him a little harder than I had Clark, and he went down, too.

Inside the room, I didn't know how to turn on the lights, indeed whether there were any lights. I said, "Eddie?"

"Here. I'm over here."

I rushed to him, unstrapping his hands first. "It's me, Eddie. We're getting out of here."

He hugged me as I got his ankles undone. "Denny and Paul and Billie have to come, too."

I felt a catch in my throat. "Them, too. Help me with them."

In the time it took Eddie to get one of them free, I'd gotten the other two up and on their feet. "Can everybody walk?"

One said, "Kind of."

The youngest said, "I want to go home."

The oldest said, "Hush up, you baby."

I spoke to the oldest boy, whose blemish crossed his nose and left cheek on the face under the shaved head. "What's your name?"

"Denny."

"Denny, can you get these other two through a hallway and out?"

"Yes."

"Good boy." I unslung the boom box, sliding it over his neck instead. "Wear this like so."

He smiled at me. "How do we get out?"

The resiliency of a child's spirit. I tried not to see the marks from the straps and "inquisitioning" on the boys' wrists and arms. "Come on."

I helped Eddie, Denny following close but kicking Wyeth hard in the crotch as he went by. Wyeth moaned but didn't rise. The other boy helped the youngest, who started to cry at the fifth explosion as we got to the courtyard and stepped around Clark, whom nobody bothered to kick. I could hear shouting from inside the Compound beyond the infirmary.

I turned to the three boys. "The explosions can't hurt you. They're friends. They'll bring out all the good people on the other side of the hallway in that building. Just run through the hall, pushing this button on the boom box as soon as you get outside again."

Denny said, "When we get outside again."

"Right. A tape will come on loud, but don't let anybody turn the thing down or off. Got it?"

"Got it," said Denny. To the other two boys, "Come on." Then to Eddie, "See you, huh?"

"See you, Denny."

They went through the door to the infirmary. I took Eddie to the door in the wall. Pushing it open, I stepped through and began moving hard. Eddie, in bare feet, couldn't keep up. I lifted him off the ground and into my left arm just as the shouting from inside the Compound was getting closer, and I heard the tape in the boom box come on.

The message, alternating my voice with Doris's and Howard's, pounded over and over again. "These boys have been tortured, and others like them crucified and killed, by Royel and Lutrice Wyeth. Go inside the courtyard and the bungalow of the Center for the Study of Sin and witness it for yourselves."

Running with Eddie, I was almost at the copse of trees when something thumped into the trunk of one of them, little buzzing noises tearing through the leaves. I dropped to the ground, cradling Eddie to cushion the impact, then letting go of him and rolling to a prone shooting position with the unfamiliar revolver as Axel Severn came on, still firing. I shot three times at his chest, spinning him around, his silenced M-16 flying off to the side as he went down.

I got up and was reaching for Eddie, whose hands were over his ears, when I heard Whit Tidyman say, "First I'll take the boy, then you."

I froze.

"Drop it, now."

I did, into the scrub grass at my feet.

Tidyman came down closer as Axel Severn, clasping his left palm on his right bicep, got to his knees. "That asshole bastard, he shot me, shot me clean through."

Tidyman had a silenced M-16, also. "I should have killed you, Francis."

I said, "Too late. Listen to the tape, the message it's sending. The people in the Compound will see for themselves what your boss and girlfriend have been doing. It's all over."

Royel Wyeth's voice came booming out of the night, competing in its own way with my tape still some distance away. "Where is he? Where is the blas-*phe*-mer?"

Tidyman turned slightly as Wyeth staggered toward him, but not enough to give me a realistic chance at the revolver with Eddie so much in the line of fire. Wyeth went right by Tidyman, stumbling a little as he came slightly downhill toward us, pointing at me. Eddie turned to my leg, hugging it and burying his face in my thigh.

"The blasphemer, back from the *dead* by favor of Satan to save his minion. It is as I fore-*told*, as I *was* told by the others who preceded—"

A six-round burst from Tidyman's weapon spat into Wyeth's back, making him stagger and fall forward, blood trickling downslope from his still body.

Severn went slack-jawed. "Well, shit, you finally done it."

"No," said Tidyman, the barrel of the silenced weapon hovering in my direction. "Francis here, he stole one of your weapons and killed the Reverend right in front of you."

Severn looked at Wyeth on the ground, then grinned like a gargoyle. "Why, I do believe you're right, Sergeant. And I'll tell that in any court in the land. Yes, I will."

Tidyman said, "No, you won't," and shot him with a shorter burst, the silencer no good anymore, the popping from the muzzle still hanging in the air as the bullets punched Severn over, his legs catching under him at the knees as he rocked back from the impact of the high velocity rounds tumbling through him.

I said, "Simpler that way, right?"

Tidyman turned his dour face to me. "Right. Only one version, mine."

I could hear sirens in the background, the sound of the Greenspans' boat racing across the channel, the voices from the Compound getting louder and angrier as they seemed to be in the courtyard now, only a couple of hundred feet behind Tidyman.

I said, "Time's running out."

"Only on you, Francis."

I stepped between him and Eddie. "You going to kill the boy, too?"

The muzzle came up. "No more options."

Then, off to the right, I heard, "Maybe one more."

Tidyman swung his weapon and fired, the M-16's report overpowered by the ringing sound of a heavy pistol's three quick shots, the forty-five-caliber slugs knocking Tidyman around like the Invisible Man was pummeling him.

Howard Greenspan came out of the shadows, limping on his left foot. "Been here sooner, but I twisted my ankle, tripping over a mangrove root. Come on."

The three of us got down to the water's edge, Doris bringing the boat in, then broaching it broadside a hundred or so yards out. Eddie said, "We gonna have to swim?"

"Yes."

He bit his upper lip. "I can't."

"I'll help you."

His eyes looked up at me, very grave. "Those men back there. They're dead, aren't they?"

"Yes."

"Good."

I put my hand on his shoulder, then squeezed once quickly and drew him toward me and into the water.

At the boat, the first thing Doris said was, "You're Eddie, right?"

"Right."

"I'm Doris. Come on, just climb up the ladder."

She helped the boy over the gunwale. We were on the starboard side, away from Little Mercy Key, anybody seeing the Aquasport 19 from shore hopefully taking it for a fishing boat that came by to see what all the excitement was about. Hanging on to the swimming ladder, I passed my fins up to Doris, then reached back to Howard, the last one in the water. He flinched when I grasped his hand.

I said, "You hit?"

"Kind of."

"Where?"

"Foot and chest. Lucky that blacktip wasn't hungry tonight."

I got Howard moving up the ladder and onto the gunwale. Then I heard him say, "Sweetheart," and hit the deck of the boat.

I was in the captain's chair, steering south instead of north toward the marina. Doris had aimed me at a light on a distant point of shore, wrapping Eddie in a blanket and putting him on my lap before propping Howard up near the engine with some boat cushions behind him. We were heading for the creek between Mercy and Plantation Key that would take us out to the ocean side and eventually past the reef.

After a long while, Eddie leaned close to my ear. "Can I ask you another question?"

"I think you've earned that."

Very quietly. "Is Howard going to die, too?"

I looked down at the boy and decided, for better or for worse, he'd been told enough lies. "I think so."

Eddie closed his eyes, and gave his grave nod, but he didn't cry. Somehow, that worried me more than anything else.

Over my shoulder, I said, "Doris?"

"Yes?"

"We're getting close to that light."

In a voice I barely recognized, Howard said, "Go ahead, sweetheart. I'll make it."

And he did.

We'd crossed the reef, me back at the helm, Eddie curled up asleep in the blanket and on some more cushions at my feet to be out of the cooler ocean wind. I was thinking about how we'd have to send a lot of gear overboard before heading back to the marina when I heard Doris say, "Good-bye, Howard." Just as she had when he and I had gone into the water earlier that night.

I turned in the captain's chair to see her cup his chin in her palm, using a tissue to wipe some blood from the corner of his mouth before kissing him tenderly on the lips. Then Doris swiped at her eyes twice before stuffing the tissue in her pocket and coming up to the helm.

I held out my hand, and she took it. "Doris—"

"You're going to tell me we can't bring my Howard back in with the bullet wounds."

I looked at her under the gauzy moon. "That's right."

A nod. "There's a place, a little further out."

After about a mile, Doris said, "This should be fine. Here, let me."

She throttled the engine back to idle, then looked down at

Eddie, who hadn't stirred. "Can you even imagine what it must have been like for him back there?"

"No."

"I'm glad he's asleep now."

I moved aft with her to Howard's body. We weighted him down, then paused while Doris said something prayerful, maybe in Hebrew, I didn't ask. Then she nodded to me, and slowly, her at his feet, me at his shoulders, we lifted the man who'd died well up and over the side, his body slipping under the surface.

I said, "If it weren't for Howard, Eddie and I wouldn't be here."

Doris took my hand again, nodding to herself rather than to me. "Thank you, John."

And then she began to cry. Softly, so as not to awaken Eddie Straw.

29

F ROM A CHAIR IN THE GREENSPAN LIVING ROOM, I SAID TO
Doris, "He still asleep?"

"Yes."

I set down my drink, another vodka on the rocks. "Hard
to figure, after all the time he must have spent in that bunk."

She looked at me evenly, spoke the same way. "He's a little
boy, John, and he's been through an awful lot."

"So have you."

A nod. "With more to come." Doris went into the kitchen,
and I heard the clink of coffee pot to ceramic mug. We'd
cruised north on the ocean side of Mercy Key, Eddie waking
and dropping off again as we bided our time before passing
through the creek between Mercy and Key Largo. Even at
three in the morning, the sky reflected the haze of official
lights and media coverage on Little Mercy to the south as we
slipped back into the canal mouth and toward the marina.
Fortunately, the docking area was deserted, and I was able
to carry Eddie, swaddled in the blanket, to the Lincoln, hun-
kering down with him in the trunk, just in case we were
stopped on the short drive to the retirement community.

I was still too wired to try sleeping, so Doris had dug

out some of Howard's old, larger clothes. I'd been watching television, the constant news bulletins interrupting the inane, insomniac broadcasting. I alternated between two channels, a Latino male reporter and a blond female one furiously conveying the impression that something "truly horrible" had been going on at the Center for the Study of Sin, despite Lutrice Wyeth's strident efforts at damage control. Clark the Clerk, however, was apparently singing his heart out, the broad outlines of events in Little Mercy's courtyard becoming clear from leaks via his official interrogators, the constant replaying of our audiotape from the boom box, and the reverent treatment, even by the media, of Denny and his two friends. So far, I was just "a man we didn't know who helped us," because I'd hit Clark before he'd seen me, and everyone else there that night was long past identifying me. I hoped it would stay that way, even as the hand-held cameras in the Compound showed more men and women with grim faces piling out of unmarked cars and vans, half a dozen federal and state acronyms emblazoned across their windbreakers.

Doris came back into the living room with a Mickey Mouse mug. "You got enough to drink there?"

"Fine."

A tired nod as she settled into the armchair across from me.

"Doris, I hate to press, but we ought to discuss details before it may be too late to invent them."

A swig of coffee. "Go ahead."

"Howard's death. How do you explain that?"

She shrugged. "Weeks ago, we talked to one of the retired doctors down here—we've got three of them you could hit with a rock from where you're sitting. One's a cardiologist, used to be on staff at this fancy-shmancy hospital in Tampa. He told us any time Howard decided to . . . just end it, he'd sign the death certificate."

"Without a body?"

"You'd be surprised, John, how many of us—the older old—just decide to sail off into the sunset. The doctor said, he signs the certificate, nobody's going to question why there isn't any funeral bill on the estate inventory."

I nodded. "You really did think this through."

"Maybe not this particular way, but other ways, yeah. We gave up the life insurance years ago, so there'll be nobody to investigate, did my husband really die, and everything else is joint name. Howard's business went well after the Marines, so a lawyer does a little paperwork, some judge waves a magic wand, and I have all I need for the rest of my life."

After another swig of coffee, Doris looked at me over the rim of the mug. "Speaking of what I need, I want to keep him, John."

I must have shown the confusion on my face, because she said, "Eddie. I want to take him north and raise him, for as long as I have left."

"Doris—"

"You want him going back to his parents who gave him away to those monsters?"

"No."

"You have a plan to look after him?"

"No."

"Then it's me or the state. Or I guess first the state of Florida, then maybe the state of New Hampshire, but then probably his parents again."

Nancy had said pretty much the same thing.

Doris set down her mug. "He's like a D.P., John."

"A Dee-Pee?"

" 'Displaced Person.' After the war, I read about what happened to the kids, the orphans the Nazis made in Europe. They wandered around, shell-shocked. They had this craving for sleep, because it was only when they were asleep that they felt safe, like Eddie in our . . . my guest room. There are ways to treat that, just like there's that laser thing to treat his birthmark. I'm going to ask my sister in New York more about that, too."

I sipped the vodka. Crystal fire.

Doris said, "Well, what do you think?"

"Of your taking him?"

She lifted her mug again. "Of course of me taking him."

I rolled the cubes in my glass. "I think he could do a lot worse."

"Huh, you're telling me?"

"Eddie?"

No response.

I shook him gently at the shoulder. "Eddie?"

His eyes came open before he focused on me sitting on the guest bed or Doris standing next to it, half-light filtering in from the hall the way it had into the bunk room back on Little Mercy. "No. No more, please? Please!"

By the time he'd gotten to the last word, Doris had muscled me out of the way and was holding him, hugging his face against her breast, her chin resting on top of his head. "It's okay, Eddie. It's okay, it's okay now."

And he started—haltingly, almost apologetically—to cry.

I stood there, looking down at them, Eddie's arms around her neck, the marks from the straps and other things still visible across his wrists. I couldn't see there was any other decision to make.

"They got roadblocks up."

Doris set the bag of groceries on the kitchen counter that Wednesday morning. Eddie and I had been watching television, both of us rising when we heard the Lincoln crunching in the driveway under the carport.

I said, "The news didn't say anything about roadblocks."

"Yeah, well, I stopped at the clubhouse—over by the pool, you haven't seen it yet—and Hank Erlandson—he's from Minnesota originally, looks like a Viking without the horned hat—he'd just finished his laps in the pool, these black goggles still on top of his head like sunglasses—against the chlorine, he says it hurts his eyes, I tell him it wouldn't hurt so much, you didn't swim in the pool for two hours till you look like a prune—"

Eddie laughed. It was the first time I'd ever heard him laugh, even with the cartoons.

"—So anyway, Hank says the highway patrol have the

roadblocks up, they're checking every car, whether you go Route 1 north or Card Sound Road."

"No other way to the mainland, right?"

"Unless you're an alligator."

Eddie laughed again.

I said, "They searching the trunks, too?"

"Hank didn't say, and I didn't want to seem too interested, you know?"

"You did the right thing, Doris."

She clapped her hands together. "So, it looks like I've got two strange men as houseguests for a while."

Eddie laughed once more. A chattery, musical sound.

We spent the rest of that day watching television and having sandwiches and watching television and doing a jigsaw puzzle and watching television and having dinner until I was developing a serious case of cabin fever. After dinner, Eddie went to bed early, but dropped off to sleep only after Doris spent ten minutes reading to him. Coming back into the living room, she looked radiant.

I said, "He agrees with you."

Doris tilted her head. "You never had kids, am I right?"

"Right."

"Too bad. They would have taught you some things."

Early the next morning, she said, "I don't like the idea of drilling holes in our . . . my car."

Looking up at her from inside the trunk, the power tool in my hand, I said, "It was kind of close in here Tuesday night, even on just the short ride from the marina. Heading north, we might have to ride back here—and breathe—all the way to Miami."

"What happens when it rains?"

"Doris, I'm drilling the holes through the bottom of your trunk."

"So, water doesn't splash up?"

"You can get plugs for the holes. There'll only be two small ones."

Still not liking it, she changed the subject. "What happens when we get to your friend in Miami?"

"You leave me, then you and Eddie are on your own."

"You don't think we ought to discuss that with him first?"

"With my friend?"

"No. With Eddie."

"I thought we'd already decided that."

"We did. He hasn't."

"Okay. We also have to stop at Mercy Lodge."

"The Lodge? Why?"

I told Doris about where I'd hidden the remaining cash from Lonnie Severn's trailer.

She shook her head. "No. It's what, a few thousand dollars? For that we risk me getting caught or breaking my ankle climbing around the rocks, maybe getting rabies from a squirrel bite?"

"Doris, I'd like you and Eddie to have that money."

"I have more money than we'll ever need."

"Doris—"

"Going back to the Lodge just isn't worth the risk, and you know I'm right."

She was. "Okay."

"Am I gonna meet your friend in Miami?"

"If you want to."

"I meet him, do I call you 'John'?"

I watched her. "Howard told you my real name isn't 'John Francis'?"

"He didn't have to tell me. Like I said, you should have had kids. You'd have learned from them, the way I did from my Mike." She grew quieter. "The way I will again, God and Eddie willing."

I stuck out my hand. "John Cuddy, Boston."

Doris shook it. "A pleasure, John."

I finished with the drill, tested each hole. Plenty of air.

Doris said, "What if we get stopped and the police search the trunk?"

"Tell them you're with the Mafia."

"After all this, I ought to join up."

He was sitting in front of the television, gorging himself on popcorn and Looney Tunes.

I said, "Eddie?"

He looked up, dropping the handful of popcorn back into the bowl rather than continuing on with it to his mouth. "Everything okay?"

Doris said, "Everything's fine, Eddie. John and I just need to have a little talk with you."

I said, "Eddie, we have to decide where you're going to go."

He bit his upper lip. "Go?"

"Yes. We can't all stay here anymore, because of what happened."

"But that was way far away from here, where the bad people were. We ran away in Howard's boat."

I hadn't thought of Eddie's orientation. All the time we spent on the water, I knew we'd just been circling Mercy Key, but he, of course, wouldn't.

Doris said, "We're going to get far away, Eddie, maybe visit my sister in New York for a while. The only thing we need is your okay on it."

Eddie looked from her to me and back again. "My okay?"

"Yes," she said. "You get your say, too. So, John and I have been thinking, and we'd like you to live with me up north."

He seemed relieved. "Okay."

I said, "Okay?"

Eddie looked at me strangely. "Yeah. Okay. I mean, I can't live with you, you're a private eye, always off doing things and helping people. You'd never be around, right?"

I tried to keep my mouth from falling open.

Doris said, "So, it's settled then."

Eddie nodded to her and me separately.

She pointed at the television. "Back to Donald Duck."

The boy gave her a twisted grin. "He's Disney, Doris. Daffy is Looney Tunes."

As he drew the bowl of popcorn onto his lap, Doris whispered to me, "You could have learned so much," and walked back into the kitchen to call her sister.

After a particularly rough jolt, I said to Eddie, "You okay?"

"Yeah. This is kind of fun."

I thought it was kind of darkly miserable, the Thursday morning sun throwing heat if not light into the trunk. I tried to keep track of the miles on my watch, figuring Doris was doing fifty or so. After forty-six minutes, the Lincoln slowed, the pebbles from the highway shoulder pinging off the undercarriage as the car pulled over. I tensed, trying to smile for Eddie, even in the dark. The driver's side door opened and chunked solidly closed, but I didn't hear any vehicle pulling up behind us.

Then it was as though a star had exploded overhead.

Through my blindness, Doris said, "Hop out. No roadblocks after all, and I haven't seen a cop since we left the carport."

Eddie got into the backseat, me into the front. Doris had thought to bring baseball caps and sunglasses, to hide my identity and Eddie's shaved head and birthmark in a way that didn't single him out. I guided Doris as best I could, from the Florida Turnpike to the airport area to the road I thought Pepe had used to take me to the rent-a-car place. Fortunately I spotted the pink skyscraper as my landmark for turning toward Justo Vega's house.

Pepe answered the gate again, the little remote box like a *Star Trek* toy in his palm.

"Hey, John Francis, how you doing, man?"

"Fine. Pepe, meet Doris and Eddie."

"How do you do, Pepe."

"Hi, Pepe."

Pepe smiled at both, bending at the knee to shake Eddie's hand. Straightening, he said, "You want Mr. Vega, he no gonna be back for hours. Had to fly up to Tallahassee, some kind of business."

Doris said, "I think we should take off then. We have a lot of driving to do."

"Doris, I—"

She waved her hand at me. "Don't say anything stupid, okay?"

"Okay."

"A hug, now, that'd be all right."

We did.

Breaking off, I saw Eddie crooking a finger at me shyly, and I bent down the way Pepe had.

Eddie said, "You kept your promise."

The voice of a young MP lieutenant said, "I tried to. And I wanted to."

Lip between teeth, more quietly. "Nobody ever did that before."

"Doris will."

A grave nod, as small as the voice.

I said, "And you will."

Another nod. Then, "When you helped Melinda and me on the road, back before that Axel man caught us, I memorized your name and stuff from the thing you showed me."

My identification holder. "That was good, Eddie."

"But I never said anything to those bad people about you. I didn't want them ... to hurt you, too."

I felt something rise in my throat. "And because of your being so smart that way, they didn't."

"Only thing is, can you write everything down, just in case ... Doris needs you sometime, too?"

The look on his face nearly broke my heart.

A little quickly, I said, "I'll mail it to you, once Doris tells me where to send it."

A better nod. "Promise?"

"Promise."

A grin, and he threw his arms around my neck, like he had the night before with Doris. Into my ear, he whispered, "Thank you, John Francis Cuddy," and then took Doris's hand and walked to the Lincoln.

As the car doors closed, Pepe said, "Hey, man, you want a Kleenex or something?"

"No. Thanks."

In a different tone, "That kid Eddie, he look a lot like some other kids been on the news, you know it?"

Doris pulled away. I turned to Pepe. "What kid?"

He nodded, slowly. "You walk all the way here from the Keys, maybe you wanna come in, sit a while."

"Mr. Vega, he gonna be very sorry he miss you."

"I really want to get back home."

Pepe eased the Escort into one of the access lanes at the airport terminal area. "I understand that. You sure you got enough money?"

"Plenty." He'd gotten my cash and credentials package from wherever Justo had stashed them. "You sure the boss won't mind your getting it for me?"

"Hey, man, that's what he teach me the combination to the safe for. Besides, he say to me, 'Pepe, you make sure you take care of Mr. Francis,' and he never tell me different after that. Mr. Vega, he is man of his word, he do no go back on it with me never."

I nodded, the fatigue starting to settle in as Pepe stopped outside my terminal.

Shifting into park, he said all in a jumble, "You go looking for that little kid Eddie I never see, you blow up the Church thing on TV down there, all because you promise him something, right?"

I started to say something else, then just agreed with him.

Pepe held out his hand. "Some of us, we going back to Cuba someday, maybe pretty soon. Take things back from Fidel, he do no give it up first. You decide you want to see *Habana* the hard way, John Francis, you give me a call, eh?"

30

I HAD THE WHOLE ROW ON THE STARBOARD SIDE OF THE AIRPLANE to myself for the flight to Washington, D.C. I'd paid cash, the ticket under the name "George Scott," who'd been a pretty fair first baseman for the Red Sox a generation ago. Looking out the window from my seat, I noticed a lot of scratches, striations really, on the double glass. They seemed to run from northeast to southwest across the panes, and I wondered what the hell could make those marks so high on the fuselage.

Once we were on the ground at National Airport, I called Nancy's office, but she was trying a case. I left a message with the secretary that I'd be back in Boston that afternoon.

Outside the terminal, I hailed a cab and gave the driver an intersection two blocks away from my T-shirt shop. After battling the traffic, he dropped me off, and I waited for the taxi to disappear down the street before walking to the store.

Opening the door, I saw Kevin, the stumpy kid from Georgetown, rising from behind a counter. Wearing a Redskins jersey, he smiled at me, then looked around as I reached him.

"I thought maybe you weren't coming back, man."

"I'm back. You do what I asked?"

A knowing smile. "Sure did. Splashed water on the soap and towels. Even took a couple showers, so everything'd look right."

I nodded.

Kevin said, "Moved your clothes some, laid on them while I watched TV from the bed at night. The clothes looked used and the bed looked slept in."

"That's pretty good, Kevin. How about my computer card?"

He handed it to me. I counted out the other hundred, plus twenty.

"Hey, what's the extra twenty for?"

I said, "Being inventive, enjoying your work."

"Kind of like a bonus, huh?"

"Right."

Kevin pocketed the money. "Cool," stretching the word into three syllables.

Outside, I flagged another taxi and went back to the chain place by DuPont Circle. Up in my room, everything looked the way Kevin had described. I dialed an airline, was told I'd have no trouble getting a seat on the shuttle to Boston, and packed. Downstairs, "John Cuddy" settled up his bill.

When I stepped off the plane and into the jetway at Logan Airport, I could feel the autumn chill of now late September, especially compared to the Keys. At baggage claim, I picked up my suitcase and got a cab right away. I had him take me to the condo first, where I showered and shaved and tried Nancy again at the office. The same secretary told me she was still on trial, so I left another message saying that I'd be by to pick her up at the courthouse around six.

I dressed in a suit for the first time in a while and went out of my way to walk toward my office along Commonwealth Avenue and through the parks. The Dutch elms on the boulevard mall that have so far survived the disease and various storms stood majestically, their leaves just starting to turn but sheltering the bay windows of the mansions along both sides of the street. The flowerbeds still bloomed in the Public Garden, the touristy swan boats still meandered in the shallow pond and under the bridge, the softball teams still played on the formal diamond at the south side of the Common and the informal ones marked off with bases of whatever was available. Good to be home and feel at home.

On Tremont Street, I walked up the stairs to my office. Unlocking and opening the door, the heap of mail inside spread out like a canasta hand as the bottom of the door moved over and through it. I gathered the envelopes and went to my desk, jacking both windows a foot to air the place out. I was halfway through the pile when I heard a knock.

"It's open."

Chief Kyle Pettengill came in, the uniform in a closet somewhere as he wore a tattersall shirt and khaki pants and some kind of moccasins that, like his black Corfams, did nothing to boost his height. The moat of baldness around the forelock of hair wrinkled a little as he hesitated in the doorway.

I tried to keep the surprise out of my voice. I expected to hear from him, but not necessarily see him, and certainly not so soon. "Chief, come on in."

Just a nod. Making no effort to shake hands, Pettengill took one of the two client chairs in front of my desk.

To keep things light, I said, "Returned your call last week, but whoever answered said you weren't there."

The low, intimate voice. "I know. Been trying to reach you ever since."

"I was out of state and didn't pick up my messages."

Another nod.

I said, "You just took a chance you'd find me in today?"

Pettengill rubbed his chin. "Not exactly. When I didn't hear back from you again, I made some calls. Friend of a friend at the airline you flew to D.C. told me when you left Boston."

"Little vacation, kind of."

"The friend of a friend tells me you stay over a Saturday, the fares are cheaper."

I just watched him now.

He said, "Of course, you just bought your return ticket today."

"Your friend of a friend again?"

"That's for true. Spend the whole time in D.C., did you?"

I eased back in my chair. "This leading us somewhere?"

"Probably."

I didn't say anything.

Pettengill looked out my window. "Nice view of the capitol dome, there."

"I've always liked it."

The nod. I remembered he did that a lot.

Then Pettengill resettled in his seat. "Got a call from the state boys down in Florida yesterday morning. Some people connected with a church on one of the Keys died kind of suddenly. Violently."

"I didn't watch the news much in D.C."

"That where you got the tan?"

"Nice weather, I walked most places."

"Where'd you stay?"

I told him the name of the hotel. "Check it out, you want to."

"Don't think I will. Isn't so hard to slip the bellboy a few dollars, have him muss up the room to fool the maid."

I kept my own counsel.

"I'm going to go on just a bit, Cuddy. Feel free to jump in, you have something to contribute."

When I still didn't say anything, Pettengill looked back out the window. "Seems one of the dead down in Florida was Lonnie Severn's brother. Officer I talked to asked me to notify Lonnie, so I drove on out there. His truck—that new navy blue GMC you came up to see me about?—that was in his driveway, but he wasn't in the trailer. I figured it would be a good thing to tell him about his brother before he heard it somewhere else, so I did a little asking around. Seems his neighbors haven't seen Lonnie for more than a week. One of them—has a hound dog loves to chase after vehicles—remembers going by his place, not seeing the truck but noticing a silver coupe, foreign job, parked kind of funny by this dried-up stream we have. Way the neighbor described the coupe, it sounded a lot like yours. Then next day, the same neighbor notices the silver car is gone, but Lonnie's truck is back in the drive. Neighbor said he doesn't believe it's been moved since."

Pettengill came back to me. "This was all about the time you were up visiting, trying to see Lonnie."

"We never matched up."

Another nod. "I took it on myself to go in Lonnie's trailer. Wasn't that much of a trick, somebody'd broken the lock on the rear door. There was a lot of pamphlets and such from different kinds of Christian places. Never knew Lonnie to be such a reader." Pettengill's eyes grew harder. "Some of the stuff was from this church down on the Keys I got called about, but it looked like there was space on his bookshelf for even more of it."

"Chief—"

He held up his right hand, like a traffic cop stopping a line of cars. "Save it. Anybody asks, I don't want to be able to say I heard any more lies I didn't follow up. Now, what I want you to do is give me straight answers to a couple of questions, and then maybe we can go on from there. How does that sound?"

Very neutrally, I said, "Why don't we give it a try."

The nod. "First, did you have to kill Lonnie?"

I watched Pettengill for a count of ten before saying, "Yes. He was—"

"Just yes or no will do. Second, will we be finding his body in a way I'll have to be explaining?"

"I don't think so."

"Not exactly yes or no, but let's pass that for now. Third, did you get the Haldon boy out of that church place?"

In for a nickel . . . "Yes."

"And will he be coming home to his folks?"

"No."

"Where is he?"

"With somebody better, somebody who'll raise him with love."

" 'Better' by whose lights, Cuddy?"

"Yours and mine both, I think."

Pettengill rubbed his chin some more. Twice I thought he was going to say something, but he didn't. Then, "There any place around here serves Dr. Pepper, this time of day?"

I felt a little relief inside. "It's a big city. We could probably find one."

"You have anything against a recovering drunk buying you a real drink?"

"Not that comes to mind."

A final nod. "Then let's get to it."

POCKET BOOKS
PROUDLY PRESENTS

INVASION OF PRIVACY

JEREMIAH HEALY

Coming mid-June
from
Pocket Books Hardcover

The following is a preview of
Invasion of Privacy

The woman choosing one of the client chairs in front of my desk was attractive without being beautiful or even pretty. Wearing a gray herringbone business suit, carefully tailored, over a white blouse and Christmas-ribbon bowtie, she seemed around forty. At maybe five-five and one-ten, her body looked trim but not athletic. The hair was a lustrous brown, curling upward and inward just above the shoulders. High cheekbones slanted slightly toward her nose while pale blue eyes slanted slightly toward her temples. Everything about the woman suggested sophisticated but foreign, and I wasn't surprised when she spoke English with a faint, precise accent.

"I am sorry to come here without an appointment, Mr. Cuddy."

I pushed a legal pad and pen to the side of my desk.

"That's all right," I said, placing the accent as eastern European or—

"My name is Olga Evorova." She pronounced it Ee-*vor*-oh-va. "I obtained your name from a computer search of recent newspaper articles."

There are worse ways. "Which ones?"

Evorova told me, then glanced away toward one of the windows behind me, the chair she'd taken giving her a view of the Boston Common as it sweeps up to the golden dome of the Massachusetts Statehouse. The trees were barely turning, the early October air on that Tuesday afternoon as mild as Labor Day weekend. When I'd come in, tourists were mobbing the guy who sold tickets to a sightseeing trolley from his carny stand across the street.

Without looking back toward me, Evorova said, "I have never before needed the help of a private investigator."

My office door has pebbled glass in the upper half, and I noticed that the reverse stencilling of JOHN FRANCIS CUDDY, CONFIDENTIAL INVESTIGATIONS bowed over her head like the arch of a medieval church. "Why do you feel you need one now?"

The pale blue eyes returned to me. "This June past [sic], I met a man. I soon grew to care for him very much, and our relationship has . . . progressed to the point that I would very much like to marry him if he should ask."

I nodded and waited.

She moved her tongue around inside her mouth, as though trying to dissipate a bad taste. "I am, however, concerned about his background."

"In what way?"

More hesitation. "What we discuss, it remains confidential, yes?"

"Unless a court orders me to talk, and maybe even then, depending."

"Depending upon what?"

"On how much I like you as a client."

That brought a shy smile. "You are very easy to talk with, Mr. Cuddy."

"It's a useful quality."

"Useful?"

"People who come to see me often have difficult things to talk about."

A dip of the chin as she seemed to reach a decision. "Originally, I am from Moscow. It was nearly impossible, but I was able to immigrate to the United States for my master's degree in finance. After graduation, I obtained a job with Harborside Bank. When the Soviet Union began to break apart, I was promoted several times rapidly as someone who might bring to the bank a certain advantage in business dealings with the 'new' country of Russia. Even though the dealings have not come so far so fast, I am very well compensated for my work." Another hesitation. "I am talking too much?"

"No. Go on, please."

Evorova looked down at my desk. "You will not take notes?"

"Not right away. I'd rather hear you describe things first."

The chin dip. "In Moscow, my family is all gone, just one uncle here I am able to help. Many died from the Nazis in the Great Patriotic War. So, except for my Uncle Vanya—Ivan—I am alone."

"And you're concerned that . . . ?"

The pale eyes glanced toward her lap, then fixed me with an executive stare. "I am concerned that I seem a 'fat cat,' a potential target."

"For someone like this man you've grown to care for?"

"Exactly, yes [sic]. His name is Andrew Dees. He is a wonderful person, Mr. Cuddy. Andrew owns his own business and a condominium in the town of Plymouth Mills on the South Shore. He is romantic and intelligent and . . ." Evorova blushed. "Soon I will be blushing."

"Then what worries you about Mr. Dees?"

"As I said, his background. Or that he has *no* background. I ask Andrew where he is from, and he says Chicago, but does not talk about it. I ask him about his family, and he says they are all dead, but does not talk of them. I ask him about his schooling, and he says he graduated from the University of Central Vermont, but he does not talk about his time there or . . . anything."

Evorova seemed to run down a little, like a wind-up toy after a long spurt. I gave her a moment, then said, "Have you done any investigating on your own?"

She looked out my window again. "Some. I ran a D&B on Andrew. You know what this is?"

"A Dun & Bradstreet credit report?"

"Exactly, yes." A small sigh. "Nothing."

"Nothing?"

Evorova came back to me. "Oh, Andrew has a personal checking account, and a business checking account, and a business credit card, which he never uses. But there is no personal credit card, no prior loan history, not even a current line of credit for the business."

"What business is it?"

"A photocopy shop in the town center near his condominium."

"That would mean some capital investment to get started, right?"

"Exactly, yes. But he paid cash for everything that is not leased."

Cash. "And the condo?"

"It is in a complex called Plymouth Willows."

"But how did Mr. Dees pay for it?"

"Oh. By cash also. Well, certified check, actually. Andrew purchased from a realty trust—do you wish the details in a banking sense?"

"I don't think so."

"Then just assume that he paid the deposit for his unit by certified check and the balance the same. Andrew also filed a homestead exemption. You know what this is, too?"

"A protection of so much equity in his condo from any future creditors?"

"Exactly, yes."

"Did Mr. Dees have an attorney represent him?"

"In the purchase, do you mean?"

I nodded.

"No," said Evorova. "Andrew told me he did not."

I'd had a year of evening law school, and the homestead exemption in Massachusetts was a pretty advanced device for a layman from Chicago to know about. "Mr. Dees is willing to talk about that transaction, then?"

"But only a little. And when we were reading in bed. . . . One Sunday morning, casually I pointed to him [sic] a newspaper article in the *Globe* about ante-nuptial agreements. Andrew laughed and said he did not believe in those things and very quickly changed the subject to something else.''

''Do you know his Social Security number?''

''Yes.''

''Do you also know there are other sources you can check by running that number through some computers?''

''Yes. And I have done that.'' The executive stare again. ''Nothing.''

''No prior employment?''

''No.''

''Military service?''

''No.''

''Divorce?''

''No, no, and no.''

I stopped. A bit of what it must feel like to sit across a negotiating table from Evorova came through to me.

She waved her hand in a way I found both alien and expressive. ''I am sorry, but this is quite . . . upsetting, even just to discuss.''

Understandable. ''Where did you meet Mr. Dees?''

''In a bar, but not as you would think.''

''Tell me about it.''

''I was driving back from Cape Cod—my best friend at the bank, she has a summer house there. My car is a Porsche, the 911 Carrera six-speed. Do you know it?''

''Only by price tag.''

The blushing again. ''One of my few indulgences, Mr. Cuddy. I even had the car custom-painted my favorite shade of orange, and I permit no one else to drive it.''

''Not even Mr. Dees?''

"No. But I have digressed. That day, when I am coming back from the Cape, I hear a noise in the engine which I do not like. So, I exit Route 3 at Plymouth Mills where the Porsche manual says there is a dealership, and while my car is being examined, I cross the street and go into a bar, to wait."

"And?"

"I am sitting at the bar, reading *Forbes*—the business magazine?—when this man on a stool nearby says to me, 'He died on a motorcycle, like James Dean.' At first I would not have talked to him, but Andrew's voice is wonderful. I do not have a perfect sense for American accents, but I have developed some ear [sic] for them, and he sounded from [sic] the Midwest. So I did."

"Talk to him."

Evorova dipped her chin once more. "For an hour, two. Andrew has very dark hair, and a very strong face. I almost forgot about my car. But when he asked me for my telephone number, I said, 'No, give to me [sic] yours, and I will call you.' "

"And then you started going out?"

Yes. Andrew does not like to come to Boston much because of his business—to leave it alone?—but he enjoys the ballet, and the symphony, especially chamber music. And we go to restaurants. Andrew does not like Italian or Indian food, but he very much enjoys the Chinese and . . ." Another blush. "Again, I am sorry."

It wasn't hard to see why Evorova was so troubled. She suspected the guy was a little off, but she was nuts about him, too.

I said, "From the way you met, it doesn't sound like a setup."

"A . . . you mean, that Andrew arranged that we would meet?"

"Right."

Evorova shook her head vigorously. "No. No, I think that would be quite impossible. The bar is one near his business, one he goes to very often, I think. But Andrew could not know I would be driving back from the Cape that day and develop engine trouble."

I picked up my pen for the first time. "The name of the bar?"

"The Tides, in the town center, also." She tensed a bit. "You will go there?"

"That depends on what you want me to do."

Evorova seemed relieved. "What I want you to do is . . . find out things. Perhaps to watch Andrew, to . . ." She admired the Statehouse again. "Find out things."

"But without Mr. Dees knowing I'm doing it."

Back to me. "Exactly, yes. I do not wish to threaten our relationship by committing an invasion of privacy."

I put down the pen. "Ms. Evorova, that won't be easy, and it may not even be possible."

"Why so [sic]?"

"It's difficult to do more than what you've done already without Mr. Dees hearing from other people that I've been asking around about him."

"You could perhaps follow Andrew, yes? With discretion?"

"Do you have a photo of him?"

Evorova looked toward her lap once more, speaking almost to herself. "He does not like the camera very much, my Andrew."

My Andrew. I brought both hands onto the blotter, folding them. "Ms. Evorova, even with a photo, following somebody isn't quite as easy as it looks on television."

"Why so?"

"Everyone can tell after a while that they're being tailed unless the followers use a team approach, like the police or F.B.I. could mount."

She seemed to digest that.

I said, "Is there anybody you know who I could talk to about Mr. Dees without it getting back to him?"

A slow shake of the head. "My uncle has met Andrew, and likes him very much. If you talk to Vanya, it would . . . get back."

"How about people from work?"

"Andrew has only one employee, and she is loyal to him, I believe."

"No, I meant at your bank. Has anyone met Mr. Dees?"

"Only my friend, Clude, who owns the house on the Cape."

"Clude?"

"She is French-Canadian, but born here. The spelling is C-L-A-U-D-E."

I wrote it down. "Last name?"

"Wah-*zell*, L-O-I-S-E-L-L-E." Evorova seemed troubled. "I would prefer you not to speak with her."

I placed the pen back on the blotter. "It might help if you could tell me why."

The troubled look grew deeper. "Probably I will talk to Claude about coming to see you. However, she has had dinner with us—with Andrew and me—twice. I think she made up her mind about him the first time, but she agreed to meet him again."

"And?"

"Claude is a very . . . instinctive person, Mr. Cuddy. She believes Andrew is hiding something from me."

"Did Ms. Loiselle suggest you see a private investigator?"

"No." The executive stare again. "She suggested I stop seeing Andrew."

I'd already heard enough not to contest Evorova on that one, but she kept going anyway. "You see, I have not had a very . . . secure life. Before I am born, my mother was pregnant with twins, another baby girl and me. When she reached her six month, my mother was passenger [sic] on a bus in Moscow that collided with a truck. Afterward, she felt sick, so she went to the doctor. He said to her, 'I am sorry, but one of your babies is dead.' He said also that it would be safer for the other baby—me—if my mother carried both babies . . . to term. She did what the doctor advised, and so I lay in the womb three months [sic] next to my dead sister." A tear trickled over the corner of Evorova's left eye. "I never met her, but I . . . I still miss her."

A moment, then, "As my other family, the ones who survived the Great Patriotic War, began dying, I dreamed of the United States, and a different life here. A secure one. And now I have that. But for me, life has been only study and work. All my time, all my energy, all my . . . heart. Until I met Andrew. And my heart tells me I cannot lose him just because my banker head—or my banker friend—tells me some things are perhaps not quite right. Do you see this?"

I thought about my wife, Beth, before the cancer took her, and about Nancy Meagher, who'd very nearly come to replace her. "I think so."

Evorova suddenly shrugged heavily. "I am sorry. I

am one professional coming to consult with another, and instead I . . ." The expressive wave again.

I picked up my pen. "We need to talk about my retainer and how you want me to stay in touch with you."

She looked at me. "You will try to help, yes?"

"I'll try."

A sense of relief came into her voice. "Thank you so much [sic]."

Evorova thought my usual rate was fine, giving me her home number but asking that I use her voice-mail at the bank, "just in case Andrew is . . . might be at my apartment."

"And where do you live?"

She reeled off the street address. "A condominium of my own, on Beacon Hill."

Which triggered an idea. I said, "You told me Mr. Dees lives in a condominium, too."

"Yes. Unit number 42 at Plymouth Willows in—"

"Plymouth Mills."

Evorova seemed pleased that I'd remembered the name of her Andrew's town.

I said, "He has neighbors close by, then?"

"Exactly, yes [sic]. Town houses on either side. In little 'clusters,' he calls them."

"How big a complex is it?"

"Plymouth Willows? A total of perhaps fifty units, sixty?"

Good. "So there's some kind of property company that manages it?"

"I believe so." Evorova's eyes seemed to search inside for a moment. "Yes, I remember Andrew saying once the name of it, when he was writing his monthly maintenance check.''

''Do you remember the name?''

More searching. ''No, I am sorry.''

I put down the pen and smiled at her. ''Can you find out?''

Olga Evorova smiled back, but I could tell she wasn't sure why.

Look for
Invasion of Privacy
Wherever Hardcover Books Are Sold
mid-June 1996